The Indigo Scarf

PJ Piccirillo

Brown Posey Press
Mechanicsburg, Pennsylvania

an imprint of Sunbury Press, Inc.
Mechanicsburg, PA USA

For information about special discounts for bulk purchases, please contact Sunbury Press Orders Dept. at (855) 338-8359 or orders@sunburypress.com.

To request one of our authors for speaking engagements or book signings, please contact Sunbury Press Publicity Dept. at publicity@sunburypress.com.

ISBN: 978-1-62006-169-5 (Trade paperback)

Library of Congress Control Number:

FIRST BROWN POSEY PRESS EDITION: June 2019

Product of the United States of America
0 1 1 2 3 5 8 13 21 34 55

Set in Bookman Old Style
Designed by Chris Fenwick
Cover by Riaan Wilmans
Edited by Chris Fenwick

Continue the Enlightenment!

For Laurie

"…that was where and how new America began. The seeds of it were scattered in lonely cabins, lost apparently in an ocean of trees.

Out of them genesis."

-   Hervey Allen

CHAPTER ONE – April 1882

If humans obey anything it is the ancient routes, which themselves followed waterways and the trails of game. They connect us through the generations, even down through civilizations, and cross all the strata we concoct within them. There have been transgressions to this rule, terrible transgressions. But this never occurred to me until after that journey.

The dank old Washington City canal, by then just a buried sewage trough beneath the street outside the station, might have run through the building that morning in April, the air so sodden that the varnish on the armrests of my chair tacked against my palms. The mahogany walls oozed their lacquered sheen and musky stink. My damp corset chafed at my sides. It was a day that made one wonder at the folly of Washington—another of humankind's great cities built on a paddy-field of pestilence.

I sat in the ladies' waiting room, a most distracting post at the Baltimore and Potomac Railroad station. For one, it served also as the vestibule of the B Street entranceway, a raucous corridor of mothers scolding travel-weary children, of the clatter of important boot heels, of one company of travelers trying to outshout another. Adding to this, the day of my journey was within the year following the assassination of President Garfield—or attempted assassination depending on one's view of the story—which took place in that room and only steps from the seat I'd taken. Though the Preacher President no longer lingered through his months of sepsis, Guiteau had yet to go to the gallows for the shooting. And so fascination led every Washington visitor to that floor tile which some aficionado had determined the dead center of the collapse.

They've since razed that hideous building with its toothed steeples, ponderous window panes, and ornamental stonework that jutted at odd angles like the trimmings of a gingerbread cake. The competing rail lines now service Washington from the misleadingly named Union Station—as if our nation's railroads are united in anything except rampant ambition.

It was in lifting my eyes to a remark from an elderly man at the floor tile—gray-bearded, monocled, trousers checked green and gray— "Well now, they all have it coming, don't they?"—that I glimpsed Benjamin James passing the entranceway of the adjacent men's waiting room. My history, all my fears and questions, walked in that man.

In the lapse of him moving to the next doorway where he stopped to bend and read headlines on the newsstand counter, I checked my impulse to approach, telling myself that ignorance is bliss. I've always found this the most fascinating of old saws with its implication of cowardice. Deciding not to be craven, and with one hand adjusting my feathered and flowered Rembrandt hat, I took up my handbag and started for the newsstand just as he stepped back to the throng and weaved into the echoing main waiting room.

Though a slow mover, Benjamin James was an expert at fading into his surroundings. He still could have stood as tall as when I'd last seen him had he not hunched his back and canted his dirty, banded, straw boater into the general stream of derbies, bowlers, and top hats. I spotted him slinking between rows of occupied chairs, burrowed into his greatcoat despite the mugginess. I started after him.

Perhaps I felt the urging of fate and feared that he, in his furtiveness, was defying it, for I broached all good manners and—worse—my station, by shouting his name. Though I'd grown indifferent to attracting sneers in public places, so many at once had the effect of withdrawing the blood from the reaches of my body; my forehead felt cold despite my cheeks burning, my toes and fingers went a-tingle.

But I'd frozen Benjamin James in his stride, the wildcat caught unawares, ready to flee, hide or fight. As annoyed passersby avoided the ten paces between us, he turned. Then his chin tilted up as he recognized me, as I knew he would even after all those years. Not that he identified me in particular—

that 31-year-old woman in a draped and bustled dress of powder-blue. The last he'd seen me I was a girl in a wilderness. He didn't have to know my face because he saw our face, that of our people, a guarded gaze nonetheless full of the pent defiance of a clenched fist. Those alone who share this trait, the descendants of two fabled men in a backwoods hideaway, endured lives that necessitated it and gained by the experience the clairvoyance to pick out the look in a crowd. We do not need a candle to know the addled egg.

So there he was, stepping my way in that space urban crowds make for the likes of me, the infamous Benjamin James, accused then acquitted of shooting to death his brother. Up close, I observed the finer signs of alcoholism—head atremble, face wan and gaping as that of a corpse. Yet as he took me in, I felt the old wild intelligence still roiling there.

He shrugged to adjust the strap of his leather satchel, parched and chafed to the hue of mortar over the years and uncountable miles. It held the entirety of his chattels, I supposed, except for a bottle and a few other items he kept at the ready in his caped greatcoat—a dusty, moth-ridden, Union-blue relic with a less faded swath on the shoulder where a stripe had been ripped away, its general service buttons gone from the cape.

"I saw you walking by," I said.

Nothing, not even a blink. But at my next words, there came a bodily shudder, faint as a candle flame at the passing of a specter. "It's me. David Sharpe's daughter."

He looked past me for a long beat while he wiped his mouth. His silence was not a matter of rudeness I am sure, rather of his deliberating whether it would be better for me that he walk away. I know now that in that instant, what would follow unspooled in his mind; he saw it all, to the last. Yet he parted his lips, so colorless that their lack of stubble alone distinguished them from the rest of his face, and looking at me, let forth a phlegmy exhale. "You've left?" he said. "Left the Kingdom?"

"Yes," I said. "A few years after the war." I offered my hand. He lifted his own and inspected it before giving it to me. The fingers were chilled and supple, delicate as pine needles.

In the ensuing awkwardness of avoiding his eyes while trying to think of what next to say, I blundered. "I left seven years after you." I immediately regretted the words; the last thing I should have mentioned was his departure from the Kingdom.

Benjamin withdrew into his greatcoat, turtle-like, and watched the floor. I groped for anything to save the moment.

"I live near Washington," I said. "But I'm traveling home for a visit."

He raised his eyes, which beneath the glaze of drink were as dark as old iron.

"There's been a death," I said. "Aunt Louise. But then there've been so many dying lately—the older generation." Which was his generation.

Benjamin took a coughing fit, exasperated I'm sure by the locomotive soot oozing through the open doorways, unable as it was to vent skyward in that Washington mug of stagnant gases. With each meager cackle, his head jerked and rested somewhere new, the bob-and-stop, bob-and-stop of a crying infant. As he continued, expressionless and patient—this apparently a condition for him—a void widened around us. Finally, with a deliberate, wheezing hack, he arrested the outburst, and breathless, said, "Who all's died?"

So, there I had it. He knew nothing of his brothers and sister, his Starret cousins or the Sharpe family, over the past twenty-one years.

"We must talk," I said. "There's so much to tell." I glanced up at the clock. "But I've only ten minutes till boarding." I reached for my bags, then realized they weren't there. "I can't even try for a later train. My luggage is loaded."

Without a second's pause, he said, "I'll go with you."

"But Benjamin, your plans. You must be off to…somewhere."

He went silent. I smoothed the skirt of my dress and pretended to search my handbag for my ticket until at last he said, "I need coffee. We'll meet in the dining car." He started for the ticket windows.

"But Benjamin," I called.

He halted, looked back.

"I can't go into the dining car."

"What's this?" He stepped toward me but stopped as I raised

my brows to suggest the obvious. "Oh that," he said. "To hell with them," and he waved it off. "If the fools only knew."

Benjamin James tottered then tipped into the cushions of the bench across the table from me, the train not even moving. I looked up the aisle to see a waiter, black-skinned and shiny as a chunk of anthracite, charging at me, finger pointed toward the door. I thought of Benjamin's peculiar facial characteristic which could play tricks on people. Given his fair skin, the narrowness of his nose, the thinness of his pallid lips, most saw only his white half. But coloreds sometimes had second thoughts. As did the waiter, who stood in the aisle beside us getting a better look at Benjamin, hat off now.

"Aw, Lawd," the waiter said to the windowed clerestory as he straightened out of his practiced stoop of servility. "Two of them."

The only other people in the coach sat at two tables toward the front. They turned our way and the waiter, catching this, let out a faint moan. "Now I'll have to fetch the conductor." He raised his brows and clenched his lips at Benjamin, a plea for us to instead leave.

Benjamin James had another look about him, this one not ambiguous at all. His features were sucked grimly and bloodlessly against his bones, his face appearing as if it had suffered a slow death separate from the rest of his body during those months he'd lived with a gallows at the edge of his every prospect, and then been blanched by the alternating rains and winds of his life on the road. Something in that look announced he still wore his coat not in memory of his service, not in tribute to the Union, but because it could hide a .44 colt dragoon revolver and a stiletto-bladed knife, right where he could reach them easily.

As the waiter recognized this, he rocked his head up and down twice, then slunk back into deference, grudging though it was this time, and walked off for our coffee.

Benjamin cast a glance at the other occupants, and in the way the lazy August leaves of a field oak turn on a breeze, their stares shifted from him. All that remained was a gulf of silence that seemed to suck the air from the coach. And I could think only to say, "Where are you coming from?"

He made a waving motion that swept the expanse of the far windows. These faced east, and so he had indicated up and down the seaboard, the pendulum of his life. I had already suspected he moved from port to port to take on stints at docks and shipyards, for I'd whiffed sea salt beneath his acrid odor of old sweat and urine, exhaled whiskey and cigarette. Indeed, the very fugacious nature of the man bespoke his mode of living. I asked where he'd last worked.

"Baltimore." He spat out the place as if it had entered his mouth on the wings of a fly. "Before that, a port in Camden. Up Jersey." He fumbled with his hat on the seat, then mentioned there'd been some trouble in Baltimore, and so he'd moved on, south. To sniff out work at the Port of Alexandria.

"Over in Virginia," I said. "Where I live."

Seeing the waiter approach with the coffeepot, Benjamin drew from his greatcoat a flask. He withdrew the stopper and as the waiter poured his coffee, added the spirit.

He downed the drink in a gulp, hot as it must have been even with the cutting of liquor. I saw he had it bad, the effort of raising the cup tremulant. The engineer set off a long, fluting whistle followed by three quick toots, and the floor of our car hummed with the air tanks releasing the brakes. As the train lurched and we backed away from the platform, Benjamin shifted his eyes to the window and asked with no expression of voice or face, "What do you do that you're here?" A pause to gather my name from the fog. "Anna Maria."

"I'm a writer." This gave me his attention, and I realized I'd better specify the kind, for he had gained an aversion to journalists. I'm sure he would have stepped off that moving train were he cornered by one, even all those years after the fact. "A speechwriter."

"For them?" With a contemptuous flick of his elbow, he indicated the window. We were crossing the mall, the city's planners and the officials of the railroad having brilliantly placed the station at its edge, sullying that public space with tracks and train sheds. We gazed at the Capitol rotunda, etched into the morning haze where it hulked over treetops. Washington has always appeared haphazard, a city not raised but dropped on an aesthetically incompatible landscape. Of all our capital's jumbled architectural plagiarisms, the spider-like monstrosity on the hill is least likely, in my mind, to settle into its place. It will forever stand there trying to appear democratic while unable to hide it wishes it were instead grand.

"For a few of them," I said. We looked out now at newly leafed trees scattered up the sweep of Capitol Hill.

His eyes lumbered back. "So you go up there?"

I chuckled. "No, I do not go there. My speeches go there. Some of them. But I do not. My writing remains anonymous." I tilted my head to emphasize again the obvious. "My writing must remain anonymous."

It was his turn to chuckle, hoarse gasps really.

Now that I'd sat and settled awhile from the flurry of our meeting, the implausibility of the encounter set in. And to think Benjamin had acted on a whim to return where I'm sure he would not have gone otherwise, the homeland he'd departed from embroiled in a murder. The extravagance had the effect of nudging the rest of my existence into the periphery of my mind. My world became distilled into the space we occupied, and my memories of our place, my movements, my very breath, had the airy quality of being lifted by a thread from above.

I should point out that though Benjamin no longer had been an accused murderer by the time he left the Kingdom, with no other party charged, he bore the stigma of having been thought the killer of his older brother, James. Known from birth by the sobriquet Jimmy James, he'd been generally loathed as a lecher and ruthless whiskey maker, an overall rogue with a lion's propensity to violence.

I had witnessed the event with as much naivety as a girl of ten could possess in the Kingdom in the 1860s. Our home was small—a cabin really, like those of all our people, with one room below and a half-story above. So my parents discussed little of the murder in those tight quarters, where nothing passed at least one of us, two sisters and three brothers.

The wisdom and judgment of Benjamin James, the withered

stalk of a man before me, once commanded as much regard as was possible in the Kingdom. Folks relied on him to mediate disputes over property lines, wandering livestock, bastardry, family beatings. Benjamin had believed that the honest work and possibilities for trade from the railroad inching its way nearer our highland might deliver us from our scourges of tippling houses, whoredom, and brutality. He was hired as a section boss but never could build us a bridge to the rest of the world. We remained hidebound, averse to any but river transportation, which suited less honest but more profitable trade, even as it kept us prisoners of the hazards.

Thus, we carried on the distinction of the most ignorant and corrupt people of the wilderness void of north-central Pennsylvania, a vast and wild tableland gouged by sharp water-cut canyons.

To this day, train travelers moving up the West Branch, their coaches squeezed more and more tightly between scarps, enter an unexpected backcountry broken only by the occasional hand-to-mouth floodplain farm. Where the walls of the valley are closest and the swift waterway bears little resemblance to the gracefully bending river left behind, rather is some temperamental cross between it and the rocky tributary they're about to veer to, the travelers come nearest to our Hickory Kingdom. Until they've ascended to the flats beyond, they wonder at the unlikeliness of such a landscape hidden within our nation's most civilized corner.

Considering how appropriately aberrant the geography of the Kingdom is to a people so full of dark ironies, I've wondered whether it's not coincidental that we settled there, rather that it had some way sought us. Outsiders might say it's been a fair deal, for among our paradoxes, we have persisted by all appearances impoverished while, in fact, have become some of the wealthiest landowners in that country.

Two generations—mine and that of the road-rotted man before me scattering specks of tobacco on the linen as he rolled a cigarette into a scrap of newspaper he must have torn away at the newsstand—have found little use for wealth other than to enable vices and evade antidotes for them. We became the self-contradictory community that endeavored to destruct itself in the very rituals of propagation.

Other than the few who've married into nearby settlements, I am the only person to have taken any of that wealth outside the Kingdom. The post-war liberalities of our federal government allowed a great deal of our money, which came to me under circumstances I would not learn until that day, to furnish me an education—though not the answers or escape I was after.

Benjamin was leaning with his elbows on the table, lighting his cigarette while sucking it. Absently, I stroked the ruffles of my neckerchief and turned toward passing farmland.

"Which ones do you go back to?" he said after a moment.

I started at this breach into my thoughts. At the sight of pastures and woodlots, I'd gone in my mind to the people and places of the Kingdom, sorting the ones I hoped to see and those I did not. As always though, reluctant to return. Benjamin dropped the smoldering cigarette into his coffee cup, a band of smoke dithering between us. With his shoulders rocking from the sway of the train huffing toward full speed, his blunted nerves hadn't the wherewithal to keep his head from jiggling. He leaned his chest into the table and crossed his forearms upon it, but this did not arrest the motion.

Caught in his aimless gaze, I decided those eyes, such a dark gray they seemed without pupils, were non-committal because of something other than drink, for they were so powerful in this generality that I could feel him plumbing my depths.

It occurred to me that I'd put my fingers to my mouth. I moved them away. "I beg your pardon?"

He went on watching and I understood he asked which of our people I stayed with. "My mother," I said. "She's still there at our house. Little's changed." He blinked twice and looked out the window.

"You remember our place?" I said. "At the corner of the cut-off road."

He nodded.

To take the subject too far, to move the conversation off my family's doorstep and onto that troubled landscape, would conjure for him delicate memories. But memories of my own, not to mention a desperate longing to solve an old, personal mystery, prodded me. "One summer," I said, "you passed our house every Saturday carrying a satchel over your shoulder from work on some section. I must have been five or six, and you were all I knew of railroads." Smiling, I glanced up at the ceiling's delicate scrollwork. "I hadn't even seen rails. Just a waiting excavation cut into the river valley the few times we'd taken the buckboard down to sell whiskey and wild onions to raftsmen."

His brows gathered just enough to reveal he was recalling. I ventured farther, up the road to his cabin, a dwelling different from the ones before and after it—the cabins of two of his brothers—in that its lot was un-cleared, a wild regrowth upon some squatter's long-before attempt at making pasture of a forest. "I remember visiting you with my father," I said. "You were so good at repairing harnesses."

The waiter returned with the coffee, and as if we'd inquired about a meal a hundred times, he announced with a show of forced patience: "There's only toast with preserves for the rest of the mornin'."

Benjamin merely lifted a hand and I said I'd like just tea. He pushed his cup to the edge of the table and removed his flask, hurrying to add the liquor as the waiter poured. Then Benjamin fished out his cigarette butt and downed the hot drink.

As the waiter left for the tea, I cleared my throat. "The lot of us went to you one day," I said. "My parents, me—only ten—my little brothers and sister."

I saw it vividly, one of those midwinter afternoons when sharp north winds daggered across the Kingdom. Snow not falling, rather racing slantwise, not settling, banking. My family trudging up the road in gaiters mother had made from flour sacks and girdled by twine at our knees and shoes—or I should say what was left of our shoes that late in winter, snow sneaking through holes, not melting though, cold as our feet were. Each of us peeped from a wrapping of wool blanket, tallest to smallest, as we plodded through drifts that restored themselves by the time of our twilight return. Benjamin's cabin came into view, a thin band of chimney smoke drafting down and compassing the walls like a lasso trick.

The waiter came and poured my tea, then half-set, half-dropped the kettle beside my saucer.

"I'll never forget that day," I said and watched Benjamin, careful of the ground I was stepping onto.

He stopped reaching into his coat for his pouch of tobacco, waited. Then he turned up the palm of his free hand, beckoning me on.

"There'd been trouble." I lifted my cup, set it back in its saucer. "I guess there was always trouble. But this time to the extent that Mother and Poppy would not leave us children home alone. Something complicated and grave enough that father needed your help to light a way through." I sipped tea, searched the car as if for an eavesdropper. A woman coughed daintily into her napkin, reached to straighten a spray of flowers on her hat.

I breathed deeply, hesitant to bring up the name. "Even as a girl of ten, I'd put together it had to do with Jimmy James. While we children warmed ourselves at your stove, I heard his name hissed by my mother, cursed by my father. Worse—" I paused, closed my eyes a second—"I'd caught him time to time around our place skulking in the woods, pretending he was hunting. But he was watching our house. I realized soon enough he was looking for my father to be away because after Poppy left for a stint cutting timber, Jimmy James knocked on the door. Mother ordered us to the corners of the room as he stole around the place. He tapped at the windows and called mother's name. 'Rachel. *Ra-a-a-chel...*'

I tugged my neckerchief, swallowed to steady my voice. "But this is the curious thing. He called my name, too." I balled my hands and pressed them down upon the table. "Benjamin, I never understood that. Why me?"

The sinewy-taught skin across his cheeks released slightly, the lips parted. But he merely leaned away from the table and pulled out his tobacco pouch, matches, and another piece of newspaper. He worked on a cigarette, lit it, returned his tobacco, and smoked.

I interpreted Benjamin's silence as at least permission to continue on about this brother who'd be the victim of a crime that would, on the very evening of the visit I spoke of, irrevocably change Benjamin's life—as I always sensed it changed mine. "I have to admit that seeing him those times, I'd become fascinated with something familiar about him. It made me realize things about myself."

Benjamin looked down where his cigarette was smoldering near his fingers.

"Does that make sense?" I said.

Without raising his eyes, he nodded, the slow certainty in the gesture growing chilly and foreboding fingers that grazed my flesh from ankle to nape of neck.

He snuffed his cigarette between his thumb and forefinger and dropped it onto his saucer. He looked up, narrowed lids quivering with concentration. "What did you realize about yourself?"

I sighed. "Differences. Between me and the people in my life."

Benjamin's chin inched toward me. "What differences?" Something near anger in his voice challenged me for an answer.

"Little things," I said. "My eyes, my clubby arms and legs. And big things—easily enough explained, but suddenly somehow suspicious." I hesitated, wrapped a finger around the handle of my cup. "Look at how different your skin was from that of Jimmy James and others of your brothers. That happens. We never know how we'll come out. In my case, it was in the opposite way, but not with such a clear-cut reason." I lifted my tea to my lips, found it cold and set it down. "When a girl suspects a loose knot in the family ties she'd taken for granted, her mind turns to her origins. Think of yourself, Benjamin. Beyond making you wonder at God's strange sense of humor, doesn't the difference between you and your brothers automatically turn your mind to your parents?"

He lifted a shoulder.

"But I knew there would be no answer from my parents. So to contemplate myself, I've always gone further back. To a person I did not know—my grandfather on my father's side, distanced by a deliberate hushing of his voice. I'm led to wonder if he's the answer I'm after."

I watched for some reaction from Benjamin that might confirm my hunch. Nothing.

"At first, I thought that by his skin color alone he could explain my peculiar appearance, given the difference between me and my light-skinned father, and of course my mother. But I recalled him being referred to as mulatto, that awful allusion to the sterile mule. That itself only further speaks of the contradiction of my looks, as I assume he was not dark-skinned. It would lead a person further back in the family tree for an explanation of me inheriting skin darker than his. But I believe that the answer in some other way lies just beyond that curtain of concealment my family stitches around the stories of him and Jedediah James."

Benjamin had given me his attention such that it had distracted his effort to hold himself upright, his body slouching toward the window. At my last words however, he straightened, nodded as if he understood, and said, "I knew George Sharpe well."

I was astonished. My father had spoken so seldom about his father that I had the impression even he'd hardly known him. I turned to the window. The hilly countryside stretched fresh and greening and without depth of shadow in that morning light restrained by milky overcast. I was well acquainted with the scenery of our route—its farmhouses, plantations, and shacks scattered among woods and rutted pastures—so I knew we'd be stopping at Bowie soon—a chance for me to excuse myself if I decided to flee what felt like a storm rolling in.

"How did you know George Sharpe so well?" I said. "They say that until his last years, he lived away from the Kingdom, down at Ferney Run."

He tipped his head—a logical question. "I worked for him until I was twenty-one. At Ferney Run. My parents—my mother really—sent me to him when I was twelve, right after his daughter Louise—the one you say just died—went up to the Kingdom and married my brother Daniel. All the Sharpe kids by then were at the Kingdom—except David—who's younger than me."

I held up a finger. "Was. My father is gone now."

Benjamin went silent a moment, then said, "I helped them run the gristmill."

Since Benjamin was the youngest James child and his

parents would have missed his help on the farm, I assumed they hired him out. "It must have been a hard decision," I said, "for them to send you away like that, so young."

He closed his eyes and gave forth a wheezy sigh; I smelled the coffee and whiskey, each remarkably distinct. "How little you know," he whispered, then looked up at the clerestory.

I could taste now that storm I'd feared looming in what I was about to hear. But it was strangely enticing even as I felt it raise a threat to my innocence, like a burlesque turning lewd. Part of me wanted to leave while another said no, that though the truth might exceed my strength, I should stay just long enough to learn the extent of any deception. "What did he look like?" I said. "My grandfather."

Benjamin pulled at the cape of his greatcoat and shifted on his seat. When he did not speak, I said, "Even as I suspect his looks don't explain mine, how can't I be curious I'm wrong? Tell me about them."

He watched himself pluck the table linen. "He was a careful man. Careful in his walk and what he said. Quiet."

"His looks, Benjamin."

"No." He lifted his head. "You let me tell you the man first. How he held to himself like no one I ever knew."

I wondered if the fugitive years as soldier and vagrant had corrupted into eccentricity the wisdom I'd known. I looked past my window reflection, grainy in the dusty glare. Where I'd just seen scattered farms now passed crowded frame homesteads with lime-white clapboards and picket fences, shanties and cows out back. The passengers at the other tables put out tips, reached for their gripsacks and inched toward the aisle.

"Before we stop," I said, "at least tell me his looks."

Who was I to think I could press Benjamin James. He reached beneath his coat, took out his flask and unstopped it, his hands shaking such that I thought I'd have to help pour the liquor—until he put the bottle to his lips, tipped back his boney head and suckled like a baby.

He re-corked the flask, empty now, and set it on the table. "Shoulders like a catamount. Good for carrying sacks of grain and meal. Big hands. Thumbs like mason mallets."

Benjamin ferreted his coat for more whiskey, pushing my patience. He frowned when he found none.

"Please," I whispered. And when he nodded—the train whistling, brakes hissing—I turned and looked not at Bowie, Maryland, but at Benjamin's face spectral and awry in the window reflection.

He let out a long breath, the smell of whiskey unadulterated by coffee now. "Had green eyes."

Like my father's, I thought, and for a moment I closed my eyes, my dark brown eyes.

"Chin split," Benjamin said. "Gouge in the middle." And I pictured that cleft in my father's chin, the chins of my little brothers and sister. I'd counted myself fortunate not to have the family "bum-chin," a consolation for knotted and kinked hair always matted with bits of grass and leaf, for dark eyes and not the pastel aqua of my siblings.

The engineer braked harder and in the window, Benjamin's head pitched backward. Out on the platform, a porter wheeled a cart of trunks. As the train huffed to a stop, I thought for the most polite way to excuse myself. Surely if I walked away, waited for a later coach, Benjamin would not follow me to the Kingdom with whatever secrets he carried. I reached for my handbag.

"George Sharpe liked me," Benjamin said. "Would've sold me the mill when he and Rosanna retired to the Kingdom. David didn't want it—too fixed on my Starret cousin, the one that many years later he finally got to marry him. Your mother."

I closed my eyes and let pass the cloud of him not referring to David as my father.

Benjamin tapped the table for my attention. "He told me the stories. Of him and my father." He tried to hold back a cough, his body quaking, splotches of color appearing on his cheeks as if fingers poked there until at last he gave in.

I looked away as he hacked sputum into his napkin. A man in a slate summer suit and white gloves entered the car and let pass the exiting passengers. He eyed me, then sat two tables away. Whatever stories Benjamin held would tear down the fence of half-truths that let our people deny some worse real truth, the stain of which we all felt and by which so many sowed lawlessness throughout the Kingdom.

Benjamin's shoulders heaved under his greatcoat as he panted, his mouth a bellows of rotgut exhalations that only added to my queasiness. I pulled my handbag against my thigh and started out of my seat, catching a wince at the movement. I shook my head; I did not want to know his stories.

But I understood that in my reluctance I admitted I needed to know. I let go of the strap of my handbag. Benjamin stuffed his phlegm-sodden napkin into his coffee cup. He took out his tobacco pouch, laid it on the table and raised his spacious stare to embrace all of me. Then he began in a voice that has infused my recollection of it all, the flat pining of a chant passing through him from vanished ancestors.

King and Queen County, Virginia

Jedediah worked not like the other slaves, their backs to the sun as they raked their windrows or planted. He always faced the big house. From just about anywhere in the fields, if he strained his eyes over the cedars, which some old Marse had planted to dampen the songs of his laborers and sweeten the smell of manure and turned earth, Jedediah could see the three upstairs windows beneath the eaves of the slated roof. He knew that Juda watched him, and to Jedediah that was the balm the other slaves found in breezes that cooled brows and shooed flies.

Juda, tending to bedding or chamber pots, knew him out there by his scarf of indigo linen. She'd made it from a length of cloth she found while sweeping beneath a shelf in the dining-room closet, probably left from a bolt cutting made into napkins, the piece saved for a patchwork or to adorn a dress back before Mistress had her outer attire sent from Philadelphia while Master was there in his sessions. A risk to Juda, for Mistress kept as careful account of her linen as she did her larder. Still, Juda had given it to Jedediah, a present upon their betrothment. The worst that had come of it was that the driver, Catman, had warned he'd let the linen's owner give Jedediah twenty lashes and an extra day smoked if it had been stolen.

No matter how far off, Jedediah looked as if he wore about his neck a band of eastern sky at August twilight—except on blustery days when he wrapped the scarf around his head in the way of the women with their kerchiefs. He paraded it without shame, and she loved that about Jedediah.

Juda stood before the sewing table in the bedroom of Missy Cornelia—soon to be Mistress Bakeraskin—alternately stitching lace onto the bodice of Missy's wedding gown and looking out the 24-pane window of wavy glass, which warped the neat blocks of field and pasture, the fence rails, as if they were under water.

Now he hunched near a mule, probably cleaning clods of earth from a plowshare with that forked stick he tucked into the back of his breeches. She watched through a window pane etched with a pin, letters and numbers Juda understood were the initials of Missy Cornelia and the year she'd scratched them into the glass—1786—when Missy and Juda were little girls and allowed to play together, even in this room, almost as sisters. Almost.

She shifted her weight enough to watch him through another pane. Voices bubbled in from the adjoining master chamber. Juda took back to stitching. Mistress chuckled over some trifle, and Missy Cornelia burst into one of those giggling fits she was wont to overdo these days as she aimed them like spiteful pebbles at Juda.

Panting mother and daughter stepped through the doorway behind Juda.

"Juda-girl," Mistress said.

Juda bowed her head.

"What's the word at the quarters about the arrival of our guests?"

Mistress always wanted the word at the quarters. "Jes dat Fri-dy—tomorra'—is de arrivin' day," Juda said.

"Therefore," Mistress said—she liked to say this after someone answered a question so she could finish with a command—"I want today to be cleaning day down there. I want all the slaves' clothes boiled. The men's hair cropped. The yard swept. Clean. Clean. Clean. And I want no slaves in the lawns of the big house unless they have a duty for the wedding. You get the word around, you hear? No one goes to bed until the cleaning is done."

Juda set down the needle, thread and dress, nodded. "Yes, ma'am."

"Juda," Missy Cornelia said and waited for her to turn. But Juda indulged a second in rolling her eyes, glanced out at that man in his blue scarf, moving now behind the mule, Jedediah deliberate and steady as his plow, unbending as his rows. *Oh, Jeddy, weren't it night time all de time. Aren't nobody torment us den.*

She turned. Mistress was bonneted, Missy's hair moused with powder, all of yesterday's curls gathered with a ribbon atop her head but for a few to cover the forehead of that pinched, pale face. Juda saw they were eager to speak, a slight tremor in Mistress's wormy lips, across that goose beak that reached right up to her plucked brows. Her daughter clasped her hands to her uncovered stays and smirked, which was all the smile a slave got from the whites around here. Around anywhere, likely.

"Do the slaves know where I will be going?" Missy said, her words oozing out in a soft, mocking song, always a perfect measure of the satisfaction she would take in some brutish infliction, always crueler when Master was away, as he was today—off to fetch the Bakeraskin family from the river port.

"Up ta Maryland's de word," Juda said. "Ta live wid yer new husband and his kin."

"No," Missy said, "we will go to Maryland only for a short visit. Then we will be off to Pennsylvania."

It mattered not to Juda. Pennsylvania. Maryland. Just words. All that mattered was being rid of her, of one more James daughter.

"Cornelia," Mistress James said, though she watched Juda, rare delight in those otherwise fault-finding eyes. "I have a gift for you and Mister Bakeraskin that I must share." She glanced out the window then back to Juda. "This present is a choice. Like picking a sweetmeat at the confectioner's—peach, nut, orange peel."

Cornelia pulled her shawl tight across her stays and exaggerated a shiver of excitement. "Tell me, what must I choose?"

"No lady should go off to a wilderness unattended," Mistress said, glancing at her daughter. "So I'm giving you a servant. Your pick."

And Juda, looking away to Missy's bed with its oyster-white quilt Juda had sewn, understood—or so she thought—what was to become of her. That warm music that had been her insides for the past year dried to punk and crumbled, leaving her empty except for some bitter rind of lost joy smarting where her heart should have been. *Oh, Jeddy.* She wanted to turn to that window, but let her eyes fall to the floorboards of amber heart pine.

"Mother," Missy Cornelia said. "Up there on the frontier, I believe Mister Bakeraskin and I would best be served by a man slave."

Juda could not help herself; she stepped ahead to embrace Missy, stopping only at Mistress's gasp. And yet Juda whispered, "Oh, Missy, I thanks you," so dizzy with relief she bumped the sewing table as she drew back.

Then Missy Cornelia, with a deliberate lift of her chin, sucked in the room's silence, pulled to herself those background sounds that only deepen quiet: the watery trill of blackbirds, the ringing of the smithy's hammer, the moans of teat-swollen cows in their stalls. Satisfaction had bloomed across Missy's face and Juda realized she'd been tricked into neglecting her own played part. Scared out of her nigger-idiocy, drawn by the leash of another white woman ploy, she'd exposed her heart and handed Missy the salt of whatever she contrived to do next. Dumb girl, bow that forehead, widen and wag those eyes.

But Mistress, too, had been taken aback by this new turn of the farce as she stared at her daughter. "Dear," she said, "step to the chamber." She forced a smile, which Cornelia did not return, put a hand to her shoulder. "Cornelia, what of our understanding?"

And then the picture became clear: scorned Mistress foiled by the spirited daughter escaping her own share of the scorn. Both of them, as usual, pretending blindness to where the blame belonged. All the while, Juda's skin going a-prickle at what Missy might be about.

Missy watched out the window. The corners of her mouth turned up in a grin—lucky, it said, that I found out. Oh, luck—just as I was to carry off mother's scorn, my scorn, and be cursed with it forever. "Mother," she said, her smile aimed at Juda now, "I've quite decided. It is my gift, after all. And given the circumstances, father can hardly deny me, don't you think?"

As Cornelia paused and looked again to the fields, a vile ichor washed into Juda's throat, a flux of the maelstrom lifting in her gut.

"Juda-girl," Missy said. "Go out to the kitchen and send the boy Aleck to the overseer. Have him say he's fetching that slave I see there with the blue neckerchief. I want him clean of field filth when I meet him at the veranda. With you."

Juda swallowed back the bile, whispered, "Please Missy."

"Get, girl. Get."

And so Juda went, her steps weightless, her hands wringing her apron as she imagined making pin cushions of their ugly dun eyes.

Whistling for another field hand to take his mule, Jedediah followed Aleck, stretching his steps to keep up with the boy as he leaped over furrows. Jedediah asked what the matter was, sure of trouble. But Aleck, reaching the peach grove, broke into an out-and-out run through the sweet pollen, his body yawing this way and that among the trees, easily irregular as a barn swallow. He bubbled out a forbidden—and so savory—slave song, safe here from the overseer, all sorrow gone from his naive rendering.

> Do, please, marster don't ketch me,
> Ketch dat nigger behin' dat tree;
> He stole money en I stole none,
> Put him in the calaboose des for fun!

The boy was out of sight by the time Jedediah jumped the fence and started along the lane toward the big house. Juda leaned against the wooden railing of the veranda, pointing him toward the kitchen. He angled across the yard, watching that sweet lustrous girl. Jedediah slowed and stiffened his steps, pulled back his shoulders, that strut she loathed because such airs vexed the master more than did walking on the lawn—and which she loved for the same reason. Her man who was really just the boy who'd stolen sugar loaves right from the table settings. For her.

As he approached the kitchen house, fowl ran hurry-scurry past the well and between the frame smokehouse and dairy of red Seneca sandstone, the overseer's tattler of a wife watching from their rooms above. He caught the glint of a meat cleaver wedged into the butchering log as he ascended the steps to the steamy laundry, which occupied this side of the kitchen. Maybe, Jedediah thought, he'd been called to slaughter a hog.

Old Anna was bent at the hearth. The fireplace, nearly as wide as the room, allowed a mere doorway to the kitchen. "Dey's a weevil in de wheat, boy," she said without turning. She shifted her clothes-iron on the grid, her fingers crooked and gnarled like the tree limbs she used to stir her wash kettle.

Jedediah took up a cake of lye soap from the table behind Old Anna, bit off a corner. He went through to the kitchen, from the acrid tang of Old Anna's laundry brew to the savory smell of root vegetables simmering on the opposite hearth, ham fat foaming at the brim of the four-legged pot. Julie stood at a table, her back to him, beating biscuit batter with a hickory stick. The way her high hips and buttocks, wagging with the work, splayed her petticoats, the slight neck which seemed too spare to hold her head steady, these stopped him with the thought: *she could be her daughter standing there.* Until she turned, that face so much darker than her daughter's, the night to Juda's dusk. And the eyes—hers creased by constant wariness, where the daughter's devoured everything.

Julie nodded to the barrel Jedediah stood by. "Don't you wash up in der. Dat's for cleanin' china. Use de sink."

Jedediah stepped to a hollowed stone trough, the shape and chill of a child coffin. He tossed in his chunk of lye soap and stoppered the drain-hole with a disk of soapstone. Then he took a pail of water from beneath the sink and poured it in.

Julie was silent behind him as he tugged up his sleeves and agitated the water.

"Dey must know," he said.

"Dat 'lil Missy up ta sumptin," Julie said. "Dat's what dey want wid you ober dat big house, where dey please dey-selves tormentin' my Judith. It sumptin dat Missy up ta."

He used the lye soap to abrade away the field dirt on each palm and wrist. He pushed back his hat brim, bent and scooped driblets of the gray water to his face, the lye burning where the wind had chafed his cheeks and lips. After removing the stopper from the drain, he shook his head and hands over the sink, then turned and dragged his palms down his shirt. "Dey know," he said. "How?"

She held his stare, abided the hint of accusation. Not taking her eyes from him, she went back to pounding her beaten biscuits, sinewy, floury forearms bared where she'd rolled up the sleeves of her shortgown. Muscular forearms, while Juda's were slight as willow sticks.

Jedediah rubbed his wet chin against his shoulder. "You think some yeller freeman gone ride in here and rest Marse's shame? Fix all de troubles?"

Julie looked down and pummeled the edges of the dough, the downstrokes of her stick slicing the air now, *whif-swak, whif-swak...* "Fill de bucket 'fore you go over dat big house," she said.

His bare feet patted and sighed against the cool slate of the covered walk. He moved soundlessly up the wooden stairs and crossed the veranda, his heart pounding out fiercer imitations of the rapping he'd just left in the kitchen.

She hadn't moved, eyes aimed across the yard. Immobile as the steam-white overcast.

"Dey knows, Jeddy," she said.

He would not risk touching her, and so clenched handfuls of his shirt. Between glances at the window by the door, he took in the curves of her cheek and forehead, roved the skin of her neck—smooth, its sheen like glass-carved walnut wood.

"Today," Jedediah said, "dey makes me feel like a slave inside a slave. Dey makes me feel squeezed so's I can't breathe."

Juda turned those hazel eyes to him, round and staunch even now, even as she said, "Der's worse news."

They turned as the door swung wide and out came Missy Cornelia in a gown of India muslin, a matching cap pulled snug by a pink silk ribbon. Her face was brimming with more than the usual sneer, lips and nose a-twitching. She motioned with her hand and said, "Step apart."

Jedediah moved away and took off his hat.

"Your dalliance," Missy said as her mother came onto the porch, "is no secret in this house. But the marriage you've planned without the permission of your master is impossible."

"Indeed," Mistress James said. "If it could be called such."

Jedediah looked down, thumbed the straw of his hat brim. "Yes'm," he said. "Me and Juda was jes waitin' til atter Missy's big weddin'. Den we wuz gone ast Marse leave for de...well, for us to be maird much as he'd 'llow. Ma'am." He could hear Juda's breathing now, her inhales catching in small hiccups. Just at the edge of his vision, he caught the brilliant, loose frizzes of her hair trembling.

"There'll be no use for that," Missy said. "I've decided to make a gift of you."

"Yes'm." He rolled his eyes like a tied heifer while he weighed what she'd said. Were they selling him south?

"To myself," Missy said.

"Pardon?"

"You'll be a servant to me and slave to Master Bakeraskin."

Jedediah tried to say yes'm but managed only a grunt.

"Speak louder," Mistress said.

He raised his head, swallowed and tried to make words. But he could only look from Mistress to Missy and back again.

"Why, mother," Missy said, "he's struck dumb." She moved half a step toward Jedediah. "All the better to hear this. You will accompany us to a place far from here. You'll have no notions about this girl and will never again see her here at Serendip. And remember this Jedediah, any bit of trouble from you or her will give me complete power over her fortune. Master will not deny me that."

She looked Juda up and down. "Wouldn't she fetch a price on a southbound coffle?"

Juda creaked out: "Missy, please."

"But have you considered," Mistress said in a final plea, "what your father will do for a new field worker this time of year? They're planting."

Missy nodded. "Juda-girl will have to go to the fields and take the place of this plowboy. How can Master prevent it if I demand it in front of the overseer?"

And this, despite the comfort Jedediah knew Mistress took in keeping an eye on Juda and her mother, seemed to be an acceptable compromise to Mistress, for it was another injury to the girl.

Missy gave her a moment. "Mother, anything else?"

Mistress lifted her chin to Jedediah. "Bow to your new Mistress," she said.

Jedediah crouched outside the door of the men's quarters in the half-moonlight. He listened in the direction of the barn, where the road passed. The still night would give away Master's approach, allowing enough time. He hoped. Each distant dog bark, each lull in the peeping of treefrogs, sucked away another breath. He glanced where Juda said she'd watch through a knothole in the women's loft. Would he have the nerve to signal and run with her to the big house? He leaned forward so he could see the whole gable. So many knotholes.

Juda turned to her mam, who'd moved her pallet next to her tonight. She breathed steady and deep now—finally, after having kept a vigil on her daughter. Juda put her eye back to the knothole. Jedediah just then turned away.

Moments later, he gave the liquid *pwip* of a whip-poor-will. Juda crawled among the scattered pallets of the other girls and women. Nothing save the ladder hole admitted light into the loft, and that merely whatever moonglow crept through the open shutters of the lower room. As she slid a leg along the ladder post, feeling for a rung, Juda reached out to steady herself and brushed little Nan who shot up with a cry of, "Mam." Patty reached for her daughter beside her, then lifted her head at Juda. Juda moaned and rubbed her stomach, and Patty nodded as she pulled her little girl to her breast.

Horse hooves rumbled on the road as Juda hurried to the peg where she'd hung her shortgown before going up to bed—when she thought her mother hadn't been looking. But it was gone. She'd have to go in just a chemise.

She found Jedediah pacing about the yard. Wrapping her arms around his neck, in half-kiss, half-words, she told him, "Settle Jeddy, we gone be awright. Dis nighttime. Our time."

Jedediah led Juda oak-to-oak along the lawn of the big house. Ahead, the team and carriage, followed by a lone rider, clattered onto the brick pavement, Hostler Harry, the coachman slave who lived at the stable, calling, "ho," at the steps. Master James hitched his mare to a post beside the black berlin, its panels lusterless beneath the silver half-moon, so mantled were they in road dust.

Jedediah huddled with Juda in the shadow of the nearest oak. He squeezed her hand and put his mouth close to her ear. "What if Marse goes in wid 'em?"

"He will," Juda whispered. "Den he be back to tell Harry where to take de trunk. You jes watch."

Hostler Harry, up on the perch, locked the brake, tilted down his hat, and hopped to the ground. He went to the door of the carriage and swung it out. Master James came around, cutting a threatening figure in the moonlight with his tailed coat and black breeches, Hessian boots, the tall felt hat with a buckled band. The greatest effects the moon could make on the man were a glint against the gold-threaded knee tassels of his boots and a milky illumination of the powder in his dangling and be-ribboned queue. He reached in and helped out a stiff little woman he called Mrs. Bakeraskin. She wore a ruffled mob cap and a white kerchief. Her "Thank you, Mister James," though a whisper, was at the same time squeaky.

Holding her hand, out came a man her opposite: tall, corpulent, and yet lithe. "A nice ride," he said, slapping the carriage. "I'd just as soon set my arse in there the whole way as spend a day on that boat from Havre de Grace."

"Why, Robert," Mrs. Bakeraskin said.

He laughed and shouted into the carriage: "Wake up, son."

A moment later, the celebrated groom, Peter Bakeraskin, tottered out, the moonlight playing in shades of gray on his light and varicolored attire. He squinted about as he swiveled his head on his tall cravat, then raised his brows to follow the high brick chimneys of the big house. He took his mother's elbow and with Master James and Mr. Bakeraskin ascended the porch stairs, his slippers falling silent while the other men's boots rasped and thumped.

The moment the door closed, Jedediah and Juda ran to Hostler Harry where he untied the trunk from the back of the carriage, mumbling about the crazy coon-hours white folks traveled by.

Juda made a "psst," and Hostler Harry spun around, palms raised. "Good Lawd, gal, what de hell... And you. Get yo asses outa here."

"She's gots ta talk ta Marse," Jedediah said.

"What she's gone get," Harry said, "is de whip an' a smokin, comin up de big house nights-time. Ah, Lawd, nekid, too."

"I's gone talk to him, Harry," Juda said. "An' you needs to tote dat trunk when I do it, so's Massa listens."

Harry watched her. "Der's no sense in a young niggah gal," he said. Then to Jedediah, "But you get yo ass away. Marse wone hear from you no-ways, boy."

Jedediah touched the nape of Juda's neck. He leaned and brushed her pussy willow lips with his own, the sweet mingled sweat of their midnight run hot and salty in his nose.

Hostler Harry moaned. "Aw Lawd, we's all gone get whipped and smoked."

Then Jedediah ran for the oak as the door swung wide, the candlelight from the hallway chandelier spreading onto the carriageway.

Master James waited at the threshold. "Harry, who's that there?"

Harry shook his head back and forth as he fumbled with the straps. "It's Juda-gal, Marse. I tried to send her off. But dis gal jes' wone listen."

Master James closed the door and descended to the bottom step, Juda holding still but for kneading hands full of chemise. "Did your mother send you for something?" he said, watching her obliquely as he glanced about.

"Oh, no, Massa, she don't even know I's here. Dey's troubles, big troubles."

Master James turned and considered the house, then lifted his chin to Harry. "Take the trunk around the back, put it inside the door."

"Beg pardon, Marse," Harry said, "but it's heavy." He rapped his hand against the top of the trunk. "I could get a wheelbarrow."

"Take it now," Master James said.

Master approached Juda where she stood behind the carriage. "Why can't this wait until tomorrow?" he said.

Her eyes went wide, her face inched forward. "It's sumsins bad," she said. "We can't wait."

"Who's we?" Master said. He glanced around again. "Are you here alone?"

"Yessuh. And 'we's' all a' us."

"Get on with it," Master said. "Before Harry comes back."

Juda took a half step toward Master. "Please Massa," she said, her words pouring out liquid and mournful. "Missy Cornelia, I know she hates me fierce. An' now she's gone get me good, get me de las' time, fer she chosed fer a weddin' gift a slave, an' it's my Jeddy, an' she takin' him offer ta some place called Pennsy-vania. An' I's gone ta de fields, an' oh Massa please, Jeddy's my ebber-thang, and dis po niggah, I's aren't troubled you fer nuttin. Or least I won'ts ebbers 'gin."

Master hissed his words. "What have you stirred up, Juda-girl?"

"Nuttin, Massa. I's jes de lil' quiet mouse you told me to be while Mistress 'sists I be near her. But you knows I can't do no right by Missy."

Master James clenched his jaw, stared perilously where Jedediah peered from the tree trunk. Blowing out a long and loud exhale, Master said, "You couldn't be content, could you?"

"Massa, all I's done's lub a man. Der aren't no pro-bitions 'gainst lubbin mans. And dat's all I's asks fer. Dat you makes so's he can stay. I'd work de fields all my days fer dat."

Master nodded and Jedediah thought he might help. Instead, he said, "You're ungrateful. You've been spoiled working in the house." He raised a finger before her face, but his attention snapped toward the corner of the house where Hostler Harry watched from beside a lilac.

"The trouble you cause, Juda-girl," Master said. "Harry, go back and carry that trunk up to the spare room. Tell Mistress I'm seeing to a loose carriage wheel."

"Beg pardon, Marse," Harry said. "I's de one s'posed to tend de wheels." But reading Master's face in the moonlight, Harry turned away.

Master grabbed Juda by the elbow, then seemed to think better of himself and pulled his hand away. "You'll not stir trouble through the quarters at a time like this," he said. "Get that nigger boy out of your head. Look at me, Juda-girl. There is no marriage of slaves, not even fornication, without my allowing it. Do nothing foolish. Or I'll have that boy at auction in the time it takes to get to Richmond." He leaned his face toward her. "Consider him lucky."

As Juda held out her hands, Jedediah knew she'd act now on that cursed sunniness of hers. He bit his lip and held his feet lest he send himself to a coffle for stopping her from uttering that damning word, full of truth and farce all at once. "Daddy," Juda said, "please."

Master's sidelong swing at first appeared it would deliver a slap—until his fist thumped Juda's temple and knocked her to the ground. When she again cried the forbidden word, this time spontaneously—the terrified and confused child's shriek—Master bent and with his hand to Juda's mouth, drove her skull against the yard.

Jedediah reached Master by the time he began swatting her face. "Marse," he said, fighting his own hands from taking hold of the man. "Sir. 'Scuse me's." He shifted foot-to-foot. He angled and bowed his head just so, turned his eyes as if the scene before him were as insignificant as the glint of dew on the fresh-mowed lawn.

In Jedediah's periphery, Master had gone still. He straightened and looked toward the house. Then, tugging the breast of his coat, he turned his eyes on Jedediah.

"Miss Julie sended me ups 'ere," Jedediah said, "ter de big house afta' Juda-gal. Sir." He shifted his gaze just so much, saw Juda lying still but for her chest lifting with jagged breaths. *Oh, girl.* Moonlight reflected in an oily sheen on the blood running down her cheek.

Master fixed his hat. Sweat glistened above his lip. He reached out and wiped on Jedediah's shirt blood from Juda's nose and tooth-torn lip. Taking Jedediah's jaw, he lifted his bowed head, and Jedediah could submit only by looking past his master's ear. "Girl," Master said. "Go back to the nigger cabins and wake everyone. Tell them this boy beat you while you tried to run from the barn. That he was trying to have his way with you before he was sent away with his new mistress. Tomorrow, before preparations for the Saturday wedding, he'll be whipped at the well. He needs a taming before he leaves Sunday. And you tell the niggers I want them to come with brooms to sweep dirt over the blood."

Now Jedediah looked down at Juda. Her lips convulsed with the effort of words hindered by pain and disbelief, and Jedediah thanked the Lord for keeping them from her. She closed her eyes as Master continued. "I want no notions from you about this nigger. You will see him tomorrow for what he is—another mulish brute that will learn by the lash. Then he will part from here on Sunday. Forever. If you do anything more to disrupt peace on this estate, I will remove you."

Juda rolled over, pushed herself onto her knees and rose to her feet. She caught in her hands strings and clots of blood. Master stepped away, and she started for the quarters.

Master rubbed his hand, regarding Jedediah. "You have the obstinate look of a mule about you," he said. "Perhaps my daughter has solved a problem. Not created one."

Which daughter dat? Jedediah wanted to ask.

First, she took her lie to the men's quarters, her ears ringing such that she could hardly hear herself call within the doorway. She sucked from her lips metallic blood as the men woke annoyed, a disturbance of their coveted peace-sleep, some not bothering to rise, even with the promise of scandal. Sam the blacksmith, in a gown, lit the fat of a crusie lamp and held the iron bowl with its smoke-oozing wick of twisted rag close to Juda's chin as others came from their places on the floor or descended the ladder. She told the tale as they leaned in from the dimness for a better look, Juda sure the swelling of her cheek, brow and lip already figured her into a monstrosity. They drew back, the meager flame making wavering shadows of them on the stripes of log and chink that walled the room, the men's cabin just a dormitory of pallets where garden rakes and hoes occupied the corners. Juda could make out the slant of doubt in their eyes, then their understanding of the sham as anger shifted their gazes to the big house. *Dey knows my Jeddy,* she thought. *Dey knows he lubs me.*

She told Master's story at the two married folk's quarters, the couplin cabins, as the slaves called them. At the first one, she watched Jedediah's father. "Damn, dem," he said, giving her lie not a second's credit. Jedediah's mother ascended the ladder to her pallet the moment she made sense of it—this woman whose other children had been sold—but only to the big plantations nearby.

At the women's cabin, Mam did her best to douse the ember of hope Juda had refused to let Master knock out of her. Old Anna lighted tallow candles and fitted them into gourds she spaced about the perimeter of the room, the redware stacked in corners and the baskets hanging by the door popping out of the darkness. She sent little Pheba to the well for a pail of water.

Juda sat on Old Anna's frame bed in the corner, her throbbing face bowed, elbows on her knees, while the women pulled up stools and the girls squatted. Juda recited it, as she'd promised Master she would, but with no passion; convincing them wasn't in the bargain. They listened, pretended they didn't suspect from the moment she started that it was a lie. All but Mam, who tried to make them question their instinct of unbelief.

"Dat rake tried to force hisself ons my baby?" Mam said. "Den dat Missy done de Lawd's kindness, takin him to Pennsy-vania." Mam stood and took Juda's chin in her fingers, turned her brow to study a lump there. None too gently. "Jes look at you. I's told you dat niggah gots de debil in him."

The women looked at one another, the girls at Old Anna, each searching for what the other believed.

"Mam," Juda said, "I's gone marry Jeddy. 'Fore dey takes him 'way."

A whispery wave rolled away from her, heads jerking back. Mam came off her stool with a hand in the air. "You gets dat notion outta yo head," she hissed. "You marry a rat dat's off to faraway, for-ebber, you jes be waitin to do sumptin eben more foolish."

"Mam," Juda said, "we's gone be 'getha 'gin. I feels it. You knows someday Massa'll..."

"Masta? Same man slap you 'roun gone free you?"

The door swung wide and little Pheba lugged in the pail of water, bursting out with, "Dey's talk ober de married cabin a' plans fer anudder weddin. A niggah weddin, now. Dis all betta den Chris'mas time."

"Hush you," Mam said. And then to Juda, finger stabbed toward the men's cabin: "If dat tom-fool try to get one dem ole Afry-cans hold de broom fer my dotter, Ise'll salt dose stripes Catman gone give him."

Juda stood. "Mam." She looked around. "All yous. Aren't all the massas in the world gone keep me from marryin' Jeddy 'fore he's taken off ta Pennsy-vania." She took her mother's still-suspended hand and held it to her breast. "I lubs you, Mam. I lubs all dese gals. But I's gots sumptin in my heart bigger'n lub tellin' me only time's gone keep me and Jeddy 'part."

A low hum of approval circled the room and her mother pulled her hand back. It felt as if she took a fistful of heart. "Please..." Juda said. But Mam stepped away and climbed up the ladder to the loft.

Believing he was condemned by the blood on his shirt and the story Juda must tell, Jedediah had burrowed into the haymow of the barn. He writhed about until the birds sang, his gut churning with the pangs of certain parting. Forever. He did not fear—in fact, did not even think on—the whipping to befall him—his first other than the occasional lash by some sour driver.

And then it came, every person he'd ever cared for forced to watch—close enough to be spattered by his blood and bile. His parents. The slaves he'd grown up with. Juda. But he did not cry out, for Master, too, looked on, and stronger than his hate for the lash of Catman was his will to hold his tongue to spite Master for not doing it himself.

When it was over, he staggered away to lie on his front in the men's loft, bare to his breeches. The pain became the steady searing of one big weeping wound, any of the interlaced gashes indistinguishable from another. At least it wasn't the biting slices that had poured forth blood and taken his breath in otherworldly agony as he knelt with his hands tethered to the posts of the well roof. Though he no longer had those few seconds of reprieve when Catman rested between volleys. Until the end when he sprinkled on the brine of pickled bird pepper, bringing Jedediah to slobbering and vomiting.

Only two things kept him going now. First, something born in him at the well this morning. Second was Juda, to ease her pain. She'd come to him here in the loft, the only other slave not wanted at the wedding preparations, her and her face of livery lumps. She laid wet rags on his shoulders and the small of his back, refreshing them in a gourd of water beside his pallet, cooed promises of their impossible reunion.

Jedediah preferred not to talk. Just the deeper breathing words required stoked the crucible atop his back. But he needed a diversion from a knot that tightened in his gut with the diminishing time they had. And she so little understood what she faced, the hopelessness of it all.

His forehead pressed into his gunny tick, Jedediah finally spoke. "Don't you sees now it's Marse turned yo mam 'ginst our marryin'?"

She stopped dipping a rag in the gourd.

"Was him we should'a feared learnin' 'bout us," Jedediah said. "Not Mistress."

Juda wrung the rag. "Seems it's Missy makin' de trouble 'bout it."

Jedediah squeezed shut his eyes, drew breath. "Marse still wudn't 'llowed it. He thinks it's a mark on him, you marries a common niggah. Less a sin to him if it's a yella one."

She bent, looked him in the eye. "I aren't no sin." Juda folded the rag and set it on the small of his back—it soothed the burning down there a little. But that knot... "'Sides," she said, "Massa 'tends I aren't even his'n."

"De only thang we can take heart wid," Jedediah said, "is I'da been sold anyways. Sout', probly."

Juda put her face near his cheek. "De thang we gots is dat we's gone be 'getha somedays." She bulbed out those buttery lips and brushed the lobe of Jedediah's ear. "Ise'll always know where Missy Cornelia is. Sooner or later, Mistress'll want rid a de 'minder and Massa'll want rid a de troubles. Slaps or not, he knows he's gots to do right by me someday. Even if he don't, Ise'll gets to you. Somehows"

The next day, Juda kept watch of Madagascar Jack where he sat on a stool in a corner of the men's quarters, the first to return from the wedding. Her only worry was that he would change his mind about marrying her and Jedediah, concede to Mam, who'd upbraided him about it.

So long as he followed through, they'd have the ceremony here, prohibited from doing so in her mother's presence, she who'd warned the women about taking part. Some of the younger ones would still come, Juda hoped.

So she had cleaned the cabin, which she realized was much tidier than the women's quarters. But then the men didn't cook, spin, and nurse little ones.

By now, Jedediah's wounds had begun to puss over. Still, he could not wear his coarse linen shirt—sackcloth, really, nearly rough as his work frock. Even the cotton flannel shirt she'd borrowed for him from one of the married men would vex the rents of his skin when it was time to put it on and come down. She wanted him beside her now. She wanted him within reach every second before he left.

Juda walked to a window opening. She swung the hinged planks into the cabin and leaned her elbows on the sill. The sun was westering, the shadows of tall oaks reclining across the meadow, blue sky blanching into that yellowing horizon of springtime dusk. She looked where the chimney of the big house rose above a row of loblolly pines that hid the quarters in their dale from the family's view. *Dem folks wid der white asses and purty close.* She heard the clatter of poles the slaves stacked as they dismantled the canopy in the yard. It was done: Missy Cornelia was now Mistress Bakeraskin. Off to some far place that might as well be the moon. No, not the moon; Juda couldn't walk to the moon. But she could walk to Pennsylvania.

A few slaves returned. Juda touched her cheekbone, her upper lip. Still swollen, hurting. *Oh, Jeddy. I wants ta look pleasin ta you. We a sorry pair for marryin.*

She smoothed the bosom of her shortgown, looked down. She hadn't even a clean petticoat to wear. *Jes dis ole day-ter-day, an' a filthy shift underneath.*

Missy-now-Mistress was probably in the dining room powdered nigh a corpse as she saw off the neighbor guests, waving her fan and sweating in the gown around which Juda had embroidered spirals of silver thread. She could see her flushing with each compliment and drawing her gloved hand to Juda's lacework at her neck. *Dat oaf standin 'side her tryin ta peek at de crook a' her arm when dat stockin-lookin glub slips past her elbow.*

Juda plucked at her hair—she wore no bandana now—used her fingers to comb tresses over her muslin neckerchief. She thought herself a fool for having considered asking to borrow Missy's beautiful veil. And a stay from her mother. Oh, to have the piece of looking glass from the women's quarters. This would have to do, she thought. But she curled her toes, wishing she had shoes.

She looked at Madagascar Jack. He'd put over his shoulder a lilac sash. Sure this was for the ceremony, Juda gave in to the good omen she'd felt when Jedediah told her about this man's strange ways.

He'd been purchased off a slave coffle coming into the tidewater from trades among the island plantations of Carolina. He'd been brought there as a young man on a slaver.

Madagascar Jack said he missed his islands, "cose teys wone stap closer to Africy, wheres all de songs comes frome."

Though he'd never married, Madagascar Jack revered fertility and so any desire to join and bear life. An inclination of the heart was the working of the spirit, and he alone among the slaves gave no heed to the separation of the couple. "Dhat noht mahtter a straw," he said. "Dey jine, and de spirit guide."

Madagascar Jack nodded to her, formally, almost a bow. The gesture made Juda feel as exalted as a queen. The four or five other men who'd returned were respectful in their own way— pretending not to see her, busy with odd tasks: sweeping ashes from the hearth; shaving tallow into the crusie lamps; straightening blankets on the two beds where Madagascar Jack and three widowers slept. Preparations, in fact. They made Juda feel a little taller, a little warmer.

She went and knelt before Madagascar Jack—gray-bearded, balding and toothless, all forehead and gums. He suffered immovably the constant buzzing and landing of flies. He returned her smile. She wanted to say thank you, and he must have understood—Madagascar Jack leaned and touched her shoulder, his eyes closed, a soft gesture giving more than reassurance about the moment to come: it was homage to a beauty he made her feel singing down inside. He took away his hand, leaned back, eyes still closed, and rocked on his hips to some chant he heard from Africa.

Juda waited at the window until at dusk Madagascar Jack rose and summoned the men from where they'd gone out to smoke and talk, all of them having returned. Not knowing what else to do, she moved to the hearth. As Madagascar Jack walked to the ladder with the broom and called to Jedediah, one of the widowers lit the crusie lamps with a candle. The oak wall-logs, seasoned and smudged as they were, awoke and embraced Juda in the warm, mottled copper of an old kettle.

Her Jeddy came down facing away from the ladder, arms extended behind him as he slid his palms along the poles. The fresh pain of the day's first steps and the chafing of his shirt warped his cheeks and brow as if he were a reflection in a river ripple. He wore his summer-allotted breeches, burlap patches already at the knees. His face calmed when he stepped from the bottom rung and looked at her. He had wrapped the blue scarf around his neck.

Madagascar Jack signaled for Juda and she went to him and Jedediah. The other men, a dozen or so, stood now with their backs to the walls, three girls who'd dared defy Juda's mother coming through the doorway and taking places among them.

Eyes rolled back so only the whites showed, Madagascar Jack held over his head the broom—a stick of hickory with one end shaven and mauled to splinterwood and lashed with a withe of dogbane, a strip of sackcloth tied around the handle for a ribbon. "De besom," he said, "sweeps away bad spir-ahts. It sweeps away all dare pas' life." His lids fluttered, his pupils descended. "De splinters is de fahmbly dat comes from de ah-mighty, de stick of de besom. De ribbon—" he moved his hand along the shaft of the broom until he touched a loop of the sackcloth— "ties de man and woe-man and chillen wit' de ah-mighty. And de whole besom is for makin' a home ta-getta'." He watched the pair. "When de ah-mighty see to it." And warmth surged in Juda's breast.

As Madagascar Jack made a rowing sweep of the bristles over their heads, Juda took Jedediah's hand. She smiled at him, but he gave no expression.

"Now listen, and look-a-here," Madagascar Jack said, his words sustained and reverberating, as in the tremble of the donged bell. "I hold de besom ober de floor behind dem. Now listen, all you. Dey bofe jump obcr togeddar. De one dat jump de highest, dat de one do de decidin'."

Madagascar Jack thrust the broom toward the couple. "Mind me," he said. "You be sho to jump high and long. 'Cause if you stumps yo toe on dis stick—" he shook the handle—"de wurstest kinda luck'll find you." He lowered the broom to his side. "If one of you does stumps yo toe, den dat's de one gone die furst." And eyes turned away in the perimeter of the room.

"You ready?" Madagascar Jack said.

Juda nodded and led Jedediah forward. They remained hand-in-hand while Madagascar Jack bent behind them and held the broom eight inches off the floor.

"You gone kiss me now, or after?" Juda whispered. Jedediah looked ahead, did not respond. Drowning, Juda thought, in pain. While in her stomach, rapture tossed on waves of worry.

"When I say 'now'," Madagascar Jack said, "you jump back. Den you's married."

Juda gathered her petticoat with one hand and held the other out from her body—all the better to keep her balance—then bent her knees. She glanced around the room at the guests, all silent where they leaned against the walls. Nary a smile.

The instant Madagascar Jack said "now," she sprang upward and back, light and sure as joy. But Jedediah stiffened, bracing, she knew, against his chafing shirt, then jumped by power of little more than his feet. As Juda landed, Jedediah's ankles knocked the handle from Madagascar Jack's hand, the guests making a great sucking gasp. When the broom struck her shins and clattered upon the loose floor planks, Juda bent and reached for it. Then all sound seemed to retreat into Madagascar Jack's outstretched hand.

Juda held out the broom where Madagascar Jack squatted. "We jes needs to do it 'gin," she said.

Madagascar Jack began humming. He rolled his eyes back and rocked on his haunches. The notes were long, changing in pitch erratically, hardly musical. Yet as the older men accompanied him with waves of fast-slow, fast-slow claps, there came a harmony, and Madagascar Jack rose, swaying to his music, eyelids flapping. He shuffled thus to his corner stool where he kept propped his four-stringed banza, a gourd and sheep's hide on which he'd painted stars in the shape of a lemur in some ancient translation of a constellation. He sat and plucked as if pulling feathers from a chicken, leading the others in a new tune that drew a quick tempo right out of his slow descant. More men and the girls joined the clapping, which emerged now as a counter rhythm. An elder produced beef-rib bones while another blew on a willow flute. Bodies began rocking.

Juda knew all the slave songs, the evening laments, the field chants with their coded mockery of masters and mistresses. She'd never heard such music as this. It pulsed through her bones as if they were the strings Madagascar Jack strummed, at the same time settling deep in her core, making her feel warm and hungry. It came from where all songs were born. Old Africy.

Juda faced Jedediah and waited for his kiss, a dance. But he stared at the broom where she'd leaned it against the ladder. She took his hands. "Jedediah, don't you worry 'bout dem ole tales Madagascar Jack sez. Dat jes mumbo-jumbo."

The other slaves watched, their claps and dancing aimed at them. "C'mon, Jeddy," Juda said. At last he looked at her, nodded. Juda released his hands, lifted her petticoat, and swayed from her hips. Madagascar Jack stepped it up. Jedediah bent at his waist until he winced. He rolled his shoulders, bobbed his head. She tried to have him smile, to kiss her, but his face was rigid as cold iron.

In the wan light of a crusie lamp, they sat in the barn loft upon a tick of chaff Juda had brought. She could not hold Jedediah, for it redoubled the pain of his whipping.

After those first songs in the cabin, some of the younger slaves had produced jugs of hard cider pilfered from Missy's wedding. The music had become livelier and everyone danced. At the end of the celebration, Jedediah grudged the well-wishers a smile. But there showed in his eyes something new in his heart, a determination Juda feared had supplanted his desire for this time in the loft.

She stood over him now, feet to each side of his legs where he'd stretched them onto the floor planks. Juda took off his scarf and dropped it beside him, then guided his hands to where they untied her petticoat at her waist, one side and then the other. She unpinned the front of her shortgown and waggled out of it. While he slid off his breeches, she lifted her shift over her head and tossed it onto the piled hay. Then she knelt over him and ever-gently undid the three cowhorn buttons of his shirt before tenting it away from his skin. As he raised his arms, he bunched his eyelids against the burning stretch of his wounds, and Juda pulled away the shirt. Then his face relaxed and his eyes swam with hers as she pressed into him, chest to chest, his shoulders raven-sheened in the lamplight as he reached around her back and held her to him.

Pushing her breast harder into Jedediah, Juda whispered his name. He gave a rumbling moan, and pangs of hunger in her own depths caved in on themselves.

But that new thing inside Jedediah took hold. "Deys gone make sho we never sees one 'nother 'gin," he said.

"Let's jes hab our now-time" Juda said. "Our nighttime." She lowered herself, ready for him. But she felt his spite, stronger than mandesire, tauten his arms. Juda rocked her hips, her inner thighs caressing his legs as she tried to tease his lust. She bent and touched her forehead to his. "I wants de leabin to hurries up—at least after dis," she said, grinning, "'cause den it's soona' we back tagetha."

He looked into the dark expanse of the barn bay. "You seen dat broom."

She rolled her forehead back and forth. "Dat was jes a signal a' troubles we ahready know."

"Why have anythang," Jedediah said, "when it's ders ta take 'way."

Juda put her fingers to the nape of his neck. "Dis aren't ders. De Ah-mighty gib it ta us. So only we kin lets dem take it 'way."

"Dey's takin' dis, ahright. And puttin' you in de fields."

"Jes hab faith, Jeddy. I feel in my bones we gone be tagetha."

The only stock in the barn were a cow and her calf rustling hay in a stall beneath the bay. The calf bleated, its mother following with a long *mawww*. Slomps of nervous hooves in muck put Juda on her feet and Jedediah to shaking his head.

Juda blew out the lamp flame and waved away the smudge. As the wheels of the barn door squealed across their tracks, she sat beside Jedediah, wrapped her arms around his waist, and rocked. Out in the bay, dust rose into the new, shifting illumination of lantern light as boot heels echoed off the floor. The uprights of the ladder crackled like old leather, a tin lantern clanging and the wide-brimmed hat of Nathan Shivelley the overseer preceding his cleanshaven face with its soul-less black eyes and the enormous purple nose planted upon it like a cluster of raspberries. Shivelley never showed emotion, whether with the whip or the slave concubines he appropriated; he might have mounted the loft for a nap rather than in answer to news from his weevil in the wheat. Before them now, Shivelley held out his light, his eyes roving Juda's naked body. He studied the pallet, weighed something while Juda reached about, found her shift, and pulled it over her head. As she stood, Shivelley watched the shift fall down from her waist. His eyes stopped at her thighs. His tongue, purple, lumpy like his nose, slid over his lips while he deliberated his demons. He grimaced and shook his head—better not.

Shivelley held his lantern over the extinguished lamp. "You dumb niggers play with two kinds'a fire." The voice neither pondering nor scolding, detached as his face. He took Jedediah's ear between his thumb and forefinger and tugged him to his feet, Jedediah covering his privates. "You lucky boy I aren't to damage yo hide no more 'fore the big trip north." Shivelley turned his attention to Juda, watched himself gather a handful of her shift. "We're gone have to break our new field nigger's house habits." His sulking face lifted to hers. "Too bad that first I have to let your mistress pick the punishin' for defyin' her. You'll wait in the smokehouse."

Juda feared not the whip nor years of toil and loneliness. But the loss of embracing Jedediah before they separated, of promising her devotion and the assurance they'd be together again, this shadowed her heart like buzzards in the sky. *I can't 'cept it. I cants I cants.*

She grabbed Shivelley's hand and fell to her knees. "Misser Shivsley, please let me hold my Jeddy 'fore you take me der. I'd do anythang to hab a minute wid him."

Shivelley held still, eyes empty of all but weighing those words. Juda waited, willing to bargain a lifetime's hard labor for a minute. Shivelley regarded the haymow as an eyelid descended, then jerked his hand away, grabbed Juda's ear and drew her to her feet. "You'll learn to beg a' me," he said.

Jedediah, in his breeches now, stepped closer as Shivelley let go of the ear and held up the lantern.

"Don't, Jedediah," Juda said.

"Do it, boy," Shivelley said. "Gimmee cause to break her for field work right here."

"Jeddy," Juda said, "you hold still. We's awright. We done had our goodbyes." She steadied her voice before taking her chance. "'Sides, we'll be tagetha' 'gin. I promise."

At this, Shivelley grabbed her hair and pulled her head back. "Remember your nigger half, gal," he said, spittle spraying, his breath fetid with the day's wine and fat and savory dishes, "'fore you talk like that. Tell this boy you got all notions of marryin' or matin' or whatever you niggers call it outta yo mind. That I don't need to worry 'bout slaves runnin' off lookin' for somethin' that's gone."

"S'like you says, mista Shivsley."

Shivelley twisted the handful of hair. "Tell him, not me."

"Jeddy," Juda said and closed her eyes. "We's had our time. You go off now and don't think nuttin' 'bout me."

Shivelley led Juda to the edge of the loft where he held out the lantern for her to find the ladder. As she turned to descend, Juda found Jedediah with his hands balled and the muscles of his jaw flexed, insensible to her, that new determination aiming all his being beyond the illuminated barn bay.

Jedediah stood thus until the nesting swallows began their drunkard-like jibes across the barn, daylight seeping between the wall slats and into his senses, his body a drinking gourd that through the night he'd emptied of his old self in anticipation of this dawning. He shifted on his feet and felt taking form within the hull that remained some hard creed of molten anger which might have been hatred had he been old and free enough to have mastered refining anger into hatred.

He unfurled his fists; there was work to do. He relaxed his neck, twisted it; there was a means to find. Then he opened his ears, catching now the squeaks and rattles of the busy birds.

He put on his shirt and picked up his shoes, which Missy-now-Mistress had told him to have for the trip today. He stuffed these half-way into the waist of this breeches and took up the indigo scarf. He turned it over, squinted where sunlight knifed through the gaps in the east-facing wall, thoughts veering, fading, flitting back—like the flight of the swallows. He didn't so much drop the scarf as it fell from his loosening hold. After a moment, he went to leave but his loins felt like ballast; they counterweighed his shoulders leaning ahead, burdened his legs lifting off.

What held him? He concentrated, tried to think beyond the urgency of reporting to the big house for the journey north, heard a call in the back of his mind to do something. The scarf. And so he took it up and tucked it beside his shoes.

He squeezed between the barn doors and looked across to the stable, found it open, the buggy gone. Long shadows stretched from the pair of oaks in the meadow between him and the big house, the air bracing, hickory smoke sweet but invisible. He started along the rutted road, the cool ground under his feet caked hard in this dry spell. He did not glance in the direction of the slave cabins, gave only a second's thought to saying good-bye to his parents.

At the big house, Hostler Harry was loading a trunk. Missy-now-Mistress, in a lavender shawl and linen headdress plumed with ostrich feathers and pink flowers, leaned out from the porch railing to watch Jedediah approach. "Nothing else?" she said as Jedediah stepped beneath her.

"Pardon, Missy?" he said.

"I'm Mistress to you now. As I was during your dalliance in the barn." She tugged her shawl then pointed at the shoes stowed at his waist. "That's all you're taking?" she said.

"Dat's all I hab, Ma'am."

Just then, Master Bakeraskin stepped through the doorway, hatless and stiffly cravated, side whiskers wet-combed.

"Peter," Mistress Cornelia said, "this is our slave. He is called Jedediah."

Bakeraskin regarded Jedediah, who sensed blood of water, muscles of sand, mind of gruel—traits Jedediah knew could work for or against him.

"Bow to your new master," Mistress Cornelia said.

Jedediah gave more nod than bow.

Mistress Cornelia turned up her palms. "Give him something to do."

"Right," Bakeraskin said. He looked about the yard, then sky-ward. "It will be warm. There are two canteens hanging from the carriage." He snapped his fingers. "Water."

Jedediah found the tin canteens and started away. As he approached the well, he saw smoke puffing from the eaves of the smokehouse. This wasn't the season for that—too warm.

He set the canteens against the stone throat of the well and turned the crank to unspool the rope. Its spindle complained against the forks of the log uprights in which it was cradled, *whumping* with each downstroke of the handle. Between these came whimpers that Jedediah finally admitted were not of the well, but human. He paused, hoped the sound would go away. It came clearer. He went back to cranking, sank the bucket, retrieved it.

Spitting into the bucket, Jedediah swirled the water with his finger. He could hear her wheezing now. He uncorked and submerged the canteens; *plump-plump-plump* came up the air. He stoppered them, left them on the ground and stepped to the door of the clapboarded smokehouse. She was in a fit of gasps. The final, deepest one shot back in a cough that set her to hacking and heaving. Jedediah reckoned her head would burst.

He put his hand on the plank door, warm from the smolder-ing fire. She'd settled into dog-like panting. "Juda," he said.

Silence. He feared she'd stopped breathing.

"Jeddy? Dat you?"

He only nodded, and as if she saw this, she spoke, voice strained to hold back coughs. "Oh, Jeddy, tell me you knows I was jes playin wid Shivsley. Dat I's sho' as ebber we be 'getha 'gin."

He looked to the ground as the coughs won out. Drops of blood had speckled the stone threshold. When she stopped and spat, he said. "Dey whip you?"

She did not answer.

"What dey use? Willa' switch or dat cowhide wid de platted wire?" He waited. The blood at his temples pounded like a cuff-ing. "Tell me," he said.

"I didn't mind de whippin," she said, then broke off, making a choking sound. "It was when dey washed me wid dat pickle juice."

Jedediah's eyes rolled back. His lips moved with a silent curse. "Get down," he said. "Dey say you breathe if you lay down in der."

Juda gasped at the shock of the fat-laden ground against her bare, torn skin; Shivelley's whip had struck even her front, spared, Jedediah knew, only her breasts. She gulped air at the crack beneath the door. "Jeddy, I scared. Nuttin scarier'n can't breathe. An' my whole body's burnin' for water. But I was mose worried dey wudn't let you come ta me." And then a rushing whisper: "I sees yer feet. Oh, Jeddy, put yer hand der."

His fists were furled so tightly they'd gone numb. He forced them open, rested his forehead against the door.

"Jeddy, don't you leabe wid'out sayin you believes me 'bout us bein 'getha 'gin. I hears dat new thang I seed in yer eyes. You 'occupied wid sumptin'."

He placed a palm on the door, then started away.

"Stop," she coughed out. And he did—as he picked up the canteens at the well.

"Jeddy, you still der? Tell me you wearin dat scarf."

He moved on. She cried out louder. "Don't you leabe wid'out wearin dat. I wants ta always know you had it on."

Jedediah paused, looked back and regarded the smokehouse a moment. He turned to the big house. Then he shrugged, pulled the scarf from his breeches and wrapped it around his neck.

He sat in the shade of a tree by the carriageway. He waited. He dozed. Woke. Across the lawn, the fume curled around the eaves of the smokehouse, thicker now, yellowish, the smell more acrid. Jedediah figured Shivelley threw in some pine full of pitch. There being no ham in there.

At the veranda, Mistress Cornelia sent Harry into the house for some trifle, both in such a fluster they'd failed to put Jedediah to work. Peter Bakeraskin came down the steps with his taut little mother and her large and loud husband. Harry returned and helped them into the carriage as Master and

Mistress James stepped onto the porch and spoke with their daughter. Master—curled and powdered—stared down his nose while Mistress sniveled into a silk handkerchief, a great cinnamon bow atop her head trembling with her shoulders.

Master walked Mistress Cornelia to the carriage. Helping her in, he looked over at Jedediah and pointed to the driver's box where Harry sat. As Jedediah approached, Harry called out, "You run ober de stable and get a sack a' oats. Dey'll want to hurry my horses, now we leabin' late. Makin me fetch ebry last stockin."

Jedediah met the carriage near the stable and tied the sack at the rear. As he passed the door, Mistress Cornelia parted the curtain and spoke his name. "Tell Harry to make haste," she said. She leaned her face closer and studied him with a twitch of her nose. "And get rid of that ridiculous rag."

He knitted his brows, not at first understanding. Then he nodded. "Yes'm," he said, and tossed the scarf to the ground.

Hunterdon County, New Jersey

Twelve years earlier, George Sharpe sat in his master's office and watched rain dapple the window. Wherever enough drops gathered, they broke free and trickled to the bottom of a pane.

Being a boy, George liked the rain, its soothing alternations between taps and tattoos on the shingles above his summer alcove in the far end of the gristmill garret. It deepened smells— the must of leaf mold that descended from the hill out back; the ratty breath of the scurrying cats; the horse-and-sweat odor of the heavy-hatted, mumble-mouthed farmers who brought their grist; and of course that nip, sharp like a shilling on the tongue, around the great spinning millstones.

Master Sharpe, who was very proud of his millstones because they came from France, did not like rain. He said its air caked the flour. It rose the river, making problems in the race. Which must have been why he was late stepping into the office where he'd told George to meet him, as he had news.

He shut the door and gave a grin. Whenever Master seemed pleased with George, something bright streamed through him, like ribbons in the wind. But lately, a reflex of his mind warned of danger in that, gave the feeling of catching himself too close to the gears of the mill machinery.

The miller hung his hat on a peg and went to his desk. He was a calculating man, right down to his stride. It was always measured as though he divided the distance to his destination by the exact length of pace for arriving on a full step. Such was his precision of hand and eye, his mouth when he shaped words.

"George," Master said, sitting and taking up a paper, "you know Caleb Farleigh."

George nodded. "He brings his grist here. He has the boys."

"Farleigh's a forward-looking man," Master said. "With a houseful of sons, he sees the need to take on more land. Which the Lord no longer makes in New Jersey."

While George wondered where on earth God was making more land, Master leaned back in his chair. He stroked his chin with its deep cleft, a feature already showing on George's face. This made George think about Master's eyes—their eyes, emerald like one of mistress's gemstones, like the eyes of Adam Sharpe Junior at school in Philadelphia.

"Farleigh," Master said, "is going west to settle land for those boys. He'll clear a bigger farm and build a gristmill. He needs a lusty boy to help. I've agreed to send you."

Caleb Farleigh was the only farmer who brought to the mill children too young to help. They ran about and chased the cats, which nettled Master Sharpe, who was exacting about the order of his granary. George was to keep them out of the stores, but they ignored him, the oldest, Caleb Junior, lifting his lip as if George were a large rat. Farleigh Senior, on the other hand, seemed very curious about George, and George, in turn, was fascinated by him, for Farleigh was one of few Quakers to patronize Sharpe's Mill. He wore a shadbelly coat of broadcloth, a nankeen waistcoat, and on his head, a bob-wig and cocked hat. His white stock hung like a bib and the buckles on his shoes were the largest George had ever seen.

Farleigh often broke from the gossipers on the mill floor to visit George where he sacked flour or meal. His inquiries about George's work were harmless enough, but George feared Master Sharpe hearing his other questions. Farleigh asked if Mistress was kind to George. He wanted to know whether Master treated George differently from Hercules, who did the milling and taught George how to dress the stones and replace sheared gears. At some point, Master Sharpe would call for George's help or come around a corner and shoo him off to some task. Later, he would say, "Those Friends better not put any nonsense in that wooly head of yours."

So George was surprised that Master, who was watching the raindrops clot on the window, had come to an agreement about him with Mr. Farleigh. Master, who rarely paused like this.

Which made George wonder if the chin, the eyes, might be tied to the arrangement, for George at twelve had come realize that their meaning made Master uneasy.

Setting down the paper and looking at George, Master sighed. "So you are going to live in Pennsylvania," he said.

"Just me?"

Master turned up his lips in an approximation of the black hairline rimming his bright bald pate. "I explained you'll go with Farleigh and those boys. And of course, that pious wife."

"I meant," George said, swallowing back a tremor in his voice, "my mother. Will she be going?"

Master started from his chair. "Aren't you a bothersome little bastard." He stopped, held up his hand as if in a reluctant truce. "Your mother will stay here." He sat. "She'll be cared for as always."

Gusts of wind drove rain against the window, the glass looking as if it shattered over and over. A gray cast and chill had taken even the room, all the gloom of the storm within doors now but the howling, so thick were those stone walls against sound. George spoke quietly, that the wringing of his insides did not come out in his voice. "I can't leave her," he said.

The miller's jaw tensed as he shifted in his chair. He tapped the paper, spoke through his teeth. "You should be thanking me. Your lot will only improve. Now let me go back to work. And you do the same."

"Please don't make me leave her, sir."

With all the force of his great hulking shoulders, Master swung an arm across the desk, letting fly the paper and an inkstand, his sand holder and quills. He rushed around to George who turned his face away.

"Do you question that I know what's best for you?" Master said.

Shaking his head no and peeping to find Master's hand raised, George said, "Can I please go to see her, sir? That's all."

"Without thanking me?"

George closed his eyes a second, waiting for Master to strike.

"Ingrate," Master said, and he went and took his hat. Then, stopping at the door, he said, "Put this office back in order. And keep away from me until you leave."

Waiting on his mother's pallet in her closet chamber off the kitchen, George could not get warm. The chill of his wet shirt slow-seeped like snowmelt deeper and deeper into his shoulders. He clutched his elbows and fought bouts of shivers.

At last, she happened upon him. "If you're not sick already, child," she said, wrapping her quilt around him, "you will be soon enough unless we chase those shakes out of you."

"Master's sending me away," George said. "I think he sold me."

She stared off a moment, then sat against the opposite wall, close enough to touch, her knees pulled up under her petticoat. Tiny Aquintice, not yet 14 when she'd had George, still looked like a girl. And so within his affection as a son was the protectiveness of a brother.

Closing her eyes, Aquintice rocked as she hummed a prayer-like dirge in a voice too deep and old for that little body. George felt himself warming.

In words raised out of the song, she began: "Master Sharpe bought me in Philadelphia when I was your age. I'd been as happy as a little slave girl could be, there in a nice house with a master and mistress that were decent-enough people. They had no problem with their own children teaching a negro to read. I had my mamma. And my daddy visited on Sundays. I hardly gave notice to being a slave." She opened her eyes, narrowed them. "But then came that day Master Sharpe visited to take care of some flour business with my old Master—a shipping merchant, he was. Master Sharpe took to me, teasing and giving me coppers. I thought he was just a frolicking, kind gentleman. But he had a mind to take me with him the minute he saw me."

"Now my old people had a debt with Master Sharpe that went back even to his father, him that built the mill. And Master was there to collect on what he was owed. I was helping Mamma serve at the table when my old Master let out he didn't have the custom he once had. That was my time, George, to have the awful feeling I know you had today. My old Master bowed his head and told Master Sharpe he could have anything he wanted to satisfy the debt, his own head if that would do, just not money, for he had none."

"George, I was a favorite to my old Master, and I could see it grieved him when Master Sharpe straightened in his chair—all pleased instead of angry—and pointed at me. 'I want her,' he said." Aquintice shook her head and looked off. "Master and Mistress brought to tears and my own mamma and me in the room."

"What was her name?" George said.

"Dear child," Aquintice said, "you're leaving here knowing nothing of your granny or grampy. It's Sylvia. I know she's still there—we promised we'd keep going for each other."

"Why don't you ask Master to keep me," George said. "He's my daddy."

She drew her knees tighter to her chest. "That would do no good. Your father has a war inside—part of him saying you're a filthy sin, fighting with another part that says he's obliged to bring up his own flesh. He thinks that by sending you off he's making the war go away."

"He needs me here," George said. "He says I'm a hard worker."

Aquintice gave a sad chuckle. "No matter his wars or what he says, you will always be to him—to everyone—first a slave. It's a backwards thing, but the more you fight that thinking, the more they'll make themselves feel right. I've been coming around to telling you how important it is to learn to just bow to that."

She waited, watching the door, saw it was the other house slave, Nackey, passing through the kitchen. "Now you hear what I say. It's what my mother taught me when I left. Even while you're bowing, don't count on Adam Sharpe or anyone for anything. Ask nothing from them. People prey on weakness. I've seen it. I'll see it in Mistress. You know she hates me. She'll think that him taking you will break me to the point I'll beg that you're treated well out there. See, if you show what you want, they'll own you by threatening it. Freedom's right there inside you. It's yours to keep or give up."

She rubbed her brow. "Oh, Lord. You're only a boy. Just remember what I said till it makes sense with things to come."

The bare plaster walls of the little room tightened around George. He drew breath and tried to shake the confusion out of his head.

"Settle," Mamma said, "and tell me you'll remember. That's all."

He went still, but his voice was a flitting moth he couldn't catch in his throat, and he thought, *What'm I going to do without you, Mamma?*

"All you have to do," Aquintice said, "is remember. Can you do that?"

George nodded. "But I'll come back for you someday. I know what she'll do to you."

"Careful," Aquintice said. "That's what I'm warning you about."

His face contorted against tears. "I'll remember what you said. But I will come back for you."

Aquintice tipped her head to the side. "Oh, child," she said. She rose onto her knees and reached her arms around him. George did not see her cry—he never would—but he felt great sobs lurching out of that tiny body, shudders of sweet-mother-cheek against his neck.

George left Sharpe's Mill riding an open wagon drawn by a mule team. The rain had tapered through the night to a mist, which promised now to rise as the sun blanched the sky over his shoulder—back over the mill and his mother and all the world he'd known. He wore new leather breeches, yarn stockings, and a black woolen short-coat over a matching waistcoat. His shoes, brogans, were the first he'd had on his feet in warmer weather, the first that were not the ill-fitting cast-offs of his half-brother.

Caleb Farleigh required that George sit beside him on the driver's box where Farleigh broke long spans of meditative silence to relate their new situation. How they would establish a farm, and someday a gristmill. That George would be his miller. During the lulls, the boy watched the croups of the mules, embarrassed to glance where Farleigh's wife, Prudence, walked alongside. Staring out from a white bonnet arched and ribbed over her head in the wagon-top style, she carried her precious spinning wheel, sparing it the merciless jouncing of a springless ride. Behind George, the youngsters sat on sacks of flour and salt, bobbling and prattling like a nest of hungry goslings. Piled about them were kettles, trenchers and redware crocks, gunny-wrapped slabs of bacon, a hand mill and cradle, waxed canvases and coiled rope. There were lamps, axes, bow saws, hoes—every manner of necessity and none of keepsake, the whole of it loaded haphazardly and exposed but for a Bible inside the box upon which Farleigh and George sat, the Good Book further protected in a wooden case sealed with wax.

Near midday, while they rested the mules in a grove of beech, the party ate pan-cooked johnnycakes and rashers. When they set out again, Farleigh, ever peculiar in his brass buckles of knee, waist, and shoe, in his softness of word and gesture, said, "Thou will find thyself in a great woods." He paused, staring ahead where the road muck baked in the noon sun, the mules' shoes chomping through the crust. "Our home will be near the west branch of the river Susquehanna, at the edge of a country even wilder." Farleigh glanced at the boy, his brows arched so high they touched his cocked hat with its great winged brim. "No white man has mapped or even seen vast stretches of that farther place, '...a land wherein no man dwelleth...neither doth any son of man pass thereby.'"

George inched closer to Farleigh and peered into a piney woodlot beyond the marching mistress, nursing now the littlest one.

"Thou might remember," Farleigh said, "a band of broken Dutch returning to New Jersey." Farleigh waited, but George had not known of this. "They were surviving settlers of the country to which we are headed. Gone to escape the trouble between the colonists and loyalists."

George nodded that he understood this.

"But," Farleigh said, shaking his head, "so many of their poor brethren perished in another butchering—that of lawful settlers at the hands of Indians who came down in an attack from that wildland. The waters of the West Branch swelled with their blood. And this only a few years ago."

George became queasy, such that the road might have been the flume of the mill before the wheel.

"Fear not," Farleigh said. "Thou may be off to '...*a howling wilderness...*,' but the Indians are gone, and we have been blessed with a warrant where we need not enter that wicked abyss beyond." He pointed westward. "'...*where the light is as darkness.*'"

They hoped to reach the ferry and cross the Delaware to Easton before dark, to be along the banks of Pennsylvania's Lehigh on the morrow. Several days hence, they would leave that river, and there would be no more road, per se.

As they descended the valley of the Delaware, the sun, pale yellow now, crowned the far ridge. George's new master squinted into the sky, lips moving silently. When the sun vanished, he sighed and gave a faint smile.

"Hear me now, friend," he said, the first anyone had called George that. Farleigh moved the reins to his other hand and patted George's knee. "I have observed thy situation for some years. At last, I quote Deuteronomy: '*He shall live with you in your midst... you shall not mistreat him.*'"

Farleigh went quiet, the thumping of the mules' feet against the hardening trace, the clatter and squeak of the wagon, a road lullaby while the children slept and Mistress plodded along as mute and persistent as a shadow.

"Friend," Farleigh said.

"Yes, Master," George said.

"I want thee not to address me as Master. Nor my wife as Mistress."

"Yes, Master," George said.

Farleigh leaned forward and frowned at George.

"Beg pardon, sir," George said, "but I don't know how to call you, then."

"Simply call me Mister. And Prudence, Madam."

George gathered his brows, looked up at the violet sky, and weighed this against his mother's words. Finally he nodded, resolved though not to say thank you.

Washington Township, Lycoming County, Pennsylvania

The miller at his work was the first black person Jedediah had seen since he and the Bakeraskins left Havre de Grace, Maryland. A mulatto man, for sure—light skin, eyes bright green. He held his head downward as he minded his spinning millstone, even as he ascended the stepladder to fill his hopper. He dressed in white linen—shirt, apron, breeches—except for a straw hat with the front of its brim rolled back. This was the first beardless miller Jedediah had seen—something about protecting their necks from flying chips when they dressed their stones.

Master had required Jedediah come to the Farleigh mill, a day's journey downriver. He always wanted him along in his travels, whether prospecting timber or making arrangements with blacksmiths for the establishment of the farm. At first, Jedediah figured he was keeping an eye on him. But he realized soon enough that Master thought of him as a kind of ornament, a watch chain hanging from his fob or a feather in his hat.

The mill stood several hundred rods from the river along a clay-bottom creek, slow-moving water unlike that of the wilderness country where it spilled fast and frigid over rocky bottoms. The valley of the West Branch stretched here miles wide, the prospect from the bridle path that sometimes mounted the hills within it splotched with irregular farm clearings, claimed warrants being hacked and burned out of the forest primeval. Following on foot his mounted master that morning, Jedediah had realized such logging would be his lot, and he could not reason—not yet—why any person would want to fell giant trees and boat loads of stone, years on-end, while cleared land abounded south and east of this wild country.

Farleigh's mill differed from those Jedediah had known in Virginia—large dual operations, half for grist, half for lumber or linseed oil. This was a two-story log barn of a structure, the wheel hidden below, the race creeping in through a hole in the fieldstone foundation. An unusual arrangement, Jedediah would come to see: the slave doing the milling, the owner's sons, long-limbed lads, the oldest perhaps 18, coming in from sundry occupations about the farm to help sack and load flour.

Master Bakeraskin led Jedediah through the dim mill, past timber posts and grain barrels and piled sacks of flour. Alongside shelves of gunny rolls, Caleb Farleigh sat at the desk where he figured the exchange of flour for wheat and corn for meal.

Farleigh was leaning back in his chair, quill in a hand at his lap. He stared off, lulled, it appeared, by the drone of gears and the spatter of the waterwheel beneath him.

Master cleared his throat and Farleigh was on his feet.

"I pray thy pardon," Farleigh said.

Master frowned, taking in the peculiar speech and dress. "You're miller Farleigh?" he said.

Farleigh gestured toward the man by the banded wooden vat in which spun the runner stone. "George Sharpe is the miller," he said. "I'm the millkeeper."

Master took hold of a bamboo cane he carried under his arm and tapped the tip against the floor. "A free nigger, have you?" he said.

Farleigh's smile of greeting faded. "Not exactly," he said.

This seemed to relieve Master, who returned the cane. "I'm Peter Bakeraskin. We've settled on a piece upriver."

Farleigh hefted a brow. "In the wild territory?"

Master tottered on this subject. To the scattered farmers of the upper West Branch and to passing hunters, Bakeraskin was always comparing himself as a pioneer. But at home with Mistress, he affirmed constantly they were distinguished among such provincials. They were timber prospectors with an established home built six years earlier by an agent of the great Holland Land Company. The house, the lone frame structure on the upper West Branch, indeed crowned them as gentry in those parts.

"Treacherously wild," Bakeraskin said with a wave of the cane. "The country bordering our comfortable home, that is.

Well, now—" he made a show of checking himself—"we have just a frame house. We're landed, of course. So are making forest into farm."

"Let all be done with diligence," Farleigh said.

Bakeraskin frowned again. "I'll get right to why we are come. My wife is a woman of the South, and chief among the deprivations she has endured is a lack of bread. "See, corn is the staple in our district by want of cleared land and any mills but coffee grinders. It's a place better fit for growing big trees. So, to the point, I'm here to buy flour. To arrange an occasional shipment."

"Thou is not the first to visit on this matter," Farleigh said.

"Then you can supply me flour?"

"Friend," Farleigh said, "we are a custom mill. We grind the farmer's grist and return the flour, less a toll to feed ourselves. Occasionally we take a fee—goods for my family." He watched Bakeraskin, who with lips puckered appeared to ignore him. "We have neither cornmeal nor flour to spare, and rye we will not grind."

Bakeraskin glanced around the room. "I see flour by the sack-full."

"Indeed," Farleigh said, "all spoken for."

"Might I deal with these men?" Bakeraskin said, "whether for flour or wheat for you to grind?"

Farleigh sighed. "I am just a millkeeper. Not a broker of grain or flour. But you must understand, these farmers have little use for currency."

Bakeraskin squeezed tight his lips and looked off, then came to attention, patting his cane against his hip. "Were you acquainted with the late Samuel Wallis?" he said.

Farleigh raised his brows. "By the generosity of Mister Wallis, we copied the design of the gristmill that stood upon his Muncy farm."

"The one he built after the Indians burned the other in that massacre the British instigated," Bakeraskin said. He lowered his voice. "Strange how his great manor was the only farm standing after the attack. Makes one wonder about his allegiance." He cocked his head and wagged his brows. "But now it stands invalid, what with the estate's disarray."

"So I have been told," Farleigh said.

"I'm involved in the dissolution of his estate," Bakeraskin said. "It is in great debt and there is nothing to offer the creditors except tracts of his wilderness land." He chuckled. "These creditors have no interest in distant, untenanted property, much of which Wallis himself had received at a loss for arrears to him. But the heirs believe as Wallis did—that the price of that land will soar the moment there becomes a means to get the timber to market. Or a market comes to it." He leaned in and lowered his voice. "See, Farleigh, I was brought in by the heirs' to make valuable that land."

Bakeraskin drew back. "The hope had been that I'd find the timber so irresistible I'd lead a charge to the legislature for a river channel clear to our mills and shipyards at the mouth of the Chesapeake. The land value would jump, the creditors would take their due, and the heirs would get rich on the rest." He looked around the room, spoke in almost a whisper. "But most of the tracts are worthless and probably will be forever because there's no way to get their trees to the river. Between you and me, I'm resigned to finding the few that have accessible timber. To make something of my move up here, I'll speculate those pieces for myself when the court declares the estate insolvent and the sheriff puts the lots up for sale. Then we'll see about a river channel."

Farleigh, bending to a cat that had been rubbing its flank against his leg, scratched behind its ears. "I am a simple millkeeper," he said and straightened. "I cannot advise thee on such matters."

"I'm merely coming around to making you a proposal," Bakeraskin said. He turned to Jedediah. "You could float pine timbers from my piece to this place, couldn't you, boy?"

"Yes, Marse."

Bakeraskin scowled and raised the tip of his cane within an inch of Jedediah's nose. "You'll be rid of that Virginia field tongue and speak as a gentleman's slave. Say 'Master.'"

Jedediah bowed his head and slowly enunciated the word. Looking up, he caught the miller at the wooden vat, his ear turned to the grind, those green eyes aimed at the pointed cane.

Master swung the cane up under his arm. "I already have a stretch of riverside timber," he said. "While I can't yet get it to a market 150 miles away, I see settlers in temporary homes and barns of crumbling log for want of lumber here. Selling flour may not interest the farmers of this valley sir, but what of trading it for pine in a neighborhood where timberland is owned by proprietors either absent or dead? What I'm saying is that if you were to establish a sawmill on your race—"

Farleigh stopped him with a wave of his hand. "Friend," he said. "I am not a sawyer. Furthermore, we have a sawmill in the valley—thou must have seen it, toward the mouth of the creek. Apollos Buckalew's place."

Bakeraskin had at first reared back his chin at the objection, but then turned an ear. "We came over the pass. I've not been downstream of your place. Is this sawyer in need of timber?"

Farleigh studied the floor. "First, it is true—many of us have outlived our log homes. They'd been meant to serve us the decade they last until we had sawmills. But as thou says, the timberland between the farms, and more to the point, timberland along the river—our means of moving these great trees— seems always in dispute. We each have our woodlot, but never in the right place. So our sawyer spends his days more as a smith." He curved up his lips, looked off a moment while Bakeraskin leaned toward him. Farleigh nodded. "I am willing to inquire whether these farmers would give thee grain in return for delivery of logs so they can then barter with Apollos to make lumber of them." He raised a finger. "But thou must know. They've little to spare and will likely partner by the log to make a few boards at a time."

"Light loads are better," Bakeraskin said. "Just one man will be hauling my flour by canoe."

"Friend," Farleigh said, "that is not the way to transport flour. One is constantly in danger of leaks or rollover in rapid water."

"Nonsense," Bakeraskin said. "Threaten a slave with the lash and your every wish is his command. Now let's sit down and discuss our arrangement. And Jedediah, go explain to that buck over there that you'll be coming for the yield of those stones soon enough."

* * *

As Jedediah approached the whirring millstone, the floor quaking through his shins, miller George pretended not to notice as he bent to a small outlet in the vat and rubbed between his fingers coarse brown flour. He lifted it to his nose, held it to the light of the doorway where horseflies slashed through the lemon sunshine of late afternoon. Finally, sidelong, he regarded Jedediah.

Tugging at the brim of his hat where it flopped over his ears, Jedediah mumbled to the floor. "Marse says I's ta talk to you."

George took up a bucket and stepped to a barrel of wheat. "Then talk," he said, and the first thing Jedediah thought was how he pronounced his words clear and complete, like a white man, and he couldn't help envying this.

"Aren't many niggahs 'round here," Jedediah said.

George stopped scooping grain into the bucket and turned his eyes on Jedediah. He held them there a moment, then mounted the stepladder to fill the hopper.

"I's from Virginny," Jedediah said. "It's wild country here."

"Not this part of the valley," George said, stepping down.

"Dey's heaps a' wolves up where I live." Jedediah said. "Howlin' all de night long."

George tossed the bucket into the barrel. "Where is that?" he said.

"Up 'da river. Up 'da Monseytown flats. Dat's as far as folks live 'fore 'da old Indian country. Marse says den it's jes' catamounts, rattlesnakes and trees. Miles on end. No roads eben."

George watched the wobbling damsel shake the grain through the shoe and into the eye of his spinning runner stone. "I heard of people settled way up there. Some few."

Jedediah remarked the size of George's hands as he brushed flour from his apron—not just their oar-like breadth, but their bulk, their pent might, the thumbs like great levers. "You talk strange," he said.

"No," George said, "you talk strange. You might do something about that around here."

It wasn't a command, more a suggestion, the voice so pacific it was almost indifferent. Mistress and Master had insisted Jedediah talk properly, but only now did he determine to learn—he trusted by a confidence this man showed in his strong stance and steady eye that it would be to his advantage. Speaking like white folks would come easy enough; he'd been hearing them jabber all his life, while the more difficult had been expected of him—making himself sound asinine.

"Marse is fixin' a trade for flour," Jedediah said. "I'll be comin' with logs for it."

George shrugged. "I just grind. Mister Farleigh arranges the grist in and the flour out."

Jedediah weighed "Mister." Something was more amiss here than the strange ways of Farleigh.

"Your master doesn't sound like he's from Virginia," George said.

"You heard him?" Jedediah said.

"Every word."

"He's the stupidest kind a' white man. Got an old gourd for a head, but 'nuf money an' fine close, anybody'll listen to all 'dat talk."

George reached up and felt for how much wheat remained in the hopper, bent and pinched flour from the opening in the vat.

"He's from Maryland," Jedediah said. "We followed de river from der." He looked to the doorway. "I never knowed mountains so close to each other as up our way. But I like dat. Never knowed water so full a' sky. De rivers I knowed looked full a' de eart'."

George rotated a wheel fixed to a shaft which descended through a hole to the ground level. The grinding ceased, though the floor still shuddered with the pulleys and belts below.

The four Farleigh boys, long-legged and somber, carried in armfuls of firewood, each wearing a hat like their father's. They stacked the wood before a meager hearth—just slate laid across the floor puncheons. Over this had recently been built an inner chimney of lathe daubed with clay.

Tautness built across George's powerful shoulders as he watched the brothers. He addressed them with a directness that turned Master Bakeraskin's attention from his conversation with Farleigh. "Save the wood," George said. "You might hazard a fireplace in the mill, but light it seldom as you can."

"Just stocking for winter," the eldest son said.

"Isn't my mill," George said, and he tightened his lips and fists as if to stop himself from saying more.

Bakeraskin gaped now at Farleigh, who returned neither reprimand nor promise of a whip at this willfulness. Instead, he said, "George, we'll all be careful. Thou knows the fireplace is only because my rheumatism will not stand another winter in a cold building."

When Bakeraskin and Farleigh turned back to their business, George mumbled to Jedediah, "Only careful that matters in this place is my careful. I should tell them—build an office. Shouldn't be a fire in a mill."

Jedediah studied him, trying to decipher the strange situation here. "Why do you go by George Sharpe?" he said. "Why not Farleigh?" He waited, but George stepped away without a word and descended through a trapdoor to the grumbling bowels of the mill.

Washington Township, Lycoming County, Pennsylvania

She appeared on a drizzly morning in March when George couldn't keep the flour from caking for the dampness of the valley and the staleness of the poorly stored wheat that came to him these days. Inured to ignoring movements in the shadows where the rats flitted, he wondered how long she'd been peering over the sacks of meal piled near the doorway. At first, he thought she frowned, but realized he mistook a fixed expression, severe, rigidly watchful.

George learned later that before Caleb Farleigh had departed from New Jersey, he'd made a covenant with her father, Reuben Wheler. They'd agreed that when the Farleigh boys were old enough to be left under another family's charge, Farleigh and Prudence, eager to return to civilization, would send word to Wheler they were ready. Wheler would pass his farm in New Jersey on to his sons, and he and his wife and daughter would come to oversee this place until the Farleigh boys, reaching maturity, would take over. Though Farleigh had known from the beginning he was no pioneer, he believed that his sons in their youth would benefit not only from more land but the forbearance necessary on a frontier. He was confident Wheler, an aging veteran of the revolt, was a stalwart and trustworthy man, of little need on a New Jersey farm his sons were more than able to work, Wheler looking for a last, brief adventure as a temporary overseer.

A whisper of a woman—slight, narrow-shouldered, sandy frizzles fringing the ruffles of her mob cap. But the intensity of her eyes made up for the delicateness, the mark of unusual strength and obstinance, like the thin stem of the mayapple with its top-heavy leaves and burdensome fruit.

Women rarely visited the mill, where men came not only to exchange grain but to smoke and impose their politics on one another. George scanned the room for a husband. She's lost, he thought. Come to the mill for help while her man tries the house. Either that or one of those Friends. But she wore neither apron nor black hood. He stepped toward her, away from his gnashing stones.

"Are you looking for your way, Madam?" George said.

"We've found our way," she said. A long blink. "And I'm not a Madam."

He moved closer. The stern face had deceived him. A girl, perhaps 16. "Here for your father's flour," he said, already knowing that was not it.

The slightest shake of her head, a tremble, almost. He glanced back at his millstones. "I have to go back to work," he said.

But she made no move, rather remained there in the shadows where on any day in the troubled times to come he might catch her watching.

He found her father at the table that evening, occupying the place closest to the door, George's seat, where during summer he could look out for customers. No extra treenplates were set out. So he stood by the hearth where Madam Farleigh gave a spin to a fowl hanging on a string in the fireplace. When the carcass stopped and revolved the other way, grease sizzling in the coals, Madam took up a flagon and poured water into noggins at the table. She spoke not a word to George.

Reuben Wheler had glanced at him, then turned back to papers on the table. George realized he somehow knew this man as there came to him across the 13 years he'd been here a ruddy and firmer rendition of the gray, slack-jowled profile. But he couldn't summon the reason it brought sour aversion to his gut.

Caleb Farleigh led his boys in from the stable, the odor of horse sweat and hog sty hanging about them in the dampness, overcoming even the aroma of roasted chicken. Stopping as the fourth son shut the door, Farleigh looked back and forth between the two men; he would not meet George's eyes.

Farleigh dismissed the boys to wash at the well, took off his hat, and fumbled with the brim. This especially put George on guard; Farleigh did not go bare-headed even at the table.

"George," Farleigh said, his wife turning her attention from where she stooped at the hearth for another spin of the fowl, "I trust thou has met Mister Wheler?" He raised his eyes only so far as George's breast. "Or perhaps thou knows him from New Jersey?"

"Haven't been introduced," George said.

Reuben Wheler paid no attention.

"Then if I may," Farleigh said, watching himself pinch his hat brim. "Reuben, I'd like thee to meet George Sharpe."

Wheler looked up from his papers long enough to deliver Farleigh a cutting glance, ignoring George who now stood at his side, ready to offer a hand. "George alone will do around here," Wheler said.

Farleigh's voice began breaking. "George," he said, "Mister Wheler, who is come with his wife and daughter—now resting above—is brother to Mistress Sharpe. Thou may recall."

And then George remembered this man coming to the Sharpe mill, rude in his dealings with him, a connection to Mistress clear now just in how he'd treated George. Still, he could not contain the question knocking always about his mind. "How is my mother?" he said.

Reuben Wheler slowly pivoted his head to see him. All of Mistress's disdain looked out from those eyes identical to hers, but George saw satisfaction too, Wheler telling him that his sister's constant punishments had not lessened with age, rather had seized upon the solitude of that remaining reminder of disgrace.

As Wheler shooed George with a whisk of his hand, Caleb Farleigh said, "Reuben, I think George can't help himself." He faltered under Wheler's gaze, looked elsewhere and tugged at his neckcloth. "Thou might see, when we discuss particulars, how this is a precious matter for him."

George bowed his head. Farleigh had only furthered a great error. In the ensuing silence, George peered to see Wheler's eyes working the table as the wayfarer fathoms a river for a ford, nodding then, as might that wayfarer in having decided his way.

Madam Farleigh at the hearth wiped her brow with the sleeve of her shortgown. She'd forgotten her fowl—it hung motionless, wings dangling, charring over the coals as the dripping grease brought forth flames. For she was locked on a new determination in the set of Wheler's mouth, something malicious showing as ice in his eye. She lowered her sleeve to her lips and shifted her attention to her husband. Her eyes shouted for him to heed Wheler. But Caleb Farleigh was stepping away to hang his coat by the door.

George would never again sit for a meal or sleep in this home he'd helped build, never be cooled in the summer or warmed in the winter by the sturdy buffer of oak timbers he'd raised and chinked.

At dawn on the bank of the head race, which he'd dug from creek to mill with pan and horse, George stood a board on-end and dropped it across the water alongside where it oozed through an arched opening in the foundation. He took up his rake of ash tines and stepped onto the board. Beneath the arch, the water passed toward the wheel through a wooden grate, a sieve of sorts that George had built, an improvement of the design he'd known at the Sharpe Mill in Jersey: George had made his pales from pine, where Master Sharpe's had been of hickory. If a tooth in this grate snapped in a spring freshet, it was less likely to break a paddle of the waterwheel.

The valley waking about him foggy and drab, George raked from the grate leaves that had washed with the snow melt into the race. White winter, which had persisted pure and downy across the valley, drudged away now with muffled gugglings beneath its tattered, sooty hide.

The board sprang beneath George with the rocking of his shoulders, which had taken on a chill not entirely of the clammy shirt brushing his skin, still damp from the night air of the mill where he'd tried in vain to sleep on flour sacks, loose burlap for a blanket. He could not call up any such thought that might warm him, though the exercise brought blood and feeling to his fingers.

Shoes squished in the snowless slough of a path that descended beside the mill. George knew it was Mr. Farleigh, sure he'd come.

"There are things thou needs to know," Farleigh said when George did not look up. "And things I can't tell thee. I only ask that thou trust my judgment."

George combed his rake through the teeth of the grate; there was no debris there anymore. "All I've figured out," George said, "is you're leaving. And that you'd planned it."

"My silence was for thine own good," Farleigh said. "And as part of a promise I made."

"To my father?" George said, looking up. Farleigh stood on the bank dressed to travel—heavy surtout, tan, buttoned breeches reaching into his boots, their tops turned down and showing canvas linings. "Did you promise my father you would keep me until his brother-in-law came?"

"This is what I must leave thee understanding," Farleigh said. "Thy father sent thee with thine interests in mind. Yet as part of those interests, he required I keep our arrangement's terms— his and mine—silent until thou is prepared for his favor."

"Favor," George said. "From the man that could have freed me. And my mother."

Farleigh, who rarely gestured, held up a finger. "He could have sold thee, just as well."

George tapped the pegs of his rake against the plank. "I thought he did, Mister Farleigh. Or Master Farleigh. It doesn't matter which one I use, really. Or am I still owned by Master Sharpe, this man of favors? Tell me, because I don't know."

"That is a complicated situation," Farleigh said, "which I am not at liberty to share. Let it suffice that I became involved only when I was sure the arrangement was to thine advantage."

George shook his head. "You couldn't even tell me you'd be handing me off?"

Farleigh leaned forward, lifted a boot heel out of the sward of the race bank, and looked into the March overcast. Beyond him, above a ragged and sallow field of corn stubble, a murder of crows, still winter-sparse of feather and luster, descended in raucous squawks and caws, alighting in a slow advancing order like a falling sheet, the lot of them hopping off and resettling again in successive waves and squabbles, finally remaining aground silent and feeding—agreed to whatever scheme they'd fussed and fluttered about.

"I had made a promise," Farleigh said. "But I would not have told thee in any case." He looked at George. "I knew that coming here would bewilder thee and that anticipating more change would add worry."

George watched two sentinel crows take wing from a hickory. When the first of these let forth a raspy *hah-hah*, the murder called back, lifting in tatters until it occupied the sky in a vortex from which one-by-one the crows broke off, forming a line of flight to some other field, some other intrigue. "You mean I might have run," he said.

"Not at all," Farleigh said. "I wanted thee to take ease in adjusting to—" he searched the slate water of the race for a way to put it.

"Freedom?" George said. He snorted.

Farleigh held up a hand. "Thou needs to understand—thy freedom, thy true freedom, is not mine to give. But—and now I've blundered into defying the terms of my promise—it was my place to prepare thee for it. That is why I allowed thee larger and larger range. Why I waited to tell thee I had been paying thee on account. And why only after thou had learned figures did I settle that account and pay thee directly in coins."

"Whose place is it to give me freedom," George said, "if not my master's?"

Farleigh turned his head to where the last of the crows disappeared beyond the limbs of sycamores sprawling over the race. George could hardly hear him speak. "I am not thy master," Farleigh said. "Thy freedom is Adam Sharpe's to give."

George threw the rake onto the bank. "You talk in circles. My master that says he isn't my master, but that my old master is again. While you leave me here to another master."

"Oh, George," Farleigh said. "I've conspired to keep the truth from thee, telling myself it was for thine own good. May the Almighty forgive me. I see I do a lesser evil breaking my promise. But will thou keep it a secret?"

"I've had enough of secrets," George said. He walked onto the bank, ignoring Farleigh's offer to help him, pulled the board across the race. He leaned it against the stone foundation, then started up the path.

"Thou should know of an act of kindness thy father did for thee," Farleigh said.

George stopped, but did not turn. "Today's the first we've spoken of him as my father."

"I've always known, George. By his decisions. By your face."

"You think anything my father could've done for me short of freeing my mother could be kind?" He turned now to Farleigh, brows raised beneath that hat brim he wore rolled back lest it bump the machinery.

"Thy father indentured thee to me," Farleigh said, "until thy twenty-eighth birthday." He stepped toward George. "He wanted thee free. I seized the chance to help a man break from bondage. Thy father arranged for gradual freedom, that thou would adapt better and learn to prosper by thine own hand. That was why I was bound to secrecy, not telling even my sons." He lowered his eyes to the muck. "But now I see the error in that. So I am speaking against my word before I further injure thee."

George was shaking his head. "You don't see you paid my father to put me out of his sight? He cast off his sin on a goat, like that man in one of the Bible stories you read to us. And he hushed you so I wouldn't be proud and come back to cause trouble."

"Even if this were true," Farleigh said, "what does it matter when thou will be free in three years."

"You mean when I would've been free." George pointed to the mill house where smoke lingered about the roofline. "Instead, you're leaving me here to this man Wheler."

"Reuben Wheler is an honorable man," Farleigh said. "I have borne that out. He understands the terms of thine indenture and has agreed to continue them. Then as a free man, thou may negotiate with Mister Sharpe for thy mother."

The chill seeped beneath George's skin now. "Does Reuben Wheler know I plan to buy my mother's freedom?"

Farleigh wormed a finger between his cravat and throat, extended his neck while he did not quite look George in the eye. "I have mentioned it."

George let out a long exhale. "You would have done better never taking me here." He squeezed tight his lips a moment, fought to keep calm. "At least tell me he doesn't know you've been paying me."

Again, Farleigh looked everywhere but at George. "I intend to be forthright about that before I leave today. I just haven't thought of the best way to explain it." Farleigh stared off, then stepped to George and put a hand on his shoulder. "Thou will fare well, George. My sons will be here and Reuben will treat thee as I have. I will require he continue to pay thee. In coins."

As George drew back and the hand fell away, he thought of all the contradictions he'd known in white men, their whims of word and action—the best a person could do with them was expect the worst. He leveled his eyes on Farleigh, who was absorbed in the downy ceiling of the valley, his lips twitching in silent prayer.

"I ask one thing," George said.

Farleigh's mouth stopped, and though his chin was still tilted toward the heavens, he shifted his eyes to George.

"Do not tell Reuben Wheler you paid me."

Farleigh's brows gathered as he lowered his head. "But George, then he would not be inclined to continue."

"It's all I ask," George said.

The old Quaker gave a smug grin and dropped his eyes. Because George had seen this all his life—the white man saying he knew what was best—he was ready with a deal, even while such was against the law of his heart. "You asked," George said, "that I never tell I learned the agreement you made with my father."

"I beg of thee."

"Then promise not to tell Reuben Wheler you paid me. If what you say is true, I'll wait three years to save again for my mother's freedom."

For the rest of his days and in spite of all that followed, George would never forget that Caleb Farleigh reached out and shook his hand.

* * *

Leading Caleb Farleigh up the slope, George caught sight of that stern-faced girl near a walnut tree not ten rods away. She wore a heavy, coffee-colored riding-coat and a muslin cap dyed to match. He was sure she'd watched the encounter, standing there arrested and as indifferent to the surroundings as was the tree itself. Closer now as he rounded the mill, he saw a strain of nerve and muscle about those dour, fixed lips, the shadows of her eyes narrowed in some manner of disapproval.

She troubled him that moonless, foggy night while he tossed beneath horse blankets on his pallet of sacked flour. Delirious, he feared her stealing about the fathomless black of the mill, imagined that her gimlet gaze would eternally haunt him with what had happened here today.

He rose hacking to a cacophony of birdsong, feeling as wrinkled and knotted as his shirt and coat. He tottered to the trapdoor and descended to inspect the trundles and shafts disengaged from the turning wheel, its paddles metrically *slap-splashing* against the race. At a bin below a chute, he took up a handful of flour and spread apart his fingers; clots dropped, steeped in the same dampness he couldn't shiver out of his shoulders.

His breath dragging ragged and acrid through his throat, George climbed the ladder. Instead of milling grist, he moved grain barrels and stores of sackcloth to the margins of the room, leaving only a cag of wheat beside his stones. Then he swept the floor planks and set to wheelbarrowing flour from his bins, throwing shovelfuls across the place he'd cleared until he covered all but a path from the door and a space around his stones, a carpet motley-brown, unsifted as the flour was.

He left open the door and swung wide a window of plate glass; he would not start a fire even to lift moisture from the room. After descending to engage the machinery, he returned and rotated his wheel to start his stones. Bending, listening, smelling the work of the grind, he noticed something was eclipsing his light.

Reuben Wheler occupied the center of the doorway, a shadow figure except for the gleam of steel buttons making an X across his breast with the inward arc of his military lapels. George knew he was surveying the floor, for the wide, flat brim of his planter's hat was turning this way and that, his queue appearing to each side of his head.

"This is how you treat the customers' flour?" Wheler said as he plodded through it with no more heed than he'd give snow, stopping where George rotated his wheel until the whoosh and mash of the stones ceased. Wheler side-kicked a swath through the flour, clumps gathering between his brogan and stocking.

"I'm drying the flour, Mister Wheler," George said.

Wheler pushed back the brim of his hat where he wore it tilted over one eye. "First," he said, "there'll be no 'misters' from half-niggers around here."

George lowered his chin. He needed to cough, resisted until his eyes watered and he hacked away.

"Second," Wheler said when the fit passed, "you'll not steal a mite of flour here or partake of bread in that house. Besides the salt pork my wife sends out to you, your provender is a ration of hominy. Cook it over that hearth I hear you won't put fire to. Start layin' by more wood. Now. Burn it to keep the flour dry and the mill warm. Only by day, though. Warm yourself at night with a blanket. Like a horse."

George met Wheler's eyes, looked down again at the strip of floor between them.

"Something else," Wheler said. "I understand your last master, full of his thees and thous and nigger lovin', would not take in rye. From now on, you will grind rye for anyone that asks. And I'll grow it here, whether for whiskey or bread, and sell it at six shillings and five pence to the bushel. Chopping or milling extra."

Cold sweat lacquered George's face. He wiped his sleeve across his brow, felt the paste of flour he left. "Yes, Master," he said, and coughed again.

"Last of all," Wheler said, George catching the toe of Wheler's shoe sliding to the edge of the exposed floor planks. "There'll be no more talk of your slut of a mother. Nor any attempts to communicate with her."

George locked his teeth together and stiffened every muscle, trying to incrust himself tight and hard as a butternut hull. The straining pinched the compass of his vision to a diminishing spot in the flour at his feet as he heard Wheler walk out the door. All of George's existence funneled and fell like the grain in his hopper into a dusky tunnel. He would not remember how long he remained there sweating, reeking of horse blankets, as in his mind he chased a fleeting terminus in that cavern of echoing regret at having learned that in three years he could have been free.

Pine Creek Township, Lycoming County, Pennsylvania

The upriver country of the West Branch was still a forbidding, lawless land, the limits of the Indian's last dominion only 17 years ago. A slave again in every manner but fact, George had been ordered many times over the past year into the foot of that abyss, the black forest as it was known, country darkened by deepness and steepness of valley and by the interlocking canopy of giant evergreen tops.

It took George a day to reach the Great Island, site of the old Indian town Cawighnowane, stronghold of succeeding tribes, last and not least fierce, the Monseys, or wolf people. This was as well the previous neighborhood of the Bakeraskins and their slave Jedediah James, that family removed upriver, closer to the timber Peter Bakeraskin coveted now, as Tantalus wanted his fruit.

One of Bakeraskin's interim enterprises—his distilling business—required a steadier supply of chopped rye than he could count on with the freshets and floods by which his slave Jedediah continued to transport logs for return of flour, and now the grain.

Unlike Caleb Farleigh and the couple millers lately established closer to Bakeraskin, Reuben Wheler accepted cash from Peter Bakeraskin—whiskey, too. And so George, tasked with milling no less toll grain, plus the rye Wheler grew, carried out the added task of tugging and heaving and—above all—keeping dry within a canvas waterproofed with bear grease, canoe-loads of Bakeraskin's purchases of the chopped rye, upriver into that country of catamounts and rattlesnakes. Subsisting on river water and jerked deer meat from his pouch, it took George four days there and back, and he made the journey once a month if the ice was out.

Past the Great Island, miles separated cabins, these occupied by mostly squatters hoping to preempt forgotten warrants. They'd taken up the scattered and meager shares of lowland that the sheer walls of the valley grudged—just grassflats where the Indians had tended their corn and inhabited their huts until the smallpox, war or migration had taken them. Each family had advanced to a plot as far upriver as they wanted to move their tools and belongings by canoe, their only choice for hauling, for the sections of valley suitable for a wagon road were separated by stretches that left no more than a bridle path, if that.

This was not the rounded landscape of the lower river valley's loamy Muncy hills, rather a looming, furrowed, jagged place, recalcitrantly rocky right down to the spadefull, the river bedded in cobblestone. It was country more hacked than created, as if chopped with tomahawks by those Indians. Nevertheless, a fiercer place lay farther on, the headwater country of the great tributary the Sinnemahoning Creek, a vast forest guttered by roaring streams, choked with rhododendron, and even then largely unknown to white men but for trappers and surveyors.

Yet George, unrested after camping fireless amidst howling wolves and rustling brush, still thrilled at starting into this stony craw of a country, something in its dimness, its infinity, the ancient and wild beauty of its raggedness. A no-man's land.

The Bakeraskin home, dismantled, hauled in pieces and rebuilt here by the slave Jedediah James, sat on bottomland rare in its long reach from shore to slope, occupying the crotch of a riverbend. George arrived at dusk, later than usual, slowed by the low waters of June. He sloshed toward the bank and shoved the canoe onto the stony strand, the scudding dulled and deepened by the dense burden of rye in the hull. Not wanting to report to the house and the miserable, whining Cornelia Bakeraskin, he whistled toward the barn out back, just a tottering, slab-sided stable with a steep roofline for a hayloft. Along with fowl and a few hogs, the Bakeraskins now kept a calved cow, for a child had come; it seemed only to add to the mistress's misery in this uncivilized land, where Bakeraskin promised deliverance to a fine estate built from the money waiting in the trees on the warrants he'd buy.

His knotted back aching clear to his hips, George watched the barn. He shivered—not from being soaked in river water, but from weariness. And his knees wobbled, to the point he needed either to lean on the stern or start ahead, which he chose. Moving through the yard, he waved away clouds of great olive-colored mayflies and wished for the strength of breath he used to have in the mill when he didn't cough while the dust rose with the grinding, much less while he swept the floor.

"You been drinking that whiskey I send your master, boy?" It broke out of the valley's birdsong and the deep *jug-a-rums* of bullfrogs. From a corner of the shadowed porch, the smoke of Bakeraskin's pipe floated into the milky twilight of the yard.

George stopped and lowered his eyes. "No, sir. I'm just not used to dry land yet."

"That rye better be dry," the invisible Bakeraskin said.

"Yessir." George swayed in the cow-cropped yard, the briny musk and muttering of the river that had glutted his senses over the past two days giving to the fecund smells and sighs of a farm—chicken manure and fresh hay, snuffling hogs, the lowing cow.

"Jedediah is up at the still," Bakeraskin said.

George squinted where in a crease in the sloped field Jedediah had built Bakeraskin's stillhouse beside a spring.

"He'll be down now," Bakeraskin said. "It's nigh dark. Start moving that rye to the barn. You know where to put it."

After George and Jedediah hauled the sacks, Jedediah hung a crusie lamp in the stall he occupied until he returned his pallet to the kitchen for winter. George untied his blanket and unrolled it across the hay-strewn dirt. His pulse dinging at his skull and the nape of his neck, he wanted food and sleep.

"So what's this news, can't be told outside?" Jedediah said, cross-legged on his pallet.

George, sitting on his blanket with his knees drawn to his chin, held a finger to his lip.

Jedediah grinned. "You mess up that white gal watches you in the mill?"

George shook his head no. He glanced into the blackness of the barn bay then watched the ground while he concentrated on the night sounds, waited. "You're free," he said, barely breathing the words.

Jedediah held still a moment, no reaction. Then he chuckled. "Sure," he said, "I'm just a goose, honked its way north."

Pitching onto his knees, George grabbed Jedediah's shirt. "Quiet," he whispered. "Listen or you're a fool."

The guard that wanted to hope, to fan that ember no slave dared feed to flame, retreated from Jedediah's eyes.

George let go and returned to his blanket. "There's people in the Muncy hills called Quakers. They help free slaves."

Jedediah spat on the ground between them. "Crackers don't give a damn about slaves but that we're the only things besides pigs lower than them."

George was shaking his head. "I said Quakers. It's a religion."

Jedediah waved this off. "Religion," he said. "It's the Bible makes me a slave."

George watched the unsteady, creamy light of the lamp flitter across the bark of the hemlock slabs enclosing their stall. He'd change this man's future with what he said next. But it mattered not even if Jedediah would be worse off. For right down to where there was peace in ignorance, the truth somehow proved more important than a man's fortune. George knew this because it touched on the error of the order that allowed masters and slaves.

He leaned forward, whispered, "They know the laws and they watch slaves, watched you. Six months after you came to Pennsylvania, you were a free man. That's the law here."

Jedediah remained silent, absorbed in a moth making sorties at the lamp.

"Either Bakeraskin's a bigger idiot than he looks," George said, "or he knew and figured you'd never find out. But it don't matter, 'cause you're free as a black man can be. They have no claim over you."

"They got somethin' over me," Jedediah said, swatting a mosquito against his ear. "Idiots or not."

"Whatever it is," George said, "the Quakers will know what to do."

"Never mind about that."

"They can take Bakeraskin to court," George said.

Jedediah snorted. "You want me to trust white people against white people for a black man?"

George reached and took down his pouch where it hung on a peg beside the lamp. "Say it in your head: free."

Jedediah gazed off toward the frog song throbbing from the marshy edge of slackwater inside the river bend, toward the unfathomed abyss of the frontier. "Why didn't they tell me before?" he said. "I been here two years."

"They knew better than to get caught coming to you direct," George said. "They looked for someone like me to pass the word."

Jedediah narrowed his eyes at George. "They'd just as likely get caught goin' to you."

"Somebody else got word to me for them."

"You're trustin' your master's daughter?" Jedediah said. "Do you know what they'll do to you—or parts of you—they catch a low-down slave with her?"

George waited a moment. "Free," he said. "Get that in your head. Find a good time to run. Like one of your log trips." He scratched an arching line in the packed dirt. "Let me show you how to find the people waiting for you in the Muncy hills."

But Jedediah was shaking his head. "If I run, I got to go to Virginia."

George thought of his mother. "There's something back there they'll take it out on," he said.

When Jedediah only looked down, George said, "You can never go back there now that you're free. You have to stay in Pennsylvania. The law here isn't the law there."

"See," Jedediah said, "a black man bein' free just means he's got things they can take. That's the white man's way of givin' freedom right there."

"But now you can buy what you have down there."

Jedediah's chin rocked with a silent chuckle. "Even if I could play that buyin' game, the last thing they'd sell me is what I got in Virginia." He took off his flopped field hat, reached up and hung it on a peg and lay on his pallet. "No, I will not run. Not yet, and never to any white man." He laced his hands behind his head. "I'm gonna wait and watch, like an old owl in a tree over a rabbit hole. 'Cept now, while I'm grubbin' stumps and totin' rye for that sot Bakeraskin, I'll be knowin' what he don't."

"That talk's dangerous," George said. "The sooner you get out of here, the healthier your hide. Wait too long, you might be wishing you'd never found out." He lifted his pouch, loosened the hemp drawcord and took out a johnnycake wrapped in linen. "You want some of this?" he said. "I got jerked deer, too."

Jedediah shook his head no. "If what you're tellin' me is true, why aren't you free?"

George put down the corncake. "I can't tell you that," he said.

"You got a secret you can't tell another nigger, even where there aren't ten in the whole valley? You're talkin' like a white man."

"In time," George said. "I made a promise."

"A white-man promise," Jedediah said. "A nigger don't keep a secret from a nigger, 'less it's got to do with a white man."

An ache at the base of George's skull reminded him of his famishment. But now the johnnycake in his hand was as inviting as a chunk of sod. He'd come here eager, bearing for his friend a rare jewel of hope. Now a pall of doubt was descending, insinuating as the ash of coalfire. He forced a bite of the saltless corncake. As it crumbled on George's tongue, Jedediah rose and lifted the lamp from its peg.

"Time to jubilate," Jedediah said. "I'm goin' up the stillhouse for a pail of whiskey. You want some?"

George swallowed and shook his head no. He pointed toward the house. "Don't get careless," he said.

Jedediah started out of the barn, the feeble light of the flame washing away as the calf bawled into the night.

Pine Creek Township, Lycoming County, Pennsylvania

So Jedediah watched and bided his time. But the Quakers of the Muncy hills would not delay—his deliverance came seeking him, without his say, with no heed for his terms or timeframe.

It came on horseback on a fall afternoon when the sun shone golden and Jedediah was where he was not supposed to be— with the neighbor girl Sarah Starret, downriver. From a sloping copse of pines overlooking the riverbank where they met on occasional afternoons—the time of day Jedediah could disappear for a couple hours from farming or distilling and Sarah could leave her aging father to his nap—they watched the lone rider pass on the bridle path. He rode the black mare at a slow amble, its head down, a sleek, radiant animal that had seen no plow. And so Jedediah knew that the rider had been pacing her over a distance and that the horse was a hostler's. He saw in the way the man sat in the saddle with his chest out, head erect, hat tilted back, that he took pleasure in rare command over such a fine ride. It was the air of bearing important business that surrounds a lower official, the minion doing the boss's bidding. A deputy sheriff.

Jedediah would have heard word of any transgression fetching the law up here. This man's business had to do with Jedediah. He looked to Sarah where they sat between a pair of enormous roots splaying from the base of a tree trunk. For an hour, they'd been plucking the fabric at their thighs, commenting on the weather or that one or the other must hurry home.

He'd heard her approaching one midday at the stillhouse, Master as usual about the country seeking warranted but unpatented tracts, Mistress napping with the baby. Jedediah stood at the stone and mud fireplace, his thumb testing the temperature of a kettle of water he was heating to make mash. The peculiarity of light feet whisking through the weeds turned his attention, bare feet for sure, steps faint and delicate as a precious old memory.

His first thought was that this girl flush with new womanhood yet showing remnants of childhood curiosity had known she'd find a black man, the reflex of repulsion he'd seen in reared chins not here.

She stepped within an arm's reach and held up a jug. "My father's in want of whiskey. For his rheumatism. We have money, pork or corn to pay."

He did not respond, just watched, mistrusting her so close, closer than any white woman would dare stand in Virginia. But all he saw was someone waiting for his answer.

He took her jug and drew her whiskey from a cask. She tarried then, as she did in all the following visits. Eventually it occurred to him—and dispirited him in a way—that the reason she remained to talk of her garden or the stock on her father's farm or—always a topic in the valley—the current depth of the West Branch, was there was no one her age in that country to keep company with. Her nearest brothers, on the closest riverplain claims, were a generation older than she, and their wives nearly so.

He came to learn she was his age, 18, and occupied in taking care of her elderly widower father. He was still somewhat capable, but tiring, his strength tolled by two wars waged under different flags and against enemies determined to inflict the cruelest of atrocities.

Neither he nor she used the word slave, but Jedediah was certain she knew he lived as one. She was wise enough to make no show of their acquaintance when she came for whiskey. Whether in the yard or alone in the stillhouse, if they hadn't already planned their next rendezvous, she would ask quietly if he'd meet the following afternoon. Sometimes he went, sometimes he did not. But she was always there.

Whether he went hinged not on his having liberty; he no longer feared being caught away from his duties; he walked about the farm a little slower now, even hummed. Besides, the baby and some strange sullenness distracted Mistress so much she quit demanding petty domestic jobs with broom or pail. Bakeraskin was gone almost always anymore, taking Jedediah with him to push the canoe and carry his satchel only on the odd day. Instead, wavering on meeting Sarah had to do, opposite of all sense, with how the thought of seeing her had stoked a bed of coals in his gut, shooting sparks through his veins. It kept him awake at night. At odd times of the day, she appeared in his mind—her figure, slight of waist and shoulders and with the taut erectness of a hickory sapling, framed by the doorway of the stillhouse. That hair, shiny black as a mourning jewel, falling from beneath her ruffled cap in thrums, the bottoms of which she cropped mop-like over her brow, her ears. He wondered at her wearing her hair like that—whether she hid something, as she seemed to when she secreted her teeth by drawing her lips over them in rare smiles. He couldn't deny that the modesty swelled his pride.

Other times, he pictured her reclined beside him in the grove of pines, her petticoat strewn across her boney hips and legs as formlessly as a dropped blanket, ankles showing where she wore no stockings, fingers, pale and pliant as ryegrass in July, folded together on her lap as though she'd fallen asleep praying. But her eyes were open, eyes of uncertain color, a flecked tea tint that in another light appeared green. The papery skin against her cheekbones, the narrow bridge of her nose, delicate as tree lichen, yet ruddily hale.

Because of that very thrill in the prospect of meeting her, he found as much pleasure staying away, fancied her anticipation in the pine grove turning to disappointment. He imagined her trudging home, pausing on the bridle path before the bend in the river to look back.

He questioned if he felt this way because of shame while he told himself it was because of loyalty. But deep down he knew it was tied to the tidings George Sharpe had delivered, to a change that happened that day.

That news nagged him like a wart on his heal, intoxicated him with unexpected notions. He'd turned his eyes to the earth; his feet had been planted there all his life, yet he'd never contemplated the idea of ground, its measure by acreage, its lay and quality. He had not considered land as within his grasp, having abided being born within the grasp of men and land. Now land had become attainable. Land and, he realized, the woman. Somehow this was why he felt triumph in, of all things, staying away.

He reached back for the tree trunk and pushed himself onto his feet. Straining to follow the horse's progress, he started off.

"Jedediah," she called, but he ignored her.

"Jeddy, what is it?"

At this, he turned and pointed. "Never call me that," he said.

He moved along well above the bridle path, a halting gait against the slope, one leg extended downhill, the other bent near to his waist as his feet clawed for a hold upon disks of sandstone detritus.

His heart drummed like a cooper's mallet as he gained the horseman. Ever so careful not to slip and give himself away, he calculated every step, looked up only to locate through the woods this man who rode slower now, sure of himself with his nearing destination. And then, overtaking the rider, Jedediah lost his footing on a leaf-hidden stone and sent it into a rustling slide.

The rider reined his horse and scanned the hillside. As he locked on Jedediah, he reached to a pack behind his saddle. Jedediah scuttled the best he could up the loose mountain scree, slipping and falling, little avalanches of sandstone in his wake. "Stop," the rider called. "Come down here."

Jedediah summoned whatever tatters of breath and strength remained to lift his legs upward against the rearing valley, concentrated for a plan. He'd mount the ridgetop, use the flat ground to make up time. Maybe he could reach the farm ahead of the spent horse, dupe Mistress into thinking he'd been about the field. But even at that, the rider would make no mistake about who he'd seen and where.

When he reached the crest, white pine and hemlock giving to a forest of pitchpine, birch, and chestnut ensnared in mountain laurel, he could not go on. He lay panting in the leaf-fall, his lungs on fire. Only after his flanks quit cramping could he rise to his feet and stumble along the ridge.

* * *

The farm sat at the foot of a furrow etched into the wall of the river valley by the diligence of the spring. He crossed its head, skirting and climbing boulders left of the slow erosion of water. Then he began the treacherous descent, falling on his rear, cutting his hands on shards of rock, nary a laurel to gain hold of, so night-like was the underworld of these hemlocks rising monstrous yet seemingly uncertain of a foothold against such a steep.

When he made it to the edge of the field, not only was the black mare hitched to the post in front of the house, Mistress, within, was shouting at someone. And Master Bakeraskin was running toward the commotion from the river where he'd moored his canoe.

Jedediah crouched and made his way to the barn where he rested inside the doorway. The marks of the rider's heels showed in the dirt, and as Jedediah's eyes adjusted to the dimness, he distinguished the faint imprints of Mistress's shoes. He crept to his stall, the scared mole to its burrow.

Squatting in a corner, Jedediah waited for his wheezing to subside, then tried to decipher Mistress's outcries, making out only the recurring, "That nigger…. That nigger… That nigger…."

He could run. And while he tensed his legs to spring for that upriver wilderness where a man could lose himself, he went lame. A figure he'd nudged out of his mind these two years appeared from Virginia. He closed his eyes. Run, he thought, then beckoned the thrill that shivered through his loins when he sat with the girl in the pine grove. All that country, man. Go.

He'd torn the towcloth patches at the knees of his breeches, blood luminescent as foxfire against his skin. His shirt was black with earth, soaked with his sweat and stench. He was a man who'd already run, back now in his stall. Master would make of that what he would. Go.

But he sat staring at the planks of his stall, and after a while, Mistress's shrieking stopped. Jedediah rose and went to the barndoor to find Master and the rider walking the edge of the field, that vast upriver wilderness looming beyond them.

Seeing now that Master carried his rifle, Jedediah determined he would not wait like a partridge on its nest. Whatever the lawman had come to redress, Jedediah would stand facing it.

He stepped out to the dusty yard of the barn, savored a moment of that idiot hunting the prey that watched him. At last, Mistress Cornelia, standing by the house, called out his presence. "The nigger's there at the barn," she called out. "At the barn."

Bakeraskin had been peering into the woods from behind a stone pile. As he turned and shouldered his rifle, the visitor reached out and struck down the barrel.

The men approached Jedediah, and again Bakeraskin levelled the gun, Jedediah noting it was not even primed. "Where you been, boy?" Bakeraskin said, poking the muzzle into Jedediah's forehead. He glanced at the torn breeches, the bloodied shins.

"By the law of this county," the stranger said, "put that damned thing down."

Mistress Cornelia, face tear-stained, capless, hair wild about her head, ran to her husband, the sow hog and its six shotes squealing ahead of her, past the barn for the woods. "Flog him," she said.

The stranger pulled from the waist of his breeches a folded document and waved it. He was tall and paunched, a narrow-shouldered man of middle age, face sprinkled with a sparse, ginger and silver beard. His eyes, unshadowed by the brim of the hat he still wore tilted back, were as pale and spangled as his whiskers. "You are in contempt of an order of the court if you do not release this—" he paused, pointed the paper at Jedediah, then looked past him. "This negro," he said. And then to Jedediah: "As a deputy sheriff, I have the authority to arrest any man attempting to bind you to his service."

Mistress Cornelia, nose a-twitch, face a-flame, stepped to the deputy and swatted the paper. "No man binds him to his service," she said. "He's mine."

The deputy must have felt his provisional authority being dishonored. He held the paper before his eyes, found a small tear and aligned the edges as if righting an indignity. "Madam, I do not know what state you quit, carrying those ideas. But I am sure of this. First, you and Mister Bakeraskin have been here more than six months and have taken residence without registering this man as a slave, which by the new law is enough to make him free. Second, you cannot by common law own property. Presuming," he said, looking from her to her husband, lips reared in an arc, "you and Mister Bakeraskin are married."

"Quite," Mistress said, the word more a hoarse bark. "By the law of a Commonwealth that protects its people's rights."

The deputy addressed Bakeraskin who lowered the rifle. "You, sir, have been summoned to appear before the court of common pleas the first Monday of November next to answer Caspar Roan of a plea of unlawful, wrongful restraint." He extended the document to Bakeraskin.

Ignoring the deputy, Bakeraskin said, "Boy, who's been talking to people downriver on your account? Was it that yellow nigger Sharpe?" He took a step closer. With the muzzle of his gun, he widened a rip in Jedediah's britches. "Where were you just now?"

"Lately he's been abroad," Mistress said. "I called for him the other day nigh an hour. He's seeing someone around here."

Bakeraskin weighed this. "Boy, is that Starret wench still fetching her father's whiskey?"

Jedediah held Bakeraskin's stare. He watched him inch his head toward the affront, scrutinize it as he did his maps at the table on winter afternoons.

"Seems," Bakeraskin said, "I'll have to speak with the venerable Indian fighter and patriot, old man Starret." He swiveled his head on the high collar of his coat. "Deputy, I quitted the Sinnemahone ahead of my surveyor. He'll be here soon. I ask that you let me offer in his company and yours a solution for your Caspar Roan that avoids any contests in the court of common pleas."

The deputy shook his head back and forth. "You'll abide the law."

Bakeraskin smiled. "To the letter. I will counter Caspar Roan with an indenture of this nigger. An indenture he will sign of his own will. And you and my surveyor would oblige me by witnessing the contract." He nodded toward the river where a man waded toward the bank, pushing a canoe. "There's young Tillman now."

"Indenture?" Mistress said. "We're not indenturing a slave we own."

Bakeraskin held up a hand. "Cornelia."

The deputy was looking back at his horse, probably weighing the long ride home, the chance of having to return here. He turned, studied Jedediah, then nodded. "I'll deliver a copy of the indenture in answer to Roan."

Jedediah had never cared for Tillman, who was approaching among the stumps and stone piles of the yard, a man a few years older than he. Tillman's face was always sour from an irritable haughtiness so caustic and outward that Jedediah knew he would never grow into it where so many come to wear their arrogance as naturally as the slopes of their noses. When Tillman boarded here, he would in his tetchiness steer conversations to politics, coming around to the threat of Tories or Indians about the country, this serving somehow as cause for raising a militia. He only added to his repulsiveness by squinting behind spectacles, which made Jedediah believe he would never become as good a surveyor as the longheaded ones he'd known to pass along the river.

Now Tillman stood frowning from one to the other: the deputy with his shoulders gathered to better bear his borrowed authority; pale Mistress; Jedediah in his ragged clothes; and at last Bakeraskin, composed now as he lifted his chin above his collar and looked down his nose at his surveyor.

After introducing the two men, Bakeraskin asked that Tillman follow the conversation closely, for he would like him to draw up an indenture. He promised the deputy a generous compensation if he would visit a justice of the peace to have the copy made. Then, in that white man way of adding teeth to words by looking not at the person addressed but at whom those words mocked, Bakeraskin watched Jedediah and said, "Cornelia, I be- lieve the name of the wench I'm trying to recall is Juda."

It took her a moment, then she understood, probably re- calling her own words on a veranda in Virginia. "Indeed," she said.

"If," Bakeraskin said, "Jedediah resists and forces us to abide the deputy's summons, shall we have her sent south? To some malaria-ridden cotton plantation in the Territory of Orleans?"

"Without delay," Mistress said.

"Jedediah would need not bother trying to save the wench," Bakeraskin said. "A letter to your mother would reach her long before he could."

Mistress nodded.

Tillman was pinching his chin, studying the ground. "If you got yourself a nigger slave, why would you bind him?" He squinted up at Bakeraskin. "He'd be free at twenty-eight instead of you having him for life."

Bakeraskin turned up a hand. "A Mister Roan has intruded on behalf of this buck. Hence our deputy's visit. Would you by chance know Caspar Roan?"

Tillman pretended to spit on the ground. "He'd be one to med- dle with a man's property."

"Deputy," Bakeraskin said, "is it true? Can I bind him only until he is twenty-eight?"

The deputy pursed his lips and looked skyward as if weighing a complicated matter. Jedediah figured he was rather counting all the shillings he was about to lose with the wrong answer. He shrugged. "They say twenty-eight's the law of the land. For a nigger. Now, a white man can only be bound to twenty-one. That's clear. But how many niggers even know how old they are?"

"Well enough," Bakeraskin said. Then he addressed his wife. "I think once your mother knows that condition, she'll make sure the wench is bred or wed before his term is over." Now he looked at Jedediah. "To rid your mind of any notions, be assured that Master James will do nothing to protect that wench if he knows it involves a nigger going free."

Bakeraskin put a hand on the deputy's shoulder. "Let's have Tillman draw up this agreement for the nigger to make his mark upon. Then you can get on your way. I'll follow in a few days to retrieve the indenture."

He bent to a tuft of sere grass that had persisted in the dusty barnyard, plucked a stalk and put it between his teeth. "Tell your sheriff and Caspar Roan they can come back for the nigger Jedediah James in ten years." Now he looked at Jedediah, chewed on the grass. "But assure them he won't want to go anywhere."

Shrugging, the deputy looked in the direction of home.

"Who is this Caspar Roan?" Bakeraskin said.

The deputy jerked his head back. "Why, he's the publisher of our newspaper."

Bakeraskin worked the stem of grass a moment. Then he nodded at Jedediah. "Be off," he said. "Wait in the yard in front of the house until we draw up this document."

Starting away, Jedediah could feel no ground beneath these feet that moved of their own; he might have walked on a plane as insubstantial as the idea of night or never. Squeezing his hands into fists, he gulped air until his mind lightened the way it did with liquor. He looked ahead, then to where the West Branch flowed green and cold from that abrupt chasm which led like a secret passage to the uninhabited wildlands. Upriver.

Williamsport, Pennsylvania

Now as it was told, and surreptitiously revealed in newspaper accounts, Jedediah's patron, Caspar Roan, was not so easily foiled. Roan may even have expected things to have gone as they had that day at the Bakeraskin farm. As Jedediah's counselor—apprentice counselor, really—Jacob Lloyd, led him into the court on a sweltering forenoon nearly two years later, he did not know it was Roan sitting, pencil in hand, in the gallery—if that assemblage of sappy pine benches at the rear of a room in a log building could have been called a court gallery.

A detail related to that incident on the farm only told, and not insinuated in the newspaper—Roan's newspaper—was that Roan had intended to wait three years—when Jedediah turned 21—not two, to make another move. But a circumstance he had not predicted had reached his newspaper office and interfered with his plan: Jedediah James's romantic involvement with Sarah Starret. The intoxication of forbidden love, Roan knew firsthand, confounded the discretion of young minds. Jedediah might veer off the road to liberty that Roan and the Friends of the Muncy hills were paving for him; he was prone to running for fear he, an indentured servant on paper, a slave in all actuality, might otherwise never possess the girl.

Jedediah, having sensed as he'd come through the doorway something confederate, intimate even, in this man's glance, studied Roan. He wore his thick brown hair curled by hot tongs, as was the fashion. He aimed his eyes and nose—aquiline as that of a soldier's statue—so intently at the Judge's bench he might have been awaiting a sermon.

Jedediah removed his hat and took a chair beside his counselor. Lloyd, plump of cheek and mouth and wearing a wig and queue, leafed through papers in a leather satchel he'd dropped between his feet. Jedediah compared the two men at the bench, merely a table, and decided by bearing alone which was the judge, the black robe meaning nothing to him. This man wore his own hair and used no powder, the graying around his ears plain. Jedediah guessed his age at 50. His brows curved in high crescents over globular and appraising eyes he was very deliberate in blinking. The lips were locked as if beyond the judgment of those eyes, words were out of the bargain.

As the judge regarded Jedediah, head tipped back into the great collar of the gray coat he wore over his robe, Jedediah wondered if the decision was being made now. Perhaps so, considering what he'd learned of the man.

Counsel had explained that the case would be affected by the background of this honorable William Hepburn, in some ways positively, but in more, negatively. Hepburn, a Scotch-Irish, was a former state senator and militia colonel. He'd commanded fort Muncy, Samuel Wallis's fortified home in the Muncy hills, during the river valley's last bloody Indian raids. Pioneer through and through, Hepburn's sympathies were hard to conjure.

On top of that, this president judge of the court of common pleas of the county of Lycoming—a county the judge himself and a few others had severed from Northumberland during his time in the Senate—had no legal learning. "He's unpredictable," Lloyd had said.

Proud, protective of this frontier county he'd wrenched from the grip of a forest primeval, Hepburn was entrenched in it clear to his arched brows, and nowhere more firmly than its seat, Williamsport. This settlement though, was still an unincorporated, swampy mire of mosquitoes and wild plum upon which no one but its two patent holders, Hepburn one of them with his tract called Deer Park, would insist a town be built. So determined had he been to have his property named the county seat, it was told, that when the competing town of Jaysburg produced an affidavit to explain to the governor that Williamsport was flood-prone, Hepburn had the document's messenger invited by persons unremembered for a drink at Williamsport's sole inn. The envoy was soon soused, and by the next day had not only a headache, but an empty portmanteau.

Barrister Lloyd had assured Jedediah during their sole meet-ing—in the barn, under the protection of two sheriff's deputies—that the force of law was on their side. Yet with his eyes cast to the dirt floor, Lloyd added that in a case of this nature, an addi-tional factor would have influence: the man who would sit beside the judge.

As Peter and Cornelia Bakeraskin and the defense lawyer took chairs only an aisle's-width away from Jedediah, he took in this other man at the table.

His name was John Burrows, county commissioner and jus-tice of the peace, renowned in the valley for his connection to General Washington. His recounting of his days with the Conti-nental Army included crossing the Delaware at age 16 on Christmas night, taking Hessians next morning, and driving the British from a thorn hedge at Princeton a week later. He fought at Long Island and Chad's Ford, endured the winter at Valley Forge, and became an express rider and courier for General Washington under the nickname "Devil Jack" for the way he rode. He claimed that at Monmouth, having his horse shot out from under him, he was personally given another by General Washington.

In after years, Burrows would hold the title "general" when Governor Snyder would appoint him Major General of the ninth division of the Pennsylvania militia. But his current ambition was finishing erection of a courthouse, the shell of which shad-owed the little log building they occupied.

Today he'd been called as a possible witness, which was a great insult to his reputation according to barrister Lloyd. In any case, since he was serving as the substitute prothonotary and recorder, Burrows would be present for the entire proceedings.

The actual prothonotary and recorder at the time was John Kidd, a dandy always in a shirt of plaited ruffles and wearing a chamois queue. Though honest, Kidd was notoriously negligent. Piles of deeds and judgments to be filed for record lay in his adjoining room, much to the annoyance of land speculators, lawyers, and justices. He was habitually absent at the court of common pleas, so proceedings could not be recorded. However, as a man of education, Kidd was in great demand; he held other county offices, right down to treasurer. So Commissioner and Justice Burrows had taken it upon himself to serve the court until he could persuade the governor's office to assign several replacements for Kidd.

Barrister Lloyd, though, had known Burrows would be at the presiding judge's table even if Kidd had offered to be available. For one, if judgment passed in favor of the person prosecuting on Jedediah's behalf, Burrows would have copied as a justice of the peace an unlawful document—he would want to make sure the record noted his inculpableness in the matter. Two, and more to the point, Burrows was keeping a close eye on cases that had disturbed the otherwise tranquil Muncy hills where he lived, an increasing neighborhood of Quakers. They were known to watch slaveholders, ready to test their least infraction of the law, or worse, some claimed, aid the escape of souls seeking liberty. Burrows held slaves.

Commissioner Burrows and Judge Hepburn were not on friendly terms. This was thought to go back to when the offices of the county were housed in Jaysburg during the dispute of locating the county seat. Burrows was said to have been a Jaysburg man. Further, the judge considered Burrows a snoop about the court; he would rather proceedings not be so meticulously recorded. Doing so just gave fodder to whom the judge called "that other snoop," newspaperman Caspar Roan, who was constantly about this log building, rummaging documents in the adjoining office so he could use "other people's business" to fill his several daily pages.

"There is no force more powerful," Jacob Lloyd had told Jedediah, "than an alliance of enemies."

Meaty and florid-faced, beady-eyed with a nose like a wheelwright's mallet, Burrows scowled at Jedediah. He looked back incurious. Nowadays, Jedediah fumbled about in a cloud of pain and fatigue. He sat there emaciated, tattooed on trunk and limb with scars of flailings by that bitter, ever more miserable bitch he'd scorned. He'd endured more punishment these two years than ever as a slave. All the while tasked with as much farm work, plus more whiskey making.

Outside, the court crier, Moses Tool, rang his bell and chanted, "Oyez, oyez. Draw near, the court is setting. Oyez, oyez." Watching the door, Burrows winced, clearly hoping no town idlers would heed the call. But a moment later, as he brought the court to order by telling everyone to rise and sit again as though the judge had just entered the room, in they came, mob-capped, aproned women, hollow-eyed men in buck-skin breeches and linen frocks of copperas and dirty whites, floppy-brimmed hats drooping about their smutched skulls. These were the weathered town-stock of the frontier, a dozen or so, all with mud on their stockings and rare eagerness in their eyes.

The counselor of the defense, the venerable wigged, powdered and well-fed Elias Mool, always in shiny broadcloth and wearing on his open coat a gold watch seal bearing a Latin verse, rose from his chair and cleared his throat. "Your Honor," he said—a kind of moan that bellowed ghoulishly from the deep well of his swollen paunch, the shirt there having caught many a dripping of gravy—"before you consider proceeding, might we simply dismiss this complaint for want of merit?" A corner of his upper lip spiked as he glanced at Jedediah.

Beside Jedediah, barrister Lloyd rose. "Your Honor, I will present you more than sufficient evidence of injustices suffered by this man on whose behalf the plaintiff has brought us to court."

Commissioner Burrows, not the judge, flapped his hand. "Sit down, barrister," he said. And now to Elias Mool: "What say under the law even has this servant?"

The broad-waisted barrister indulged a smile. "The servant has as much say as allowed by the indenture upon which he made his mark." He turned to where the surveyor Tillman had taken a seat among the curious. "A mark witnessed by a disinterested party."

Young barrister Lloyd was red in the face now. "Your Honor," he said, pointing at Jedediah. "This man is not the plaintiff."

The judge's great brows arched ever higher as he glanced at the documents before him. "Is that servant not the so stated Israel Tuke, plaintiff?"

Sighing, rubbing his forehead, barrister Lloyd said, "Your Honor, we are aware of the difficulties involved in a supposed indentured servant filing a case against his master. I trust you read the petition. Israel Tuke is the complainant on behalf of this man."

Quill in his hand, Commissioner Burrows was nodding wildly, assuring everyone that he unlike the judge had read the petition. Then he held up a finger. "However," he said, "it is necessary the accuser be present."

As Lloyd turned to the gallery, Jedediah glanced back at the young man he'd noticed on the way in. However, another among the spectators stood and said, "I am here," a man of late middle-age in tight breeches who had not, despite being within doors, removed his hat, a broad-brimmed, tall beaver. His coat was long and drab and without collar, his cravat dirty from work in a field, and he had great silver buckles on his shoes. Jedediah recalled Jacob Lloyd explaining he would be here thanks to some anonymous benefactor, that he'd been watched by members of a group that helped people in bondage.

Lloyd turned back to face the table. "Your Honor, that is Mister Tuke. He is a man of humility, and wishes to attend from the gallery."

Commissioner Burrows shook his head. "That would be quite irregular. The accuser must present himself to the accused."

"And so I have," Tuke said, looking at Peter Bakeraskin. Then, with not another word, he took his seat, and the judge and the commissioner could do no more than look at each other.

"Does he own property in this county?" Judge Hepburn said.

"Indeed," Lloyd said. "A hundred acre in Pennsdale."

Hepburn nodded as if that explained it all. "Meddlesome Quakers," he mumbled. And then to Burrows: "I suppose you know him, then. He's from your neighborhood."

"Heard of him," the commissioner said, narrowing his eyes at Tuke. "One of that lot that might have sat by and watched us butchered by the Brits, happy to bow to the king for eternity."

"Your Honor," Lloyd said, "may I now address the court, as it seems the defense has already done so?"

The judge sorted the papers before him. "Explain your case," he said.

Barrister Lloyd took a step toward the table and tugged his cravat. "I will show the court that Mister Peter Bakeraskin coerced Jedediah James into signing an indenture that is unlawful, as its terms are in violation of a statute prohibiting the service of freemen beyond 21 years of age. I will first reaffirm how Jedediah James was a freeman."

Lloyd dabbed his brow with a handkerchief and withdrew a paper from his satchel. "I will read from an act of our legislature dated March 28, 1788. 'For preventing many evils and abuses arising from ill-disposed persons availing themselves of certain defects in the Act for the Gradual Abolition of Slavery...'" He paused and looked around the courtroom. "'...all and every slave and slaves who shall be brought into this state, by persons intending to inhabit or reside therein, shall be immediately deemed to be free.'"

Judge Hepburn tilted his head to the side and slowly blinked the great orbs of his eyes. He let out a breath and said. "Enough of the bloody law, young barrister. Let's get on with the defense's opening."

Elias Mool waved this off as if it were a waste of time in a trifle such as this.

"Then to your first witness, barrister Lloyd," the judge said.

"I call Jedediah James," Lloyd said.

Now Elias Mool was on his feet. "A negro cannot bear witness in court."

"Your Honor," Lloyd said. "I've cited the law upon which I will now prove with testimony that Jedediah James was a freeman the day he entered this Commonwealth, and so can testify."

The judge looked to Commissioner Burrows, who shrugged.

Pointing at Jedediah, Mool said, "I'll not disgrace 25 years on the bar by questioning him."

"So be it," barrister Lloyd said, approaching the table.

"Then I demand," Mool said, sitting, "that the court take this testimony for what it is worth."

Lloyd eyed Mool as a curiosity and scratched his head. He nodded and turned back to the bench. "I certainly hope it does," he said.

Wanting of all bearing, Jedediah leaned ahead and looked to the only people he knew here for direction. Mistress Cornelia's nose was flared and fluttering, the hate and discontent that fermented in her veins frothing at her eyes. Master mouthed, "God damn you."

Jedediah shifted to see the gallery. The young man he'd felt a connection to on the way in, whom he decided now must be the newspaperman Caspar Roan, smiled encouragement. On the bench beside Roan, but not so close they appeared together, Israel Tuke sat cross-legged, eyes gray and austere as gun metal, his great beaver hat tilted across his forehead. He hardly looked a friend.

"Go on, now," Lloyd said to Jedediah. "Sit in the chair beside the table."

He rose but remained hunched as he'd been in his seat. Master had given him new brogues and demanded he wear them today, the sturdiest shoes ever on his feet. He was dressed in an early issue of the wardrobe he always received just before winter: leather breeches and wool leggins, linen shirt. Master had also required that he crop his hair, which was shaped now like a box atop his head. He shuffled more than walked to the chair.

Jedediah sat, spoke his name on request, and swore upon a Bible, which the commissioner extended to him as if feeding a bear on a chain.

Barrister Lloyd stood with one hand on the back of the chair, another holding a document before Jedediah. "Do you recall," Lloyd said, "how long you were in Pennsylvania before you made your mark on this indenture?"

Jedediah barely gave a nod, his head so low already. "More'n two year, sir."

"And until then," Lloyd said, "had you been led to believe you were slave to Peter Bakeraskin?"

"I object," barrister Mool said. "Whatever the buck chooses to believe does not make my client culpable. The document is in question, not what a servant thinks."

Judge Hepburn tilted his head this way and that. "Sustained," he said.

"Very well," Lloyd said. "Indeed. His thoughts are not what is in question."

The room went silent. Jedediah looked up, first at Mool, then Commissioner Burrows and Judge Hepburn. Their faces were no longer stiff with impatience; they instead appeared as if they'd been caught with their fingers in a pie. Jacob Lloyd must have tricked Mool into what he'd said.

"Jedediah," Lloyd said, stepping around the chair and looking into his eyes. "Was your mother a slave?"

"Born so, sir."

"Was your mother a slave in Pennsylvania?" Lloyd said. "Ever?"

"No. Virginny, sir."

"And you were born in Virginia?" Lloyd said.

Jedediah nodded. "Right down on the Serendip farm."

Barrister Lloyd touched his nose and watched the floor a moment. "I have no more questions for you, Jedediah. You can go back to your seat."

As Jedediah slugged away, Lloyd called Peter Bakeraskin.

"I'll be damned if I'll answer to that nigger."

Very calmly, barrister Lloyd said, "You are responding to Israel Tuke. And as the defendant, if you do not take my questions, you are in contempt."

"I'll not sit up there," Bakeraskin said. And he crossed his arms.

Lloyd raised his brows to the Judge, who said, "Just answer from there, sir."

Shrugging, Lloyd stepped to Bakeraskin, beside whom Mistress waved a fan, face squirming like a pail of worms. "Do you own your home in Lycoming County, Pennsylvania?" Lloyd said.

"Of course I do," Bakeraskin said, eyes aimed straight through Lloyd's waistcoat.

"And you've lived there more than six months?"

"I'm known up and down the river, you damned fool."

"Had Jedediah James, whom you call your indentured serv-ant, been here with you more than six months prior to his signing the indenture?"

"Objection," Elias Mool said.

But Peter Bakeraskin responded anyway. "Damn right. He's been my nigger since the day I married Cornelia."

"Commissioner," Mool said, "strike that."

Burrows lifted his quill and glanced at the judge, who nod-ded.

"Carry on," Judge Hepburn said, slouching now—though the gallery was stirring with murmurs.

"Last question, Mister Bakeraskin," Lloyd said. "Though it would not have mattered, did you register Jedediah James as a slave with the county of Lycoming during your first six months here?"

Bakeraskin went to respond, but caught himself. Barrister Lloyd made a great show of looking away to politely give his wit-ness time to think this over and for counselor Mool, eyes on the ceiling as he sorted the web of slave laws, to make his objection.

Bakeraskin could no longer forbear. "I do not recall," he said, and Elias Mool added that he had no questions for him. Nor would he call a witness, and so Jacob Lloyd rested.

The gallery was sizzling now with whispered wagers on the verdict. As Judge Hepburn called for order, Jedediah looked back. The wags were weighing him as a cock before the fight. He caught the sour face of Tillman, whom Jedediah had gained an-other reason to hate. Master Bakeraskin, upon his suspicions of Sarah Starret, forbade Jedediah to meet with her at the still, and then had tasked Tillman with delivering her father's whis-key.

This reduced Jedediah's time with Sarah to rare but costly afternoon trysts. Listless though Mistress had become, Bakeraskin required she be more vigilant of Jedediah when he wasn't making his river deliveries to the Wheler mill. So on Mis-tress's more lucid days, Jedediah was likely to be caught returning from the pine grove, and to pay the price he bore on his battered body, wounds he kept hidden from Sarah.

He knew Tillman hated him back, hated anything he thought beneath him. Though Tillman never smiled, Jedediah recognized morbid delight in the coloring of his face and fluttering of his voice when he brought mealtime conversations around to not just the damned Indians or Tories, but to some minor negligence in Jedediah's work about the farm—an un-set fox snare by the poultry yard, an un-swept room in the house. He went red with ecstasy upon the fury and lashings those complaints triggered from an ever more distempered Bakeraskin. A good share of Jedediah's welts had their source in Thomas Tillman.

Barrister Lloyd stood and began his closing by descanting on how courtesy should be expected from citizens of one state toward those of another. The pair at the table ignored him. But when he mentioned that a Virginian, in ducking the laws of this proud Commonwealth, had affronted the good people of Lycoming County, so many of whom had earned their pieces by emolument after enduring hell in the rebellion, they cocked their heads. Soon enough, indignation narrowed their eyes as Lloyd suggested that Bakeraskin, who never even attempted to register with the good County's offices the slave he thought he owned here, had been so presumptuous because he underestimated the people of this place. With a crescendo of voice and a wave of his arm toward Jedediah, Lloyd ended on his plea: "I ask that you relieve this man of this fraudulent contract."

Just as Jedediah thought Lloyd might prevail, a shout volleyed from the back of the room like thunder through the valley. "Lift thy sleeve, man."

Jedediah did not need to search out the source. The tone, sober as a command from God, matched to a stitch the manner and dress of his benefactor, Israel Tuke.

As the demand boomed again within that drum of log and mortar, Tuke adding, "Heed me, Jedediah James," and as the judge pounded the table, calling the outburst a contempt that must cease, Jedediah stood and began to roll up a sleeve.

Peter Bakeraskin was on his feet. "Stop," he said. He started at Jedediah, Elias Mool seizing his coat as Bakeraskin cried out, "Do as you're ordered or I'll flail you to the bone."

"There'll be no chicanery in this courtroom," Commissioner Burrows said. "Stop him." Then, beside Burrows, Judge Hepburn's brows reared to his hairline as he leaned toward the forearm Jedediah revealed.

His skin was dark and luminous as polished carbonado, but that did not obscure the plum bruises, a geography of vivid new lumps among paler old spots shaped by daily doses of the hickory sticks of Peter and Cornelia Bakeraskin.

Quiet descended against the rustling of coarse linen shirts and petticoats, the sighs, as the gallery strained and saw. And then soundlessness as the several factions, each in its own interest, clawed with their minds at time, this one wanting to pull it back, that one to thrust it forward. One, to seize it in utter stasis, for there was no escaping the past, no promise to yearn for.

Again, the voice resounded from the back of the room: "Would thou, Jedediah James, have more such markings on thy back? On thy thighs? Tell them, man."

"Enough," young barrister Lloyd said. The finality in his voice as he swung around to Israel Tuke told Jedediah their spoil had been lost. Whatever outrage had been stirred to their advantage in the two at the table was about to be turned back on them, for Israel Tuke had faced the judge and commissioner with a far greater indignity.

While Judge Hepburn regained his composure enough to echo Lloyd's command, Jedediah realized the exchange had discovered the informant. Only Sarah Starret could have spied what festered beneath his shirt. Maybe she'd glimpsed a wound near his neck, felt the swelling of his sleeved arms.

Barrister Lloyd stepped toward the table, determined, Jedediah saw, to arrest another outburst. He motioned for Jedediah to sit as he passed, then with a humble bow of his head, said to the Judge, "We rest our case."

Hepburn's eyes did not move from Jedediah's forearm. He frowned, pondered something even as Lloyd, returning to his seat, whispered for Jedediah to unroll his sleeve.

Barrister Mool labored to the table. "What a performance," he said with a chuckle, facing the gallery and smoothing his lustrous lapels. "A cheap appeal to the passions of our esteemed judge. I've not seen anything like it in my 25 years on the bar. Desperate souls pray pitiably, don't they?" He shrugged and raised his palms. "Nevertheless, I represent an upright, enterprising landowner of this county and ask only that the court honor a contract he made with a man who, were it not for my client's generosity, would still be in bondage in Virginia." He turned, and tugging on his watch seal, locked eyes with the judge. "I hope you will take into consideration the negro's good fortune before we release another indigent into the charity of our county."

As Mool returned to his seat, the judge's brows shifted this way and that, as if weighing the force of the law against the dear order of his county.

Beady-eyed Commissioner Burrows waited for the judge to look his way, tapping the feathers of his quill against the edge of the table, clearing his throat. His patience evaporated and he tilted his fleshy face toward the judge and whispered for more than a minute.

The judge deliberated, then nodded. "The indenture will stand," he said.

A satisfied hum of murmuring followed from the gallery. Jedediah, who had no expectations, awaited instructions from the Bakeraskins.

But Judge Hepburn had something more to offer, in fact as much as barrister Lloyd had told Jedediah to hope for. "It will stand for one year," Hepburn said, "in accordance with the laws of this Commonwealth until the subject of this proceeding, Jedediah James, turns 21."

Commissioner Burrows motioned for the judge to carry on. Hepburn grimaced. "I'm getting there," he said. And then to Jedediah: "You will heed these two conditions, Jedediah James. Or this Commonwealth will bind you out to indefinite servitude to recompense society for the burden you will surely bring upon it if you cannot follow such orders. First, you are to abide for the next year the terms of your indenture unerringly. Second, upon completion of your service and in accord with our various negro codes necessary for maintaining peace and decency, you will re-move from the county of Lycoming."

Jacob Lloyd shot up from his seat. "Negro codes? When were negro codes enacted in the four years of this county's exist-ence?"

Judge Hepburn and Commissioner Burrows were on their feet, the judge holding a finger out at Lloyd pistol-like. "Don't you question my authority, young man, in maintaining law and order in Lycoming County. I'll see to it what manner of rogue inter-copulates or idles about our streets."

And then from the gallery came a voice, "A sham," and all turned to the scowl and tall hat of Israel Tuke, yet cross-legged on his bench, in his eyes the wrath of an arbiter of much greater dominion. "I've grubbed the stumps and tilled the dirt of this land since long before it was called Lycoming, when as many men black and red as white trekked it. There are no codes here having to do with a man's skin."

The voice of Commissioner Burrows caught up with his mutely flapping jaw. "You be quiet, sir, or I'll have you removed from this building." A buzz of excitement met this until the met-tle fell from the eyes of Burrows for want of finding about the room a constable to act on the promise.

At his bench, Caspar Roan had stopped scribbling at the pa-per on his knee, his brows gathered over the noble-looking nose. "He's right," he said. "I've reported every meeting of commission-ers, juries, and judges in this county. No black codes exist."

Burrows lurched forward, bumping the table and spilling his inkwell. "You meddling coxcomb. You've as much impertinence to disrupt a court of law as tamper with my daughter. Feeding her and the readers of your so-called newspaper the emancipa-tion drivel of these hypocritic Quakers. You come courting her, turning my wife and children and servants against me. And you conspire for my job. Begone," and he waved his arm.

Now the glee of the gallery was beyond restraint: the onlook-ers leaned in their seats and whispered, sought acquaintances.

Young newspaperman Roan remained calm. "Sir," he said to Burrows, "those you refer to as servants would, in fact, be your slaves. And I endeavor not to take your job—commissioner—

rather to relieve you as prothonotary in the regular absence of Mister Kidd by petitioning the governor for an appointment."

When Burrows slammed his fist on the table, Judge Hepburn snatched his coat sleeve. "For God's sake, John," the judge said, "think before you incite these talebearers."

Burrows took in the faces hungering for more. He glared at Caspar Roan, then sat.

Peter Bakeraskin meanwhile was hissing into Elias Mool's ear. The counselor stood. "If I may, Your Honor."

"What now?" the judge said.

"My client has business in town," Mool said. "We would like permission to house Jedediah James in the gaol tonight."

Hepburn closed his eyes a moment. "You try my patience, counselor. We established that Jedediah James is not a slave. I cannot lock him up."

"You expect my client to house a nigger at the inn?" Mool said,

"Elias, I don't care if he houses him in hell. It is dinner time, and we are adjourned."

With Mistress Cornelia sobbing beside him, Peter Bakeraskin shouted to the gallery. "Not only has your court let loose a shiftless nigger, but one that's been off alone with the daughter of your august Samson Starret. The fools."

As the gallery gasped, John Burrows became very serious. "You refer to the daughter of Captain Starret?"

"Indeed," Bakeraskin said, starting for Jedediah.

Burrows looked off, the first he seemed at a loss today—until he nodded, something becoming clear.

Jedediah set his hat upon his head and cowered as Bakeraskin approached—the dog accustomed to the lash. Then a voice broke from the din of the courtroom.

"God is watching over thee, sir." Israel Tuke had not moved from his seat. "As are those who fear Him."

Everyone exiting turned to catch the encore. Bakeraskin, watching Tuke, grabbed Jedediah's ear and tugged him to his feet. He twisted the ear until Jedediah, yielding to the point his head lay on his shoulder, thought it would tear. Then

Bakeraskin waved Mistress Cornelia out the door and followed with Jedediah.

The courthouse grounds, enclosed by a fence of slabs to keep out the swine, was but an acre hacked out of a swamp of plum and alder, which other than a cluster of shops and cabins, was yet to be Williamsport. The stacked logs and slab roof of the temporary county building appeared more a rubbish heap for the main events of the grounds: the nearly-completed official courthouse, and the gaol, which served also as the sheriff's home—the only stone structure in that country.

Before the former building—a stiletto-steepled affair— Bakeraskin stopped and let go of the ear. Jedediah watched the crowd, dejected for want of a good flogging or hanging, mope out of the courtyard. Then Bakeraskin kicked him toward the muddy trough called Third Street.

The courthouse bell tolled with the crier Moses Tool's noon pulls of the rope to the belfry. It was known as the Burrows bell, for not only had John Burrows insisted the county have one, he paid for it and escorted its delivery from Philadelphia. He'd made the trip twice, having pronounced the first bell too feeble to sound the song of justice of so large a county.

And so overhead the glum gongs plodded, as did—before Jedediah—Mistress Cornelia, tugging her petticoat above her ankles as she moved this way and that upon assorted slabs of slate and lumber thrown for a sidewalk along Third Street. All the while she whimpered that because of a froward nigger she'd had to leave her child in a wild country with neighbors she hardly knew.

They passed a mishmash of log structures, all a story-and-a-half, sleeping quarters above, shops below, none identifiable by a sign, rather particular waste and wares scattered in the yard: the saddler, the tanner and weaver, the cooper and blacksmith, potter, tinsmith, wheelwright. Then on a street corner stood the Russel Inn. Square-timbered, shake-roofed, it boasted a chimney of brick through its middle. The place's greatest distinction was not that the first courts had been held there, rather than at one such session, proprietor James Russel had been the defendant, indicted for, of all things, keeping a tippling house.

Bakeraskin told Jedediah to wait beside the lone tree outside the inn and went in with Mistress to rent a room and have someone tend to the horses they'd boarded out back. No sooner had the couple gone through the door than the bar patrons, generally the crowd at court, poured out to see what might have become of Jedediah. They nosed about him like moths at the lamp until a man in buckskins black with grease pointed over the Bald Eagle mountains. "Look at yond smoke cloud," he said. "Methinks there's a house afire downriver. Past the Muncy bend."

They all forgot Jedediah, forgot even their tankards, and started for their canoes. For nothing beat a good fire for exciting the miscreants of the borderland, dross who, upon finding the convenient combination of cheap drink and odd work at the last outpost before a new country, had lost the wind of adventure that had pushed them northwestward.

Bakeraskin returned alone, Jedediah looking up just enough to see fresh menace in his eyes. "Thanks to the devil you are," Bakeraskin said, "I had to pay a boy to carry word downriver. Since I can't trust you right now to continue on with the canoe for rye like we planned, I'm having nigger George deliver the goods. And to somehow use this trip to my advantage, I summoned that idiot tenant Wheler to meet me here in the morning. I'll set some new terms, given the Farleigh mill's no longer the closest. The price of the messenger will come out of your hide. For now, you'll have a long night in the stable to think on what I'm about to tell you." He bent to better see Jedediah's face. "Are you standing there asleep like a mule?"

Bakeraskin reached beneath his coat and pulled from the waist of his breeches a folded document. "In case today turned out as it did," he said, "I requested the help of your former master." He held out the paper and Jedediah recalled the coat of arms stamped in the red wax seal—the same as the one cast in iron and hanging in the hall of the big house. "I hold here a promise from him that if you attempt to break the original terms of your indenture, he will take it out on that wench you left at

Serendip. Mind you," Bakeraskin said, using the edge of the document to raise Jedediah's chin, looking more like he was about
to spit than speak, "the man's sense of duty has been exhausted. He has grown weary of his wife's complaints about the
girl."

He watched Jedediah a moment. "You understand that if you
try to leave in a year, the girl will be sold South?"

"Yessir," Jedediah said.

Bakeraskin wagged his brows. "A pretty sum, she'd fetch, if
you know how I mean."

Jedediah nodded. But he was more than saying he understood; he was acknowledging to himself that somewhere over the
past months, while the scent of freedom had made fair and
tempting the countenance of a white woman and the prospect
of a wild upriver valley, he'd already forfeited this ransom of
sorts.

For three years the smell of river had soused his every breath
and seeped into his veins. Today, it lazed stifling, fecund and
fishy under a vaulted haze. It intoxicated him. Jedediah
straightened from his servile stoop and looked away. He turned
from it all, toward the river, the smoke of distant fire spuming
against the low, white sky. And fighting back a pang of remorse,
he could not help savoring that for the first time in his life, he'd
had a chattel valuable enough to command a trade.

Washington Township, Lycoming County, Pennsylvania

Because the heat, having singed George's eyes, had fogged his vision, he could not distinguish that the person stepping out of the crowd between the headrace and the creek, approaching through the smoldering rubble of ash and charred timbers fallen into what had been the ground floor of the mill, was a boy. Not until he spoke as he balanced across a beam bridging the gurgling inner race: "I've come with a message from Williamsport for Mister Reuben Wheler. From Mister Peter Bakeraskin."

Kneeling alongside the race, George only squinted.

"Why, you sure isn't Reuben Wheler," the boy said, standing before George now, bearing crooked teeth as he curled up his lip.

George pointed to the man in shirtsleeves pacing and raging atop the foundation stones yet standing, these built into the bank. Then he returned to sifting the debris for the crock of money he'd hidden all these years in a cavity gouged out of a beam. Presently, George rested. The boy was moving toward the creek, head down, in want of a reply, of any reason from the man who raised his fists and demanded of God the millstones restored, oblivious to the surviving three Farleigh brothers. Black with soot, they sniveled about a steaming lump in the ash, the smoking black timber upon it a headstone of sorts for the eldest, Caleb Junior, who'd be here still to build a new mill were it not for the mad-cap on the foundation.

The cats had saved him, waking him from his nightly dream: a search for his mother always ended at the verge of delivering her from what he could only understand to the extent it was accursed. It started with him meandering exhausted through a pine barren, at last emerging to see her at the doorway of the old mill house in Jersey, Aquintice's face still young, her body, though, stooped and faltering with the brittle bones and stunted nerves of an old woman. His perceiving that some agony of the heart ravaged her insides sent him sprinting. But every time, as he reached to take hold of her, she turned from George, stepped into blackness—no, worse than blackness, for that was something; worse than utter emptiness, for that was the lack of something. Beyond that doorway, even the exclusion of existence was not credited. Nothing to aver, nothing to deny, no yea, no nay, neither tenet nor heresy, heaven nor hell. Just an awful in-between.

And on his side of the threshold was only the memory that she had denied him simple touch. He stood wavering, wanting to step through to find her while something whispered he must turn away. This had been his dilemma when the guttural caterwauling and frantic scratching of the cats broke through.

Glowing smoke gushed out the open trapdoor into a churning, yellow cloud-ceiling. The opening coughed out rats, dozens scurrying from the ladder, around George, atop him, some rat sense of mass survival overcoming their impulse to secrete themselves, overcoming even their fear of the cats who'd lost their evening egress down past the conflagration or up along the smoky rafters. And so cat and rat scratched together at the door and the shuttered windows in a brotherhood of terror.

By the time George ran to the door and swung it wide, the animals racing out, the floor planks were hot against his feet and the smoke hung to his shoulders.

At the house, Reuben Wheler, awoken by the hounds and already at the door in his gown, sent George for the Farleigh brothers at their bunkhouse with orders to enter the blaze with axe and lever. "Save the stones and irons," he cried, raising fists toward dawn's softening sky as the mill George had built, Caleb Farleigh's mill, began disintegrating through its eaves in an updrafting river of ash.

George woke the brothers and told the second son, Isaac, to spread word for neighbors to come with buckets. He sent the two younger ones to the rope walk on the far side of the barn where hung the latest rope Wheler had George making to sell, and then with the eldest, Caleb Junior, ran to the yard between the house and the mill. But Caleb, goaded by Wheler's cries and frantic about saving his father's legacy, took from Wheler the axe and pry he held out and went to the race to soak his shirt. And though George tried to stop him, begging he wait for the rope, Caleb, shirt tied over his mouth and nose, started in with the tools.

The eaves were exhausting like a bellows now, the doorway, clear of smoke, sucking air in huffs George could feel twenty feet away. As the boys came stumbling over the dangling skeins of the rope they shouldered, George pointed to the roof. He shouted back to Wheler that the only hope of saving his stones, of them not dropping into the ground floor and the building falling in a firestorm, was to get to that roof and pull slabs. They might control the fire by vent and so have a chance of dousing it. And save the man who'd just gone in.

Wheler was shaking his head and pointing to the door, his gown wafting in the hot breath of the eaves. "Get those stones," he said, "or I'll whip you raw."

George went to where the Farleigh boys peered through the doorway for their brother. "Wrap an end 'round you," he said to the youngest and lifted the burden of coils from the shoulders of both. As the boy tied a loop around his waist, George unsnarled the rope as best he could, pulled tight knots where the web of it was too complicated.

"Damn the rope," Wheler called, the building emitting now a low rumble, waves of heat smarting against their foreheads. "Get on with it."

George re-coiled the loose rope and took it to Wheler. "Feed this to us so we can follow it out," he said. Then he returned and pushed the boys to their knees, arranging the youngest ahead of him, the eldest behind.

Just inside the doorway, backlit by flames that they could not see, the smoke rolled in a reverse cascade. With the first inhale upon breaking through, George was already drowning. Each of them lowered his head and laid a cheek against the floor to suck at a sediment of air there. In this way, like a catfish in the murk, George by memory steered the boy in the lead among bins and stacks of grain bags toward the stones, the heat scorching

George's skin and the bloating explosiveness of the mill squeezing at his wits.

Then, coughing more than breathing, the boy hissed out that he'd found his brother's pry bar.

"Go on," George said, pushing his rear.

A crawl-pace later, the boy jerked back. "Caleb," he said. "Caleb."

George felt his way to where Caleb lay face-down, pulseless, axe in hand. Rearing into the smoke so he could take up an ankle, George fought for breath enough to speak. "I've got him." Bending, gulping air at the floor, he said, "Start back along the rope. Gather it as you go to save it. I'll follow by touch." And he straightened again that he might pull Caleb along.

The gasses at the ceiling, pregnant with ash, ignited with the huff and boom of cannon shot, a gust of embers knocking George flat. Blazing slabs fell, enkindling flour sacks and bins, the brothers screaming, all of them covering their heads, scorching then their hands as they lifted inflamed pieces off themselves and crawled across smoldering ends, George dragging Caleb.

The draft of the opened roof set aflame every spark in the room. This and the thinning of the smoke made visible a few rods about them. George stopped, and kneeling, let go of Caleb, sucking at the scant air as the boys crawled toward the illumination of the doorway. He squeezed shut his eyes to quell their stinging, then glanced back to find Caleb's shirt catching fire from a fallen board, which he tossed away.

Each suffocated breath drove spikes of pain into his temples. The fury of flame and heat gathered into thrusting, upward gasps as he looked toward the doorway and wondered if he had the strength to drag himself, much less Caleb, out of here before the floor collapsed into the machinery beneath him.

Leave Caleb or take him? The simplest solution was a third way—quit fighting for air.

His mother came to him, as she always did when he had a choice; she'd given George a rule to follow, framed somehow by all she'd told him. So though there seemed no more reason for returning to the whims of the Reuben Whelers of the world than for going the way of Caleb, George knew that his mother pointed him onward, into the daylight, alive.

George spied a glint in the ash, rose and started toward it until a bed of embers scorched through the holes in his soles. He stepped back, a dilatory, dizzying effort, and heard Reuben Wheler shouting, "Nigger George, get over here."

George ignored him, stepped around the hot spot and bent to see what reflected the irradiated white sky. Just a charred piece of roof slab.

"God damn you, I say, come now."

Go to hell, George thought. But the crazed fool would just keep at it. So George lumbered toward him, meandering smoldering coals and the black bones of the mill's frame timbers. He saw the blame in the narrowed eyes of the three surviving Farleigh brothers as he passed.

Wheler, flushed, hatless, tassels of his white hair wild over his neck, had dressed into a shirt and waistcoat. Not a trace of ash on that ever-sour and slack-jawed face.

Standing beneath him, George was bold in his speech and direct in his stare. "What is it?" he said, the words snapping off his parched tongue like a cat-o'-nine-tails.

"What are you looking for over there?" Wheler said.

George held his stare, made Wheler watch the green eyes and riven chin of his brother-in-law.

Wheler nodded where the brothers tried to pry the timber from the lump of sodden ash that was their brother, the bar still too hot to hold long enough to make purchase. "You'll begin rebuilding my mill tomorrow," Wheler said as the youngest brother wrapped his shirt around the tool and drug it to the edge of the ruins where the race flowed out. He dipped it in a pool made by the toppled foundation stones, paddles of the wheel and its hub bobbing in the water.

George snorted and looked to the heavens. The man thought him as much a daff as himself. "It is not your mill, Tenant Wheler," George said. "It is Caleb Farleigh's. And it would have been the mill of the man who is buried in it."

As Wheler burst into curses, swinging his arms to keep from falling, his daughter, Rosanna, approached from the house. Always fixed-mouthed and stern-eyed with her wisps of hair cropped tight to her head, she stopped behind Wheler and watched him threaten whippings.

"It's your greed burnt down Mister Farleigh's mill," George said. "And killed Caleb Junior." I told you those belts could not spin so long on a hot day. Flour dust hanging like tinder in the air."

"Father?" Rosanna said. "Is that true?" She looked from one to the other, wrung her petticoat.

"Get up here, half-nigger," Wheler said.

"No," George said, glancing over the waste, the onlookers craning their necks toward this sequel.

"Mother wants those strangers gone," Rosanna said. "And we need to do something for those boys." She indicated the three Farleigh brothers lugging a piece of beam for a fulcrum. Little good that'll do, George thought. Unless those idlers help.

"Look upon your groom," Wheler said, pointing to where Caleb Junior lay.

George had never seen Rosanna so much as turn the edges of those wafer-thin lips in a show of emotion. Now they quavered, as did her voice, as she said, "What can you mean, Father?"

"He means he had notions for you to marry yon dead man," George said. "And so he'd have his mill. Am I right, man?"

"I'll whip your brown hide until it's a bloody wattle," Wheler said, and then shouted to the onlookers. "Hear this saucy nigger insult a white man."

"I'm a freeman now," George said. "You knew that the day I reminded you I turned 28. I been waiting on my pay since then."

"I'll see you in the barn," Wheler said. "Go," and he pointed that way.

Rosanna stepped beside her father on the foundation stones. "Why did you keep the truth from George?"

"Filthy minx," Wheler said. He seized her shoulder and jerked her toward him. "Defiled by the black sin of your lecher uncle."

Gasps emitted from the bystanders at the *thrack* of Wheler's fist against Rosanna's cheek, that opaque and creamy flesh that in never bending to joy or anger had only increased George's affection. For in the moments they talked after he'd find her watching from a corner of the mill, he'd become taken by the honesty of her attention, her interest in his work and past, her admiration of his feats of strength and cleverness.

Had he all his might, George couldn't have mounted that yet-baking wall; something else pulled him to the top. He gained his feet between father and daughter, Wheler stepping back red with outrage and George flexing his hands as he fought crushing the man's throat beneath his thumbs. Rosanna, trying to steady her breathing, whispered, "George, don't."

Wheler called to the crowd across the race. "See this half-nigger meddlin' with a white man that's disciplinin' his wayward daughter. For God's sake, go for the sheriff." Then to George: "They'll hang you if you touch me."

As the rabble bobbled heads with approval at this fortunate turn of events, thunder trundled down the valley from where clouds had banked over the Bald Eagle Mountains, ripe with storm and electricity.

"You will pay me," George said, the words rasping in an acrid whisper across his scorched throat, "back to when I turned 28. You will pay me to rebuild Mister Farleigh's mill and be your miller until I can buy my mother. Or I will go back to her and my father now, and my father will know you have not kept your terms with Mister Farleigh."

As a flash of triumph crossed Wheler's face, George realized he'd just defied what his mother had warned him against.

The haze overhead had lost its luster, curdling and sagging as the cloudbank pressed in. And so the shadows of Wheler's jowl-wrinkles had faded, as had the murk beneath the great eaves of his brows, his entire face returned to its waxen pallor, all concern erased from his eyes. "What a fool," he said, the white tresses at his collar lifting in the fore-breeze of the gathering storm. "You will never have your mother."

Rosanna moved between them. "Father," she said, seizing his shirt. "Tell him the truth. Tell him what you forbad us to say."

"To hell with his slut of a mother," Wheler said.

Rosanna's eyes were closed when she turned to George, head tipped away from an expected strike by her father. "Your dear mother…" She peered at Wheler who growled out a no, and her words raced: "A letter came from Caleb Farleigh to his boys. She has been dead these six months. They were to tell you, but father would not allow it."

What little breath remained in George left him in a croak and he doubled at the waist. Thunder ranged across the valley in contours of sound imitative of the lightning that spawned it— skeins of grumbles spidering out from each bole of rib-drum-ming boom. George mouthed for any surrender that would make this a lie. But he could only mew, "How?"

Wheler stood over him now, inches away. "She wilted," he whispered. "Dried up like a leaf. Going back to when you left Jersey, boy. When my sister started making amends. I seen that. The wench must'a just fell to pieces."

The pain balled into the hate George had forsworn. It bloated against his chest and he straightened. For the first time in his life, he let the bile of revenge trickle across his tongue, cold and steely as the blood of a cut lip. His breath, though shallow, was clipped and hissing, glancing off Wheler's face and lifting his locks, so close was he.

As Wheler shrank back, George looked to Rosanna. "Run away with me," he said.

From that face that seemed cut from slate, Rosanna fixed her eyes on her father, who looked from one to the other as he made a humffing sound. She held out a trembling hand. Then, her arm still outstretched, she clinched tight her fingers, turned to George, and nodded. And as she started through the yard, George felt cool leaden drops of rain plunk upon his shoulders.

Pine Creek Township, Lycoming County, Pennsylvania

By that evening, Jedediah heard from a stable boy about the ruin of the Farleigh mill. There was also talk of a canoe stolen from one of the onlookers, the man's rifle gone with it. Jedediah inquired about the miller. The boy assured him that only one person had perished, a white man whose roasted body, the rumors held, had "stinked more'n the burnt flour."

Though the stable was without walls, the fresh, trodden dung was sharp enough to sour even an empty stomach. The place teemed with biting flies, and when the storm surged, rain dripped through cracks in the shingles. Jedediah tossed about in an empty stall, the hay beneath him moldy, its dust, even in the heavy humid air, making him sneeze.

He cared not whether Bakeraskin knew about the mill, would not seek him out. But later, he came to the stable with a tallow candle, irate, wet from the rain. "You niggers are nothing but trouble," he said, leaning over Jedediah, the melted, rancid fat of the candle dripping onto his shirt. "I'll bet that idiot mulatto lit the place afire." He kicked Jedediah's leg. "I need rye. Soon. You start off with the canoe at daybreak and tend to the farm while I waste the day making arrangements with one of these tub mills around here. When I get home, you'll be on an errand for grain." He turned, the candle disappearing before him. Then the feeble flame reappeared at the end of the stall. "Don't get any ideas." The light tottered as Bakeraskin pulled from his waist the letter and waved it.

Hours later, the storm passed, rumbling and flashing southeast. Jedediah dozed, waking to stand and snort away snot. Only by dawn—a jaundiced, hazy, reluctant illumination—did the tepid belt of dampness lift out of the valley.

Carrying his shoes, he stole along the woodsline behind log homes, his summer hat of rye straw pulled close to his eyes. When he found a cow and a calf tied apart from each other in a pen, he watched the house. Then he crawled beneath the udder, and jerking a dug, suckled, the calf bawling at him, straining.

His thirst quenched, but still hungry, he slipped to the river, the last tinkles of the night's katydid fading into the crows of roosters and the barking of dogs.

All manner of canoes strewed the riverbank. Some were shelled in the bark of birch or elm, pieces sewn together with tough filaments of tamarack root, their joints calked with turpentine. There were dugouts carved from pine and walnut timbers, big enough to hold a score of riders. Humblest were the stinking skin tubs. Their crude gunwales and ribs were of bent saplings lashed together with withes and covered with the assorted hides of deer, elk, panther and wolf, smoked and greased for preservation, sewn tight to the frames with the sinews of deer—mangy, beast-like vessels, what with the hair still on the skins excepting where it wore off. Since the settlers often helped themselves to canoes, some owners of the less hideous craft hid them in the Indian fashion: they sunk them in pools under the weight of great stones.

Jedediah set his shoes by the water's edge and crawled beneath his keeled, birchbark canoe. It was thirty-feet long with a wide, steady bottom, and had proven watertight. He'd built it and one for Bakeraskin under the guidance of neighbor William Starret, step-brother of Sarah, who lived on the farm across the river from her and their father. Jedediah raised the canoe on his back, just forward of center, and carried it to the water. Wading to his knees, he grabbed each gunwale and rolled the canoe over his shoulder.

He retrieved his shoes, pushed the stern off the sandbar, and stepped in. He knelt on one knee at the center of the canoe, and before he could un-lash his paddle from the thwarts, the current, even here in a riverpool, swung him downstream.

The storm-swollen water surged murky as dark rum, dimpled with eddies. Jedediah swung the canoe around, and though he paddled close to shore, out of the main current, he merely maintained his place. He took his pole from the bilge. But instead of pushing himself along, he spent his effort fighting the bow from turning.

So, he untied from the front thwart a rope of the strands of inner hickory bark and pulled the canoe in shore water to his waist. His destination was Sarah Starret's farm. He needed to be there before dark.

By midmorning, the sun was burning away the haze, and the horizon was retreating farther and farther into the cup of the escarpments, the shaggy washed coat of the forest roaring into its late summer glory of emerald. Fatigued, but cooled by the water, he pulled the brim of his hat over his neck where the rays seared, and slugged along, his breath crossing his tongue with the river's mineral taste of wet iron. In the sky raced flat-bottomed heaps of curd, the great skiff clouds of August. He'd had the river to himself, seen among the few settlers' places an occasional woman at a garden or a child at play. The women never waved during his journeys, but the children always did. Some few men.

The flat water of the riverpools hid large rocks. Though he knew many by memory—the like of road ruts to the stage driver—Jedediah knocked his shins and toes, the going slow. By midday he was ready to give in to his hunger—he'd eaten only a few plums snatched from the riverbank. Ahead grew corn at Great Island, council ground of the Delaware and Shawanese only thirty years ago, and before then, domain of races who'd left not even their names, only mounds of stone that still dotted the field. William Dunn now owned these two hundred lush acres, reputed to have been had from the last Delaware chief, Newhaleeka, for the price of a musket and a keg of whiskey.

Jedediah kept to the riverbank, wading well past Dunn's cabin at the tip of the island until he found a shallows, where he crossed. He tied his canoe to a Sycamore that leaned over the water and crawled up the bank where red tassels atop the tall canes of Dunn's corn swayed in the hot breeze. Jedediah stood still, and when he was sure no one was about, slipped in among the rows to where he could still see his canoe wagging on the water, the papery yellow tips of the corn leaves hissing dryly about him.

He snapped an ear from its stalk and peeled back the husk. The golden kernels bloomed full and lustrous. He crunched into the corn, milky juice running down his chin onto his shirt. He ate and ate, dozens of ears, sugary as maple candy. He knew he should stop, for he would get the itchy, mystery sickness. He shrugged, famished.

Then he saw them wading the river, a woman and a black man who pulled a dugout. They kept a wide berth around Jedediah's canoe. Jedediah stooped, strained. He deduced by the smoky skin and hulking shoulders that the man was George Sharpe, recognized Rosanna by the scowl. You old fox, Jedediah thought.

Still crouched, he stepped toward the water. The moment George spotted him emerging from the corn he moved amidships of the canoe, reached in and retrieved a rifle.

Jedediah waved his arms, gestured to himself as if to say, "It's just me."

George stretched his neck, returned the gun. He nodded to Rosanna and they waded across to the shallow water before Jedediah. George surveyed up and down the river. "On your way to the mill?" he said.

Jedediah couldn't keep his eyes from Rosanna. Her soaked petticoat and shortgown divulged her woman shape, the slope of her breasts, their points patent and rigid as the set of that jaw. She crossed her arms.

"I'm travelin' upriver," Jedediah said. "From Williamsport. All that business 'bout settin' me free."

"So you free now?" George said, wringing water from the hem of his soaked frock shirt.

"I been free," Jedediah said. "You know that. But their judge says I have to wait a year and Bakeraskin says I have to wait eight." He brushed a fly off his cheek. "But I won't." He looked back at Rosanna. Good God. He'd have his own. Soon. "Where you headed? White girl and all."

"Upcountry," George said. "Where you told me a man can disappear. The Sinnemahone."

"That's a rough country," Jedediah said. "That's a howling wilderness. And you got winter comin'."

George looked to Rosanna, spoke more to her than to Jedediah. "We got time. I was headed to you to learn the way and lay of the land. We could draw a map."

"I know about the mill," Jedediah said. "And I'm guessin' that old bastard ran you off, now that he's got no stones. But I know he don't 'prove of this." He looked from one to the other, glanced down the river. "He'll be huntin' you."

When George didn't answer, Jedediah asked if they were hungry. George nodded and went in among the canes to snap off ears. Then the three of them sat on the bank, George and Rosanna each holding a lapful of peeled ears, chomping back and forth along the cobs, careful of loose husks not blowing into the water, lest settler Dunn detect his thieves.

The fog of fatigue Jedediah had been fighting evaporated, leaving him the easy mind that came with a noggin of hard cider. He caught himself kneading one hand into the other, waggling his foot. A hankering set in to be back on the river, to get to Sarah Starret faster, and it came by more than his reaction to Rosanna. George's plan helped his own.

To his torment, the two lazed on the riverbank, sat picking their teeth, searching them with their tongues. They talked of putting up a cabin before snowfall, storing in venison and firewood, nuts and berries. Although George had lost his savings in the fire, they had a little bartering money Rosanna had taken from the family stores. By spring, George would have their future figured out. A farm. A mill. Who knew?

"No millin' up there," Jedediah said. "You'd want for custom. Hardly a settler."

George shrugged. "We just need to take cover awhile. Things settle. Then we can move downriver." He looked about the valley. "Maybe 'round here. Aren't but a couple tub mills up this way, what I hear."

Rosanna eyed George. "We'll find a preacher then," she said.

George's jaw tensed. But then he nodded. "Or a justice of the peace."

There are no preachers up this valley, Jedediah thought. And to ask a justice to marry them? He pictured the great rope in their canoe noosing George's head. Even so, the idea of George having Rosanna as a wife put his heart near to punching through his shirt, for it made his own plan seem all the more real.

"I'm makin' a move upriver, same as you," Jedediah said. "With my own woman. The one on the next place down like I told you about, George."

Rosanna watched George until he nodded. Letting themselves trust the luck, credit the possibilities.

"A year, and I'm free," Jedediah said. "All free. Even the free of judges. Knowin' that's so close, she'll run with me if I ask. 'Specially now."

George and Rosanna met eyes again, and Jedediah saw doubt there now. George touched Jedediah's knee. "Wait the year. They'll be huntin' two of us this way."

"Can't," Jedediah said. "There's a problem."

Then Jedediah told the story, how after Bakeraskin warned Sarah's father about the couple, the venerable veteran took action on his daughter. Starret, who depended on her in his domestic affairs as he had his wife, forbade the trysts. Later, suspecting that his daughter defied him, he suited her to a more than willing Thomas Tillman, who'd represented himself to the captain as not only surveyor to Peter Bakeraskin, but as a land speculator in the making. Sarah despised Tillman almost as much as she grieved losing Jedediah. But her father determined the couple would be married after the coming harvest moon when Sarah's sisters downriver could join her two neighboring sisters-in-law in arranging the wedding.

"I was hopin' to reach her by night," Jedediah said, "'fore Bakeraskin and Cornelia get home. We'd be gone by the time her father and that snake Tillman find out I'm free in a year." He pointed to his canoe. "But I'll need that, and haulin' it's slowin' me. If I could run the river trail, I'd make it."

"Wait," George said. "Weigh out your moves."

Rosanna leaned ahead and looked over at Jedediah. "If you wait until tomorrow I can talk to her."

Jedediah considered this. Maybe. Hearing from another woman might make a difference if Sarah wavered. But he shook his head no. He stood, stretched his back.

"Then let's meet," George said. "We'll run together."

Rosanna's chin fluttered with her nods, the serious eyes spirited.

As a knot loosened in Jedediah's gut, George pointed upriver. A lone paddler in deerskins moved downstream. They crept into the corn and watched him study their canoes. But the current was so fast he couldn't have approached had he wanted. When he was out of sight, they stepped back to the riverbank.

"Agreed?" George said.

Jedediah knew he needed every advantage. And he respected no man in this world except George Sharpe. He looked at Rosanna. Traveling with another woman might make Sarah more inclined. He nodded.

George and Rosanna each let out a breath, everyone grinning. "I'll pull both canoes," George said. "You move on ahead, talk to her."

"No," Jedediah said. "You'd go too slow. The Bakeraskins would catch up and see my canoe. And he knows you." He looked up at the sun. He sure could use the time. "I got an idea. After the river bends north, you'll come to where the mountain on the east rises straight from the bank and forces the trail to ford. Wade along the steep side 'til you come to a creek. You'll know the hollow—there's two gravestones behind the charred foundation of a cabin burnt during the runaway. Hide the canoes. Watch the ford from there. You'll see them. Late in the day. Mounted double."

George's eyes swam, trying to picture it. He bobbed his head. "I think I have it."

And it was only then, hitherto distracted by his fatigue and urgency, that Jedediah noticed George's own exhaustion. He fought for his wind even as he stood there. His eyelids sagged and his head trembled. Something else, some sadness. Jedediah took hold of George's hand. He squeezed and the men met eyes. And at that moment, Jedediah felt pass between them the understanding of allegiance they would carry to their graves despite all that was to follow.

Jedediah took his shoes from the canoe and sat on a rock to put them on. "Keep movin' after the Bakeraskins pass," he said. He described the Starret farm along the riverbend. "Where the river turns west again. It's on the south side. One brother's place is across. By then, you already passed the other brother's farm. Keep goin'. You'll come to where giant pines grow on a high bank. Even in the dark you'll know it, 'cause the branches reach out over the water. You can feel them. We'll meet you in those woods in the night."

They considered provisions. George and Rosanna had taken a needle and thread, a tinderbox with flint and steel. A kettle and a sack of cornmeal. Jedediah and Sarah would need their own, plus blankets, coats, axes, knives, and whetstones. Jedediah should pilfer cloth—wool if possible. Noggins and spoons of cattlehorn, of pewter if he could find them. Seed: rye; corn; flax. A faggot of bar iron, a saw, and grubbing hoe. Broad-ax, spade, and gimlet. Of course a gun—the old Brown Bess Bakeraskin had let him use for hunting—powder, flints, bullets, and a mold. Leather for moccasins and strap hinges. Jerked deer meat and gammon. Flour—he sure knew how to keep that dry. Wouldn't chocolate be nice? A crusie lamp and candles. "Whiskey," Jedediah said. He'd take the still. To hell with Bakeraskin.

"But by God," George said. "Make sure you find salt. It'll get us through winter."

On the energy of ripe corn and river water, Jedediah whisked through the goldenrods of the island shore until he reached its tip and splashed across a shallows to the riverbank. Gaining the trail, he followed it, ford to ford. On he went, weighted only by the apprehension of being found out. West and north.

He arrived at the farm two hours before dark and went right to carrying the supplies to a thicket by the river. He began at the house, taking only items that would not immediately reveal his leaving. Next he worked the barn. With an hour of daylight remaining and minutes before Bakeraskin came leading the horse upon which mistress now carried the baby, Jedediah re-moved from the stillhouse the tubing and kettle. He made himself seen about the barn while the Bakeraskins retired, her attention on the baby, his, Jedediah guessed, on whatever ar-rangement he'd made for the rye he planned to send Jedediah to retrieve. Then Jedediah slipped away. He'd have half an hour once he reached Sarah.

But on the porch sat Samson Starret watching midges effer-vesce in the twilight over the river. And hitched to a tree in the yard was Thomas Tillman's horse. The longer Jedediah stood sweating in the shadowed underwood bordering the barnyard, torn between storming the house and abandoning his hopes with Sarah, the more the sight of that horse roiled his fatigue into wit-crippling fury, and wits he would need if he were to coax Sarah. Still, he'd have to get past Captain Samson Starret—not the man himself, rather that bearing and legend that may as well have been their own brigade.

Everyone on the West Branch knew Starret's story, whose face was as much a composite of contradictions as had been his life as a warrior. His brown eyes—deep-set, radiant orbs—were warm, inviting, almost matronly. Yet his club of a chin, his lips, drawn over his toothless gums tight as wicker, the concave cheeks and greats palms of ears, were molded in the shape of ferocity gained through a hell of wars. A bastard child who'd survived the squalor of the London streets in the 1730s, he man-aged by the age of 21 to achieve sergeant with the 44th Regiment of Foot. Samson followed his service overseas during the French and Indian War. Full of cockney accent and the barbarity of a British soldier, at 25 he survived Braddock's bloody defeat. He was then assigned to the 60th, the Royal Americans, and after marrying the mother of Sarah's half-siblings, went with General Bouquet and Colonel Forbes to retake Fort Duquesne. He butch-ered Indians and Frenchmen. Duty in New York and Montreal followed. Then he and his wife settled near Philadelphia where the first son, Samson Abel, was born in 1762.

And then the rebellious turn of allegiance from crown to self, from red coat and tricorn to butternut and beaver. But Samson

Starret had only abided the tendency of the colonial character. Acted by the logic of one who'd chosen, rather than been born into, the path of the warrior. For the thing that had inspired so many impoverished Londoners to pledge allegiance to the crown—the same smoldering mettle that made other men sailors or pugilists—was the stuff of the patriot. The American. That spirit was ignited into an inferno by all that land, all those trees. So much space. Property.

It was deep winter, 1759, between his engagements at Duquesne and Montreal, when Samson first came into the vicinity of the West Branch. His company was pursuing Indians up the frozen Susquehanna. They encamped on the outer grounds of Fort Augusta, overlooking the forks of the west and north branches. From the deck of the fort's watch, Samson took in the valley of the West Branch. Several soldiers of the garrison, men gangly, famished, wearied by the constant harassment of Indians, described that place to him. The black forest, they named it, the darkest and least-peopled place of the northern frontier. There, over the campfires of savage war parties, dried the scalps of the children of settlers.

He looked on fascinated, as only a young rover of a soldier could be with a country that in its borders bared teeth in the cragginess of its ridges and that in its interior sulked beneath an unbroken shroud of ancient evergreen. A land of awful and dismal beauty.

A fellow sergeant observed his interest. "The Indians," he said, scowling in that direction from which all manner of atrocity had descended on the fort and where nineteen years later such would befall settlers such as Samson Starret. "They call it *Otzinachson*. Demon's Den. Where the evil spirits hold their revels."

Samson and his wife would have two more sons and three daughters as they followed the advance of the Pennsylvania boundary, moving on to establish new farms when Samson became restless and eager for better ground. In 1774, he took possession of West Branch bottomland at an ancient Indian settlement known as the Monseytown flats. Two more sons were born. In June 1778, while most of the men of the valley were fighting on the plains of New Jersey, the slaughter that led to the Great Runaway of the West Branch took place. When a band of Senecas and a Tory ranger from the Royal Greens appeared in the yard, Samson and his two teen sons moved inside the house and fired from the doorway. They turned the party away, but as they reloaded, had to endure watching the Indians disembowel Mrs. Starret, who'd huddled by the stable where she'd been gathering eggs. She was yet alive and screaming as they took her scalp for the bounty they'd get from the Crown.

And so Samson and the eight children, the youngest a nursing infant, fled by canoe with Mrs. Starret's body to the family who'd taken their previous homestead along the Juniata River. They were back on the West Branch in a year, along with Samson's new wife, a woman of prominent people from near the mouth of the Juniata. Her sister would a year later marry Commissioner John Burrows. In 1780, at 50 years old, long-impatient for the moment and accompanied by two sons now of service age, Samson left his wife and six other children on their farm in the wilderness. The three men traveled back to the valley of the Juniata where they signed on to fulfill their compulsory two-month service rotations with the Seventh Battalion of Pennsylvania's Cumberland County Militia.

They took on other assignments over the next several years, hiring out as substitutes to patrol the frontier for loyalists and Indians. Samson did not serve as a captain but was regarded as such, for the seasoned veteran was the chosen leader of any reconnoitering or work parties not accompanied by an officer.

Upon his return in 1783, he fathered Sarah. By 1787, his oldest daughters had married among settlers near the Monseytown flats and the first two sons had built farms there. At 57 years of age, Samson and his wife—with his middle son of 18, two sons not yet teens, and little Sarah—moved upstream, starting over again where there were only cabin ruins, trees, ridges, and river.

He couldn't keep up with the farm after his second wife died early in 1799. The third and fourth sons helped from where they'd cleared plots and built houses nearby while the youngest, Benjamin, left for the Ohio country with his father's penchant for wandering. But Samson still had his Sarah at home.

He sat there bareheaded, collared, eyeing Jedediah where he stood off the porch rolling the brim of the hat he held. Jedediah had always felt—absurd as it was—connected to Starret. A galvanic force hummed in his hawkish scrutiny, a chain that though each tugged at, somehow—against all the laws of their universe—allied them. Jedediah knew this troubled the old veteran, all the more for he despised Jedediah, who confronted him with an unsolvable riddle—this, Jedediah had read in his eyes.

He once mentioned it to Sarah. She gave a flutter of nods to assure him that yes, what he saw was real. Her words, though, he could not decipher. "He is this country," she said. That was all. But from that day, Jedediah believed Sarah Starret was more than a simple settler girl from downriver.

He stepped onto the porch, nothing between him and the door except that fortress of history surrounding Starret. The valley, washed in the dusky white of old bones, buzzed with cicadas. They sawed away at the seconds, might have been Jedediah's legs pleading for him to move them. He pictured Tillman in there, holding Sarah if not in his arms, then within his black heart. And at that, Jedediah's rage knocked about his insides like a sacked wildcat and freed his voice and lifted his feet.

"I have to see her," he said, starting ahead. Samson drew back in his chair. His mouth moved to call out an assault, the soft eyes helpless. Jedediah had broken through the margin of honor, but the riddle, roiling in the old man, had hamstrung his tongue.

She sat on a bench before a slab table, the handle of a coffee mill in her hand, a linen cap ruffled about her sheaves of black hair. Dusk barely breached the greased paper window, the room swimming in the towy glow of a half-dozen candles impaled in hooks along the walls. Instead of surprised, she looked concerned. Tillman occupied a stool harmlessly across the room from her; he even wore his tailed coat of brown broadcloth. He placed on the floor a quill he'd held and a paper that had been on his knee, rose squinting through his glasses. "You have word for me from your master?" he said.

"I come to talk to her," Jedediah said. "Alone."

Tillman's top lip twisted up beneath his nose as though he sniffed something foul. "I'll not leave her alone with a nigger," he said.

Sarah was studying Jedediah. Not worried now. Probing. That flesh so thin, almost transparent, stretched across her narrow nose, the bones of her face—not at all Rosanna's full, glowing dough-skin. But she would be his, by God, this girl so gentle and obliging.

"Thomas," she said, the familiarity goading Jedediah, "he's come to talk to me. I want you to leave now."

Tillman picked up his paper and quill, an ink jar. "I'll be here tomorrow night," he said. He rose and snatched his satchel and hat from a peg, then fumed past Jedediah and out the door.

Sarah stood. "You look so tired," she said. "But hurry. Father will be in at dark."

"I came to get you," Jedediah said.

She looked to the floor. "It's too late for that."

"You don't have to marry him," Jedediah said.

"It's my father's wish," Sarah said. "That's my duty."

"Thomas Tillman is a lootin' blacksnake," Jedediah said.

Sarah neither answered nor looked at him.

"I got another way for you," he said. "I'm free in a year."

Now she raised her eyes. "You learned this in Williamsport?"

"We can run off now," he said. "Den up 'til I'm free. You'll get outta marryin' him."

Sarah gripped together her hands and glanced at the door. "You never asked me to wait. How could I wait if I didn't know if you'd be there at the end?"

"I had a reason," he said, trying to rub away the pain at his forehead. "But I don't anymore."

"I hoped and hoped for you to say something." She started for him. Thought better of herself. "I would've done it, waited the eight years. Now I can't even wait one year. I gave my father my word, and besides, he needs me here."

Jedediah pointed to the door. "He's a son across the river. Another downstream. And your brothers know Thomas Tillman, so they got to be against it."

"Oh Jedediah, I feel nothing for him."

"There's more," he said. "George is goin' with us. Him and a woman named Rosanna."

The promise in this turned her eyes to the window. A grin. "I think of my mother," she said. "She would've despised Thomas Tillman. Who's to say I can't do right by her?" She gathered her apron and petticoat and sat on the bench. "But you need to know something."

Jedediah shook his head. "We don't have time."

"I will not decide unless you know it all," she said. "Then we'll see if you still want me."

"For Christ's sake," Jedediah said. He reached and pushed the Indian bar across the frame, rested against the salt barrel that made for a wash tub.

"I knew why you were in Williamsport," Sarah said.

Jedediah gave a hum from deep in his chest and nodded. "You kept lots a' things from me."

"You told me George came to you once with news. He said people from downriver watched you. When they tried to get you free, you didn't trust them."

Jedediah tapped his heal against the barrel. "So you're circlin' around to tellin' me our times together depended on me gettin' free. Didn't happen quick enough, you moved on."

"I came to you even after the first try didn't work," she said.

The door clattered against the bar. The creaky cockney voice of old Samson Starret: "Sa-a-r-ah."

She went to the door. "Father, I'm fine. Give me a moment."

"I'll not 'ave ya 'lone wif a blackie."

"Sit back down," Sarah said.

"Ates dark aahhht-side."

She stepped back to the table. "I can't explain it all now, good as I should, but the man you saw yesterday, Commissioner Burrows, is my uncle. He married my mother's sister, and he is a slave owner. Those people in the Muncy hills conspire against him as they do Peter Bakeraskin. And they do not give up."

Sarah waited, eyes on the door. When her father stopped shuffling about the porch, she continued. "My aunt hates havin' slaves in her house. My cousins grew up as I did—taught by their mother people can't be owned. They aren't Quakers. They're just learned and never use the Bible for their own advantage. But these others—Quakers in the Muncy hills and people friendly to them—are workin' with lawyers in Philadelphia and my cousins to free their own father's slaves. It is a great scandal for John Burrows." She closed her eyes a moment, gathered herself. "And so what I'm sayin' is that these people use others to help them."

"The man Caspar Roan," Jedediah said. "He's one of them, even though he's from Williamsport?"

Sarah nodded. "One of the smartest. He shall marry my cousin someday."

"So these folks I don't even know thought I needed help. And you're tellin' me you came to me all those times to be their spy. That's how they always know my situation."

She rapped the table beside her. "Every time I saw you was by my choosin'. I been fond of you since we met."

"I was the only one you had around here."

She stepped to him and took his sleeve in her hand. "You are a strong-minded and upright man with a mighty hunger, Jedediah James. The only thing to stop you from makin' your own way is an old chain of lies. I see you as you are. I do not pretend meanness in a man's skin. I would have hoped for you to want me anywhere." She upturned the corners of those thin lips in the slightest smile. "All of that and thoughts of my mother are what I'm decidin' by. If you'd still like me to go now that you know I tried to help without tellin' you."

He thought of turning away and there came a thrill in that, in spiting all their pity. Even if there was no denying he couldn't run at all were it not for those people in the Muncy hills, Caspar Roan, this girl. Then he pictured George having Rosanna.

Samson knocked on the door. "I'll naaht be locked aahhht me ahn hice."

"I'm comin', father," Sarah said. She gave Jedediah a look that said *what do I do?*

Jedediah rubbed his forehead. Think, man. He swung around, paced, returned. He'd be damned if she wouldn't be his. "After you get the old man to bed, make for the jakes. Bring a coat. Anything else you want. Then sneak off to the pines. But go the way I'm goin', along the river, not the bridle path, in case Tillman's hidin' to see when I come along before he goes to the Bakeraskins' for the night."

Sarah watched the door. "I can't bear leavin' my father." She allowed a smile. "But it's just a year 'til I can visit." She took his hand. "Are you sure you want me? I add to your chance of gettin' caught—I'll double the attention."

He shook his head. "There aren't no attention where we're goin'."

She let go of his hand and lowered her eyes, pinched together her lips, and Jedediah did not like the frowardness in her thinking him ignorant.

There came again the knock at the door. "Sa-a-r-ah, is 'e molestin' ya?"

She rushed off to a shelf to take down a Bible and leather satchel, and Jedediah started away.

"Wait," Sarah said.

He turned as he reached for the bar, old Starret rattling the door by the handle. Sarah approached, lissome even now, and stood before him. She tugged at his shirt and kissed his lips.

They stood thus, avoiding each other's eyes. Then Jedediah threw back the bar and nearly toppled Samson Starret as he burst into the fuss of katydid and cricket song shuddering through the valley.

The Sinnemahone Country, Lycoming County, Pennsylvania

Beyond the conflux of the Sinnemahoning Creek with the West Branch, the forest, in its virginity and dankness, its enormity and gloom—a sulking black presence, it was—felt as if it had been waiting for him since the first dawn. Now, with daybreak, it breathed the fetid smell of having festered through the ages, while the evening before, as they'd waded onward, it had howled and screeched as something having grown more feral all those years.

The Sinnemahone was a land with no history, seen by few, that expanse of creek canyons and headsprings, of ancient Indian paths crossing monotonous plateaus, a swath blank on every map of the Commonwealth but for a guess at the meanders of the main waterway.

On earlier journeys into that country, Jedediah had seen only two settler's places and these near the mouth of the creek. Spread miles between there and the first fork stood three bottomland sheds of itinerant trappers and hunters built upon the charred cornerstones of past squatters' cabins. Those cornerstones now dated 25 years and beyond, when this land still belonged to the Indians and the proprietors forbade any colonial from entering. The law hadn't needed enforced; it had been dispensed by the Indians, the penalty: death and scalp—not always in that order.

Bakeraskin and Thomas Tillman had brought Jedediah here to push their canoe against the fitful current of this stony tributary. It rushed with all the icy urgency of the wild streams and springs gushing from that sun-less abyss, even while it was by breadth as much river as what it left of the West Branch curving away to its own reaches, southwestward.

Jedediah had trekked these woods, too, carrying rod and chain, quadrant and ruler, as Tillman surveyed to find the bounds of creekside Samuel Wallis warrants, Bakeraskin crossing them off his map, gripped with seeing them all, with estimating the value of their timber—which was astonishing. He would agonize about having to wait for the sheriff to put them up for sale, fret whether pioneers would dare preempt him by squatting such steep and wild warrants. And as if he were two halves of one man, he cursed and argued aloud about the risk of showing his hand should he lobby already for a river channel to move these trees to the great mills and shipyards of Maryland. "It all better be had for a song," he would say. "Wallis and his troubles."

"Traitor," Tillman would snarl. He spat whenever he spoke the name, for this was in keeping with his politics, his detestation of suspected Tories, even while Wallis had been benefactor to him.

"Now, now," Bakeraskin would say. "Speak well of his departed soul. He'll be our man if we mind our manners and keep at it." Then he'd look northwestward and move on all the hungrier.

Tillman was otherwise quiet on the matter. He watched Bakeraskin's outbursts, licked his lips and squinted through his spectacles. And Jedediah, catching the slightest quivering grin, knew that Tillman schemed.

Jedediah waded this creek today remembering well those three flats with hunter's hovels and parts already cleared, where a man might more readily settle. These had enraged Bakeraskin. They cut into the Samuel Wallis warrants in odd-shapes, not following the typical square in the checkerboard plan laid out by the Commonwealth land office. They abided the banks of bottomlands and extended to the ridges of the steeps behind them. Neither Wallis nor the Holland Land Company had been able to warrant these tracts because, as with the two farms downstream, pioneers had already done so. Having squatted there before the Indians sold the land in 1784, these families held warrants recognized by what the land office called previous settlement and improvement. "Damned preemptors," Bakeraskin said. "The best tracts stolen."

During the great runaway of 1778, the squatters of the Sinnemahone and upper West Branch who weren't butchered had fled to the lower Susquehanna. If any from the three unoccupied places had survived, they had decided against returning and fighting the winters and isolation. They had claimed their warrants in 1784 while absentees, in case a road would be built. If they hadn't survived, heirs had made the claims.

Bakeraskin said he'd have those tracts as well one day. Absent warrant holders wouldn't bother to file for patents until someone contested their claims. And he'd be the one to do it—once he figured out how to work the damned land laws such that he'd have the upper hand when they found out.

The rain-swollen river had begun to recede by the time they'd started their journey up the West Branch last night, an early and bright moon overhead. Jedediah had dozed beforehand as they waited in the grove of pines for Sarah. George woke him, Rosanna gasping in a panic. They pointed to a monstrous silhouette approaching where a reflection of silver moonlight trembled upon the water, a shambling creature of sundry misshapen limbs and distensions. But soon they saw it was Sarah as she stumbled across a shallows, suspending and repositioning a ladder-back chair on one shoulder, a spinning wheel on the other. Around her neck, she wore the thong of her leather satchel. It held, they later learned, the Bible and a folded, flower-printed gown of chints and lace. They'd been her mother's, as had the chair.

The women had made their way among the stones of the emerging shore. Where they could, they took to the bank for easier walking despite their fear of rattlesnakes. But along the Sinnemahoning, the steeps crowded out both bank and shore in most places, so they waded with Jedediah and George, often to their waists.

At the set of the moon, they moored the canoes at a hemlock flat on a bight in the creek. They undressed from their wet clothes and each to his or her own blanket slept on the mold of decaying needles.

Now, at daybreak, they cooked bannock on sticks over a fire, and on hot flat rocks each fried three of the eggs Jedediah had stowed in hay in the bow of the canoe. They sopped the yolks with the bread, raked and sucked pieces of the whites off their plates of stone, and licked at the caked yellows at the corners of their lips. Jedediah, savoring the creamy after-taste, grumbled they would not eat eggs for a long while—chicken eggs, anyway. But having slept, sitting at ease, he felt the airy cheer of freedom. For the first time.

He watched George through the smudge emitting from the throbbing coals, saw no trace of victory. Where Jedediah could not help glancing about with thoughts of this place's possibilities, George's eyes were turned inward. He'd fumbled along yesterday in a daze of exhaustion and now had woken only to brood over this new situation. The women were no different. Faces bowed. Thinking.

Sidling closer to Sarah, Jedediah thought, *my woman*, a warmth in his loins he hadn't allowed in a long time. He took a lock of her hair between his fingers. She smiled, flushed as she peered across at George and Rosanna. But when she looked at Jedediah, the color drained and her jaw loosened—she saw what he felt inside. Jedediah lowered his hand. Though he'd seen this in women, the guard of modesty—not innocence or reluctance—he couldn't help resenting even the suggestion of her rejecting him.

Rosanna leveled those severe eyes on him like musket barrels. "We'll be needin' a reverend or a justice," she said. "We'll be needin' to marry."

Jedediah chuckled. "This is the edge of the world. There's no justices or preachers here." But now Sarah was nodding her agreement with Rosanna.

"Edge of the world or not," Rosanna said, "we'll live by rules and not debauch ourselves."

Jedediah took a stick and scattered the coals. When the ash settled, he breathed in the musk of hemlock and pushed away the sting of Sarah's coolness. Then into his mind crept this thought: while he may never eat another chicken egg or wear more than moccasins on his feet, no man would own him again. He'd die first.

By noon, the heat of the sun so sharp the haze it burned through might have been glass, they passed an island of ten acres or so, then rounded a gentle bend in the creek and stopped in the shallow headwater of its pool to behold the valley of the first fork branching to the north.

George tied around his waist the rope of his canoe. He bent, cupped water in his hands, and rinsed his face. Straightening, he waved away a halo of punkies and nodded toward the fork. "What's that country like?"

Jedediah turned the other way, downstream, straining his eyes beyond the island where they'd passed one of those deserted claims. That place had been on his mind since they'd started out this morning, a most inviting piece, 80-acres or more of level, arable tree-stubble—plus a reverting Indian cornfield, half of which had been worked by the settler. The mouths of mountain runs, pouring out of the unmapped wilds, flanked the stretch.

He had stopped before the tract and asked Sarah and Rosanna up on the weedy bank whether the trapper's hut still stood. They shaded their eyes and scanned the clearing. "I don't see it," Sarah said.

"Stones," Jedediah said. "Do you see the stones it was built on?"

Sarah lifted her petticoat and started through the weeds, stutter steps as she watched for snakes.

When she came back, he saw she was eager to give him the report, to please him. "I see stones. Large ones. For the corners? And an apple tree besides. I think it's bearing."

Jedediah grinned. By God, the apples were a sign. One day he'd have that piece. After a year hiding away from the creek. Then his gut twisted like an eel for fear of the land getting away. He squeezed the rope in his hand as if he choked that eel, and when he growled out at Sarah, "Never mind about apple trees when it's a spring I'm looking for," the smile she'd worn vanished.

Now, in answer to George's question, he turned to him, shrugged, and said. "I don't know the country up that fork. Bakeraskin sniffed around this creek—" he nodded up the Sinnemahoning—"as far as the next branch—four, five miles."

"Then we should go up one of the forks," George said.

"No," Jedediah said. "We need to stay 'round here." He glanced downstream at the steep, verdant cradle of the upper run's hollow. Border of that abandoned stretch of sandy loam. "The forks run too shallow to canoe in summer. And that country's thicker'n this with rattlers and painters."

George had been soaking his hat in the creek. He withdrew it and flapped it about his head to wave away the flies alighting on his cheeks and neck, cool drops of water peppering Jedediah's face. "Those'd be reasons to go up the forks," George said.

Jedediah shook his head. "This is the country for us. The shad come this far in spring. A hundred shad'll bring a bushel a' salt."

"Don't say shad," George said, putting his hat on with one hand, rubbing his stomach with the other. "I could eat one 'live 'bout now."

Jedediah pointed downstream where the water eddied deeply back on itself within the crook of the creek. "I have fish hooks," he said. "And a horsehair fishing line." He pointed to a boulder slanting into the pool from the steep cut of the bank. "There'll be catfishes in the deeps on that slow side. Suckers for sure. It's shady there."

They had the women wade upstream to a cove of flatland at the mouth of the first fork. They would gather firewood in a stand of walnut, locust, and sycamore while Jedediah and George swam the deep pool to the rock. The men thought of taking a musket but knew they'd never keep powder dry, so loaded one for the women. Rosanna was reluctant, but Sarah took it and said she could handle a gun well enough.

Upon the sloping stone, Jedediah lay back holding a hickory branch, waiting for a nibble on a worm. He motioned across the valley. "Up past these tops is the unmapped country," he said. "No-man's land. "

George tipped back his hat and squinted across the creek. "Then that's a country for me. A man don't even exist if he aren't in a place at all. But I can't climb that wall carryin' stores."

"Wouldn't have to. Follow that little run we saw just down from here. It'll head-up on a flats miles beyond, like all the runs do in this country."

The horsehair line described a circle in the water. Jedediah sat up, pulled back on the stick. Missed. He tilted his head where the canoes were moored. "Up there by the fork," he said, "is wide bottomland. But squatters kept away from it. Too dangerous. The Indians could a' come down on them from two places. And it was their campin' grounds." With a snap of his wrist, he jerked the tip of the stick, plucking the line out of the water and the hook onto his lap. He inspected his bait and cast it out again. "That's where Grove and his boys massacred the Indians in '80. The story is they spotted them from the ridge behind us. But now," he said, shaking his head up and down, "squatters will come to the fork. I need to keep downstream of them."

"And squat right in this valley? A black man—escaped, consortin' with a white girl and sportin' it on a highway of a creek? Word'll spread before the first frost. You might as well put the rope around your neck now."

Jedediah shrugged. "I'm not sayin' I wanna squat right out along the water. Not now. Just close enough I can keep an eye out. We'll need to make business with trappers and hunters that pass. Remember, I have a still and they hanker for whiskey. We can trade for grain, seed. And there's fish and beavers in the creek. So one of us should stay handy to it. Now, you recall that piece down a little ways, the one I had Sarah spy out? Across the creek from it, there's a wrinkle in the valley with a spring and a slope not too steep. A man might clear a few high acres where he can hide while he still has a good chance with a bullet if someone comes up the hill huntin' him."

George pulled his hat down over his forehead. "We should stay close together. For the first winter at least. We'll share the burden and tools. Even the heat if we keep one cabin. 'Sides, the women won't like it if we split up—not bein' married."

Jedediah traced the current to where it curved away. Toward that piece just out of sight. He would not leave the vicinity of that place until he had it. Before anyone else, by God. "There's an advantage to splittin' up. We cut the chance of them findin' us both." The horsehair line made another circle. This time Jedediah was ready. He raised the stick and it bent and shuddered. He stood and lifted out a writhing sucker, its jar-top lips contracting and opening against the hook. Jedediah took hold of the fish and cracked its head against the stone. He withdrew the hook, the worm still impaled and tossed his line into the water.

"We'll build my cabin on the slope," Jedediah said as he sat. "We'll girdle the big trees, fell the small ones, and lay by firewood. Then we'll set off for the no-man's land to find you a place on the flats where there's water and good ground. We'll be a couple hours apart—close enough to help. And by winter, be ready to den-up like bears."

George sat looking at the sucker; a foot long, slime adhering to the rock around it, blood seeping from its gills. "The wilderness is a mean country," he said. "We'll have a hard time of it."

"Country aren't mean," Jedediah said, and he set the hook on another fish. "Country just don't care."

Jedediah caught five more suckers and an eel as long as his leg. No catfish. He and George met the women on the bank at the confluence and roasted the fish on a skewer and spit Jedediah contrived of green spicebush limbs. They dipped the pieces in sweet oil they skimmed off a kettle of boiling white walnut kernels, nuts the women had gathered and cracked with the flat side of an axe. They cooled the nutmeats and ate them as they sat about the coals and spoke of swollen feet and aching thighs and delighted their flight was soon to end. Then the men shared their plan.

"I'll not separate from Sarah until I'm wed," Rosanna said, brushing bits of nut from her petticoat.

"Right now," George said, "we have to plain survive. That means makin' it through winter and waitin' Jedediah's year. That means putting up huts, huntin' bear meat and opossum, and layin' by food. I won't stay down here and Jedediah won't

go up to the flats, and besides he might have a point that separatin' cuts the odds of us all bein' stole back. Now, aren't our
promises we'll marry you good enough to get you through the
year?"

The women looked at one another.

"I don't have a promise," Sarah said.

Everyone looked at Jedediah. "Rosanna don't have one neither," he said.

"I promise," George said.

Rosanna reached for George but stopped herself. George
turned to Sarah. "You can go get your Bible."

Jedediah, kicking dirt onto the coals, felt their eyes on him
again. His heart pounded and his fingers tingled and he wished
they would leave him alone and if not, that he could just run
with Sarah and leave all these predicaments, run to that apple
tree. And it angered him all the more that he wished to run away
from having run away.

He looked up to find them glancing at one another, and then
they avoided each other's eyes. Sarah tilted her head down and
covered her face.

What he said next wouldn't matter, he thought. Words. And
yet he fumbled for his voice and found it frantic and feathery. "I
just need to go slow," he said. "I don't see what the difference is,
promisin'."

"The difference is a sin likely to start happenin' next year,"
Rosanna said, "if you won't be willin' to marry this girl and she's
got no place to go."

"I'm not sayin' I won't marry her."

"You're not sayin' you will," Rosanna said.

"Well then," he said, "I'll marry her."

Sarah studied him a moment, then let out a long breath. "I
still think we should stay together," she said. "But if separatin'
means someone has less chance of goin' back to all their troubles, then I'll live out the year with Jedediah."

Rosanna hadn't stopped watching Jedediah. "I'm not agree-
in' to separate," she said, "'til Sarah gets that Bible from the
canoe. Not until one man and then another places his hand on
it and swears."

And so Jedediah laid his hand on the Bible and swore to God and these mortal witnesses he would marry Sarah Starret. Yet he as he took up the kettle and sulked away, he could not help feeling low and dirty.

The canoes glided through the curving pool and its swift tailwater, the creek *blib blib blibbing* against the wedges of the bows, the air heady with pollen, with the buzz and rattle of insects. Overhead, cobalt sky spanned the valley haze-less and unbroken now but for the swift bird-swooping of peak summer. Then, past the island unfurled that strip of bottomland. But Jedediah led them paddling to the other shore where they unloaded the canoes.

High above here, the work of spring seeps had over the millennia creased the descent of the valley, the lower sweep of the fold splaying, sloping gradually into a small flat pinewoods a later settler might find sufficient to clear for a house and a garden, a little pasture. But the trough was not so steep just up from its base that an acre couldn't be planted and a cabin erected. Those tall pines would hide Jedediah and Sarah from waterway travelers. While he watched that piece across the creek.

Sarah protested that she could not grow a patch of flax on a hillside only partly cleared, that she'd need a steady source of water close-by when it came pulling and soaking time. Jedediah pointed across the creek where a meandering rill bisected the old settler's field. He'd clear a quarter acre for her before winter and she could plant her flaxseed there.

Before they'd even removed from their canoes, they'd decided how substantial the structures should be. They'd build Jedediah and Sarah's to last the ten years a good cabin survived in that clime. Jedediah was silent as the others reasoned it might serve as a permanent home if he found trade as a hunter or such, which wouldn't require a full farm. But he did add that if he and Sarah claimed a place better fit for the plow, they'd have good luck selling this one to some pioneer—there'd be the value of both the structure and of a year's settlement toward preemption.

George and Rosanna, they supposed, would stay only a year up in the wilderness. There'd be little chance they could sell. Their cabin would still need a watertight roof and sturdy walls, but it could be smaller, so such could be the girth of its logs. And that was well, for they feared they'd find few manageable trees among the giant timbers of the topland.

The men compared materials, designs, methods—the best trees, the ideal building height, the machines they'd construct to raise the timbers. What pitch and style should each roof be? They had considerable experience to draw upon. George had been a hand in building and maintaining a solid log home, mill, and barn. Jedediah was the more practiced carpenter; Bakeraskin had hired him out to help raise every cabin and stable for 25 miles down the West Branch.

After they overturned their canoes in the pinewoods, protecting their goods beneath them, they hung their food and seed in sacks from treebranches with withes of grapevine. Then they found a level spot low on the trough, treeless but for a few hemlock saplings and sufficient to accommodate a cabin ten feet by twenty. It gave a glimpse of the creek through the trees. They grubbed up the saplings, and from the rock-rubble in the nook of the gully, rolled the four largest stones they could manage for the corners. These they half-buried. They cleared the needles and a layer of loose humus and tamped the black dirt of their floor with a beetle Jedediah had made from an oak log, its handle a hickory branch he'd fitted into a hole drilled with an auger.

Then in a nearby depression left in the slope eons ago by the uprooting of a great tree, they constructed their temporary shelter. They chopped two fallen branches of all but Ys in the ends and planted the bottoms for the front posts of a lean-to. They cut more branches, and for a slanted roof frame, lashed one in each Y with thongs Jedediah sliced from the sheet of leather he'd taken. He likewise secured ribs across the frame and bound over them sheathes of bark scored and stripped from birch trees near the creek. They laid in a mattress of hemlock boughs.

At dusk, while the men dug up a spring in the stony gutter of the draft, the women simmered ears of corn George and Rosanna had stowed from the Great Island. They sat around the fire and roasted on sticks live crayfish plucked from beneath stones they'd overturned in the creek shallows. As George raked white flesh from the tail shells and nipped every kernel from the cobs, cheer flashed over his lately listless eyes.

The wilderness night fell black as coal tar as Jedediah lay on his blanket, his head swimming in the babble of innumerable treefrogs *krek-ek, krek-ek, krek-eking* through the valley. Delicious sleep soaked into his limbs, pooled in his loins, washed his thoughts.

The beam of a crystal moon woke him. Its reflection stole from the shimmering creek like silver ghost-smoke through the great black boles of the pines. As wolves let forth ghoulish halloos from the rim of the unmapped land, Sarah seized his arm. She lay trembling, clutching him till dawn and birdsong filled the valley.

This day was one of rest and fishing, for Sarah and Rosanna insisted they observe the Sabbath. So not until the next morning did they set to home building.

Jedediah and George began felling the wall timbers, thankful they'd excavated their spring, for the dense ceiling of leaf and bough did not blunt the heat of the burning sun. Jedediah would have liked his pick of trees. But with only four people, rope, and ingenuity to roll, skid and ramp logs there in a forest so old that small trees were few, he had to take what was available and upslope.

They'd raise the cabin ten rounds. In addition to these 40 logs for the walls, they'd need at least ten for the roof ribs and a dozen more, though successively shorter, for the gables—not counting smaller timbers for the chimney. But that many trees 10-inches in diameter and less were scattered halfway to the ridge.

The valley up there reared nearly plumb, so only with a stay rope and tree trunks as snubbing posts were they able to ease to the cabin site the timbers they felled. Still, in two days they had their first 40 trees.

When the women weren't helping skid logs, they pulled rushes from the creekbank and spread them there to dry; these would be mixed with clay to daub the chinking. They fished and dried their catch over a fire, laying the flesh across a woven rack of green sticks lashed to a tripod. They salted the pieces of fish and packed them in sheaths of birchbark until they could store them loose in the rafters. Sarah came to bed smelling of salt-fish and smoke and sweat, a delicious odor to Jedediah that made him hungry for her tired as he was. How could he wait a year?

The women worked also at the edge of the pines using the broad-ax to peel the massive limbs of a fallen black oak. Jedediah chopped these into lengths. Then, with a beetle and gluts he'd fashioned of ironwood, he split the logs into roof planks, and boards for the door and table. A window-frame maybe. These the women smoothed, employing the broad-ax as a draw-knife. And at the cove of flatwoods by the mouth of the fork, they gathered walnuts until their hands were stained black, then picked from blackberry canes that had overtaken an Indian cornfield across the fork.

Before dusk of the second day, Jedediah and George trimmed the wall logs of knots and bumps and whet their axes; they were ready for the raising.

In cabin-building, the axe was the reigning tool, greater even than the knife to which it was second in all around pioneering. The axe to the cabin-builder could be feller, saw, hewer, ruler. But never abused as hammer, mallet or hoe. Knowing he'd break helves, Jedediah kept spares of ash wood he shaped with a chunk of bottle glass, charring and seasoning them by the fire they burned at night to ward mosquitoes.

At dawn on Wednesday, while the women boiled a kettle of samp, Jedediah and George axed nooks into the long-side bottom logs to fit them over the cornerstones. They rolled the logs into place and adjusted them to be square using rope marked against the scores in Jedediah's axe handle. Before they notched the first course of end logs, George, using iron staple-dogs he'd been farsighted enough to pilfer, secured them to the ground so they would not turn as the men chopped, one claw of each pounded into the log, the other into the black earth.

Jedediah chose the bottom-notch style, a trial for when he'd build his place across the creek. He'd test against the claims of less rot if only the lower half of each log was notched.

And so they rolled the logs up pole ramps for each successive course, but always stopped before the last turn onto the cross-logs below, propping the log there on the ramp with long forked sticks. Only then, for accuracy, did they chop out the notches.

On the second day of the raising, the walls now too high for the men to handle the timbers, the women helped roll them. And when the height of the ramped logs made them too unwieldy even for the four of them, George snubbed the middle of his rope to a tree on the side of the cabin opposite of wherever they were rolling, tying the ends to the log to check it. Jedediah was fatigued in leg and shoulder, calloused on hand and foot. But the sight of a home rising in the wilderness was a tonic, and the exhaustion that overcame him as he lay down at night was like a draught of warm sweetened laudanum.

Before they started the roof, Jedediah and George chopped and sawed an opening for the fireplace in the eastern wall. They cut out a doorway and a window, which Jedediah framed with boards he drilled with a gimlet and secured with pegs.

The last course of end-logs projected 18-inches longer than the rest. This would create eaves by supporting what Jedediah called the butting poles upon which would rest the edges of the lowest tier of vertical roof planks. Jedediah bored matching holes in the long end-logs and the poles, then rounded pins with his knife to secure them together.

They put in place the triangles of gable logs and across these mounted the timbers of the roof ribs, which like the butting poles projected beyond the gables for side eaves. This was the hardest work, as the logs were longer and the ascent higher, and so required trestle scaffolds and George's skill with his rope while Jedediah and the women used lever poles to ease the logs upward.

Again it was the Sabbath. After a morning of everyone berrying, nutting, and fishing, Sarah read from her Bible while they dined on eel meat at the great rock in the creek bend. The women bathed while the men sipped from a jug. Their tongues loosened and they spoke of their childhoods as slaves.

On Monday, they set across the roof-ribs the planks Jedediah had split, each row lapping the one below. These they held in place with press poles running longwise and knees of heart timber up and down between them. They placed flat rocks upon any boards still loose, and Sarah remarked they had best not put the bed below these. "Beds," she corrected herself.

It was too dark when they finished the roof to bring in their hemlock boughs, so they spent one more night in their lean-to, a soft, dripping fog having settled in late that day. The women in their spare moments had leveled a path to where they'd been digging a jakes in another windfall depression. Sarah whispered to Jedediah that with an axe and some little instruction from him, she and Rosanna could fell small trees at the edge of the pine flat. They could section them and carry them to the jakes where they'd notch them and build a privy shed. His blood pounded in his ears and he snapped no, that the women should be fishing and a-berrying. That there would have been light by which to settle in the cabin tonight had they gathered pine knots. But once that was out and Sarah turned and tugged up her blanket, his heartbeat shrank in his chest and he could not swallow away a ball of pride for this woman—his woman.

Jedediah reached under her blanket and around those ribs spare as dove quills. He found her hands clasped at her breast. He held her wrist and whispered that her idea was a good one, that in the morning he would show her how to line up the logs to measure the notches.

They would have raised the chimney today, but low, pearly rainclouds had settled on the country, downpours alternately overtaking drizzles. The men, shirtless, retrieved their supplies from beneath the canoes and untied from the vines the food and seeds, which they hung from the rafters where Jedediah would, over the winter, build a loft. Sarah set up her spinning wheel and chair in a corner and said she longed for flax and a weaver. Glancing at one another's soiled and torn attire, they all agreed they'd need cloth long before winter.

"When the leaves turn," George said, "me and Jedediah will be in buckskin. You women can have all the cloth we brought and use it for petticoats and gowns and blankets. You can even have these," he said, plucking his breeches, the earthy color now of the woods.

Rosanna, bold as her gaze, said, "We'll want for more cloth than we got. Women have monthlies to stanch." Sarah flushed, looked away. "And," Rosanna said, "there'll be no sycamore leaves in the winter and no cornhusks and cobs to save to clean ourselves at the jakes. George and I will be atop a mountain with no runnin' water to clean rags, so what we got won't last a week."

George was shaking his head. "We'll gather mosses and smooth stones. We'll survive this winter until we can lay by cobs and husks."

Wednesday dawned in a fog so heavy the cabin's sour smell of fresh cut logs and sweaty, smoke-ridden clothes made the throat smart. But the rain had stopped, and despite a chill that made Jedediah want to stay cocooned in his blanket, he rose to start on the fireplace and chimney, the last big jobs in the raising but for the chinking.

While Sarah and Rosanna worked on the privy, the men dug away black dirt outside the hole in the wall to make the hearth, which would be large enough for a four-foot backlog. They covered the space with flat rock and clay from where the women had excavated the jakes. Next, they constructed over the hearth a miniature three-sided cabin of logs, two sides of which extended inside the hole a few inches. They laid midway across the top rounds a heavy lubber pole of green oak, which they further supported by stacking stones beneath it as jambs. From this, they would hang three trammels fashioned by Jedediah from white oak branches, each of a different length so Sarah could adjust the kettle over the fire. They mixed clay with nibs of the grass the women had dried. This they applied to a lath of oak splints on the inner walls and packed it between the stones of the jams. Outside, they chinked the interstices of the fireplace logs with moss and woodchips left of the notches and packed about these their plaster.

They moved on to the chimney, which would stand free of the cabin and so could be pushed away if it caught fire. Jedediah would keep handy the poles they'd used for the raising in case of such an emergency.

Because they had to chink and daub as they went along, their chimney work was slow. They reached only the top of its taper by dusk. But from there it was a straight-up square, and by the next evening, having worked from the roof and a split pole ladder of hand-carved rundles Jedediah made to reach the loft, and with the women trying to outpace the men with their project, they finished both the chimney and the privy.

Over the next two days, while Jedediah constructed a door and a shutter from oak boards, the others chinked the cracks of the cabin with moss and notch-chunks of heartwood. They dug out more clay in depressions left by uprooted trees and hauled it to their worksite in baskets Jedediah had fashioned from birchbark bound with willow withes. They added to this the dried grass and daubed the calked interstices. Late afternoon Saturday—George and Jedediah sharing a jug—they all stepped back and admired the cabin. The pine and hemlock boughs and the fat leaves of oaks and poplars ordinarily made those woods sunless as the tomb. But now, with a dog day haze vaulting over the valley and soaking in sunset, light seeped somehow beneath the canopy so that even the bark of the rearing pines shone golden. And the cabin, with its daubing of yellow clay covering even the unpeeled logs, glowed as if ringed in an aureole.

Jedediah took a nip of whiskey. The hot sparks prickled down his throat, singed the walls of his belly. He exhaled and nodded. Their cabin was earthy and cool inside, and though it would be dim and smoky in winter, it would keep them warm enough— most of the time. Home.

September had closed in on them. Though each had a hair plucker and razor, Jedediah and George wore beards now for want of a mirror, George's wispy and scattered across his chin like the hairs on the head of an old man. They spent several days furnishing the cabin—a slab table and a pair of 3-legged stools to start. There was the matter of a bed. Jedediah raised the subject as they sat before the cabin eating ashcakes and roasted trout from the first fork. Sarah brushed a shuck of hair from her temple. She flashed her eyes at him. "Two beds," she said as the others looked away. "For a year."

And so they would sleep one above the other. At head height, Jedediah mortised two pole joists into opposite long-side logs, across which he placed boards for the end loft—the warmer place to sleep, and so for Sarah. Into a nook he gouged into the outer of these joists he fixed a support post that would serve also as the corner of the lower bed. This he socketed to receive the bedframe poles, which spanned at right angles to notches in the wall logs. Upon planks that he fitted between channels in the long frame pole and the facing wall, and in the loft, he spread beech leaves and grass to dry—mattresses for beneath what meager bed-clothes they'd make of rags.

Then Jedediah bore holes and hung pegs around the room for their wardrobe and the musket, shot pouch and powderhorn. He considered the home done. There would be one more outbuilding—the stillhouse. He would finish that by spring; they may have means for grain by then.

They needed to make haste to explore the unmapped country. Sarah and Rosanna protested being left alone, but finally agreed it best they fish and gather while the men proceeded. And Jedediah and George could construct a hovel well enough on their own. They would need all hands on the next trip, carrying goods into that abyss.

At nightfall, after collecting pine knots so the women would have an abundance of torches, they roasted two raccoons George had shot at dawn where Sarah and Rosanna—while cleaning trenchers or bathing—had often seen them amble along the creek.

The next day, which broke clear and cooler, they breakfasted on what was left of the 'coon meat. The women set to rendering the fat in a kettle for soap while the men readied to leave. Then Jedediah took Sarah inside the cabin. She wrapped her arms around his waist and pressed her cheek into his chest and breathed him in. She squeezed tighter, trembling. Jedediah closed his eyes and touched the nape of her neck. He needed to leave. He had to leave, for he could not bear her body against him like this. Sarah tipped her head back and waited for his kiss. He caressed his brow across her forehead and then they simply softly pressed their lips together until Jedediah moaned and Sarah smiled.

George left his musket, powder and shot and reminded the women how to load and prime. They moved the canoes into a deadfall and all said goodbye. Then the men started for the creek, Jedediah carrying his Brown Bess, both of them wearing packs they'd made of birchbark and leather thongs, their shoes and axes tied to these with willow withes.

They crossed a shallows to the island and then forded to that bottomland Jedediah knew he'd own someday. They reasoned it safest not to have a direct route between their houses—they'd gain the unmapped lands by route of the farther hollow, the one that flanked the lower end of the flat.

The tract moved Jedediah all the more. At its back edge, white and black walnut hugged the bank of a woodland that sloped gently to the sudden ascent of the valley. The stubble of trees bordering the reverting Indian cornfield included fence-worthy locust. Grapes drooped within arm's reach from the shrubs and saplings taking over the field, the middle of this more lately cleared and hardly grown over. And the spring descended the bank and crossed the plot right where the old cabin corner-stones remained.

Like all runs entering the Sinnemahoning Creek, this one flowed not so much through a valley as a boulder-ridden, narrow-bottomed canyon, the stout boles of pines, birch, and oak clutching to walls so steep a man climbing them could touch the ground in front of his nose without bending. The chatter of the water and the sharp scent of damp sandstone drafted through the shadowed hollow. They filled Jedediah's head, they heightened the airy exhilaration of liberty that in this untamed country had been healing his hide and heart, strengthening him to work and now explore—every fall of water a wonder, every passing bird a song, every breath as sweet as a quaff of springwater.

They were alarmed to find a path weaving through the hollow among long-toppled trees, decaying boles higher than their breasts. But there was no print of foot, shoe or moccasin. Two miles on, they saw the first blaze where a steeply ascending side-hollow, known in that country as a draft, split eastward. Jedediah recognized the marking, chest-high in a hemlock, as a tomahawk gouge. It faced the trail, a square carved to its left.

Jedediah pointed his musket. "The blaze says the trail follows that draft."

They lifted their eyes to trace its rise. The ravine was so sharp there was no bottomland, just rock-jumble in the crease, water gushing and splattering through it in white falls. The path was etched along the southern flank. Jedediah knew others such as this, excavated into the detritus of the steeps by travelers over eons setting aside stones, footways no wider than mule trails. Yet dead trees would obstruct the way and they'd have to scale loose, flat stones to get around them.

George nodded. "Steeper grade means we're quicker to the top. I say we go that way."

"But then we're keepin' to a path."

George considered. "Doesn't appear used anymore. With the Indians gone. Trappers maybe."

Jedediah did not argue. He had a notion about this trail. Traveling the backcountry, he'd become aware of an internal compass. Bakeraskin and Tillman had relied on him times they'd gotten lost. Word was that an overland Indian path shortcut the great arc in the West Branch, avoiding the constant river fords and continuing to the Sinnemahone. This sharp turn had that feel about it.

And so they followed that ledge of scree. Treacherous. Of the fallen birches thwarting their progress, they were glad for those few small enough to chop away.

After a mile walking, clambering and clearing, they gained the head of the hollow, a box of a basin scored by springs at two corners and rimmed with a gloomy brow of hemlock and pine.

"I like this," George said as they took off their packs. He nodded where the farther spring broke from the tableland. "We'll look on the flats that way for a plot to clear—away from where that spring seeps through the woods but close enough we can tote water from it at some spot we'll grub for a steady flow." He indicated the hollow behind them. "Once we have the path opened better, we won't be two hours apart."

"Snakes'll be bad up here," Jedediah said.

George nodded. This was snake country for sure. "Just a year," he said, then grinned and winked.

The lowering forest was remarkable in its variety: among tracts of great pines, there abounded hardwoods of beech, yellow poplar, birch, maple, oak, cherry, chestnut. The ground was a dank, mottled mold of leaf-fall and needle droppings where decaying dead boles meandered their travel and sparse ferns and rhododendron made for the only undergrowth.

After two hours reconnoitering, they spied an intrusion of sunlight and pursued it along the faint depression of an underground headspring. Its terminus was a seep matted with willow wisps, a half-acre meadow hemmed by saplings. George took it in and declared this was the place.

"Bear huntin' will be good in these woods," he said. "I saw where they shat. And holla' trees plenty big for them to den in and me to smoke them out. Their meat and hides will get us through winter." He was nodding, his eyes sweeping meadow to woods. "We'll girdle and fell trees in the good soil beyond the head of the break. Half an acre. I'll grub all the rock I can until the ground freezes. Rosanna and me'll plant corn in the spring. It'll give us a little harvest before we move on. Or if we stay longer, we'll have a start on a field."

With no sign or scent of rain, they forewent a temporary lean-to and set to clearing ground at the edge of the meadow for the cabin. They slept that starry night without a fire, the blankets they'd rolled into their packs ineffective against the chill of the highland and the coming of autumn. Jedediah shivered through to morning, unsure of whether from the cold or the wolf howls that ventriloquized about the forest, from near or far he could not tell.

They spent two weeks opening the corn plot and building the home, living on opossums, squirrels, and johnnycakes. They began by girdling the hardwoods they could not manage; this would keep them from leafing next year and so admit the sun. If the couple stayed, they'd burn these on the stump when they dried in afteryears. They felled the others, chopping some of the branches into firewood, arranging the rest into a fence of odd, slanting sections edging the half acre.

On the second day, something peculiar happened. At the edge of the plot, they'd felled a pair of tall, broad-boughed pines. Near noon, when the steely rays of the September sun reached in, Jedediah shouted to George, pointing across the fallen boles. Steam poured like smoke from the forest floor where the break let light shine upon that ancient moist humus for the first time since—who knew? George closed his eyes while he inhaled the mustiness. "God, that's good ground," he said. Then he shook his head and voiced what Jedediah was thinking. "Too damned rocky to bear wheat without a team to grub the deep stones." They stood with their axe heads planted at their feet, handles against their thighs, and watched the vapor rise, Jedediah sensible of an anomaly, of time standing still.

With the smallest timbers, they constructed a cabin of ten feet square, a stick and mud chimney. They daubed the interstices and peeled birchbark for the roof. It was a dim, low-ceilinged den, a bandit's lair, but George proclaimed it satisfactory. A place of his own.

Then at dawn, they descended the unmapped wilderness. Jedediah was hungry and sore of back and shoulder as he placed his feet carefully along the trail lest he stumble on a stone or step on a rattler. Still, he felt a galvanism twitching through his muscles from this ground. The place was fresh and alive in the nose, lush and noble like no other country he'd seen. And though the forest canopy hung heavy and dark, he liked feeling as if his head were hooded and hidden. A man's future here felt as vast as the Sinnemahone. This was where he wanted to be.

The Sinnemahone Country, Lycoming County, Pennsylvania

Jedediah swung out the shutter to find Samson Abel Starret walking with a rifle up the slope, scanning through the trees their little field. The creek was in flood. Potsherds of ice, splintered from winter sheets which lay now invisible in the deep pools, jounced along, sopping up the chocolaty, eddying water, some colliding into a jam at the head of the island, crunching, scraping, the shards nosing, burrowing, lifting the mass near to the height of the sycamores that flailed in the deluge breaching the banks of the bottomlands. Which meant Samson Abel had been walking the woods away from the water and had stumbled onto the canoe. He'd probably looked for them in the fall but from the creek. Damn the flood, Jedediah thought, the warm spell.

Sarah had been stitching buckskin in the light of the open doorway. He told her to run to the unfinished stillhouse before her brother spotted the cabin. Then Jedediah took down the musket, powderhorn and shot pouch from where they hung from a set of buckhorns. He wrapped his leg around the gunstock, poured a measure of powder down the barrel, and pressed a cloth patch and lead ball into the muzzle before sliding his hickory ramrod from its rings and shoving these home. Then, as Samson Abel huffed to the edge of their little level, Jedediah half-cocked the hammer, tapped a dash of powder into the priming pan, and stepped out.

Strange how a man aged not steadily, rather in sporadic and remarkable ebbs, as the mill dam breaches by interval of storm. In the seven months since Jedediah last laid eyes on any of Sarah's half-brothers, Samson Abel had taken that middle-age turn toward looking like a forebear; in this case, his namesake. His hair, longer than Jedediah remembered it, fell now in frosty fetlocks from beneath his floppy-brimmed beaver, parting around his great ears. He seemed more than before to share the elder Starret's warm eyes, incongruous with that warrior's face of furious concavities.

A step out the doorway, Jedediah shouldered his gun. Starret's remained in the crook of his right arm, muzzle just off the ground. He seemed more interested in Jedediah's appearance, eyeing him head to toe.

"You been eatin' bar meat," Samson Abel said. "Look like one. Hairy. Skinny and filthy like you just crawled outta the den." He sniffed. "Goddamn."

All true. Jedediah could even feel against his nose the wild hairs springing from above his lip. His hat had become tight on his head while his wrists were so narrow Sarah could wrap her fingers around them.

Sarah. Samson Abel wouldn't know his sister. She was a ghost of bones, sick all the time, same as Jedediah. The flux. Their gums hurt and bled and their teeth felt wobbly when they chewed. They craved every manner of vegetable. For all they ate was bear meat, but for an occasional opossum or porcupine. Not even fish, what with the ice, not since catching a few trout from the run across the valley during a thaw in February. Deer were scarce; they'd shot only one last fall when they ran crazy with the rut. They'd yet to see an elk. The bullfrogs still hid in their mud lairs.

Their skin was covered in scurf and dirt. And now that the days had warmed, the fleas were busy in the bearskin blankets, chewing at their wrists like moths at the wool. In fitful sleep, Jedediah and Sarah scratched up the prior night's scabs; during the day they bled into their sleeves. The lice seemed to burrow to their brains. They stank of rancid candles and sour smoke and had long ago quit caring.

Jedediah had thought air could never be so harsh as in January, until the first of March when dampness leached to his bones. All he could do to ward the chill was remind himself he was free. And remember the piece across the valley. He leveled the muzzle at Samson Abel's head. Like hell this man would keep that place from him.

Starret chuckled. "Word went 'round you were up here some-where." He glanced into the valley. "A land agent seen you at the fork. Ought to be glad it was me found you first. There's nigh a posse after you and my sister." He pointed at Jedediah. "'Spe-cially you." He looked around. "Where's the other one?"

"Other what?" Jedediah said.

Samson Abel eyed him, ran his hand along the barrel of his rifle to wipe away mud that had splashed from his moccasins. He nodded. "The other man that ran off. The miller."

Jedediah shrugged.

"Sarah," Samson Abel hallooed, looking over the cabin roof. "Come down here. I seen you run up the hill."

"Quiet or I'll shoot," Jedediah said.

Samson Abel ignored him. This time louder: "Father's sickly, gal. It won't be long." He cupped his free hand beside his mouth. "I know you run off 'cause it was too hard on you. I took up Pappy's farm. C'mon home now."

By the time Jedediah had his hammer fully cocked, Samson Abel had raised his rifle. "Stupid-ass fool," he said.

Jedediah steadied the barrel. Upon the report, it was not by pain he knew he'd been shot, rather the sharp blow to his shin that nearly buckled his knee. As Sarah shrieked his name from the stillhouse, the searing set in. He collapsed beside his fallen musket, the trigger of which he'd never had a chance to pull, and seized the shank of his leg, his stocking drenched already in blood. A hot poker had been plunged into him and now it sawed barbs through his flesh. He grunted down to stop his gulping breaths, tried to form a thought, then groped for the musket. But Samson Abel's foot was on it, he who'd already taken out his knife and cut away a strip from the hem of his shirt. He knelt beside Jedediah who swung for his face. Starret caught the fist readily as he would a flipped coin and pinned it beneath his knee.

"You're a idiot," Samson Abel said. He doubled the band of linen and tied it around the leg, blood already blossoming from where it covered the wound. He pressed against the stain and Jedediah shot up, grabbing with his free hand Samson Abel's arm.

"Lay down," Samson Abel said. "You're lucky I know how to shoot. It's through the outside meat a' your leg." He pressed harder and Jedediah howled and fell back. "Grazed the bone," Starret said. He turned to find his sister rounding the cabin, charging him. Starret tucked his chin as she tried to push him away from Jedediah.

"You shot him," she said.

He held her away with an extended arm and a handful of shortgown as he studied her. "Pappy saw the sack a' bones you become, he'd a' shot him in the head." She tried to release his grip, gave up.

"Your fool went to shoot me," Samson Abel said. You ought to be happy I hit where I was aimin'. He ought to be happy for where I aimed."

Jedediah let out a quavering moan. "Get me whiskey," he said.

Starret nodded at this. "And linens." He warned off Sarah, then untied the bandage and peeked beneath, tied it again. "We need to stop this bleedin'," he said.

"I'll kill you," Jedediah said.

"Enough a' you," Samson Abel said. He pulled Jedediah to sitting by the front of his buckskin shirt, a greasy black rag it was, and struck him at the temple with his palm.

He opened his eyes, shivering and parched, apprehending he'd been gripped with the agony even in his insentience, a piercing burn in his calf so intense the source had to be other-worldly. Demon fangs.

The weight of death pressed on the bearskins that covered him. "Whiskey," he called into blackness. He tried to sit and the fiend clenched its teeth. He groaned and felt Sarah moving beside him, leaving this bed they had not shared. He heard her stirring coals, saw a pitchpine splint ignite. She stuck this candlewood into a notch above the hearth, then lit from it a tallow crusie lamp. Returning with the lamp, she set it on a log on-end beside his bed and took his hand as the feeble flame steadied.

"Where is he?" Jedediah said.

She kissed his cheek and felt his forehead. "He's gone for George and then to get help. George and Rosanna will be here in the mornin'"

Jedediah pressed his elbows into the tick, tried to sit. "You told him the way to George's?" The walls of his throat grated as if he'd swallowed emery. "And sent for others? They'll hang me. Damn you, Sarah."

"We need George and Rosanna here until someone can come and mend you. You bled so much." She held his shoulders as he tried to rise again. "Samson Abel's goin' to my cousins in the Muncy hills. He took the canoe and promises it back."

"No."

"Shh. He wishes you no harm, Jedediah. He wants to help. Think of it—he could have forced me away with him."

"He shot me, for God's sake."

She closed her eyes a moment. "Why would a man who shot someone admit it unless he means well?"

He woke thinking he was consumed in hellfire, but instead found the wrath of God. Or at least its countenance. Israel Tuke, his scowl wreathed by the tilted, broad brim of his hat and set upon a fresh cravat, leaned over Jedediah. The eyes were cold and leaden as thunderclouds. He reached beneath the bearskins, his fingers slinking along Jedediah's body, and probed under the dressing. Jedediah stiffened, the hand a knife of ice against the fire of the wound.

"He'll live," Tuke said in the tone Jedediah recalled from the courtroom, temperate and firm, indisputable. Then he realized other faces peering down. He could not hold his eyes long enough to recognize them. "A day or two, anyway," Tuke said. "Unless thou strips me the bark of slippery elm and boil and mash it. And find me maggots. Leave out rancid flesh if thou has to. I need them soon. Then we'll see whether the leg lasts or I cut it off. Is there a saw?"

Jedediah recoiled into his tick. And then came another voice, a boyish tone to this one, which he could not quite put a name to. "Israel, I would never question your skill as an animal doctor. But perhaps there are different considerations for a person."

Tuke turned and Jedediah strained to pick the man from the figures that had dispersed into the dim distance. There was George, tall and straight and broad-shouldered despite the winter they'd endured. Rosanna beside him. And Sarah. He made out curled locks on the last person, a proud eagle's nose. The one who'd spoken—Caspar Roan, the newspaperman.

Tuke's reared chin might have been a cudgel as he faced Roan; everyone leaned away.

"May I at least give him the laudanum?" Roan said.

The tall hat wagged. "Not until thou finds me maggots." He glanced at Jedediah who could not imagine why he wanted maggots. "For that, he'll need laudanum—it's an unnatural thing, repugnant to a man's body and mind."

He lay four days in a stupor prescribed by Tuke, taking doses of that tincture of opium when Sarah and Rosanna woke him to spoon-feed broth and change the clothes he soiled. He learned later the maggots had been easy to find—the blue flies had emerged with the thaw and the crows had yet to pick away the pile of raccoon and opossum innards Jedediah discarded by the creek. George had suspended a blanket from the loft, shielding Jedediah's exposed lower half from his eyes. Each sup of medicine soothed his stomach and made him drunk until he drifted to sleep only to come-to half-conscious, half in a maudlin nightmare in which a pulsing swarm of toothed creatures devoured his leg in mad nibbles. He screamed or so he thought, his skull going numb from trying to make sound. He strained to scratch, to dig his nails into the flesh of that itching and seething limb; yet no matter how intently he willed his arms to move, they lay invalid at his sides. And then he'd remember George tying them to the bedframe.

He woke to find Israel Tuke and Caspar Roan returned, the cabin alive with the light of their lamps and with blazing pitchpine splinters stuck in the fireplace jambs, with murmur, too, including George's deep whispers; it was a comfort just knowing he was still there. The blanket had been taken down and while Roan held aloft Jedediah's calf, Tuke wiped the wound with linen, entrance and exit. On the bed stood a pail into which Tuke, using the blade of his folding penny knife, scraped the squirming larvae from the cloth, sour rot in the air. And yet the misery in Jedediah's leg had taken a turn, no longer a furious, needling burn, but a rawness he knew without contemplating was the hurt of an injury on the mend.

He called for Sarah, who came and took his hand. She wore a new shortgown and petticoat of linsey-woolsey instead of her filthy shift and coat. And so he knew the creek was no longer in flood, for Roan and Tuke had brought goods.

Tuke placed the pail beneath the leg while Roan lifted it higher. Each side of the wound was a red mass, full and sore with the movement, but bearable. George stepped alongside Tuke and handed him a whiskey jug. Jedediah reached for it but Tuke poured the spirit over the entrance wound—he might have been slicing skin away with his knife. Jedediah shot upright and George held down his arms as Tuke poured whiskey onto another rag and wiped the calf where the bullet had left him.

"Thou can keep the leg now," Tuke said, then pulled away the bucket and applied a fresh linen. "I needn't even stitch it."

Jedediah sat at the edge of his bed and devoured jerked deer meat and ash bread from a platter of hickory bark—the first wheat he'd eaten since their flight. Roan had brought ground coffee, too, Jedediah's piping hot cup as aromatic as the oily meat of a roasted chestnut.

He tried crutches George had made of dogwood, but was so lightheaded he needed help going outside to relieve himself. It was a warm dusk as he leaned alone against a hemlock, the valley a-gabble with the peeping and moaning of frogs; the fresh air was a balm in his lungs.

Back inside he wanted to sit at the table. He took a stool, extending his leg before him; it throbbed from his having moved. Sarah knelt beside him, bathed and not so thin anymore, the company stepping to logs on-end around the table. Rosanna, too, wore new clothes, stern as always, silent. Yet there was anticipation in her stare, same as in the eyes of all the others.

"The lot of us have to talk," Sarah said.

Jedediah shook his head up and down. "Sure do. About putting your brother in gaol."

"In fact," Caspar Roan said, "he and her other brothers have to do with this. But we'll come around to them."

Jedediah felt strength from the food seeping into his arms, his mind, the fog lifting. Let them talk.

Sarah eased onto her haunches. She glanced at Rosanna, then watched the dirt floor. "We can get married. Now. In the Quaker fashion. We don't need a justice or a preacher, just two witnesses, and we have them here." She looked up at Israel Tuke who lowered beneath the brim of his thimble-like hat, hand clinching the breast of his waistcoat. He nodded.

But Jedediah remained silent, and Caspar Roan, pressing his chest into the table, spoke out. "I understand your concern," he said. "Trust us, a self-uniting marriage—a Quaker marriage—is as old and legal in Pennsylvania as vows before a justice. And we're more than willing witnesses, aren't we Israel?"

Tuke said yes by closing his eyes a second, and Jedediah saw a man determined to make a point with this wedding. Damn them. His indenture remained and they'd agreed to wait. He'd had a long time before he had to worry about this.

Roan leaned back and studied Jedediah, head tilted. He put a hand on the table. "It's unnecessary, but I'll even record the license with the county. I'm prothonotary now. Would that satisfy you?"

But for the soft crackles and sighs of green wood smoldering in the fireplace, the room was silent. The wavering illumination from the pitchpine splinters pulsed upon the walls like sheet lightning, Jedediah's heart pounding in accompaniment. George tapped Casper Roan on the shoulder. "I think it's the other thing botherin' him," he said.

"Of course," Roan said. "I should have begun there." He tucked his chin into his cravat a moment. "I'm sure it wouldn't surprise you that Peter Bakeraskin posted a reward for your capture. He and Thomas Tillman searched for you themselves until the snows came. They had decided you went upriver after nobody the other way reported seeing you. We know their moves because a group called the Friend's Committee On Protecting

Black People kept an eye on them. I'm sure you suspected someone was watching out for you."

"I didn't ask nobody for that," Jedediah said.

"We wanted only to help," Roan said. "Thomas Tillman is bitter." He paused, glanced at Sarah. "I fear a seed of vengeance
has sprouted in his craw. You were in more danger by the day.
Rosanna's father tried to send the Farleigh boys after her. But
they were too aggrieved to do it, so he went to the sheriff—he
was calling up deputies when I warned him that Rosanna is
twenty years of age. When we learned a surveyor had seen you
on the Sinnemahone while Peter Bakeraskin was already
searching this country, we let out a rumor you'd fled from here
and gone far up the West Branch."

Jedediah adjusted his leg. The throbbing was subsiding, and
though his frustration at being backed into a corner bloated his
mind nearly to bursting, he could concentrate. What if they
hadn't watched out for him? No, they would not make him answer that.

"And so," Roan said, "I've come to the matter that will ease
your worries. The moment Judge Hepburn and Commissioner
Burrows learned you'd violated their ruling, they too went to the
sheriff. But as it happens, when he stopped by the new prothonotary's office to see the order, it could not be found." Roan
searched the rafters. "It must never have existed." And then
back to Jedediah: "You are free of any indenture and at liberty
to marry."

Sarah slid her arms around Jedediah's waist. But he could
not return the embrace, could not move for feeling a snare had
been set for him. She let go.

Israel Tuke glared at Jedediah. He thumped the table. "God
sees all," he said. "All." He looked from Jedediah to George and
Rosanna. "Marry, or it is debauchery."

Sarah raised herself onto her knees, facing Jedediah. "There's
somethin' else you need to know. Two of my brothers are comin'
to live near here. They'll be a great help to us."

Jedediah started up, stopped when the fire set into his leg.
"Like hell," he said.

"Not that brother," Roan said. "Hear her out."

He settled back onto the stool and let her go on.

"My brothers by my father's place," Sarah said, "want to keep ahead of settlers. William will come here and start a farm at the first fork while Samson Abel's eldest son moves from the Monseytown flats to take over William's place. Samson Abel and his wife will also leave the Flats. The will live with my father."

Jedediah was shaking his head no.

"Hear her," Israel Tuke said.

"The younger of Samson Abel's sons is takin' the other farm near my father, the one Stephen lives on. But Stephen is not the second brother comin' here—he's claimed land on a great hickory flats above the West Branch, far upriver. It's my youngest brother, Benjamin. He's returned from the Ohio country. He is a hunter and wants to come to the Sinnemahone, for it is a wilderness, but one where he can keep close to a brother. Since he needs only a little piece, he'll build a cabin on the next bottom downstream." She caught herself. "The one on this side, not across."

She leaned back from him, ever so slightly, but away. "Jedediah, you won't be able to farm or hunt on that leg for a year. We need my brothers. They're willin' to help."

"A Starret tried to kill me," Jedediah said. But when all eyes fell from him, he realized they knew better.

"We need to marry before they come," Sarah said. "They'll not move here with a scandal on the family."

The room had dimmed, the candlewood smoldering. Sarah waited while Rosanna went to the fireplace, lit two more splints, and returned to her log at the table.

"There's something else," Sarah said. "I have to see my father."

"Hell no. You promised."

"He is dying," Sarah said. "His last thought cannot be that I would not come to him." She closed her eyes a moment, linked her fingers. "But I will not go until I am married to you. I must first make my vow. Then there aren't no manner of leaving you, no matter where I go or what happens."

* * *

* * *

Jedediah lay in his bed until the fire died such that he could hardly see George and Rosanna beneath a bearskin at the hearth. Bet they didn't wait, he thought. Above him in the loft, Sarah drew the widely intermittent breaths of deep sleep. He raised himself to sitting and his gut roiled from the after-effects of laudanum.

The flagon by the door was distinguishable by a faint luster where the embers reflected upon its leaden glaze. He lowered himself off the bed and crawled to the whiskey. He slid back the Indian bar and pushed on the door, and though it stuttered and screeched against its sill, no one called out. Outside with the jug, Jedediah squinted over at the lean-to he'd left standing, Roan and Tuke motionless in the moonlight beneath their blankets. He continued on all fours to the lip of the little flat, rolled onto his hip, dragged his leg around, and sat with the jug between his thighs. He shivered and wished for a bearskin, sucked at the flagon, the whiskey roaring through his belly like a fireball with a tail of sparks. The leg felt better already.

By benefit of the bright gibbous moon, which was entangled in the limbs of upvalley oaks, glimpses of the creek glimmered like quicksilver along the valley floor. Jedediah traced the course best he could through the trees until he beheld a pale opening downstream along the far bank—the reverting field he would have someday. By God.

Once he'd drank enough to do it, he raised his eyes across the valley. South. Through thin upper tree limbs, he marked the shoulder of the far ridge cutting crisply into the pewter heavens. He concentrated on that horizon. After his eyes adjusted to the luciferous sky, the feeblest wink of a southern star broke through. No, not feeble; brilliant enough to outshine the moonlight. It flickered, it faded. It brightened. He wanted it to go away.

Damn the star. Damn the mess white men made even of freedom.

He raised the jug and guzzled. But he did not take his eyes off that point of light.

As a little boy, what he'd known of twilight had trickled through cracks between wallboards in the loft where he lay on his pallet, a time of trusty sounds: birds twittering out nest songs; the sigh of dirt turning against wooden shovels as the slaves worked in the garden, their songs a sadness that soothed. Night came on smoother than the velvet curtains of the big house. It was transport to sweet slumber, to dreams and waking to a new day when even work, for a while, was a kind of play where he could breathe again the comfort-smell of fresh earth upon each tug of the hoe, chase butterflies and hopping toads, run off to toss a line into the murky mystery of a fishing hole.

When was it that night went brittle, a territory of the mind where stale wishes that had hardened into fears and worries, jagged and cold like hoarfrost, began crumbling and falling in an endless spate? They mounted as he lay wanting sleep; they eclipsed all thoughts but those of the anger and hate by which he tried frantically to disentangle the rubble, to arrange it into sallies he might one day launch. Such scheming was his only comfort, could ease him into the delirium that was as close as he came to sleep anymore.

A question struck him. He almost said it aloud to that southern star. If he'd never known her, would it be like this?

He'd drained the jug to where the whiskey spilled down his chin as he drank—for want of tilting his eyes back from that star—and soaked the front of his shirt. Not until dawn blanched an arc of eastern sky and the songbirds stirred did Jedediah lower his gaze. He stretched his neck this way and that and nearly toppled, then shot a glance back at the lean-to where Israel Tuke sat coatless, his shirt drawing the new light of the day. That look of wrath engulfed Jedediah. How long had he been watching?

"What have you done?" Sarah said when she came to him where he'd collapsed pulling himself to the cabin. He lifted his head but hardly recognized her, for she wore her mother's dress and a new cap and he could not keep his eyes from crossing, the world a whirligig.

Sarah stooped to look into his eyes, pulled twigs and leaves from his beard. She turned toward the lean-to. Jedediah started looking that way but stopped himself as the distance only sped the spin of the earth.

"Help me get him to the spring," Sarah said. Then the shadows of Caspar Roan and Israel Tuke were upon Jedediah and billows of the liquor lapped at his gut.

As they dragged him, Jedediah retched out clear, fruity-smelling fluid. Then coughing up gruelly phlegm that stuck in his beard, he cursed their poisoned whiskey and called them sons of bitches.

They plunged his head into the pool of the spring, then stripped his filthy shirt, which Israel Tuke ordered burned.

Inside, the door and window shutter opened to the warming day, they put him into a new linen shirt and set him on a log where he slouched into the table. He buried his forehead in the crook of his arm and shivered as an icy headache set in, even as his leg was afire.

"We'll come back another time," Caspar Roan said. "We have work to tend to."

"I'll not wait," Rosanna said. "And Sarah needs to go to her father."

Jedediah raised his head. They all watched him, Sarah crouching by the fireplace.

Israel Tuke stepped to the table. "Girl," he said, "come here and make thy vow."

She watched Jedediah, waited.

"Bid her," Tuke said.

Jedediah turned up his hands where they lay on the table. He nodded, and Sarah came and stood beside him.

"Be on with it," Tuke said.

He shut his mind to it all the best he could and used the table to lift himself onto his good leg. At this, Caspar Roan ran to a satchel in the corner and brought two rolled papers, a quill, and a corked jar of ink.

"Say thou takes the other," Tuke said. "That thou is free to do so. Forever in the eyes of God and the laws of the Commonwealth. Go on," he said. "Each in thine own words."

Sarah bent and looked up at Jedediah, his head bowed. She took his hand and squeezed it. "You first," she whispered. "I want to know you're sure." She smiled. "I love you, Jedediah."

"I can't remember all a' what he said."

"Say thou wants to be her husband," Tuke said. "And that thou does it freely."

Caspar Roan had taken a seat at the table and inked his quill.

Jedediah closed his eyes, his palm sweaty in Sarah's hand. "I take Sarah for my wife," he said.

"And thou is free to do so?" Israel Tuke said. "Tell her."

He opened his eyes and nodded at Caspar Roan, who dipped the quill, having written what had been said so far. "He already told her," Jedediah said. "He said that indenture was gone."

"And nothing else constrains thee?" Tuke said.

Jedediah glanced out the doorway. A raucous cawing of crows accompanied wild March winds huffing warm and heavy against the treetops, scent of creek water and earth breezing into the cabin and mixing mustily with the stink of deer fat burning in the lamps. He shook his head. "There aren't nothin' else to stop me from marryin'," he said.

And so Sarah, in her mother's wrinkled cotton dress and a new ruffled mob cap, a band of white ribbon wrapped around the crown, looked into Jedediah's eyes on this Friday, the ninth of March, 1804, and said she took him with all her heart and was free and pleased to do so. Caspar Roan finished the document, then drew up another as George and Rosanna made their vows. Roan and Israel Tuke added their signatures as witnesses, and the quill was passed among the brides and grooms. Rosanna Sharpe and Sarah James signed their respective covenants, then George marked an X beside Rosanna's name. Jedediah took the quill last. His hand was shaking; he told himself it was the effect of whiskey. And as he made his mark, more a wobbly christcross than an X, he wondered how he could feel both joined and separated at the same time.

A child was born to each couple before the year was out, the wife of William Starret delivering Sarah's baby, George himself mid-wifing Rosanna in their own little hovel during a blizzard just three days later. Jedediah asked Sarah that they name their son George. George and Rosanna called their daughter Rosa.

Confined to his cabin in the depths of another sharply cold winter, but bolstered by flour and stores of pumpkins, apples and potatoes shared by the neighboring Starrets, Jedediah learned the bliss of fatherhood. The greatest surprise was the satisfaction of simply holding a baby, a little person of his own flesh looking back awestruck.

Jedediah's cheer uplifted Sarah, which was much to say, for even in uncertain times she maintained ease and optimism. She sang and smiled and spoke of orchards and the field of flax she'd grow, buoyant in Jedediah's pleasure as he lay on a bearskin before the fire playing with his little boy. Her papery skin was not so pale now, and thanks to the provisions, rich milk engorged her breasts and plumped the baby despite the grip of winter. When she was ready—Jedediah impatient, having pestered for a month—he found her aroused and hungry, his joy her joy.

Sarah was showing with child again by spring. And as the valley went mild and shrilled with frogs peeping along the creek, Jedediah realized he himself had warmed—to his brothers-in-law. When they arrived last April, he would not see them. They gave him room. They cleared their pieces and built their cabins without what help a man on the mend might give, asking only that Sarah visit every few weeks when they transported goods from William's former farm to the new one. They sent William's wife, Mary, to beckon Sarah, Jedediah watching first from the doorstep where he whittled some toy, then, by last June, from their little field—his leg healed enough to bear labor part of the day. Sarah took the path along the creek or, when the load was large, waded with a canoe. She returned not just with comestibles, but piglets, linen, tools and redware, pullets and apple seedlings—these, Jedediah planted across the creek. He was privately pleased with the advantages the deliveries brought, as he was when Mary inquired through Sarah for his opinion on an overland route whereby her husband could more easily bring a horse, eventually a cow, oxen and sheep. And now there was the luxury of Sarah's books, which in addition to her Bible, she read aloud by the fire or where they sat on logs outside the doorway at dusk. He always asked for his favorite, the one where Crusoe was lord of his own island. Jedediah never could understand why he left that place.

One afternoon the previous July, while Jedediah knelt weeding potatoes, he watched Mary Starret meet Sarah in front of the cabin. Sarah fell to her knees before her sister-in-law, and so Jedediah knew she'd just learned that her father had died.

He limped over, drew Sarah to her feet, and held her as she sobbed.

When Mary disappeared toward the creek, Sarah said, "At least I went to him and tried to make my peace."

Through openings among the treetops, Jedediah watched a procession of crows flit down the valley, sunlight skimming blue against their flapping wings. "I suppose you'll go for the burying," he said.

Sarah drew back from him, wiped her nose and nodded. "And I don't expect you to come, Jedediah. I know you don't want to be around Samson Abel. Though he means you no harm."

"I don't give a damn about him," Jedediah said.

He weighed it. Told himself to do right by his wife, resisted. Until he realized Peter and Cornelia Bakeraskin would be within sight of her. Thomas Tillman. His blood burned at his temples. "I'll go," he said.

She summoned a faint smile of gratitude. "William passed word there'll be a little money," she said. "I want to buy a cow.

Next spring. We'll want for milk after I wean the child. I'd like a butter churn, too."

Jedediah strained his eyes into the valley until he found an opening to that bottomland he'd have. "I'm needin' some copper for a bigger still. We'll put rye in the ground next year—when this leg's healed to where I can go across the creek every day to work our new place."

Jedediah would not hear of staying at her father's place, considering Samson Abel lived there now. So they waited to depart in their canoe until the next morning, the day of burial.

The riverbank before the Starret farm was strewn with canoes. Jedediah tarried by the water while Sarah, already plump of belly and wearing a clean linen petticoat and shortgown, ran toward the house where her father lay in state. A crowd on the porch parted for her. When they saw her gravity, they turned their heads to where she'd come from.

Sarah returned, tears drying on her cheeks in the sharp midday sunshine. "The grave is ready up back. They waited on us. Can you come now?"

Hand in hand, they went and stood in the yard before the house. With Samson Abel leading, the five brothers carried the pine box through the crowd, which couldn't seem to decide whether to watch the coffin or the couple.

Shielding his eyes against the sunlight, Jedediah soon made out the faces of those on the porch who watched him alone: Peter Bakeraskin, gray cravat up to his side whiskers; Cornelia, looking more like her sour apple of a mother; and Thomas Tillman, wigged—the fool—squinting through his spectacles as his eyes shifted to rove Sarah's belly.

Jedediah recognized former neighbors coming out the door; he'd helped build their cabins and stables, delivered their whiskey. In the perimeter, old soldiers leaned on porch rails. They held military coats, some drab, some blue, all with bright buttons, and they wore hats of the old styles, a few tricorned. These men, with the keen warrior's eyes he'd known in Samson Starret, glanced only. But however brief the exchange, Jedediah felt them falter on that impossible kinship. The riddle.

He followed Sarah as she fell in with her sisters behind the coffin, a minister with his Bible and the others bringing up the rear as the procession rounded the house.

When they reached the grave, dug on a rise at the back edge of a mown hayfield, the brothers lowered the coffin with ropes. The minister made his way into the circle and read:

He cometh up, and is cut down, like a flower; he fleeth as it were a shadow, and never ...

As Sarah squeezed Jedediah's arm, he held his hat at his waist and watched the ground, ignoring who might be in his periphery.

The minister finished and stepped away. Samson Abel sank a spade into the mound of earth, Sarah shuddering as the first shovelful fell upon the coffin. And so continued the *swish-thump, swish-thump* as the brothers joined in with their shovels and all the onlookers but family left.

When her brothers finished, Sarah let go of Jedediah's arm. "Go to the house with me," she said, and they turned and started away. But as they descended the slope, they saw the Bakeraskins and Thomas Tillman waiting at the back corner of the house.

"They wouldn't dare, here and now," Sarah said, and took Jedediah's sleeve, trying to urge him along as he slowed his pace and the rest of the family moved well past them.

But they did dare. As Sarah led Jedediah along the side yard, Cornelia called out, "Thieving nigger," the veterans stretching their necks to watch from the porch where they'd returned to lean on the rail.

Sarah kept walking, still gripping Jedediah's sleeve. They were near the porch when Bakeraskin called out, "They sold the wench south."

Jedediah halted. He went stiff as rawhide.

Sarah looked back, then watched Jedediah. "What is it?" she whispered.

Jedediah turned to find Bakeraskin rushing ahead of the other two.

"She went well smoked," Bakeraskin said, stopping within arm's reach. "She went well used. Old Nathan Shivelley wrote me. Says she's quite the minx."

Jedediah squeezed shut his eyes. Her name crawled into his throat, burned like the brash. He swallowed it back before it came out and it went down rough as gravel, caught in his craw. He forced open his eyes.

Cornelia stepped alongside Bakeraskin. "You've every right to seize him, Peter. He robbed us." Her lips and nose went a-flutter and it seemed for a moment she might not master them. "He took our things, he stole himself." She flapped a hand. "Take him, for God's sake. He's yours. There are no Caspar Roans or Israel Tukes to make a fool of you." And at this, Peter Bakeraskin snatched a handful of Jedediah's shirt.

"Let go of my husband," Sarah said. "Leave this property."

"Husband?" Cornelia said. "Husband, indeed—of a wanton slut."

In the silence that followed Sarah slapping Cornelia, silence utter but for birdsong snipping at the calm valley air, they all turned to the metallic click of a rifle cocking. Samson Abel stood beside the porch, the venerable veterans appraising the piece in his hands. He leveled the gun on Peter Bakeraskin. "You get outta here you son-of-a-bitch." He shifted the muzzle toward Tillman. "Either a' you come 'round my brother-in-law agin, I'll plant a ball a' lead 'tween your eyes. One or the other or both," and he waved the gun between them.

Awash in well whippings and smokehouses and lovers cut asunder, Jedediah grabbed Bakeraskin's wrist and removed his hand from his shirt, then twisted Bakeraskin's arm until he fell to his knees. It may have only been for the moment, but he owned his former master while he held him thus, and Jedediah liked how that made him feel. This must be freedom, he thought, this was why he'd determined to be a man who owned things.

Bending, still clutching the wrist, Jedediah moved around Bakeraskin, pulling his arm behind his back near to dislodging it from his shoulder.

And even at that, even with a rifle aimed at her husband, Cornelia railed in shrieks against wastelands and negroes and ungentlemanly husbands who could tame neither.

Jedediah pushed Bakeraskin downward and with his other hand at the base of his skull drove his nose into the dirt of the yard until he cried out for the pain. He coughed and spat out that sandy loam and begged that Jedediah stop, that he spare his arm, for God's sake. And Jedediah never felt so free.

Cornelia lost her wind, giving way to the veterans on the porch commenting on this extraordinary event, some cackling, "Say what?"—hard of hearing as they were from the boom of cannon and rifle.

Samson Abel waived the muzzle at the Bakeraskins and Thomas Tillman. "Outta here."

Jedediah wrenched Bakeraskin's forearm until the elbow was ready to snap loose as the green limb from the sapling, then pulled him to kneeling, let go and spat on the ground. Bakeraskin, sniveling and limp-armed, rose and walked to his hat, chicken dung smeared among the buttons of his plum, short-waisted coat.

But that was in the past. The birth of little George had washed away Sarah's melancholy along with her questions about Jedediah's exchange with the Bakeraskins, her content-ment only increasing with the second pregnancy.

By the end of the July before the second child, they'd pulled flax from the half-acre Sarah had planted along the rill on the piece across the creek. Like the Sharpes, they had at their own place a little field of ripening corn, while Jedediah had put in some rye near the flax and was already distilling whiskey from it.

For the benefit of both families and the neighboring Starrets, George had constructed a mechanical hominy block at the foot of the James property, its mortar a hole he burned into a log he placed beneath the springy bough of a pine, the sweep on which rode the pestle. This he fashioned from a round of hickory through which he bored two holes, the lower to hold a dowel— the handle by which the person would stroke the pestle—the other to receive the end of the pine branch. In place of a bolting cloth, George made a sifter from deerskin in a state of parchment, sewing this to a wooden hoop and perforating holes with a hot wire.

Upon completing the hominy block, George announced plans to establish a mill. He'd start with a quern near the mouth of some fast stream beside which he'd then build a tub mill, fashioning the stones himself. But it would have to be down in the country of the West Branch, where there'd be more customers.

The news fell heavily on Jedediah. He wondered how he'd have gotten by without George—not just because of his generosity and wisdom through the difficulties of building and growing a back-country farm, in facing catastrophes of weather and famine, but because the diversion of his company was Jedediah's only comfort against some new, nagging need to keep watch over his shoulder, a wish to see past the bends in the creek, behind every tree.

Curiosity led Jedediah to speaking with his neighboring brothers-in-law. Under pretense of fishing, he'd watched their improvements take shape. William and family's place along the first fork aspired to a full farm with its crop of children and corn, an orchard, pasture for sheep, even a little wheat. And only a five-minute canoe-ride downstream, at the mouth of a brook called among the trappers Mantuer's Run—though no one knew anymore who Mantuer had been—Benjamin the hunter built his small bachelor cabin between a garden and corn-plot.

Jedediah noted their manner of clearing fields and making fences, the construction of their cabins. He'd waved to them in June. And now, September, the brothers, where they worked together at one or the other homesteads, would come to the creek, inquire on his crops, the baby, the forthcoming child.

During pauses in their conversations, they stared off at the water, chewing the quandary of this brother-in-law. At the end of October, after the son he named Jedediah Junior was born and it came time to ask his question—a favor—Jedediah saw that through their deliberations, the brothers had rested on looking beyond the nonsense. Part of this was necessity—

survival on the frontier called for blind brotherhood. It allowed with only a little disapproval such marriages; there was plenty else to occupy the mind. Besides, what was the alternative? Thomas Tillman, whom the Starret brothers detested?

Jedediah started with William where he bailed water from a saw pit beside the sheep fold he was building. It was a damp day following a week of rain, low, lacy clouds racing over the valley. Little Starret boys and girls in chemises of linsey-woolsey peeped out from the writhing roots of stumps small enough to have been grubbed and dragged and turned on their sides for a fence to keep the cow and hogs from the crops, maybe the wolves from the hogs.

William lifted his head where he bent knee-deep in the muddy water.

"I want to raise a new place," Jedediah said. "Bigger."

Like his brothers and father, William was a mule of a man, big of shoulder and hand, long of features, deliberate and patient in deed. At last, he ascended his ladder, bare-footed, breeches rolled to his thighs. "Family's growin," he said, and stepped to Jedediah. "Aren't hardly space there for fields, a hillside."

Jedediah shrugged. Let them account for the move as they wished.

"I 'spect you mean the place downstream from you," William said, "on the other side. You got a claim on't? Warrant?" He dried his hands on his shirt. "I wondered at settlin' that piece myself. But seen it's been improved."

"Don't need no claim," Jedediah said. "I have a summer's worth of occupyin' it with Sarah's flax field, an orchard planted already. That starts my right to it over anyone tries to get it. Or anyone that left." He took in William's cabin and stable, the farm plot he'd hacked out of the forest. "I'm wantin' a big lay. Bigger'n this. A barn and twenty acres cleared. Hmm."

William looked past Jedediah, up the valley of the first fork. His answer had a residue of reluctance, and so Jedediah supposed he thought the idea unwise, and he did not like that. "I'll help raise your cabin," William said. "And you'll have use of my horse for clearin' and pullin'." He narrowed his eyes at Jedediah.

"But you need to find the story on that land. You need to get a claim on it by the law, in the daylight. I seen trouble boil right outta the ground when more'n one man fixed his head on the same piece."

Later that day, Benjamin, with a shrug, agreed to help Jedediah. He echoed William's warning, however—Benjamin's more a matter of commiseration, adding: "Man can't keep ahead of meddlers no-how, no matter how far he roves. Bastards find him. Trouble him with particulars. Details. Horseshit." He spat and looked toward the far ridge, the deep woods he preferred. The hunter.

By blazes he found on trees, Jedediah decided he owned not only the flatland between the twin streams, but the sloped step of woods above it, and the steep forest of great pines clear to the brow of the ridge.

He wanted for a house a story-and-half, 24-feet square with a roof of red oak shingles and puncheons under their feet. A foundation of stonework to keep the bottom rounds a foot off the ground. Every log oak. To last. A bottle-glass window, maybe two. The front eave extended for a porch. From which he'd look out at his piece.

Sarah merely nodded as he went on with his plans, a reserve and caution about her he resented. The Starret brothers approved of the foundation but complained of the weight of oak logs and warned against the upper half-story. "Wouldn't call attention," William said, shaking his head the windy Hallowmas they met at the property. Benjamin agreed. "A simple cockloft cabin'll be outta sight of the creek. 'Sides, don't spend too much'a yourself buildin' a place some land hog might steal."

Jedediah ignored them, pointed up at the bench of woods, the place from which the little rill beside the cabin site seeped. "I'll want a spring and a springhouse up there. We'll cut a trail to it crosswise up the bank." Turning the other way, he said, "The barn'll go between the house and the creek."

But William was shaking his head. "Call it a stable, 'cause that's what we're givin' a hand in buildin'. A man needs to lay out his farm small pieces at a time. Else it falls in on itself. Or eats him alive."

While the weather held, Jedediah, George, and the Starrets laid the stones for the house and barn—a barn in Jedediah's estimation, for he'd prevailed on them to enlarge the structure enough for a main bay with stalls and a mow to each side, one end for a horse or two, the other for a cow. They felled and skidded timbers and dug a jakes and sawpit. Then they whipsawed walnut boards for the floor and the frames of windows and doors.

When the others were occupied on their own places, Jedediah split shingles. In the woods above the site of the home, he dug his spring in a low spot where the subterranean source waters of the rill coursed, then he excavated a groundwork around it for the springhouse. Farther up, where a trough in the forest floor terminated against the sharp rise of the valley wall, he grubbed stones for another spring. A pool bubbled before him—his cooling and wort water. Nearby, he set four rocks as the corners of his stillhouse.

The bitter north winds set in by Christmas, as did the ice sheets upon the creek and the driving snows across the landscape. Work on the place ceased, though Jedediah's plans and the disquiet of his mind to be there only festered.

With neighbors to visit and cousins for little George to play with came both relief from their near-hibernation, and constant sickness. Someone that winter was always down with catarrh or influenza, little George's face constantly in snot, Jedediah Junior's infant lungs rattling through the night. Sarah fretted and cried in his weakest moments, and the several times the baby went listless, Jedediah reached hysteria, pounding the walls of the cabin. Yet the child prevailed.

Despite the sickness, Jedediah would prize those winter months of early 1806 as an interlude between calamitous times. He would recall moments of bliss as he basked in the company of a little tumbling brood and a wife who adored them all.

In April, upon completing the house, they agreed to sell their other place for $200 to a man William recommended. Wash Bartholomew, with his wife and aging father—a veteran of the revolt—wanted to move from their piece at the Monseytown flats, weary of sharing it with Wash's drunken brother. The Jameses moved across the creek in May, Sarah again in the bloom of pregnancy, their corn planted, flax growing, the house grand and aromatic of the musk of fresh-cut logs. Though she did not remark on the luxury of a larger home, Sarah admitted the convenience of a wooden floor. "Yes, it was a trouble to pack and sweep the dirt," she said.

Jedediah went right to finishing his stillhouse, and as soon as the Starret brothers harvested rye, they brought it to him for whiskey. They, along with George when there was moon enough to light his way home, helped Jedediah build the barn after their own work. At twilight, they sat on porch benches sipping whiskey and smoking pipes of the tobacco William shared, their feet propped on the railing of locust.

In August, just before the James's third son, Jacob, was born, Benjamin delivered Sarah's cow by way of the new Ellicott road, cut through the wilderness by the Holland Land Company to make accessible its remote tracts to the north. More a bridle path, it spanned the far top to bypass the tortuous narrows of the creek, descending then a mountain run and crossing the first fork just upstream of William's place.

A person on the Sinnemahone was forever scratching at the body or swatting at mosquitoes and flies. More vexing were the wrist-nipping punkies, miasmas of them always about the head, nettling at the temple.

Rattlesnakes descended through the sultry months. The more of them Jedediah killed, the more he found beneath the porch, sprawled upon rock piles in the field, coiled in tall grass near the woods edges. He took vengeance butchering them and having Sarah, who feared the children being bitten, stew their pairs of white, stave-like flesh.

By fall, the Jameses had an out-and-out farm; corn, rye, turnips, a few melon plants. A hoe would not do to plow anymore, for they'd cleared the brush from almost all of Jedediah's desired 20 acres and felled or girdled the sparse river birch, oak and sycamore upon them. With plenty more grassy bottomland for pasture, they could have a mule or horse—no more borrowing the Starret's. They'd need then a harness and saddle, a shovel plow for the first settler's field, another with a strong iron colter for the land newly cleared. A good stumpland harrow. Better scythes and sickles. Other wares from a cooper and a black-smith.

The money left of Sarah's inheritance and the sale of the other place would only go so far; it was time to buy his larger still.

He could not raise enough rye to run a whiskey business, nor could he cut into the corn he planted for his family. Yet without an operation, he had no whiskey to barter for these or for a supply of flagons and kilderkins.

In his days trading for Peter Bakeraskin's flour and rye, Jedediah had mastered moving logs down the West Branch. Barefooted, holding a long hickory pole across his waist, he could steer a pine around or through rapids by leaning or, in running fore and aft, adjusting his weight upon the log, all the while handling the rope of a canoe.

Jedediah worried that the slight limp of his leg injury might impair him in floating timbers. So, one day in late October he felled and made a saw log of a pine at a narrows downstream of his place. With lever poles, he rolled it into the water, hopped aboard, and as sure-footed as a cat, steered the log around a bend and through a chute where the creek congested at one side of the round island. He went ashore and ran home, returning in his canoe with a sack of jerked deer meat and johnnycakes, a blanket, his musket, and all the money.

He camped that night at the mouth of a stream just upriver from Williamsport, in sight of the first sawmill he'd spotted from the water. But in the morning, the proprietor, an old man with the stare of a goshawk, was already shaking his head when Jedediah asked if he wanted for a straight and sound pine. "I saw my customer's logs," he said. "Don't pay for timber."

"I'd take rye for it," Jedediah said.

The old man spat on the puncheons of his mill floor. "Get outta here," he said.

Beyond Williamsport, a saw birthing off boards sent screeches and groans across the valley. The sawmill sat along a stony brook in the middle of 10 acres cleared, an open, log affair with an upstream millpond, apple trees lining the race. Jedediah spied corn stubble and a patch of cut rye out beyond stacks of drying lumber.

Two young men tended the saw—twins identical in every way but for one chewing a shaved birch twig. Their names were Ivan and Irvin Reed, though they explained that everyone called the place the twins' mill.

Jedediah saw something malleable in these boys. He went right to work as they turned back to the walnut log easing ahead in the carrier, the chattering sawblade, set in a sash, gnawing away by drive of crank, shaft, and waterwheel. "Hard to make a mill pay on a frontier, I'll bet," he said.

"Shit," Irvin said. "Everyone wants lumber, but for nothin'. Not like back in Harrisburg."

Jedediah arched up his lips and rocked his head to say he understood the economy of this new land. "How do you come by timber?" he said. "Not many trees of use left in this hollow."

Ivan shrugged. "Used ta be folks would float us a log and come back for boards. But all the easy trees been cut. So they come just wantin' lumber. We go upriver and buy a tree where we can. Find one up the hollow, if it's where the donkey can drag it down for us."

"That's what led me this way," Jedediah said. "I got all the timber a sawmill could cut. And a reason, come spring, to bring you a log or two every week."

The boys looked at one another. Jedediah saw Ivan catch himself. He shifted the birch twig from one side of his mouth to the other. "They your logs?"

"Course," Jedediah said. "Up the Sinnemahoning."

Irvin whistled. "Way up there? Devil's den." He took up a paddle of tallow mixed with tar, and between a rise and fall of the sash, greased the channels in which it rode.

Jedediah liked what he'd said. Wished the whole Common-wealth thought the same. "I got a white pine out by the river," he said. "Your donkey could drag it right up the path. Come look at what good sort of timber I cut. If you don't got two dollars for it, I'd take just a couple bushels of rye."

Now Jedediah knew his log was worth only a dollar and a half, but he wanted the rye more, for he could get three dollars in whiskey per the bushel. So his design was to make the grain seem like a bargain. "And maybe next year," he said, "you could charge rye from a few of these farmers for your sawin'. They always have grain to spare. I'd barter every saw log for just two bushels." And Jedediah liked a little barley for a malt, and told them to keep an eye out for that grain. "Just a wee-bit a' that's all I'd ask," he said.

And so began his trade as a lumberman, likely the first on all the West Branch. Then he went to Williamsport to make purchases for his distilling venture and to establish his custom. First, he paid $20 to have a 60-gallon still built, the leather-aproned, thick-armed tinker promising that within a week he'd have the copper tubing rolled and sealed and the boiler built.

Jedediah bought supplies with the rest of the money—except for sixpence, which he placed on the bar of the Russel Inn, an empty sack stuffed in his shirt. There they were, huddled about two tables, a few faces replaced, but in effect the slag of Williamsport that had watched the trial, drinking whatever earnings would hold them until they had to find again stints of labor on the big farms or gristmills of the Muncy hills.

James Russel, the merry publican, poured him a noggin of whiskey. Jedediah was satisfied that the poor liquor Russel stocked was of a potato mash. And having such a low standard for his distiller, Russel probably served wood whiskey in the dead of winter without knowing, making a few poor souls blind beggars come springtime. So, Jedediah thought with a flutter of pride, he was doing a public service. A kindness, for these churls hadn't had a decent sip since leaving Jersey.

He put his hat in is hand, his eyes to his feet, and shuffled to the closer horde. All the chairs were occupied, cackling men and women leaning on elbows between them. Everyone was barefooted and in rags of linen and paid no attention to Jedediah—just another ne'er-do-well wanting in on the game of cards sure to break out at any moment.

A middle-aged man in a ridiculous old tricorn glanced at him, then back again. "Why here's the slave they had in court," he said. Both tables took note, then turned away, likely remembering the disappointing verdict. But the tricorned man, well into his cups, struck up a conversation with Jedediah about a fortunate turn of events after the trial, describing a fire and an altercation between another slave and his owner. "A two-for-one day," he called it.

Jedediah led the discussion to the quality and kind of liquor to be found about town, then mentioned the dainty of his own variety. Now the rest of the table turned ears, and soon the other party had gathered around. Many a lip were wetted as he attested to his whiskey's purity and flavor. With a glance back for Russel, Jedediah pretended a grand idea struck him. His farm always had a surplus of grain, and it seemed a waste not to distill the excess. Why, he could deliver a canoe-full of flagons every week, starting April next. To be fair—considering it was surplus—he'd let it go for one dollar a gallon. He'd even sell them three gallons for two dollars if they wanted to pool their money, maybe sell some on the side. The happy tricorned man said it was a bargain, by God. "Look what we pay for a tankard-full of this rotgut."

"Come a good freeze next fall," Jedediah said, "I'll siphon off some applejack. And only charge half the price of whiskey."

"And three gallons of the 'jack for a pound?" asked a toothless lady. They all waited with their chins edged forward while Jedediah squeezed together his lips as though he'd been driven to the margin of his means. In fact, he needed the pause, for he had a hard time figuring his gain in thirds without sticks or marks in dirt. "I'll do it," he said with a sigh and nod. "Just for you kind folk. But not a word of this to Russel." And he put a finger to his lips.

Quitting the barroom, he went around back, knowing from his night in the stable that the tavernkeeper placed empty bottles outside the door lest he draw in fruit flies. Jedediah filled his sack with nine blue-green bottles. Turning away, he stopped himself, stuffing another, cobalt, behind the waist of his breeches. Then he slunk off for the river.

The problem was how to pierce holes through the shards of glass he chose from the two bottles he'd smashed—one blue-green, one cobalt—having used the others to make his pair of bottle-glass windows. He'd smoothed the pieces with a file he borrowed from Benjamin, then polished them with clay and a strip of goat shammy. He consulted William, who produced a fine drilling brace, its frame a curved limb of rhododendron, a grinding bit fixed into the chuck. "Keep it wet," he said. "And if you got any rot of the tooth, use that to bore it out."

And so, taking a burning pitchpine knot to the barn on milder evenings that winter, Jedediah ground through the pieces of glass, wood-clamping them one-by-one against a table he'd built beneath a window opening. The squeak of the button atop the brace and the rasp of the bit against the glass accompanied the chomps of the cow and her calf—sired by a bull William bought.

He strung the pieces of glass on a thong of buckskin, assorting them in size and shape but in no particular arrangement of color—for he thought that most pleasing to the eye—and gave the necklace to Sarah while they lay in bed one night in March, little George, Jedediah Junior and Jacob asleep in the upper half-story. The foresticks of the fire still burned brightly, the backlog of green cherrywood just starting to crackle. They were naked under a quilt Sarah had just finished from linen scraps gained over three-and-a-half years on the frontier, its wool stuffing from William's sheep. Jedediah held her within the cup of his body, his arms crossed at her breast. Her buttocks were warm and soft against his thighs, and he was eager for her. He nuzzled his nose into the nape of her neck and whispered he had a present.

"I bet you do," she purred, giggled.

He reached beneath the sack of goose feathers that was their pillow. The disks of glass clinked as he drew them out and he felt her breathing go still. He slid the necklace over her head. Sarah lifted it to see the jewels gather the firelight in an aqua gloss. She sighed and squeezed his arm. Then her shoulders quaked, and touching her cheek he found it wet with tears.

She was a quiet one. Quietly observant, and more than he liked. But there were the children she gave and the charms he'd discovered in the most unlikely places. Like the dooryard or hearth where she worked with such finesse and proficiency at her spinning wheel. She pumped the treadle and managed the two spindles of her double-flyer immersed in the task even as he knew her ears were alert for the slightest peep from the children.

And Sarah was a skillful seamstress and flax farmer—this on top of all else she did: birthing and rearing babies; tending garden; keeping house; feeding chickens and hogs; cooking meals; gathering firewood; helping at the plow. She even raised and spun extra flax for the Sharpes, in return for which George paid their fee to Elton Burch, a weaver on the West Branch who told Jedediah the skeins of thread he delivered were the best quality he'd known.

That day two years ago when they'd crossed the creek to stake out her flax patch, Sarah had taken charge, the straps of her cap loose at her jaw, her features broadened and brightened with the prospect of the job ahead. Her eyes searched the lay of the bottom for the best course of the story Jedediah was to see unfold in the transition of flaxseed to linen. She walked about and kicked up sod, tested it between her fingers. Thought.

She had decided on a humped and therefore better-drained acre across the rill from the piers of the settler's cabin. Tilled in years past, the ground would have fewer stones. And the run of water beside it would make the retting easier. They'd add to the crop as time went by, for, as Sarah explained, a quarter-acre of flax clothed a grown person for a year.

Jedediah helped her turn soil and broad-cast and rake the seed fast upon the final frost, that her flax might have a start on the weeds. She watched the plants. When in July the stalks started to yellow, bearing just the ripeness for the finest quality thread, the Jameses and Sharpes set their babies in baskets in the shade of the apple tree and pulled the flax, Sarah leaving a corner of the field standing for good planting seed.

They knocked dirt from the roots and laid out the flax to dry. When Sarah deemed the stalks ready, she spread out a blanket and rippled them over it, pulling handfuls through an iron comb she'd had Jedediah mount to a trestle. She gathered into a sack the fallen seed bolls, which she would save and sell someday to an oil-man for pressing into paints and varnishes and such.

According to Sarah's design, Jedediah had dug a trench for retting, a lint hole, she called it. Now he shoveled out a water channel from the rill to fill this ditch, then dammed it. After letting the sun warm the water nigh a week to take away its freshness, the lint hole full of the tiny tadpoles of bullfrogs, Sarah sorted the stalks into sheaves of similar lengths and colors, tied them with twine, and submerged them, top ends down. She had Jedediah cover the ditch with pine boughs and left the flax to rot of all its gummy mucilage.

The longest fibers spun into the best thread: if she let the flax ret too long, it would break into small bits. Yet if she took it out too soon, she could not remove the chaff, rendering the thread too coarse. So every morning, Jedediah and little George accompanied her to be sure the stalks remained submerged and for Sarah to reach in and feel them, the water growing more putrid by the day.

After a month, she spread the sheaves to bleach in the sun, turning them daily until they reached the paleness she desired. Then it was time to separate the herl, or bark, from the woody core, to make the hair and straw, as she said, the hair being the outer fibers for thread, the straw the smashed chaff of the core.

They canoed the flax across the creek, baby George in his linen dress bobbling about the stacked bundles. Up on the little flat before the cabin, Sarah went right to what she called breaking. With a mallet Jedediah had made from the burl of a walnut tree, she pounded each bunch of flax crosswise on a squared beam standing on pole-legs. She worked with great dexterity and effect, slight as she was, her black locks swaying, her lips squeezed tight as she swung away and moved the flax across the beam.

Next came scutching—clouting away the straw she had broken from the fiber, a violent operation out of harmony with Sarah's meek temper. During her rests from the winding work, she shook her head no as he tried to take the scutching knife, a tool of seasoned white oak two feet long and planed on one side to a sharp edge. She'd wipe her forehead with the sleeve of her shift and attack again the bundle of broken flax she held across the beam, turning her work as she went. With each whack, bits of straw fell to the ground—chaff for their ticks—the fiber in her hand becoming more lustrous.

She gives me the oaf-jobs, Jedediah thought when Sarah let him heckle. And even at that, she kept watch as he pulled handfuls of flax through clusters of standing nails on wooden boards, first coarse, then fine, the passes straightening and cleaning the fiber. Sarah gathered the tow that fell at his feet, some for tinder, some to clean the musket or twist for wicks, the rest to spin into coarse yarn for satchels and towels and the grain sacks George wanted in anticipation of the mill he'd build. Occasionally she caressed the flax he worked. "That's enough," she'd say. "Don't over-hetchel." And he'd have in his hand the smooth hairs of a brushed horse tail, shiny and white as river sand.

Afterward, Sarah grouped the finest bundles for shirts and her shifts, the coarser for britches, hunting smocks, short-gowns, and bedclothes. Then she rolled a great hive of flax onto her distaff to spin.

As Sarah's shoulders went still and she held the necklace at her breast, the wonders of those capable hands and her satisfaction with his gift buzzed through Jedediah like the song of cicada. He pulled her tight, but with the undue force of that urge to clutch all he had. He made himself relax. She wagged her bottom and pressed against him. Jedediah kissed her neck and she gave a purr. Her hair was fragrant of woodsmoke and the fresh out-of-doors and the sweet sweat of her day's work.

In all, these past few years had been good ones. The babies, Sarah and her flax. He recalled a verse girls sang at scutching parties while he and Bakeraskin delivered whiskey. It chanted through his thoughts:

Since all here assembl'd to card and to spin,
Then, girls, be nimble and quickly begin
To help neighbor Friendly, and when we have done
The boys they shall join us at set of the sun;
Perhaps as brisk partners, shall lead us thro' life,
And the dance of the night end in husband and wife.

"Hold me tight as you want," Sarah whispered. "Just take me all up in your arms and have me." Then with a slight shift of her hips, they were together.

At dawn on the first Saturday of April 1807, George Sharpe set out on a Sinnemahoning freshet, humming *Alouette* in an elm bark canoe, Jedediah riding alongside atop a pine log, this the first of his trading trips. Upon the split sapling ribs of George's canoe stood eight of Jedediah's flagons packed in hay, whiskey distilled from rye the Starret brothers had exchanged for their own cut.

George intended to have a look around the upper West Branch as he planned his move to where there'd be enough custom to support a gristmill. In the two years since George had revealed the idea, Jedediah had pressed him to reconsider, to keep his farm and build a tub mill at one of the runs on Jedediah's piece. George would not relent.

Over winter, he had helped Jedediah fell and limb twenty pines on the bank of a downstream warrant. Jedediah chose nice straight ones, not too ponderous to manage with a lever pole, yet big enough to make the trade of grain seem a bargain to the sawmilling twins. George asked one day who might own this land and whether Jedediah was taking liberty with the trees. "They're mine to take," Jedediah said. His eyes swept the valley wall. "What man would want such a steep piece?"

For four years, George and Rosanna saved every penny as he occasionally broke away to scour the lower hollows of unoccupied runs. The family continued to tend their little upland farm that produced more stones than corn. Communication by a steep forest trail was trying. If it hadn't been for the neighborliness of the Jameses and Starrets, they would not have survived the wilderness winters, which George had blamed for the death of their fourth child, a croupy infant, in January of 1809. They buried the boy at the edge of the woods in a shallow grave, what with the frozen ground. The sight of the stones piled to thwart animals, the knowing they must one day abandon him in this wildland, compounded the gloom.

Their farm offered nothing for trade, so George was more a hunter and hired hand to the others, earning a little pork and chicken, grain and linen, an occasional coin. He had to borrow tools and depend on William for his ironwork. He could feel the need of aid cutting across his grain. By the end of winter, 1811, it was time to go.

Rosanna was pregnant again. Rosa was seven, a great help to her mother, learning to spin with a drop spindle, gathering firewood, and fetching water from the spring. George had named Caleb, five, after Mr. Farleigh. Though he wanted to accuse the man of abandoning him, by his code, George would not hold the notion. He would remember that Caleb Farleigh had shaken his hand. And that within all the muck of George's past, Caleb Farleigh had given him something clear and firm to have for his lifetime. Finally, there was three-year-old Berneta, full of bouncy cinnamon curls and George's green eyes.

George fancied a hollow seven miles downriver of Samson Abel Starret's place, its stream called Ferney Run. The lay of the land lent itself to the construction of the succeeding types of mills George envisioned, and the location satisfied several requirements. Only four hours distance by canoe, he could service the Starret brothers and Jedediah James while the site was not so far downriver that he'd compete with the established gristmills beyond Williamsport. And since the run was on the opposite side of the river from that rutted, meandering trough of stones and mudholes called a road, he called no undue attention.

During one of his journeys the previous fall, George visited Caspar Roan in Williamsport. Roan had known George's story at the Farleigh mill and had sworn any assistance in keeping Reuben Wheler away from him and Rosanna. "A dastardly bastard," Roan had called him.

George found Roan in his office in the stately, steepled court-house where he was well established now as prothonotary—in part because he'd written favorably about the governor in his former newspaper. The centerpiece of the room was not a desk, rather a table overspread with maps, documents and thick volumes. Roan jumped from his seat, came around, and they shook hands. "George," he said, "a pleasure," and directed him to a chair at the table.

Before George finished explaining his plan, Roan stood and pulled to the top of his piles a large map that showed the arc of the West Branch, its oldest improvements identified with black dots and what George guessed were the names of settlers, most at the mouths of streams. He was speechless when Roan pointed to the exact location he'd hoped for.

"Have you considered this place?" Roan's brows drew to-gether over the aquiline nose. "It's untenanted."

George nodded. "But I haven't a lot of means. Yet."

Roan dismissed this with a wave. "You've more than means," he said. "You have mettle. Discipline. You've been deliberate. Now, let's see." He reached to one of the great volumes at a cor-ner of his table and leafed through it. "Here we are." His eyes shifted back and forth across the page. "Good. It's not tied up in the Samuel Wallis mess. Warranted, of course. But not pa-tented. A hundred acres." He looked up at George. "Enough?"

"Plenty," George said.

Finding a ruler, Roan marked his place and closed the book. He tugged down his coattail and sat. "I know the warrantee of that tract," he said. "Let's say I offer him fifty dollars and he settles for seventy-five. Should I make it a deal?"

George was already holding up his hands. "I only got so many pounds saved. I'll not go in debt."

"Understood," Roan said. "That's why I'd arrange a loan se-cured in such a way you're beholden to no one. First I'd purchase the warrant outright. With some of your dollars as a deposit, you could postpone installments until you start your trade. If you have to back out before making payments, I have whatever portion of the deposit is necessary to cover costs I may have incurred. And I promise that if you decide you cannot keep our terms either before or after you start the loan, I'll be happy to have bought the land. I am none the worse for the investment."

Roan explained how he'd afterward help with the patent, then waited while George weighed the idea. "If it makes you feel better," Roan said, "I'll be charging you interest." And only then would George nod agreement.

Now it was time to move to the other topic George came to discuss. Though he shunned involving himself in another man's business, he would make this exception: "Might you do something like this to help Jedediah James with his property?"

Roan leaned back in his seat. "I'm aware of Jedediah's move across the creek." He pursed his lips a moment, laced his fingers. "Yes, I want to help. But I can't—even while I fear that if I don't, he will desperately need me someday. You see—" he looked down at the edge of the table—"he must ask. He must come to me." Then back at George. "I think you understand what I mean."

"I do," George said

They sat in silence as sunlight broke between clouds and through the room's only window. It beamed across the table and gilded the map, caught with a syrupy luster on Roan's tong-curled locks.

The light swept away and Roan gave the sigh of one getting back to business. "I understand Jedediah has a whiskey trade."

"It's a hot one," George said. "I s'pect he's made quite a pile."

"I see no harm in a little side work in whiskey," Roan said. "But when it becomes a business, it opens a man to trouble. He could become beholden to the wrong sort. Or the wrong sort become beholden to him."

Roan rose and went to his window. "But more than that," he said, holding the high rolling lapel of his blue cloth coat, "I wish it were harder for him. Do you know how I mean?" He turned to George.

George nodded. Jedediah could bear wealth only as a burden, at least so soon.

"It will rob of other things," Roan said. "I'd rather he settle into his farm. The honesty in the struggles preserves a man." He turned back to the window, leaning with his hands on the sill. "Have you heard that Thomas Tillman purchased the newspaper I owned?"

"I don't read newspapers," George said. "I don't read, sir."

"Yes, yes," Roan said, turning back. "I thought perhaps word got to you, even up on the Sinnemahone."

"I heard at the trading store he writes things," George said. "If that's what you mean. I heard he writes things against negroes. Especially free negroes. He has a burning hate for negroes. I think I know why."

"I want you to understand—and I want you to tell Jedediah—that I despise every word Tillman writes. And please tell him I did not sell the newspaper to Tillman. He had a middleman—a trickster who represented himself as a newspaperman from Lancaster." Roan shook his head back and forth. "Tillman's a sneak," he said. "And all of this together worries me. It worries me for Jedediah James."

On a drizzling morning in March of 1811, George and Rosanna and their three children gathered with the James and Starret families on the creekbank in front of the James's place. Over the past weeks, the men had constructed the shells of a log cabin and a mill building at Ferney Run. They'd cleared a tiny creekbottom cornfield with the help of a mule George bought in Williamsport, spavined but good enough to plow such a little plot and to tug a scoop in the building of a race.

They'd also helped George set up his temporary quern—a pair of hand stones fitted in a box. After working on finishing the mill each day, George and Rosanna would by firelight rotate the quern's runner stone with a stick socketed into a nook.

Benjamin Starret, long of hair and a winter's beard, in want of a bath and wearing his filthy hunting shirt, pined for George's hidden hovel deep on the plateau. "I should'a saved and bought'n that place off'a you," he said.

George was shaking his head. "You wouldn't be happy. I've seen cressets from my doorstep at night. It's best that Sammy bought it." He referred to Samson Abel Starret's son, Samson the third, now 29. He and his family would take over the farm and expand it with the help of his cousin Arthur, who'd settled farther out the plateau at the great hickory flats where their uncle Stephen had moved to in 1804, a place known now as the Hickory Kingdom.

Benjamin spat. "Man can't be at peace. I ought'a go to the Louisiana Territory. I'd rather be troubled by Indians than meddlin' squatters."

While Sarah and Rosanna planned the long distance economy of garden truck and linen-making, George stepped up to Jedediah. "We're still neighbors," he said. "Just a canoe ride apart."

Jedediah, expressionless, watched the creek. It was muddy and swollen by the melt of snow, remains of which clung beneath the mists at the brows of the ridges, the back-glance of grudging old-man winter who'd left these pioneers skinny and short-tempered.

George had watched this man in a few years amass three more children—Sarah, Daniel, and Henry, now six total—and a fortune. Jedediah never admitted the money, and no one would detect it. For he was miserly. But George in his occasional journey with Jedediah to Williamsport had seen his custom grow from a swapping of jugs with the rabble from the Russel Inn to the delivery of kags George helped roll up the riverbank and lift into the wagon of Williamsport's new general trading store.

Jedediah said at last, "I'll see you when I come through every Saturday anyway."

"We'll be together more'n that," George said. "We'll be there for each other the rest of our days."

Jedediah shrugged, preoccupied—he was always preoccupied these days.

He posted the notice, written with charcoal on a parchment of deerhide, beside the doorway of the little log mill:

TERMS
GRANES MILLED FOR TOLL
TOLL 1 PART IN 10
NO MORE

NO LESS
NO CREDIT

FLOUR AND MEAL FOR SALE BY POUND 2
CURRENCY OR EQUAL BARTER

Rosanna, transcribing for George, had warned the sign was proud. Especially for the new miller on the branch. But George would eat cornmeal alone and starve by the mystery sickness before he'd go into debt or have any man indebted to him.

The first customer to come to the new structure, a rough settler named King who'd swallowed his pride to avoid the long haul to the mills near Williamsport, took up the van and made it acceptable to do more than just a little quern business with a black miller—the mulatto miller, they would come to call George. With his sack of last year's shelled corn slung over his shoulder, King sneered at the sign and said he was outraged by such airs. It made no difference to George.

From that first transaction, George had Rosanna keep a record of every bushel brought in, every portion held back as toll, every pound sold. For the rest of his days as a miller, he would have her read him the accounts before bedtime.

He offered his share for sale from the floor of the mill, which stood along the creek downstream of where the cabin, stable and field occupied the slope of that dark and hidden hollow. Passing trappers and traders hungry for ash bread or johnnycakes paid in venison or money from pelts or wares. The blacksmith accepted flour for his work on George's irons and rifle. The tinsmith had his pots, the tanner his hides.

George had been his own millwright, building his tub mill with much careful planning and the benefit of his years maintaining a mill. And by trial and error—particularly error.

First, with stone and timber, he had dammed the rushing run upstream of the mill. From it, he built a gated sluiceway, a string of ten logs he troughed with an adze and a smoldering fire. He and Rosanna muscled these into trestle legs along the stream, each downstream end feathered and layered over the next log.

The site he'd chosen for the mill flanked the creek just beyond a six-foot waterfall. A final, shorter section of log sluice plummeted alongside the falls to where he built the tub of the turbine, and so was the flume that cascaded water to power the mill.

For a short distance past the falls, the bank, conveniently wide of the waterway, continued on-level high above the stream. This is where he built the mill, 12- by 14-feet, partly situated on the bank where George placed his entryway, the rest suspended on piers over the turbine tub on rocky ground along the creek. In the floor, he cut out a circle to receive the shaft that would turn his runner stone.

His was the simplest of mill designs, eliminating cogs with its one oak shaft, the bottom of which was mounted to the horizontal rotor in the tub.

He carved this rotor and a spare from a poplar log, each hub and its blades of a piece. The tub, a large half-barrel of sorts built by a cooper in Williamsport, made for an economy of energy, for it constrained all the water surging from the flume to powering the wheel.

George knew enough about what he did not know to be successful in spite of not knowing it. He understood there were many mathematical and hydraulic considerations in designing a mill, having to do with pressure and horsepower and the sundry pieces that made for the ratio between the turn of the rotor and that of the runner stone. But in choosing a site with more than a sufficient head of water, and using this plain design and the right sized rotor, he avoided all the calculations of water volume and gear teeth and so much more.

He dug a short tail race from the overflow of the tub to the stream, Molly the mule pulling a drag pan of flatiron to scoop out stone and sand, George wielding the reins and the pan's two handles.

With the help of a hired mason, George cut and dressed millstones from the hard red sandstone atop the Bald Eagle Mountains. The runner was 25 inches in diameter, the bed stone 27. Using trees as snubbing posts, the men lowered the stones down the mountainside on a sledge tied to George's rope.

They rafted them up the river and had Molly skid them to the mill.

The instant he glanced out the window, cut into the mill wall for a view to the mouth of the hollow, George knew them by how they carried themselves—Reuben Wheler on his black mare, Joseph Farleigh following on a mule. Wheler scanned the hollow, strained his eyes up to the field, studied in its foreground the cabin that blocked from his view Rosanna on the other side tending garden with week-old Edward bundled at her bosom in sackcloth. Then, having moved close enough for George to see the odium in his eyes, Wheler locked on the sloped yard where the three other children must have played.

Though the steamy heat of August oppressed the hollow, provoking swarms of punkies and mosquitoes that nipped at the ears of man and beast, Wheler wore his military coat with its polished steel buttons and stand-up cuffs, their braid dull as his black eyes. His jowls sagged more flaccid, more grayly furrowed, and beneath the brim of his hat, worn low to his brow, the wisps of long locks hung scant now as milkweed fluff. Reuben Wheler had turned an old man, just a meaner old son-of-a-bitch.

As they pulled up before the mill, George scooped buckwheat seed into his hopper. He reached down to the meal spout, rubbed the falling flour between his thumb and forefinger. Then he stepped through the doorway where he'd yet to install a door.

Wheler merely glanced at George and dismounted with a sigh, Joseph tilting back his straw hat and narrowing his eyes at George as he got down from his mule. He wore a pistol girdled at his waistcoat and George did not like in this display the dishonor of their past; he'd been good to those Farleigh boys.

His chin cocked, Wheler walked to the edge of the stream bank and stooped to the extent his frame would allow. He wore breeches with thongs laced along his outer thighs, and high black boots with tassels at the knees. Peering at the underworkings of the mill, he traced the turning shaft, the chute, studied the splattering wheel. He waved off punkies and shouted against the rapid slaps of sluice water striking home, "You burn my mill, take my custom."

"You know what started that fire," George said. "And I made sure there were four mills between us."

Just as Joseph brandished the pistol—the lock and severed barrel of a musket mounted to a curved chunk of wood—George caught the three children running toward him ahead of their mother. "Caleb," George shouted, "take your sisters to the house."

But they kept coming—until they saw the pistol, stopping steps from George, Caleb shrinking against his older sister Rosa who took the hand of naked Berneta.

Reuben Wheler had swung around, upper lip flared, eyes on them. "What did you call that nigger bastard?" he said.

Rosanna stood behind the children now. "He called him Caleb. And the other two are Rosa and Berneta. How is mother? Tell me."

"You named a nigger boy off'a my brother?" Joseph said.

Wheler had not looked up at his daughter, clouted as he was by the sight of these children.

"There's another one here," Rosanna said. She folded back her sash of sackcloth to reveal the napped, tottering head of their little Edward. He let out a squawk and she put him back to her breast.

"Whore," Wheler said, and he started for his daughter while George stepped in front of her and the children.

"Named after my brother he kilt and my Daddy," Joseph said, and then repeated it.

With the children crying, clutching at their mother, Wheler stood now inches from George, who instead watched Joseph. "You have that thing aimed in the direction of children," he said.

Wheler raised a fist at Rosanna. "Run off to live in the woods with the sin of my sister's husband. We disowned you the day you left and I'll not stand you and your nigger taking my trade."

"She should'a married my brother," Joseph said, voice cracking. "'Stead a' the one kilt him." He tried to steady the pistol. "'Cause a' him, Caleb's dead and the old mill's burnt and we got a poor mill now and hardly no custom." He spat toward the children, and George fought the fight blood surging to his fingers.

"More than one mill can burn in this valley," Reuben Wheler said, and Joseph rocked from foot to foot, mumbling, "I want to kill him. Just want to kill him." Then he cocked his pistol.

"Rosanna," George whispered over his shoulder, chary of tipping the boiling kettle, "take the children away from here."

"Jezebel," Wheler shouted.

And then George caught movement downhollow—a black man creeping tree to tree. Jedediah.

"Go," George said.

Instead, Rosanna ordered Rosa to take her brother and sister to the house. "Father," she said as the children ran, "do something about Joseph."

"He has his own score to settle." Wheler stepped away to give Joseph room, then lifted his chin to the sign beside the doorway. "Even your lecher understands squaring accounts."

Rosanna came around George and clutched him so tightly she smothered the baby. "Would my father watch his daughter be murdered?" she said.

George tried to tear her away as the squirm of the infant became a mere pulse against his stomach, suffocating inhales coming in clipped croaks. Joseph Farleigh moved closer, the unsteady muzzle inches from Rosanna's linen cap.

Forcing himself and Rosanna to crouching, George closed his eyes and took her head into his great hands. Had he known other than a nonsensical world where truth was lie and lie was virtue, where men could corrupt heaven into hell and call it providence, he would have wondered at the absurdity of death by whim of this madness. Rosanna whimpered out that ultimate plea for deliverance from iniquitous injury: "Oh, God, Oh God, Oh God..." It rang impotent, hollow with its own doubt of being heard, it was a voice calling out to the great reason, muted against a wasteland of unreason, and so in a place, George feared, without the bounds of God's heed.

The baby, quivering in spasms, had gone silent. George opened his eyes. Thirty yards away, Jedediah shouldered his musket. And though it would have taken less might to rip bark from an oak, George forced away Rosanna's arms and shouted a diversion: "Jedediah, don't shoot." Then he sprang on Joseph as he turned and fired at Jedediah, George wrapping an arm around Joseph's neck and taking him to the ground.

Immediately, Jedediah was standing over them. "Son-of-a-bitch tried to kill me," he said.

"Easy," George said, pinning Joseph. He looked over his shoulder at Rosanna, still crouched, slapping limp and gray-skinned baby Edward. She blew in his face. The child coughed, vomited, cried.

Jedediah pressed the muzzle of his musket against the crown of Joseph's head, forcing his face into the straw hat that had fallen to the ground before him, muffling his curses. "Second bastard that tried to kill me," Jedediah said. "What the hell do they think I am?"

Reuben Wheler, white of face, looking around not knowing what to make of it all, said, "I'll tell you what you are, what the lot of you are…"

"Shut up," Jedediah said. "'Bout now, I don't care who this bullet kills."

He nodded at the spent pistol Joseph still held. "I want that at least." He let off Joseph's head and jammed the musket into the back of his hand until it gave the soft snap of tinder under leaves, precipitating shrieks from Joseph, then took up the pistol and stuffed it into the waist of his buckskin breeches.

Rosanna was standing now, stroking the cheek of the gasping baby. "Father," she hissed, "leave. Take Joseph with you. Take him and the violence you people sow everywhere you go."

Before the cabin at dusk, the children and Rosanna in bed, George built a smoky fire of green stickwood, for the gnats and mosquitoes were making meals of everyone. He set logs on-end and sat with Jedediah who held between his thighs a flagon of his finest.

They stared into the flames, George shifting the firewood with the toe of his moccasin, muffled cracks and lazy sparks emitting from new embers. Jedediah took sups and waved away smoke. George occasionally reached for the whiskey.

When the raspy scrapes of katydids and crickets ramped with the cranks of treefrogs and the hollow darkened even as the river valley yet cupped western skylight, Jedediah spoke: "I can't keep up with the farm. I need for a cradle fixed to my scythe. I need a tumbril sledge for takin' in the hay. Me 'n Sarah could use a apple barrow, the orchard producin' finally." He held the flagon out for George, but he waved it off. "I'm askin'," Jedediah said, "that you might build 'em for me. I'll pay you good."

"You should build your own," George said. "Keep your money for hard times."

"You mean harder times," Jedediah said. "Times are always hard, up the Sinnemahone." He coughed from the smoke. "You know which wood's springy, which is strong. To use hickory here, ash there. What lumber'll make a peg that'll grow tight. And you can blacksmith. I'll pay you in coins."

George watched the firelight flicker upon Jedediah's face, chose his words. "The more you ask for help, payin' or not, the more people got a piece of you. Things are different when you get 'em first-hand."

Moonlight described the roofline of the cabin, the stable, a palisade of mighty pines bordering the steep orchard and field beyond the jakes.

Jedediah set down the flagon and handled his pistol—pulled the cock, eased it to rest, tilted the barrel toward the fire. "Why d'you still hide out? You're like a spider in a corner back here." He aimed into the silver moonlight that pooled over the mouth of the hollow.

"I might live like a hermit," George said. "But I don't show the bastards what I want for. And we'll own this place before long." He leaned toward the fire. "I tell you, man, you got to slow down on the business. Put more time into takin' care of that farm."

Jedediah laid the pistol on his thigh, took up the flagon and sucked at it.

"You tell me your youngest child's whitest of 'em all," George said.

"Damn right," Jedediah said, wiping his lips with his sleeve and raising the whiskey. "Straighter hair than a bear's."

"How's that make him so different from the others?" George said.

"You know how." Jedediah put down the flagon. "You know better'n I do."

"I thought that was it." George took off his hat and tapped flour from the brim. The specks fell into the flames, igniting in tiny sparks. "So that makes him better than the rest?"

"No" Jedediah said. "Makes somethin' easier. Ownin'."

"So you're sayin' they're right. It's all theirs to give and take to and from what men they please. Their rules are the right law of the land. And I'm someways halfway ahead of you 'cause I got more of them in me."

Jedediah spat into the coals, the spit sizzling. "There aren't no right laws or wrong laws," he said. "There's just the law a' the land."

One more try. "Do you really think," George said, "little Henry's head a' hair's what could make a difference for him?"

Jedediah studied his thumb petting the grip of the pistol.

"You know it's not," George said. "Don't that tell you you're dancin' to their song? Make that boy see the lie they rule by. Give all them children a law of their own."

Jedediah went still until he stood and tucked the pistol beneath a band of linen he wore to gird his fringed smock. Then he picked up his flagon and walked from the light of the fire into that of the moon, which near to swam now with katydid song.

At daybreak, George went to the mill to sack flour. An hour later, he stepped outside to find Jedediah approaching from the stable where he'd spent the night. He carried his empty flagon and musket, his pistol banded at his waist where he would carry it the rest of his days.

"I'll harness Molly to sledge your rye to the river," George said.

"Keep at your work, old friend," Jedediah said. "I'll get her." He smiled, and George dared think maybe he'd be fine, that it might sink in before it was too late.

Jedediah glanced skyward. "Haze burns off, it'll be a hot son-of-a-bitch." He leaned his musket against the mill, set the flagon beside it, and turned for the stable.

George watched him walk off. Then, starting through the doorway and seeing that his sign hung crooked, he reached and made it straight.

He pieced it together the second he saw a horse tied by the barn, before he could have said for sure its color. The automatic certainty of menace in the first whiff of death. In a like sense, the events of the day would leave a tang that forever tainted his home, even as his determination for the place burned.

He moored his canoe, took up his shot pouch, loaded and primed the musket. Crossing the barnyard, he did not give a thought to the children other than that their absence about the place bore out the sin he was about to redress. Red hens dusting in sand scattered before him; they must have sensed the tight grip on the musket, the ire behind eyes locked on that house, quiet with its door closed despite heat sharp against the cheek even in the shade.

He glanced at the chimney—smokeless just before the midday meal. Noticed that the dog, given him by Benjamin Starret, an old long-legged, flap-eared, coon-hunting bitch that at least appeared Virginian, was not about. Yes, all was still in the face of that intrusion simmering before him in this bake-oven of a valley.

Stopping before the porch, he watched and listened. He closed his eyes, put her spread-legged and a-sweating on the bed, Tillman's drooped shoulders and white ass over her slight body, Sarah wild with some passion she'd contained these years he could not in his anger account for other than she'd been his woman, moaning there cuckolding even the children she'd sent off a-fishing or berrying. Tillman groping, groping something that belonged to Jedediah James.

He opened his eyes, certain of all he'd envisioned and more he could not imagine and tiptoed in his moccasins across the porch. His heart flailed at his ribs, echoed at his temples. She had not even thought to pull in the thong that lifted the inner latch. He wrapped his left hand around the grip of the musket and in a motion jerked back the latchstring, kicked open the door and rushed in before it swung shut behind him.

The room was dim. Dust drifted in the faint blue-green light before his bottle-glass windows, the walnut slabs of the table a-flutter in the thin towy glow of a tallow lamp setting there with the coffee mill and her pipe, a littering of papers. His eyes were slow to adjust as he surveyed the place, made out the hominy block and splinter broom in the near corner. Kilderkins of cucumbers, their ever-hovering fruit flies invisible now. The salt-barrel washtub by the ladder, its ewer hanging from a rung. Where the hell were they? He could even enumerate the articles on shelves: cattlehorn spoons and Sarah's precious bone-handled forks of pewter, stacks of trenchers and platters, redware crocks, the noggins, ladles and bowls he'd carved—most cracked and in need of repair with pitch. He strained for the cradle of hickory bark and the table with Sarah's Bible and books by the bed. The bed. It made no matter that neither were near it, that instead he found Tillman, brows arched over his spectacles in his fear of the musket, squatting beside a bench at the table, and then Sarah standing five steps from him pressed against the wall among the coats, hats and blankets hung on pegs.

The pistol would be easiest for the first shot. He palmed it. Already a thing of his person. No, he had not yet even a mold for the right-size bullets. Next whiskey run. He braced the musket. One shot, he thought, two targets. And so he took the gun by the barrel and raising it over his head, started for Tillman as Sarah cried out, "Oh my God, no."

Like a cornered kitten, Tillman sprang on all fours for the door and Jedediah was ready for this. He was on him within feet of the table, landing the corner of the gun's stock into the back of his skull with the dead thump of the beetle when the glut finds the knot in the rail. Tillman collapsed into the floorboards and Jedediah lifted his eyes to find Sarah standing beside him.

"Slut," he said, drawing up and pointing the musket. Her eyes snapped large in bafflement and for an instant he wondered at his instincts, could not see her clothed and capped had she defiled herself. When that passed, he poked the muzzle into her neck.

She squeezed shut her eyes and fell to her knees, trying to push away the barrel. "For God's sake, Jedediah." She looked up at him and he saw she understood that he knew. "Jedediah, listen to me." She winced and retched as he pressed the muzzle into her neck. "He wouldn't leave. I tried all mornin'. He threatened me. Us."

"He's been comin' here every time I go to Williamsport."

"No," she said. "Put down the gun. Think of the children." She shuddered to her haunches. "Oh, Jedediah, I'm so scared. Please stop."

"You been sendin' my kids off and screwin' that white snake in my home."

Sarah was sobbing now, her words more whimpered than said. "I sent the children to my brother for help. To get them away from here. Jedediah, he said he'd take our land and home."

His hand was wet on the grip of the gun, his shirt sticking to his back, yet his throat was so dry he couldn't swallow. Salt burned at the corners of his eyes. He curled his finger around the trigger... Why? He held his breath, tried to steady himself and answer that question.

Sarah, sensing the pause in his determination, checked her sobbing, watched him.

Nobody was going to take her, that was why. Yet he sensed a dilemma in that.

So accustomed had he become to listening for the sigh of the thong passing through the hole in the door, fearing some man with papers coming to steal this place, he'd have heard it against a rainstorm. Before the latch bumped its pine stopper, Jedediah swung around and shouldered the musket.

The white light of the muggy midday seeped in with the opening door, followed by the figure of a long-faced man in a broad-brimmed hat, big hands brandishing a rifle. William Starret. He stretched his neck toward this strange scene: Jedediah a sweating wreck aiming a musket his way, prone body beside him, Sarah sobbing on her knees, reaching out to her brother.

"I come too late, sister?" he said. He stabbed the rifle in the direction of Tillman on the floor. "What the hell?" He took a step closer. His eyes moved person to person, pawing it out, settling then on Jedediah. "He gone mad?"

Like hickory hulls raining down in a gust, erratic footfall pit-apatted across the dirt of the yard, followed by the six children bursting into the room, led by the tallest, George, who carried little Henry. They stopped fast when they saw their daddy with the gun. The youngest ones called for their mamma while Jedediah Junior, six now, pointed where Tillman was stirring. "What's the matter with that man?" he said.

William swept the children behind him. "I told you to stay back at the canoe with your auntie."

Jedediah raised his finger, beckoned them. "Come over here."

Henry, naked but for a length of towcloth wrapped about his bottom, was squealing in George's arms, pushing away from his breast, that head of jet gossamer bobbing as he looked around the room. Not another child moved, just watched their mother and the musket aimed at their uncle.

They aren't lookin' in their daddy's eyes, Jedediah thought. "Dammit," he said, "get your asses over here." But they only peered as they had, two-year-old Daniel mumbling, "Mamma."

Turning and pushing the children away, William said, "Get back to your Auntie," and they ran out the door. He stepped to Tillman, telling Jedediah, "You're fool enough to shoot me, you're fool enough to hang." He bent, set down his rifle, and slid his hand beneath Tillman's forehead, slapped his cheek. Tillman moaned and William pulled away his hand, touched the bloody lump on Tillman's skull.

"Bastard," Jedediah said. "Comin' 'round here every Saturday I'm gone. And this slut sendin' my own children off to her brother."

William had been keeping one eye on the musket. In a motion, he seized the barrel and swung it upward, the hammer falling with a *plip* against the pan. Sarah jerked away and Tillman, dazed as he was, looked toward the sound.

Standing, pointing the muzzle toward the ceiling in case of a late charge, William wrenched the gun from Jedediah's grip while with his other hand he took his throat. He squeezed at Jedediah's jawbone until it might snap, dropped the spent musket and tossed the pistol from Jedediah's waistband, then released his grip. Picking up his rifle, William stepped to Sarah, whom he lifted to her feet. "Sister," he said, "what went on here?"

"Whorin' went on here," Jedediah said, his jaw in the palms of his hands. "That son-of-a-bitch stoled my wife. Tried to take my land."

William leveled the rifle on him. "Mind your mouth," he said. Then he rested the butt of the rifle on the floor. "Sister, you tell me the story here. Or I'll take 'em both to Williamsport and show the sheriff what Jedediah done to the other'ns head."

Sarah stepped to the table and sat at a bench, squeezed together her hands. "Jedediah," she said. "You listen to this. You hear it all." She looked to William. "Now I haven't seen Thomas Tillman since father's funeral. This mornin' I was breakin' flax by the barn when he came ridin' up, the kids followin'." She swallowed, closed her eyes a moment. "Yes, he come right out and asked me to run off with him."

Jedediah started at her but William took a step, extended his arm, and had him by the neck. "Hear her," William said, and Jedediah pushed himself away, went to the wall where he leaned sucking breaths.

"'Course I told him to leave," Sarah said. "I didn't know what to do. I thought to tell him that Jedediah would be back soon. But then I was afraid he would stay and try to hurt him." She sniffed and rubbed her cheek against her shoulder. "He was talkin' foolish, like I been waitin' for him all this time. Said—" she glanced at Jedediah—"he knew I never meant to marry Jedediah. Then he talked crazier, sayin' I should leave for Jedediah's sake, that he'd let him keep the farm. He told me he had papers under his shirt. Maps of warrants that showed he could take the farm right out from under us if I didn't run off. He knew Jedediah was downvalley, said he knew everything Jedediah did. Now I really feared for what to do. And all the while the kids watchin'." Sarah let out a sob, gestured sharply at Jedediah. "So there. Ask Georgie if you don't believe me."

"Then what?" William said.

Sarah drew a breath and shivered. "I made like I wanted to talk to him. It was to protect the kids. I said, 'Thomas, let's sit on the porch and you tell me about those papers. I'll send the children and that barkin' dog off to their auntie.' I called over Georgie and told him to help the others ford one-by-one at the low place in the creek. Then I hugged him and whispered to send Uncle William quick. When I looked up at Thomas, I could see he thought me sendin' off the kids meant I'd run." Sarah struck the table with both palms. "For God's sake, as if I'd think of leavin' my babies." She looked at Jedediah. "Of leavin' you."

William crouched in front of Thomas Tillman, who'd raised himself to sitting. "You know where you are?" William said.

Tillman's spectacles rested crooked across his eyes, his skin slick and sallow like a corncake dunked in bear grease, his mousy hair pasted around his crown. "I'm where a wayward nigger tried to kill me." He snaked his tongue out to lick snivel from his upper lip. "I'm on a farm I'm going to own."

Jedediah started for him until William swung around with his rifle raised. Jedediah pointed from Tillman to Sarah. "Then what were they doin' inside the house?"

William stood and waited for his sister.

"He was startin' to scare me," Sarah said. "When we got to the porch, he kept harpin', 'let's go, let's go.' He said if I didn't hurry, he'd waylay Jedediah with a pistol he had in his saddlebag."

"Son-of-a-bitch," Jedediah said.

"I kept dallyin'," Sarah said.

"It took me a while, sister," William said. "I was out for firewood."

Sarah wiped her eyes. "I said I had to go inside and see about my things. I thought I'd latch myself in, but he had hold of the door before I could close it. So I told him he had to show me the papers before I'd make up my mind. He boiled over, ran in and threw them on the table, kept swearin' about Jedediah."

Cradling his rifle in the crook of his arm, William went and studied the documents, then turned and frowned at Jedediah. He took the papers to the fireplace, set them on the gridiron and withdrew from the tinderbox a chunk of flint and a bar of firesteel. Striking sparks, he leaned in to blow them to a flame, then eased back onto his heels and waved the fire to life.

"Copies," Tillman said, more a wheeze. "I'll have new ones tomorrow."

"Please get him out of here," Sarah said.

"You touch me," Tillman said as William rose and approached him, brows gathered as if he were deciding the fate of a calf born blind, "you'll be in the gaol by nightfall."

William bent and lifted Tillman by the tails of his cravat, Tillman only helping him as he clutched the wrist, lest he be choked. William let go to see if Tillman could stand, and when he remained on his feet, made a fist and pressed it into the soft concavity of his upper gut, just below the ribs where his waistcoat came together, and pushed him to the wall. This put Tillman to heaving, to fighting for his breath and trying to tear the hand away.

"You hear me," William said. "You're in my country now. The law of this land starts and stops with this hand I'll shove clear to your throat, you don't agree to my words. Look at me and quit your bawlin'. You send a sheriff to anyone on the Sinnemahone, I'll hunt you like a coon. I'll shoot you outta lair or tree and I don't care if it's on a street in your county-seat town. Leave here and never come back. And don't in no way trouble this piece with your papers and lawyers and land offices." William thrust harder until Thomas Tillman drooled, nodded violently, and prayed in gasps he stop. William pulled back and Tillman tottered toward the door, lifting a corner of his upper lip at Sarah, then at Jedediah.

"You leave that saddlebag in the yard," Jedediah said. "With the pistol in it. "

Everyone turned to William. He nodded, then followed Tillman out the doorway.

When the horse clopped across the barnyard, Jedediah retrieved his musket and pistol and started for the saddlebag.

"Jedediah," Sarah called out, "tell me you didn't mean it."

He stopped, turned only his eyes to her. Then he walked outside where William waited on the porch.

"He had warrant maps," William said. "This piece, the pieces up and downstream."

Jedediah leaned against a porch post. He eyed the saddlebag, hoped the pistol in there was of the same caliber as the one at his waist.

"This warrant unclaimed," William said, "might mean somethin' for him. Or it might not, you improvin' the place these six years. I don't see how he can take it without a fight in front a' one a' their damned fat judges. But that don't mean he won't. You go down to Williamsport tomorrow. Find those fellows helped you at court. Tell 'em you want this warrant. Tell 'em you want a survey so you can patent it. You might just turn out lucky this happened. 'Less that little bastard's ahead a' you already. Then we see."

"I own this piece," Jedediah said. "Own it by right of improvement. I don't need to kiss no Williamsport asses. Now you go over to the creek and send my children back here."

William had pulled a bone pipe from his shirt and was about to reach down for his tobacco. He stopped and regarded Jedediah, turned his attention to the doorway a second, then looked out at the sky heavy with hot haze. He tugged out the neck of his shirt and returned his pipe before starting across the field, the up-valley half of which Jedediah had left unbroken and fallow this year. At its edge, aster and milkweed already encroached from the creek near which Jedediah had left stand brawny-boled oaks, that their roots buttress the bank and so stop floodwaters from robbing any of his land.

This was the tip of the splinter that breaks off, that a man can't dig out. It rankles with pus, becomes a constant bane—first to the hand and then the mind. Finally, it spreads forth the feverous blood poisoning that consumes.

Jedediah lay, starting that night, on a bearskin in front of the door, his pistols of a like caliber—so was his luck—charged and within reach, his musket no longer hung on the wall, but leaned against the jamb. He'd gouged a hole into a door plank eight inches from its bottom, through which he could see clear to the creekbank if there were moonlight. He occasionally dozed. Never again would he sleep soundly.

Sarah came to him on an occasional evening after the weather turned bitter in January, the heat of the fire enfeebled by icy drafts through gaps in the daubing. With little effect, she stuffed into those voids cow manure, its stink overcome by the ordinary odors of a winter home: hinds of deer meat, gammons and ver-min-ridden bags of seeds hanging in the rafters; burnt animal fat from their lamps. And the bodies of two adults and six chil-dren, the littlest one's underlinen scraped of soiling for days on end, Jedediah loth to daily axe ice and wash cloth in the upper run. For the cold of it disabled his fingers until he held them for hours by the fire, his work hung there to dry on a peg, still filthy for want of his scrubbing it with lye.

Jedediah was obliged already this season to chop logs of fro-zen, fallen tree limbs; he had not kept up with firewood cutting over summer. Nor did he have enough feed for the horse, cow, and calf. He at last told Sarah to ask William for fodder, to say he'd pay him in whiskey when he could distill again. Sarah hauled the hay by tumbril sledge across the frozen creek, a bushel of apples at the bottom on the first trip. The charity in-furiated Jedediah, even as he knew his family needed the fruit now that they'd exhausted their own, everyone craving it, every-one sore of gum.

He thought and may have wished she'd stay beside him those nights, but always before daylight Sarah crept back to the bed. There gaped a void between them colder than riverstone, even when he loosened his grudge enough to return her embrace, when his desire outgrew his obstinance and he would let her have him wholly. She was patiently meek around him otherwise, gave an ear when he spoke of some simple matter about the house, assisted him with a chore if he asked. But Jedediah was always sour by choice, by lesson, by a revenge he wouldn't allow was undeserved.

And all the while she refused to despair, as if confident a goodness in his heart would prevail.

Little Henry, that precious boy, only two years old but smart as a crow. Little Henry, fair of skin and straight of hair like his mother, black of eye like Jedediah, stood beside him one dawn in March where Jedediah lay on his bearskin by the door. Jedediah reached and clutched at the boy's shirt—he was always grasping one of the children, squeezing a shoulder, keeping them, as if they'd be taken. And he felt them uncomfortable in his grip, afraid even. Ever since that day.

"Papa," Henry said, that little liquid voice bubbly and pure as the tumbling water of their mountain runs. "Why you sleep der?"

Jedediah had a mind to send him off, chide him not to pester. But the face was furled in perplexity, the eyes probing in such earnest.

"The wolves," Jedediah said.

"Wolfs?"

With his free hand, Jedediah pointed toward the south ridge. "I want to hear them."

"Scary wolfs," little Henry said. "You 'tectin' me?"

"Scary?" Jedediah said. "They're a comfort." He looked at his handful of the boy's linen shirt, thought for a better way. "They say no one's out there. Wolves mean we're alone. You see?"

Henry's top lip quivered, the half-light of dawn through the nearer window swimming bottle-blue in his welling eyes. "Dat's why wolfs scare me, Papa."

The hound disappeared in late June. Jedediah was well soused these days, his trade back to busy. He hadn't noticed her missing, though the dog had daily followed him up to the stillhouse, laid about in the shade of the woods snapping at flies.

The children saw her one day at the far edge of the stump-ridden, downvalley field. They called to her from where they weeded the garden near the house. Jedediah stepped out of the barn, Sarah looking up from her flax patch. The hound paced the makeshift fenceline of stones and treebranches. Head down. Everyone shaded their eyes, squinted, the dog lethargic, limping. Then she stumbled, fell on her side. Rose again.

Jedediah thought he caught a wound in the ham. He started off, noted the horse sidled up to a corner of the barn, ears pricked, mane quivering. Halfway across the field, Jedediah saw that the dog, standing now, head turned toward him with eyes drunkenly imprecise, had a bite in her thigh. A piece of hide the size of Jedediah's hand hung as a flap, the underskin matted with leaf mold, the muscle of the leg slick, pink. That dog's always barkin' at every damned thing, he thought. Silent now.

He moved closer, stopping within 20 yards. As though she woke to a fly at her nose, the dog yawned out a lazy snap in his direction. Slaver fell from her leathery lip. Jedediah confirmed his suspicion by the tumult in her eyes—fatigue vexed by an afflicted urge to attack. He'd already discharged his pistols, did it every morning for practice and so that he'd load fresh powder should he need to shoot during the day. He pulled one from the band at his waist, half-cocked it, reached to his hip where hung his shot pouch. While the dog tilted its head, mildly interested, Jedediah worked open the throat of the bag, felt for the powderhorn, found it, a ball. Where the hell were the patches? The dog growled, a phlegmy rattle that trailed into a cough and then a body wrenching heave, eyes pushing at their sockets. She fell to her side, straining, gagging, legs jogging in vain against the stems of weeds. Jedediah put the ball into his mouth and held the powderhorn in his underarm. He looked into the bag and fished out a patch. The dog, having gone still, caught her breath, face wet with drivel. She scratched for footing and rolled onto her stomach, stood. Using his teeth, Jedediah plucked the thonged stopper from the horn and tapped powder into the barrel—no time to measure with the fawn's hoof in the bag. She stepped toward him. He spit the ball into his shirtsleeve where he made a crook with his arm, returned the powderhorn to his armpit, and rubbed dry the bullet. The dog sniffed the air, licked at drool, then made a wobbling turn. By the time Jedediah pushed the patch and ball into the barrel, she'd slipped through an opening in the tangle of treebranches. He withdrew the ramrod, seated the ball, and shook powder from the horn into the flashpan. Closing the frizzen, he clambered over the fence. He watched and searched. But he could not find her among the brush and scattered trees of the bottomland he hadn't cleared.

The children had watched with their mother from behind the fence of laced bramble about the garden.

"Stay the hell away from that dog," Jedediah said as he approached. "You see it, come get me." He caught little Henry peeking through an opening. "You understand, Henry?" The child only frowned at the pistol in Jedediah's hand. Jedediah went to fit it into his linen band, remembered it was primed. Dammit, a wasted bullet. He would have discharged it right there, or better yet, let six-year-old Jacob try, but he couldn't bring himself to it with Henry's sweet face looking out so confounded.

Two nights later the hound let off somewhere near the spring above the house. Awful, hoarse huffs, the gasping kecks of a man taking blows to the gut. Jedediah watched the moon-washed yard through his peeping hole lest the animal trouble the hens in their coop, the calf in the barn, the hogs.

Little Henry called out from his pallet in the upper half-story, "Goggy." He kept on with it until Sarah pattered up the ladder. She soothed the boy with soft *shishes*. But he went back to repeating, "Goggy, goggy…"

Then the hound ceased, for the wolves began their ululations on the ridge—a clamor of brays and whinnies, hoots, sobs and sniggers, resolving into that mass lament a body felt at the base of the skull more than heard, gruff cavernous roots levitating into a dirge of wobbling wails and squeals, the pups puling and squeaking in frenzied accompaniment. The outcry orbited the valley, sounding at one moment distant, the next at arm's reach, gloomy as the shadows of vultures.

Henry wept as his mother in whispers tried to calm him. Yet to Jedediah this was a siren song, and the wolves transported him to a rare doze.

* * *

The next afternoon at the stillhouse, as Jedediah poked his fire with a stick and held his other hand to the boiler to feel the temperature of his mash, the children panted up to the doorway. Turning to point them away he found them a-snivel—Jedediah Junior, Jacob, Sarah, three-year-old Daniel. "Where's George and Henry?"

"We told, him, Daddy" Jedediah Junior said. "We told him to stay in the field and look for strawberries."

"Told who?" Jedediah said.

Their eyes went white as they shifted glances.

"Henry," Sarah said, her hands full of her dress of butternut towcloth, more a rag with a hole for the head. "He kept sayin' that this mornin' he saw the dog out by the fence. We told him he didn't see nothin, but he kept talkin' about his goggy."

"We were just pickin' strawberries," Jedediah Junior said. "Then he was gone. And George went after him."

Jedediah looked to the irradiated woods edge where the bank dropped to the farm. "Where's your mother?"

"Washin' clothes in the creek," Jedediah Junior said.

No way that child'll find the dog, he told himself. No damned way. "Jedediah, when you last seen Henry, was he closer to the creek or the woods?'

Jedediah Junior creased his eyes.

"C'mon," Jedediah said.

The boy nodded. "The creek," he said.

"Now you all find your mother and tell her to go lookin' with me beyond the field. Git."

He stood on the bank eyeing brushy openings among river birch and silver-leafed sycamore. He shouted for George, for Henry. He shouted to stay away from the damned dog.

The moment Jedediah saw the child, George leading him from the lower run, he knew. He ran to where they waited in the shade of a spicebush. Henry, face wet with sweat and tears, resisted as Jedediah pulled away the fist he held at his breast. Finding both sides torn by canines, seeing the bloodstain on the shirt, his little Henry fearful of him yet trying not to cry, Jedediah loathed the tongue that scolded the boy, the heart that shattered, that he knew had, on the day he was born, been turned to glass and ordained to break at this moment, upon this threshold to perdition.

"Sorry," the boy said over and over. "I petted goggy."

Jedediah carried him doubled over his arm, Sarah running after them from wherever she'd been searching. He did not stop his stride at the head-high creekbank, rather jumped to the shore. Henry squealed out at the whipping of his neck as Jedediah landed, his knees buckling, their caps crashing upon stones.

He plunged the boy's hand into the waters of the Sinnemahone, scoured the cuts with a disk of sandstone. Pinned over Jedediah's knee, Henry screamed for Papa to stop, reached back and clawed at his arm. And Sarah pleaded over Jedediah's shoulder for what had happened.

"Where the hell you been?" Jedediah said, blame just the chimera they had recourse against whatever wickedness was as rooted and indifferent in this place as the boulders simmering in sunlight on the far creekside.

"Henry," Sarah said, hitching her petticoat and wading around Jedediah. She touched the boy's cheek and he stopped writhing in his father's hold.

"Goggy," he said.

"Oh, God," and the panic in Sarah's voice sent the boy back into a fit. She tried to take him into her arms. "I'll get my brothers to fetch a doctor from Williamsport."

Jedediah shook his head. "Aren't no doctor but a witch can fix this." He drew Henry up, pushed to his shoulder the head of soft hair, wild and pliant as September ragweed, rose and turned and looked at that silently witnessing ridge, border of his land, bounds now of his hell.

Sarah tried to hold the two of them, but Jedediah pushed her away, her petticoat catching in the slow current of shore water as her eyes went wide and her breath departed, finally returning in quaking suspirations.

Why couldn't a child be as worthless as a lame old donkey? Why should a man have to suffer what was about to happen? An awful quandary cramped into his brain: the best he'd be able do for this boy's comfort would be to break his little neck, even while he was beautiful and strong. Jedediah was as damned in having to endure the truth of that impossibility as he'd be in bearing the weeks to come.

God, do you hear this?

No, he thought, not here—if He'd ever heard him anywhere.

He would not lose sight of the child, sometimes embracing him for minutes, and so terrified the boy and redoubled his fervency for his mother. But Jedediah warned her and the other children away from him. He made Henry sleep at his side on the bearskin by the door.

Other than to tend to a meal, Sarah kept a vigil. After the third day, she gave up trying to speak with Jedediah; his only words had been to forbid her from telling her brothers or sister-in-law; he did not want them about. "But let them know we won't be at no Fourth of July. Ask them to tell the Sharpes not to come. A run of the flux."

The boy quailed in his father's shadow and all childish restlessness left him. He looked back at his mother as she followed wherever his father took him, whether to brood on the creekbank or rock him on his lap against a stall in the barn. Jedediah knew not the expression or depth of Sarah's pain, never wondered at the willpower or fear that stopped her from forcing herself up them, for he gave her no attention. He quit the farm work, his distilling. He minded only the boy, fed him jerked meat from the rafters and had him sup from Sarah's kettle in the fireplace. As for him, he drank, but did not get drunk, rather subsisted in a malaise of having drank.

Only prisoners and soldiers endured such waiting as did settlers on the frontier. They shivered through winter nights with nothing to rise to but idle, snowbound days. Waited daylight to dusk, weeks on end, for the deer to pass or the elk to come to the lick. Only to miss. Wives watched from doorways as husbands set out for goods or business fifty miles away, not knowing when or if they might return. Families brooked the silence of no post while the wheels of the world turned for better or worse and distant loved ones flourished or suffered, lived or died, who knew? A soul prayed through pregnancy that the birth not go bad—for mother or child or both, there in country destitute of midwives and doctors.

Children. They lived months in want of fruit or vegetable, biding the attendant scaly skin, fallen hair and sores of the gums while there were only samp and sour meat to eat, cravings boring into their brains and stomachs like flyworms. Come spring, thin as their rags of linen, hollow of eye and too weak to convey their perplexity, they pointed into the gardens at potato tops, and mothers suffered retching cries of starvation from their own flesh as they tried to explain the necessity of leaving the plants be.

But no manner of forbearing prepared a man to wait for his still-hale son to die.

It may have been a week, may have been longer, sun and moon passing without Jedediah's heed, until Henry showed the first signs.

Jedediah emerged from a fitful drowse to the heat and tremor of the boy's fever. It had crept across the bearskin they lay upon, it shuddered through their blanket. He pulled the child to him and pressed his lips into the sweat-dampened hair.

They remained in this posture until dawn blued the room enough for Sarah, on her watch from the bed, to decipher the turn of circumstances, realize they'd reached the precipice. "Oh, dear God," she said. "Our baby."

As a boy, he'd rafted hogsheads of tobacco through the Dragon Swamp to skiffs docked on the Piankatank River. He'd thought of the black water that sucked at the great splayed ropes of bald cypress bottoms as death having reeked out of the place where corpses went by way of graves. He rose now to the fetor of that swamp's muck, tugged out of the way of the door the bearskin with the boy upon it, he who'd not the desire to lift himself as he complained, "head hurt, head hurt," and went out to a phantasm of just such a deluge covering the ground of his place, sucking at his ankles, defiling every thought and thing.

He stood in the mist-muddled dawn and thought of the pool of the creek bend and of drowning himself and the boy. He thought he would have done it, if for anything to end the ache in his gut, but for the dilemma of being a hand in just what death had cursed upon him.

After the phantom flood cleared from his vision—though the smell remained—he went back inside and ordered the children to chores about the farm, then lay with Henry. He continued thus for two days, making water in a basin and letting Sarah spoon him and the boy the broth she brewed of chicken bones and livers. The whiskey was gone. He left the house only once—to defecate—returning to find Sarah holding the child, and so chased her away and voided from then on into his crock of red-ware.

On the third day, Henry began moaning for the pain in his throat. By twilight, he was thrashing and chewing at himself, at anything in his sight. He bit off mouthfuls of bear hair, his fair little face, wet with sweat and drool, bearded with it. He screamed of many-headed wolf-monsters, of wolfmen in the corners, of his hands having become spiders, which he clutched one with the other and tried to tear from his arms as if gloves of fire. His shrieking rattled the potsherd left of Jedediah's heart. The boy would not be calmed. Jedediah pinned his shoulders to the floor and Sarah begged he free the child and let him purge his torments. The other children bawled in terror until Jedediah ordered them away, commanding George to make them pallets in the barn. "And do not tell your cousins any of this."

In days that followed, Henry would sometimes become tranquil, lay still and reach out to his mother where she watched from the hearth. Jedediah would embrace him, think beyond hope he'd been cured, imagine the fever gone. Only to watch him relapse into worse suffering.

And then came the torturous stage that gave the malady its name, the aquaphobia, terror of water, the sight or thought of anything suggesting drink intensifying wringing spasms of Henry's throat, even as he thirsted. Fighting for breath with agonal sucking sounds, groping at his neck, he pressed his back into the wall as he tried to kick away from the kettle at the hearth, the bottles and bowls and cups about the shelves. All these Jedediah ordered Sarah to throw outside, the steam of the passing kettle provoking a frenzy of hiccups as the boy covered his face with his arms. His response to the very swinging of the door revealed another phobia, a terror of breezes. Henry fell onto his back in a seizure and they could do no more for him than hold his head from slamming the floor, the child terrified of the pain of his each next breath.

The un-human gulps, the strangled *homp-homp-homps* of the gosling seized by the fox, clawed at Jedediah's ears. Worse was knowing that each attack on the child's throat was like the increasing, wrenching twist of strands by the ropemaker while the natural spasm of the throat, as of the rope, was to fight the wring.

The moments the fits subsided were no better, the breathless child with his hollow and jaundiced eyes panting out, "Make stop. Make stop."

Jedediah could no longer keep Sarah away. He had not enough spite, let alone strength, to inflict his grudge in the face of this. Even as he resented how the boy clung to her after all his attention.

And so with the other children orphaned under George in the barn, Jedediah and Sarah sat by the door and rocked their writhing, croaking Henry in the stink of fever and watery excrement.

In after-years, Jedediah would realize how lonesome the child must have been until then, deprived of his mother. And so Henry endured not only his agony, but seeing the coming of the end—any creature would have known what such hell foretold—while estranged from her who'd nursed him.

Then one night in the sallow light of a crusie lamp, as Sarah hummed to soothe Henry who trembled and groaned against the howls of the wolves, he slackened in their arms, and with ebbing strength and increasing terror of the eyes, grasped the loose linen of Sarah's shift, trying to keep hold but bungling, falling, falling, fading, losing control of his hands, helpless, and—oh so scared—imploring of her the answer to the unanswerable question, whimpered in the frightened say of a name, the question that asked why all was answerless: "Mamma?" And Henry, having in response only Sarah's dismay, her powerlessness to hide the dread of what such a plea meant, tried to put his arms around her, but they went lax. With a weak staccato gasp his features popped wide and he fell into a catalepsy from which he would gape and not rise before his heart stopped the next night and Sarah petted his brow and whispered, "Come back, little Henry, please come back," and Jedediah went mad.

The stench of the Dragon Swamp filled the house. The walls and ceiling went aflicker, sight, sound, all sensation pulsing between sensibility and not: Sarah's sobs, the touch of his shirt against his skin, glimpses of the lifeless body on his lap.

Taking up Henry, Jedediah swung open the door and stumbled across the porch and into the yard. No moon. Just a silent dome of crystal stars suspended across the ridges, a purple nebula besmearing the apex like a stain of clabbered blood.

He could not see the barn, circumvented it by vague awareness of his footfalls sounding back from its walls. The sky flashed down on him. It rained like a meteor shower. Yet when he looked heavenward it hung there brooding.

Then he heard the mutter of the creek, apprehended its eggy surface, corrupted reflection of the starlight. Still his senses wavered, matched the throbs of katydid cries coming across his field. In between, all was blank, all was the dead silence underneath.

Finding the edge of the creekbank, he dropped onto his backside and pulled the yet limp body to his breast. He'd thought when it happened he would blame the meanness of this place, haunt of catamounts and venomous serpents and what other insidious menace lurked in its heavy treetops and shadowed stream chasms. But it was something worse than meanness. It was indifference run amok in the black heart of a country unheeded by God.

He buried his lips in the soft nook of Henry's neck. When he surpassed reproach, realizing there was no help even in hating back what had taken his son, he wept.

How much later he could not have said, but he broke from a delirium in which the grief had maimed his power of mind.

Mosquitoes buzzed in his ears, nipped at the lobes, the crotches of his fingers. The moon had risen; it lacquered a chattering sheen upon the creek's riffles. All but two persistent stars edging the south ridge had disappeared. He spat and cursed these, he accused the moon. A cloud scudded across its face, a burst of silver gauze. A jeer.

"Goddamn," he said. "I been whipped and beaten. I been shot and starved." He snatched a breath. "Now..."

The wolves broke out in a round of bays.

He let them unite in mass ululation. When they trailed into scattered barks, Jedediah howled back, strained wheeze though it was. But the wolves paused not, they raised again into the ancient otherworldly voice of an eternally impervious universe of which man was doomed to bear witness, maybe hearing him, maybe not.

The next evening, Sarah, upon a bout of sobs muffled into her blanket, called out to Jedediah where he lay by the door with Henry next to him in the wooden box of a sledgebarrow. She asked him to come to her.

"Oh, God, Jedediah, please. I need you so."

But he turned away and peered through his hole in the door, out into the barnyard, every feature of weed, wall, and rubbish having assumed a rank of gray as allotted by the moonlight.

And still, the following day, Sarah searched him out where he sat sprawl-legged on the creekbank mumbling words incoherent even to himself. She must have thought it would help or that she'd better get out with it before they buried the body. "I'm pregnant," she said. "I been. It'll show soon."

Then followed the Christmas when Rosanna Sharpe stopped speaking to Jedediah. This despite the remaining years and associations between their families, her silence coexisting with George's patient attention to Jedediah.

The Sharpes and Jameses had over the years kept ties as if they remained neighbors—holidays and work parties, the sharing of tools and venison, cidering, husking and threshing, planting and pulling flax. No sooner had Sarah gone to her brothers to relate Henry's death than George arrived to help bury him, Rosanna along to attempt consoling the inconsolable mother and her children who more than suffered their grief— they feared it by extension of the affliction they witnessed consuming their father.

In the months after Henry died, Jedediah supped from the kettle when hunger overcame the maelstrom in his gut. He craved whiskey, and having none, saw in his woken nightmare phantom jugs in every nook. But George, who showed on odd days to mend a plow or lay-by straw, began to bring Jedediah back to his senses by stirring memories as they went about the farm, Jedediah mute at his side. George spoke of what he knew of Jedediah's youth, ventured on what he did not. He recounted hard times they'd shared, plans they'd made. Early in those months, only threatening shadows inhabited Jedediah's' mind; these retreated. By Christmas, something of his old constitution, its pulse the wag of a feather, tottered to its feet. He agreed to celebrate at his family's house, as had been the tradition for inclement gatherings, theirs the larger, the Sharpe's place preferred in the warmer months when the children could camp in the yard or stay in the stable.

Beneath an iron sky and in zigzags of snowfall, the Sharpes came afoot in blanketcoats the day of Christmas Eve. George led Molly the mule, fitted with a wooden packsaddle from which hung grain sacks of food and gifts.

Starting midmorning, the James children had taken turns watching through Jedediah's peeping hole until Daniel screeched and jumped to lift the latch. They and the four Sharpe children were off to the barn to see the elm bark toboggan George James had made, he and his brothers and sister barefoot and coatless in an inch of snowfall, but Sarah letting them go. And so on the porch she stood with George and Rosanna—both women pregnant and flush—suspended there in the sulking watch of the gaunt and pistol-wearing figure in the doorway. Until at last he nodded and stepped aside.

The families were settled into the house at dusk, the small ones a-tumble and giggling in the upper half-story, everyone else at the table about a platter of roasted chestnuts and a heap of biscuits with a bowl of maple syrup for dipping. Sarah and the children had decorated the ceiling beams with the boughs of pine and hemlock trimmed with twigs bearing deep red winter-berries. They'd threaded garlands of popped corn and festooned them among the evergreens. The fire, stoked tall and blazing be-yond Jedediah's usual economy, huffed into the room a lively golden cast. Sarah lit two luxurious, sweet-smelling candles of beeswax, gifts from Rosanna. Jedediah looked up from his nog-gin cup and remarked he had not breathed such a warm smell since he was a boy. When Sarah's features softened with cheer where they'd been strained for months, Jedediah drew a sip from his cup and let forth, "I killed and plucked two gooses to feast on tomorrow."

The Sharpes might have been bloated sheep with pins stuck in their sides as they eased at their seats, stern Rosanna even allowing a grin. George shouted toward the ceiling. "Children, we're eatin' roasted goose meat tomorrow," and their assorted shrieks trilled through the ladder hole.

It had been whiskey in his noggin—from a share surrendered by his brother-in-law whose ire had mellowed into sympathy. Now on Christmas morning, queasy and chilled, Jedediah sulked in a corner, sitting with his knees pulled up, hands linked at his shins as candlelight wagged across the ceiling. The smell was not so warm in a head full of ache and irascibility. The children jumping about in the upper half-story since before daybreak, Sarah and Rosanna chattering at the hearth, only nettled him. And he had geese to roast. There was nothing to do for it but start already on the whiskey.

He went up the ladder, passed the children playing on mattresses in the dim light of a fat lamp, and took down the birds hanging among gammon and sacks of seed in the stink of the rafters. At the hearth, finding Sarah had banked the fire for him into a bed of embers, he spit the birds on a rod of iron. He inserted the point into a hole in a jamb and suspended the other end from the trammel hook, having slid it to the far side of the lubber pole. Under the weight of their watch, he retrieved the bottle he'd hidden behind a stack of treenplates, unstopped the corncob with his teeth and filled his noggin. He sat at the fireplace and sipped while he turned the meat, Sarah stealing glances, Rosanna scowling, and everyone giving him his room, for all but the youngest knew now what was in the cup.

Still, the others celebrated. The children drank chocolate, the adults, hard cider. George set two laden grain bags on the table, igniting squeals in the little ones. To each of the five James siblings, he and Rosanna presented a gift. For Daniel, a whizzer made from a disk of leather, a loop of twine coursing two holes in it and strung through a pair of wooden handles. Young George came and showed his brother how to twist the twine then work the handles to spin the leather circlet. "Whish, whish, whish-sh-sh," Daniel said as he watched each pull, then took the toy to try on his own.

Such was the prize George Sharpe gave his namesake it interested even Jedediah: a barlow knife.

"Oh, Georgie," Sarah said. "Don't lose it. Keep it in your shirt with a rope drawn at your waist."

George called for Jedediah Junior and handed him a wooden box with hinges of leather and a loop of cord pulled over a nail for a latch. The boy stared at the chest in his hands. "Open it," Daniel said as he jumped from the bench and ran to stand beside his brother, everyone leaning to see the better, Jedediah too. Jedediah Junior stretched the string over the nail and with the yawn of the lid a smile lifted his cheeks. Dominoes filled the box snug as puppies. He drew one out, a six-over-three, cut of the white sapwood of tulip poplar, its pips the singe-marks of the head of a rose nail. In an instant, the boy was at the table setting the dominoes on end in a curving row for a great fall.

Seven-year-old Jacob and little Sarah, five, unable to contain themselves anymore at their seats, ran to George's elbow.

"But I have nothing for you," George said to Sarah, upon whom the balk was not lost, for she smiled all the more. "Maybe ask Rosanna," George said, "if she's got a girl's present."

Sarah turned to Rosanna who pulled a straight pin from her shortgown and withdrew a pair of cornhusk dolls, one an aproned and capped girl holding a broom of blue jay plume, its quill stripped of feathers but for a fan at the tip. The other was a man with a brimmed husk-hat and a basket woven of tiny shreds of rush.

"Is that everyone?" George said, ignoring Jacob even as he crawled onto his lap. All but George looked where lumps remained in the sack, until at last he took notice. "Did I forget someone, Jacob?" And the boy's frizz of hair shook with his nods.

George pulled from the bag three balancing toys sculpted from wood. He set them at the edge of the table and tapped each to start it rocking. Jacob put his nose to a smiling boy working a hoe up and down. On one side of this, a man rode a horse, and on the other, a blacksmith swung his hammer over an anvil. Everyone at the benches rose for a better look.

Then Sarah went to the bedstead and crouched best she could against her burden to find her own sack. Face flushed, she returned and presented Rosa, Caleb, Berneta and Edward Sharpe each an orange, maple candy wrapped in tow linen, and a flat piece of slate with a pointed shard of stone for drawing.

Jedediah wanted to ask where she'd gotten money for the oranges. She'd been into the jorums of liquor money, he guessed, had her brothers bring the fruit from Williamsport. But these first drams of whiskey were lulling the tetchiness.

Then George and Rosanna were standing before him, George holding out a pewter tankard big as an ewer. "For you and Sarah," George said. Jedediah nodded and took it into his hands as Sarah came to him. They'd made it into a candle lantern, having punched with a nail the shapes of three stars about its circumference, lines radiating from their points in the manner of twinkling.

Rosanna handed Sarah another beeswax candle and Sarah clutched hold of her friend and thanked her while Jedediah looked away to turn the roasting geese.

By midday, when the skins of the birds were crispy and glistening and Sarah had moved her pot of wild plum pudding to the coals, Jedediah had lightened enough to step away at intervals to inspect the children's gifts and inquire with George for news of the West Branch. He felt the spring of tension he'd made of the room relax, heard Sarah speak more merrily.

Each child had come to the hearth to watch the birds and draw in the aroma, to say how hard it was to wait. Finally, Jedediah announced it was time, and Sarah climbed the ladder and returned with an oaken platter long as the table was wide. She and Rosanna spooned into bowls a stew of root vegetables they'd heated in the kettle on an outside fire. They broke hunks from a cake of wheat bread while little George went to the springhouse for butter the children had churned. George and Jedediah wore mittens to move the spitted geese from the fireplace to the platter and to remove the iron rod. As the others squeezed onto the benches and waited, Jedediah took up a knife, and holding one of the birds, sliced at the flesh, releasing a savory steam that made the children writhe and sigh.

But as Jedediah thought of those faces aglow in candlelight, the liquor lapped at his ribs and the cheer in him dissolved, for among the warbles of laughter filling his home, a void pronounced itself all the more. He stopped carving and glared around the table where there was hardly room for another body, much less the thought of little Henry. Forgotten. Stolen of this moment, this meal, every rapture of a child on Christmas day.

Sarah was watching him. She asked if he wanted a treenplate for the meat. Asked tentatively. Jedediah did not respond, looked at the knife, the carcass of the goose. The table went silent and he met Rossana's severe gaze, her lips set rigid as hickory boles, her capless, wiry hair pulled back against her skull. Judging, he always felt.

She was waiting for something. They all were waiting.

"And we'll pray now?" Rosanna said.

Jedediah turned the handle of the knife backward in his palm, a knife George had helped him make from a file, the tang fitted into a notched rhododendron root and bound tighter with time by the threads of the sinew of deer spine. He raised the blade before his face, the aqueous light from a bottle-glass window catching there. "Damn a God that takes a baby," he said, and with a furious stroke, drove the tip into the platter.

Late the next morning, George shook Jedediah out of a stupor where he lay in the barn. He'd sipped whiskey through the night while shivering beneath the horse's tow linen blanket, Rosanna's reproach rattling about his head: "You condemn yourself and your family, Jedediah James. You blaspheme God."

The barn was dim but for shafts of milky light described in the steam drifting over the stalls from the nostrils of the cow and her calf. He told George to leave. "I don't want to hear I mistreated your wife," Jedediah said. "I know what I said and I said it in my own house."

George was squatting before him, his blanketcoat tented from his shoulders. He slipped a hand through the overlap and stroked the stubble at the cleft of his chin. He remained so a moment. "Caspar Roan wants to see you," he said

Jedediah snorted. "There it is. Now the two a' you gettin' together to talk about ol' Jedediah."

"Trouble's brewin'," George said. "You're like to lose this place. Roan knows what to do."

Jedediah pulled off the horseblanket and forced himself to sitting. The liquor sloshed and something vile flushed into his throat. He swallowed it back with tears in his eyes and waited for the barn to steady. "I'm not givin' up this place. Not alive, not dead."

"The law will take it either way," George said, "if you don't see Roan. He'll even come to you, but you have to say so." He moved his hand from his chin and touched Jedediah's knee, George the only man Jedediah would let touch him. "Do it for me," George said, warmth seeping into the leg.

Jedediah answered by not answering and saw this was sufficient for George, who reached and shook the bottle. Empty. He sniffed the air. "You pissed yourself." He glanced around the barn. "Get off the teat. Mend your tools and dress your coulter. Clear more field. Come spring, get back to farmin' for all this land's got to give." He tossed the bottle into the hay Jedediah had lain in. "Stay outta the whiskey business. It sticks your neck out to trouble. You risk your farm while you make a pile you can't do nothin' with."

"I had a good custom," Jedediah said. "I owned the whiskey business in Williamsport."

George was shaking his head. "It owned you."

"I got timber that sawyers want. I got a good still."

"You got a nice piece way up the Sinnemahone," George said. "That's what you got," and he touched the knee again.

But Jedediah had heard enough. He rose and tottered out of the barn and toward the house where he'd dry his breeches by the fire.

At a stool by the hearth where he spooned lead from a crucible into his brass bullet mold, Jedediah heard a horse blow in the yard. Using a hickory stick, he knocked the balls from the jaws into a square of leather on his lap, then set his work aside and went to the peeping hole. Caspar Roan and another man sat their horses, watching the house. It had been only two days since he'd given George permission to send Roan, or at least had not denied it. He glanced back at Sarah who, knowing nothing of the visit, watched from her chair with her head cocked, wary.

He drew back the Indian bar, opened the door and stepped onto the threshold. Roan waved and the other man nodded, his name coming to Jedediah: Jacob Lloyd, the barrister from the day at court.

They tied their horses to porch posts and approached Jedediah, Caspar Roan reaching out from the cape of his overcoat and grabbing Jedediah's hand. "Thank you for inviting us."

Jacob Lloyd, well into manhood now and not so round of cheek, stood glancing between Jedediah's eyes and the pistols at his waist. Jedediah surveyed the barnyard, which glared with snowcover in the crisp sunlight, then looked to the far ridge where the pine tops were a-waggle in a fitful wind. He extended his face out the doorway, felt the chill against his right cheek. East winds always brought trouble. "So, what do you need with me?"

"Would mention of Thomas Tillman be enough to allow us in?" Roan said.

"You tell Thomas Tillman to go to hell," Jedediah said. "You tell him he comes 'round here, I'll put a musket ball through his neck. Then I'll piss in the hole."

Barrister Lloyd winced, even more when Caspar Roan nodded and said if he had such an opportunity he would be pleased to do so. Jedediah credited the man for that.

"Our horses are tired," Roan said, plucking a kid riding glove from his hand. "We've traveled since last night. We'd like to warm ourselves by your fire."

Jedediah looked into the dim house. "No," he said. "Go away from here."

Roan tugged at the collar of his overcoat. "I'll stand here and speak through that door if I have to. George Sharpe said you gave him his word."

Jedediah tightened his lips, exhaled through his nose so loudly the horses pricked their ears. "Sarah," he called out. "These men are comin' in to talk. Keep outta' our business." After he gave her a moment to ascend the ladder, he let them pass, then shut the door.

"She should hear this," Roan said as he led Lloyd to the table. He squinted around. "Where are the children?"

"At their cousins'," Jedediah said, going to the hearth. "Coasting."

"A fine day for that," Jacob Lloyd said. He and Roan took in the room as their eyes adjusted, Lloyd's nose curling at the smell. But Roan looked to be at home, all grins and admiring eyes as he unbuttoned his coat and studied deer antlers Jedediah had hung as hooks for the children's blanketcoats and mittens, Roan ignoring the bearskin and moth-ridden blankets behind the sweep space of the door.

Jedediah removed his crucible from the coals, threw on a log. He turned to Roan eyeing the bullets lying on the leather.

"How has the hunting been?" Roan said.

Jedediah shrugged. "The deer are few. Market hunters shoot up the elk or drive them into the portage country. The bears and coons are holed up."

"The wolves," Roan said. "I know they are hard to compete against this time of year."

Jedediah said nothing.

"You look well," Roan said as he and Lloyd tossed their gloves and hats onto the table and twisted out of their overcoats. But Jedediah knew he did not look well. He was a frayed wire with a headache and hollow eyes. Come April, he'd get better.

As Roan hung the overcoats from antlers close to the fire, Sarah came down the ladder. She'd changed into a clean petticoat and apron, a fresh linen cap, and a kerchief over her shoulders. Roan met her at the table and squeezed her forearm, offering his sympathy for their loss of little Henry. Then with a chuckle, he pointed at her gravid midsection and said, "Soon, soon, soon."

She took down the lantern the Sharpes had given them. Jedediah tried to stop the extravagance with a shake of his head. She ignored him, went to the fire and tipped the beeswax candle to the flames, then took the lighted lantern to the table and bade the men to take seats. She returned to the hearth, hung a kettle of water from the trammel hook, and sat on the stool. Now she would serve them chocolate and he could do nothing to stop her.

The men pulled up benches, Jedediah to his own side, Caspar Roan clasping his hands before him.

"Lydia Wallis," Roan said, "the widow of Samuel Wallis, died in September. You're aware of the countless warrants her husband held, the enormity of them pieced together from the Muncy hills to the state of New York. Wallis's estate has been a chaos. Very complicated with people he owed and people who owed him. Made more complicated because he allowed debts to be paid in land that remains worth nowhere near what was due him. It had fallen to the wife to salvage what she could of the shipwreck. Now the court will sell all his pieces of land at whatever price can be had, and pay from the proceeds at least a few crumbs to the people owed. The sheriff is posting the warrants for sale, some of them already patented, all of them cheaper than Commonwealth lands. The vultures are descending."

Jedediah had little interest, doubting this had anything to do with him. But when Roan said, "Now enters Thomas Tillman," he drew up with attention.

"As prothonotary," Roan said, "I know beforehand each tract the sheriff puts up for sale. But Thomas Tillman, owning my former newspaper, controls when—or if—they are advertised. And I am seeing a fraud take place."

Jacob Lloyd spoke up. "Tillman culls for himself the arable tracts and those where the timber can be rolled to the water."

Sarah came and set before each man a noggin of chocolate, pipes of steam swaying amber in the lanternlight. Jacob Lloyd lifted his cup and examined a black stain about the rim. He returned the chocolate to the table. Caspar Roan, though, thanked Sarah and sipped. Then he watched Jedediah, who'd burrowed into the shoulder cape of his winter hunting shirt, hooded up against the chill he felt here away from the fire.

"Jedediah," Roan said, "sometimes you can predict a man's determination by looking into his past."

"I don't need to know nothin' about any men," Jedediah said.

Jacob Lloyd raised a brow at Roan.

"But you may discover," Roan said, "there are no limits to his ambition." He leaned toward Jedediah, whispered. "You learn how seriously to take a man. Realize that the pistols at your waist will amount to mule shit if it's the law he's going to bring at you." He drew back from Jedediah. "Please excuse my language, Sarah."

Jedediah leered from beneath the hem of the cape. "To hell with your law."

"Law or not," Roan said, "heed the depth and danger of the man's resolve." He placed his forearms on the table and touched together the tips of his fingers. "The tale of Thomas Tillman, as I have gathered, begins in Scotland. His father was a drunk who hung himself from a tree in a sheep pasture when Thomas was a small boy. The man had survived eviction from the highland farm he and his ancestors had tenanted, but could not endure the squalor of the croft he'd been relocated to, where sea winds plucked seed from the hand and blew children off cliffs. Thomas, sent out by his mother to call his father home, found him dead. Crows had already picked out his eyeballs."

Roan glanced toward the hearth where Sarah stirred the fire, making as if she were not listening.

"To bury the past," Roan said, "Thomas's mother assumed a new surname, the English one we know, and took him to the villages of the lowlands to scrape by on what work she could find and probably some she would not admit. She learned of a way to gain passage to America with a guarantee of employment and a roof that did not leak. She went to the waterfront and found a ship captain who drew up papers that gave her and Thomas passage in exchange for their indentures, which he'd sell in Philadelphia."

He supped from his noggin, pulled from his waist a handkerchief and wiped his lips. "Surviving weeks at sea was more common than one would think for such traffick—dead indentures do not draw profits for captains, so they keep the cargo alive—just so, I have been told." Roan returned the handkerchief. "Then, off the Walnut street wharf, an agent for Samuel Wallis, land king of the West Branch, found the house servant he was looking for—with the bonus of a boy to work the garden and fields of the Manor of Muncy. They stayed on with the Wallis family even after receiving their freedom dues, for Thomas was apprenticed to the surveyor of the land holdings by favor of Mister Wallis. And so, until she died of yellow fever in her son's arms, Mrs. Tillman's luck turned for the better."

"Those were bad times for yellow fever," Roan said, shaking his head back and forth. "Within a year, Samuel Wallis succumbed to it while traveling. Since then, Thomas Tillman has prepared for this day when he can corner the sheriff sales of the Wallis warrants he prefers. He aspires to be the new land king."

"Where's he gettin' the money?" Jedediah said.

"Peter Bakeraskin makes loans to him," Roan said. "He uses to advantage Tillman's mania over owning land, taking the timber on the best warrants as added interest. This is his way of finally getting droves of it to his family's mills in Maryland without having to buy the land itself, which would have been a burden to him. I've been told he's spending a lot of time in Harrisburg, lobbying for a deeper river channel, and in Maryland, readying for the influx of logs."

Jedediah snorted. "No, he's stayin' away from the bitch."

Roan watched Jedediah. "We've arrived where the story concerns you."

Jacob Lloyd withdrew from beneath his waistcoat a map and unfolded it onto the table. Jedediah recognized the course of the Sinnemahoning and its first fork spanning across the paper.

"This shows the warrants in this part of the county," Roan said. "You see the squares marked across it?"

Jedediah leaned, nodded.

"A man in the Commonwealth land office who'd never seen this country drew this map," Roan said. "Now look at this piece." He pointed just below the fork by a bight in the creek, a smaller, rectangular parcel. "Your place."

"You may wonder," Roan said, "at the strangeness of someone hundreds of miles away carving out of the surrounding squares a four hundred acre property that follows a stretch of bottomland."

But Jedediah was shaking his head. "I know all about that."

"So you understand," barrister Lloyd said, "that when the land office chunked up these Indian lands, they first honored claims by anyone who proved settlement well before 1784? That this is not a Wallis warrant?"

Jedediah nodded. Roan watched him a moment. "This property had been improved before you came along," Roan said. "A house and a field."

"Just the stone base of a cabin and a spot cleared for corn," Jedediah said. "No way anyone lived up here long, Indian times."

"Likely not," Roan said. "But that was enough to stake a claim for title by improvement."

"And in an effort to buy the rights," Jacob Lloyd said, "Thomas Tillman already tried to track down the man who applied for the warrant in '84. But that failed because he's dead and there are no heirs and it has fallen back to the Commonwealth."

"And now," Roan said, "because you have this land by right of improvement after it went back to the state, the only way he can gain a superior title is by claiming he had it before you. Which I'm sure he'll do."

Jedediah was on his feet. "Like hell he will." In a motion, he had one of the pistols aimed toward the ceiling. "Goddamn him," he said and set the cock.

Jacob Lloyd leaned back so far he had to grab the table to catch himself.

"Jedediah," Sarah said, though with little alarm. "Please."

Whether or not Caspar Roan knew the pistol was uncharged, he remained calm. "Then come to Williamsport," he said, "and we'll help you patent this property."

Jedediah waved the pistol from one man to the other. "I don't need papers to live on a place I been for six years."

Roan shrugged and Jedediah lowered the pistol to his side. Sarah had already turned her attention back to the fire.

"Please sit," Roan said. "But let off that cock first."

Jedediah looked down at the pistol. They weren't going to leave until they finished their say. He released the cock, sat and put the pistol on the table before him.

"It's a simple matter," Roan said. "Jacob, please explain."

"You appear before a justice," Lloyd said, "and make proof you've lived here at least five years, that you built a home and improved at least—let's see, you have four hundred acres, so you need to state you have tilled at least eight."

"And a witness?" Roan said.

"One of the brothers-in-law would do," Lloyd said. "Both would be better." He looked at the pistol, swallowed. "Then there is the matter of money."

Jedediah pushed back his hood, shook his head no.

"Go on," Roan said. He sipped from his bowl, nodded his approval to Sarah, who'd glanced up from patching the upper of a child's shoe. She looked down, pierced the shoe with an awl and wove through the hole a hog bristle with a thread of linen waxed to it.

"The Commonwealth requires seven pounds and..." Lloyd lost his voice.

"Seven pounds and what?" Jedediah said.

"Just seven pounds and ten shilling per the hundred acre," Caspar Roan said. "And then you've patented the warrant and no one can contest it."

"No," Jedediah said.

"If you don't do this soon," Roan said, "Thomas Tillman will claim this land. The minute he files an ejectment suit, you've lost your chance to have a title. If it's the eighty dollars—"

"I don't need your eighty dollars," Jedediah said.

Roan leaned into the table. "As you consider this man's cunning, his story and ambition—" he paused here, glanced at Sarah who was staring into the coals. "As you consider your history with him, do you not see he won't be stopped short of your ruin. Unless you prevent it. Unless you allow others to help."

All was silent, Jedediah's brooding as heavy and dark as wet black fleece. Sarah bent and blew on the coals, then set down the shoe and awl and bristle and went to the table. She said only one thing before stepping away for the men's coats: "Don't let Thomas Tillman browbeat you, Jedediah."

He found himself eager for the day, hated how this admitted he was wanting of a present. Their alms. All because of Thomas Tillman. The man had reduced him to a beggar, had tainted his possessions.

He would not ask his brother-in-law William to witness. He did, however, approach Benjamin—who was more than willing to go to Williamsport with pelts to trade and a need for lead—and the man who'd purchased from Jedediah their first home across the creek, Wash Bartholomew. Benjamin was Benjamin and Wash a man with a look of yes in his eyes, and for no reason other than it was his nature—not pity, not artifice. But with William, there was about him a feel of patron.

And so each man to his horse, they set off at dawn on an appointed Monday in January. The day broke in a glare upon the brilliant white that blanketed ground and bough, the sun so bright it muted the sky to a pale ice-blue. Their steeds stepped high against two feet of snow, a fresh, gritty, top layer scattering like sand with the rise and advance of their knees. Steam as thick as cream curled about the mouths of man and beast, sharp cold certainly of near zero degrees stinging cheeks—but it was tolerable, for no wind blew.

They rested their horses all afternoon and rode through the night, arriving in the morning at the office of Prothonotary Caspar Roan. They stomped snow from their boots and rubbed their hands together beneath their blanketcoats. Talked to Roan of the thickness of the ice and the floods that would follow. Then Jacob Lloyd conducted into the room two justices of the peace, silent, nodding men who went to the table and took up quills.

Pens enough for everyone else lay about the table. The affidavit was read, quills dipped. The tap and graze of wetted tips against paper, they were the sigh of relief Jedediah held back, that he resented.

He marked his christcross where he was told. He paid in coins his thirty pounds. And with that, he held title to his land. No man would take it from him.

Before the steepled courthouse, as the men unhitched their horses from saplings planted by the street, and against the ten dongs Crier Moses Tool tolled on the Burrows bell—the resistance to satisfaction fell away as the root of this reared into view, vivid as that lemon-yellow sun of winter.

There came a peace in the clarity of just the antagonizer—that fixed problem one could align himself against—so much less complicated than talk of affidavits and warrants, patents, deeds. On it went, their gab. Most about laws, which were least clear of all. Concentration. That's what he'd needed.

By the time Jedediah arrived home and lay down with the moonset early the next morning, he was a newly determined man. At daybreak, sleepless as usual but not tired at all, he went and sat at the edge of the bed. He felt about for Sarah beneath her quilts, finding the swell of her womb. Resting his hand there, he knew she awoke by the change in her breathing. "The oldest two," he said. "How old's they now?"

She did not answer, not until he said, "Damn it, tell me."

"George is nine. Jedediah Junior is eight."

He nodded. Old enough.

She waited. "Why do you want to know?" she said. "What is it?"

Jedediah watched bottle-tinged daylight catch like green filigree across the bark of the joist timbers. "Gonna get back to 'stillin'. Time they learned so someday I can pass on the business."

"Not that, Jedediah. Leave them out of it."

He slapped her stomach. "Don't tell me what to do. You and your Thomas Tillmans. And speakin' a' him, he been 'round here?"

"For God's sake, Jedediah."

"I'm watchin you," he said. "I'm watchin' everything."

A little foot slid along the wall of her womb like a mouse under a blanket. Sarah tried to take Jedediah's hand, but he pulled it away.

"When's that baby comin'?" he said

"February."

"A month

"Mm-huh."

He glanced where she hung a new calendar twelve times a year, a grid drawn on a sheet of birchbark on which she slashed off the many days of winter.

"Jedediah?"

"Huh?"

"What should we name the baby if it's a boy. I know you like to pick the boys."

He shrugged. "Call him James."

"James? He'd be James James."

"Then that," Jedediah said.

* * *

He'd lost his trade, but the wags of Williamsport were always thirsty. He'd build back business a flagon at a time and by spring be delivering kags again for the general trading store.

The boys. He'd start them out making applejack from a hard cider they'd ferment in the house. As soon as a thaw came, they'd distill corn liquor—until creek and river became navigable and he could barter trees again for rye.

The applejack would be his stepping stone back to the churls at the Russel Inn, something to whet appetites for that favored nectar soon to come. He'd meet with the trading store owner and undersell whomever had taken his place. Until he could call his price again for the quality of his whiskey.

So they culled bruised fruit from the cellar-cave he'd dug in the bank behind the house and crushed it in a tub hollowed out of a sycamore log, then filtered the juice through his horsehair sieve. They half-filled a barrel in a day, and Jedediah shared his secret of throwing in a little precious sugar from a box he kept in his stillhouse. "To get it goin' good." Sarah kept herself and the other children away—housekeeping in the upper half-story; out by the barn tending to the chickens and hogs; across the frozen creek visiting her brothers.

He covered the barrel with an ell of linen held down by two boards. "Now we keep the house warm and let it work."

The cider hardened in two weeks. After the evening meal, Sarah took the younger children above while Jedediah handed the boys noggins and made them drink from the barrel by the hearth. "A little kick, eh?" Jedediah said. They tried to quell coughs that came at last, eyes bulging, watering, sleeves mopping their mouths. "But that aren't the good stuff," Jedediah said. "You'll see." They took smaller sips, and though they swallowed hard, did not cough anymore.

They shuffled with the barrel out the door and into the yard. "Still good and cold at night," Jedediah said. "Maybe zero degrees. That's the best." Then he brought another board from the barn to fully cover the cider. "In the mornins'," he said, "we scoop off the ice. When the ice quits comin', we got our liquor. One sip and you'll see the difference."

Then up they went to the stillhouse. With a fire burning for warmth, Jedediah explained the parts of his still—the boiler and head, the tank for cooling, its coils. He revealed the mystery of making liquor, the boys following his gestures of hand, nodding each time he said, "You understand what I'm sayin'?" They spoke questions with low voices in deference to this awesome occupation and in keeping with its covert setting, in sacred secretness there in the wake of their mother's disapproval. Eyes flittering with the nervous gumption of wanting to please their father, they stepped right into whatever task—bringing in firewood, polishing the walls of the boiler with a sheep shammy—eager to take part in a man's work, but restraining themselves with that measured quietness and careful, furtive manner of doing something naughty. It all satisfied Jedediah immensely.

He drilled them on and on, keen they master quickly the art, learn the trade, taste the stream of money—protection against the Thomas Tillman's of the world, now and forever.

Though the day, damp and dun as a mussel shell, was cold to the bone, the door of the stillhouse had remained open. The boys were chilled by dusk to the point of shivering despite the fire. "Do we got to leave the door open?" Jedediah Junior said.

Jedediah looked outside, down through the woods where in the twilight a far hedge of a lighter gray hinted the cleared bottomland. "We got to watch out," he said. "For someone comin' after our place down there. Or after your mamma."

He was in the barn shelling corn when George ran from the house toward the creek, a floating fur-topped tent, the boy was, with his raccoon-capped head poked out of his blanketcoat.

"Where you off to, boy?" Jedediah called through the door-way.

George was out sight when he shouted back. "Fetching auntie. Mamma's ready to have the baby."

Jedediah waited in the barn. Half an hour later, Mary Starret came plodding through the snow with a sack over her shoulder. He'd heard Sarah's occasional moans, cries of, "Help us God," her grunts of agony. This had been a painful pregnancy; toward the end it had exhausted her, keeping her in bed some days until afternoon. Her skin was so light and transparent it appeared as sheer muslin wrapped across her skull with the orbs of her sunken eyes suspended in shadow.

After Mary entered the house, Jedediah went to the door. He cracked it open. The room flashed yellow with blazing pitchpine knots. Sarah lay still, legs spread before her sister-in-law who knelt at the bed, Sarah's shift pulled to her breast to reveal the great swell of her womb. Jedediah thought she'd died. Then Mary spread the pudenda with her fingers and Sarah squalled so fiercely Daniel and little Sarah cried "mamma" from the upper half-story. Jedediah strained his eyes that he might catch sight of the baby's emerging head. But it was not the head Mary exposed, rather little buttocks starkly purple against Sarah's frail white thighs.

"You got to push when I say," Mary said.

"It's dead, aren't it?" Sarah said.

"It's not. But it's gonna be if you don't push."

"Oh it hurts so. It's never been like this."

When Mary pressed down on Sarah's womb and worked her fingers around the little bum, Sarah arched her back and howled such that the baby must have been a candent coal.

"Now push," Mary said. And in a burst of pale fluid and a bloody tear of perineum, the little buttocks lurched onto Mary's palm, the legs turned back into the womb.

"Oh God Oh God it hurts it hurts. Why does it hurt so 'cept this baby's died on me."

"It's a backwards baby," Mary said. "It's just comin' out wrongways." She grasped the baby's hips between her thumb and middle finger. Now I got a hold of it—no it's a him. When I say push, you give it all you got."

"I can't," Sarah said. "Oh I can't." Fast, shallow pants, terrified eyes seeming to read omens in the pumping of shadow and light across the ceiling. "Where's Jedediah? I want him here with our baby if it's dead. I can't stand it alone no more."

Jedediah leaned away from the door until Mary said, "Never mind him. This baby'll be fine if you give me one more push. Now I'm countin' to three. One, two—"

But before Sarah could fetch her strength she screamed as a great convulsion quaked across her womb and thrust the baby out to its neck. "Oh Mary," she moaned out, "he's still in there, I can feel his little head. He aren't breathin', I know it."

With both hands, Mary clutched the baby by the trunk and pulled as she twisted him, the neck stretching such that Jedediah thought she'd tear him apart. Then Sarah sent forth their child and Mary slapped his bottom and swept his mouth of fluid, making him wrinkle his forehead and pucker his face as though he'd been fed a lemon. When he rasped out a hollow croak of a cough, Sarah bawled to the ceiling, "Thank God."

Mary took a linen from her sack and wiped oleaginous film from the baby. As she stood and passed him to Sarah—the blue, glistening cord still connecting mother and son—Mary said, "He's an odd one. Don't cry, but he's healthy. See him staring off mad at the world. Looks like Jedediah. Contrary."

Sarah gulped for breath and kissed the baby's fuzzy head. "Cry," she said. "Cry, little Jimmy James."

By the time the James family set off for Ferney Run for the marriage of George to Rosa Sharpe, the boy at sixteen was nearly as good a distiller as his father, and better than him at piloting logs through the bends and rapids of the Sinnemahoning Creek.

Jedediah had expected the union, and not just because bride and groom had so few choices in that backwoods. With George and Jedediah Junior sometimes transporting the whiskey now, their visits at the Sharpe place were more frequent. Jedediah figured Jedediah Junior and Berneta would someday follow.

They were three miles downstream by sunrise that second Friday in October, plodding along in their canoe and another borrowed from William. White mist sagged across the bluffs, fingers of fog dangling down wrinkles that springs had etched into the valley over the eons.

Jedediah and Jedediah Junior navigated their canoe hauling offerings for the celebration. George and Jacob—14 years old and plying the whiskey trade with his brothers now—paddled the other, the rest of the children and Sarah on board, Sarah lately keeping an even greater distance from Jedediah, seeing how she was a spark and he amadou.

The creek was low, so until they broke onto the river, all but the two youngest stepped out to push the canoes through the riffly shallows, legs soaked to the tops of stockings.

The elder of these two littlest was Jimmy James, seven now. He sat amidships and stared ahead with no interest in the world about him, even as his scowl said he was enraged with it. Something about him repulsed Jedediah, this one among the bunch always vexing him with no cause he could name. Yet the more Jedediah tried to ignore him, the harder the boy tried for attention. Too often, Jedediah found him at his elbow: "Daddy won't you play wif me?" And though his insides rent as he did it, Jedediah would send him off with curses, knowing that in a day he'd come back, some irrepressible hunger inhabiting the boy.

Beside Jimmy James, leaning over the gunnel with all the wonder and curiosity his brother lacked, the last child Sarah would bear stretched his fingers to break the tips of tiny curling waves. He was five years old, born a February morn when Jedediah was top-heavy with liquor—long winters were the times of his worst drinking bouts, in the throes of which he accused Sarah of making him a cuckold. "I smell snake shit 'round you," he'd say. "Tillman's been here."

And yet when the baby was born and Jedediah came to inspect it, his sister-in-law stepping away disgusted at the sight and smell of him, Sarah still deferred to Jedediah to name the child, as it was a boy.

"What do I care?" he said, words windy and slurred, a-float upon his liquor. "They're all bastards anyways."

Sarah, weeping with the baby at her dangling breast, sniveled out they would name him then after her brother the hunter. Benjamin Starret would come to take great pride in having a namesake, and favored the boy until the last he saw him when the younger Benjamin fled that country.

They moored their canoes at the mouth of Ferney Run where George met them with a sledge led by one of his mules—he had two healthy ones now. They loaded their effects and followed the sledge up the bridle path, past the mill, to the house.

George had improved his mill, increasing its capacity in pace with families settling between here and the Sinnemahone. He'd hired a millwright, and now the water from his flume spun a sturdy rotor of iron. The wright had affixed a toothed gear to the main shaft, and this, meeting a lantern wheel, powered a system that allowed George to load his overhead hopper by wooden conveyor. And on a subfloor beneath the stones, a belt turned a silk-covered bolting drum that separated flour from bran.

The Sharpes had doubled the size of their home, added a covered porch, shingled the roof, and put in four windows of plate glass—rare extravagance for George.

"Don't go up there and catch sight of your bride," Sarah told young George where she'd halted everyone on the bank before the cabin.

"Don't matter," Jedediah said, and waved it off. "Wives tale."

"She's holed up in the loft," George Sharpe said, lifting a sack from the sledge. "You won't see her 'til the preacher comes."

Where the James yard had become a weedy sty of defective farm tools, barrels and bottles, animal bones and ash piles, the sloping lot of the Sharpe place was mowed and clear of all but the rows of apple and pear trees among which the children ran with trailing skirts and shirttails in a game of tag.

Jedediah and Sarah waited on the porch while George carried the bags into the cabin. This was his busy season, but the betrothed had pestered so since summer that everyone conceded to letting them marry now. The mid-afternoon sky had broken blue. The bridegroom stood at the porch step squinting down to the trestle-supported, wooden sluiceway that replaced the old end-to-end logs. He was stiff in a waistcoat and cutaway tailcoat he'd bought in Williamsport, a linen kerchief gorgeted around his neck for a collar. He held a new high-crowned hat that Jedediah knew he was embarrassed to wear.

Rosanna stepped out, passed Jedediah as she glanced at his belt of pistols, and embraced Sarah. "I always knowed this day would come," Rosanna said and flicked up the corners of her lips in as much of a smile as Jedediah had ever seen her make.

"It's just as it should be," Sarah said. With a pointer finger, she touched away a tear at her lower eyelid.

Jedediah noticed that Sarah, her coat over her arm now, wore her necklace of bottle-glass outside her shortgown—she never took it off, but had long ago come to keep it beneath her clothes.

George came out, leaned over the porch banister and looked up at the sun. "Preacher'll be here soon," he said. "Nice enough day, we can have the weddin' outside."

"We'll eat inside, though," Rosanna said. "Much as I cleaned the house."

"Your house is always cleaned," Sarah said.

"There he is now," Rosanna said, pointing down the bridle path.

Young George paced while a rider approached on a black horse, its legs glistening from the ford. The preacher was a frail man of 30, fair of skin and hair, which he cropped straight back from brow to nape of neck. He walked the mare right to the porch, turned her askance, and nodded all around. "Everyone here?" he said, a whispery, congenial voice.

George confirmed they were and stepped off the porch to take the horse to the stable. The preacher, like others of his occupation who traveled that backcountry for marriage or interment, wore black that was not black, for his frock coat, knee-breeches and gaiters were dusted brown and had gray frays from briers, cockleburs, and unfriendly dogs. His broad-brimmed hat, though, the preacher kept well brushed, as he did his horse.

Dismounting, he sneezed and complained of a cold. "The weather," he said, indicating the sky. He unclasped a saddlebag, withdrew his Bible and asked to speak to the groom.

"Out in the yard," George said, "pacin' like a toe-trapped wild-cat."

The families gathered among the fruit trees, facing the house. The preacher and the boy George stood before them, backs to Rosa who stepped alone off the porch, eyes to the ground. She held a nosegay of autumn flowers: purple aster and goldenrod brilliant against the bleached linen of her high-waisted and ruf-fle-hemmed dress. She wore a linsey shawl over her shoulders, and on her head was a turban bonnet about which she'd wrapped a silk ribbon, copper-dyed by dogwood berries and tied in a bow above her right brow. Oiled ringlets dangled at her tem-ple and neck.

Flashing grins dimpled Rosa's cheeks when she reached George. A smite of tenderness surprised Jedediah for the pretty innocence of this girl who'd be his eldest son's wife.

The whispering of the children ceased as the preacher eyed the onlookers. "I spoke to the boy," he said, wiping his nose on the shoulder of his coat. "I'm satisfied this couple is ready to be wed. But you all need to solve the problem you been havin' about where they're goin' to live. It's tearin' 'em up."

The subject lingered like a polecat in the rafters as everyone sat for the meal in the cabin, the room washed in sunshine through the windows and in the smell of roasted pork and fresh-baked wheat bread. Little was said after the blessing but well-wishing for the bride and groom who sat stiff at the head of the two tables George had arranged end to end. The adults carved at their meat and waved away flies, avoiding that discussion the preacher had ordained necessary. Their mood caught with the children.

Jedediah rose and offered around his jug. All declined but the preacher. Jedediah poured his burl noggin full to the rim, and he liked the preacher for the cool proficiency with which he downed a heavy dram. Years of experience rinsing the dust of the road.

Rosanna threw her pewter fork onto her treenplate, a twang of the room's harpstring of tension. Two-year-old David started in her lap and set to crying. She rose and stepped over her bench, clutching the child at her hip. "I had it with this quarrel no one wants to finish," she said. "George needs the boy's help and I need Rosa's. The boy could learn a decent trade here. Someday he could go off and set up a mill a' his own."

"You got Caleb and Edward and the one you're holdin' for help," Jedediah said. "And two girls, too."

When Rosanna did not reply, Jedediah said, "George works for me in a trade he already knows. I need him that his mother learnt him to read and write."

Rosanna spoke to the ceiling, addressing only the subject, never Jedediah. "This couple needs a honest living. Not furnishin' liquor to cads in Williamsport."

George looked over his shoulder. "Rosanna," he said, and pointed to the squawking baby at her hip.

"Not this time you aren't defendin' your poor sufferer friend Jedediah James. He aren't takin' my eldest girl and makin' a' her another drunkard's wife." She made a sweeping gesture around the table. "This'll be the doom a' all these kids and them to come."

Now Sarah was on her feet. "Enough," she said, "of you disgracin' my husband in front of these children."

Jedediah nodded his approval.

"He disgraces hisself," Rosanna said.

The preacher had not stopped working at his second piece of roast pork, head bent over his treenplate even as he reached into his shirt and withdrew a handkerchief to wipe his nose. There came a hiatus during which the children braved biting into hunks of bread and sipping their chocolate. The preacher looked up, contemplated his cup of whiskey, and emptied it down his throat. He waited, then frowned at Jedediah who reached over with the jug and replenished his drink. The preacher held a finger in the air. "I got a wild idea," he said. "Why don't you let the bride and 'groom say where they're goin' to live." Then he went back to his pork while everyone turned to the couple as if they'd sneaked into the room.

For the sudden size and darting of young George's eyes, the preacher might have asked that he rise and repent of his sins. But Rosa looked at her mother and asked her to sit, please. Rosanna waited for her husband to say something, and when he did not, she stepped over the bench and lowered herself onto it, the child going silent.

"We've made up our mind," Rosa said.

"Boy," Jedediah spoke out, "I'll give you two hundred of the acres. Split the farm down the middle." He leaned ahead and looked each way at his six other children. "It's for all of you when you get married. Build cabins. Plant more ground. Take the timber." Then back to his son George: "So long as it's put on a paper you'll never sell it outta the family."

The room went quiet but for the preacher masticating. Rosanna pushed her treenplate away. "Now I want what their decision was before this all come up."

But Rosa was watching her new husband's eyes. Everyone was trying to read them.

"Two hundred acres," Jedediah said.

The boy studied a dish of butter on the table. He glanced at his wife.

"You're the man of the house now," Jedediah said.

Beside Jedediah, Sarah drew a deep breath. "I think maybe—" She grabbed hold of the table. "I think it's best they stay on here, Jedediah. I never meddled in your distillin', but I'm askin' this."

When Jedediah took her by the wrist, even the preacher looked up. "Rosanna been tryin' to turn you against me? You and your sneakin'. Boy," he said, not shifting his eyes from Sarah, drawing out his words, "you take that property, or you don't step on it so long as you live."

"Yessir."

Sarah did not move but for pinching together her lids to wring away tears.

The preacher set down his fork. He wiped his nose with the back of his hand and reached for his noggin. "You get that paper drawed up and I'll come witness it for you. For a fee, now," and he laughed as he raised his whiskey to his lips.

It was a simple covenant between Jedediah James and his six sons, minors though they were. As such, it would not have been worth its weight in parchment in a courtroom. The body of it read:

Witnesseth that the said Jedediah James Senior, in consideration of the sum of one dollar, doth agree to give his six sons George, Jedediah Junior, Jacob, Daniel, James and Benjamin and any who may follow a certain part of the lower end of the property. The division line is to be marked by the lower end of the house that the said Jedediah James Senior now lives in. And the line is to run in the same direction that the said house stands in and the line is to extend from the Sinnemahoning Creek straight back to the back line and the said Jedediah James Senior is to reside on his upper part and is not to make nor meddle but for shared farming with the said sons' part. And the said sons upon their lawful marriage is to reside on their part and not interfere with the said Jedediah James Senior's part but for shared farming. And further the said sons agrees not to sell or dispose of said land out of the family or to any person except themselves as witness our hands and seals this sixteenth day of October eighteen hundred and twenty. Witnesses Benjamin Starret and Washington Bartholomew.

Beneath this were the signatures of the witnesses and of the James brothers old enough to write, the names of the other two and Jedediah written in a single hand, Xs marked beside them.

There'd been no time to accept the preacher's offer. The morning after the wedding, Jedediah rushed to Williamsport and paid a justice of the peace twenty dollars to travel to the Sinnemahone that Monday.

Within a month, George and Rosa's cabin stood at the far end of the field. Soon afterward, Jedediah and Sarah learned they were grandparents to be—the following August, baby Nancy would be born.

Jedediah had moved his bedclothes to the barn, had done so the Saturday night they returned from the wedding. He took the stall closest to a plank door that opened to pasture, the creek beyond. During the cabin-raising, he sawed boards to enlarge the stall, enclosing it around the doorway as a room. He left another entrance from the barn bay and curtained it with a double-layer of bear hide which he'd replace with a door before winter. Then he cut an opening through the bottom logs of the exterior wall. He laid into the earth a clay hearth, constructed a small plastered fireplace, and raised a stick chimney.

He planted a pole in a hole in the dirt floor, the other end fixed into a notch in a joist of the hayloft above him. This became the corner post of his bedframe, across which he suspended slats of hand-hewn limbwood. He stuffed a tic with corn shuck and over this threw his flea-ridden bearskin and motheaten blankets.

No longer would he have to lie on a drafty floor to listen to the wolves. And through a window of plate glass that he framed into the logs at the height of his bed, he could look out.

Certain weeks, the pack held silent. Maybe they departed from that mustering ground on the ridge where the incessant wind swept a bald at its brow, a floor of moldering boulder around which a scurf of stunted, east-leaning pitchpines, scrub oaks and laurels abided a withered and knotted existence. Dour witness to flood and famine in the valley of the Sinnemahone. But he liked to believe that the wolves ghosted there still, muted by some unknowable shift in their conjunct blood tide. Even so, these were his most restless nights.

Something was different that April two years following. He was uneasy the first morn after the quiet, had a notion the turn was not by the normal workings of that voiceless current arranging every twitch of nerve and muscle into the order of hunts and haunts. For a man who looks out, who lives in endless anticipation of calamity, is sharp to the irregular. Keen as the beast. By sudden and subtle absences he detects something new in his midst. Perhaps birds common of a daybreak song hush, evening bullfrogs cease ronking from the mud in the bight of the creek, the cow quits the pasture, is found by the barn looking off to the fenceline.

The silence on the ridge was aberration in reflex to aberration. Something in the locale was awry. The wolves had smelled it, he felt it.

In a few days, the scheme crystalized, the irregularities of the moment set in relief to the remembered machinations of men in times past.

Now he could picture him up there watching, knew what he was about. What remained was who brought him—which of two. He didn't consider it was both.

* * *

He lay in bed, head propped on clumped burlap, face tilted toward the window. Dawn seeped like run lead into the lower wedge of the valley. The little frogs peeped with the fever of spring, ignorant of a rogue in their midst.

The first matter was to see his brother-in-law Benjamin. Jedediah was a skilled enough hunter, but he'd never stalked a man. He needed to consult someone whose livelihood was killing creatures of many kinds.

And should he take it on alone? He stroked his beard. Odds were better with someone watching his back. Benjamin would not accompany him given the prey. But the sons held a stake. For what would become of all Jedediah James had mastered if the wretch studying his farm from the ridge prevailed?

He rose from bed, thrust his pistols behind the band at his waist, and untied his moccasins from the stock of the Brown Bess. Setting off for his son's cabin, he said not a passing word to Jimmy James, who was on his way to milk the cow.

There was great risk in leaving the property in daylight. The abrupt lulls had told him the sonofabitch had been hereabouts, learning every egress and ingress. He supposed that now he watched by spyglass, his plan to waylay Jedediah upon a return. And so George must go with him to Benjamin's; that kind up there wouldn't take Jedediah in the presence of another.

In ten minutes they were in his canoe. "We're just goin' down the stretch to your uncle's," Jedediah said.

George shrugged, incurious about an impromptu trip—the business of whiskey making had habituated him to them.

They rode the current, watched ahead for the wavelets that underwater boulders made. "This 'tains to somethin' you never tell no one," Jedediah said. 'Cept your brothers—but not for a long time."

Again, George said nothing, used his paddle to turn the bow as they neared Benjamin's short stretch of bottomland.

They moored the canoe and tied it to a river birch; the creek could rise in an instant this time of year. Each took a jug of whiskey for Benjamin. Atop the bank, Jedediah turned and tilted his hat brim against bright white cloud cover as he traced the treeline of the far ridge. He found the break where trees could not find footing for the floor of stone, where wolves announced their revels.

The door was cracked open. Jedediah swung it wide and they entered. The cabin was a windowless, loftless, smoky black cavern illuminated only by a crackling fire of green wood and the doorway light behind them. Jedediah's eyes adjusted to the dimness. Peltry, stretched on boards, appeared against the walls, loose hides in the rafters. Wire traps in a heap. A blood-stained butchering table in the center of the room. The place was sour with chimney soot, putrid flesh, jars of the animal urines Benjamin used for trapping lures. They thought no one was about until a pile of furs stirred on the bed in the corner and Benjamin called out, "Who's there?"

"It's Jedediah. And my boy George."

Benjamin did not move for a moment. They thought perhaps he'd gone back to sleep. "Is it day or night?" he said.

"Morn," Jedediah said.

"Then I 'spose," Benjamin said, and he emerged from the covers, fully clothed: buckskin breeches fringed on the outer seams and blackened by animal fat and smokings to waterproof them; caped and belted hunting shirt of linsey; even knee leggins with a knife strapped beneath one of the tasseled bands, moccasins on his feet. He stepped past his visitors and just out the doorway where he pulled down his breeches and made water.

Returning, he stirred the fire, coughing at the smoke that backed into the cabin. He tossed a fagot against the backlog, pushed a gridiron over the coals, and set upon it a coffeepot. Then he lighted two sticks of candlewood and stuck them into cracks above the fireplace jambs.

As he plopped onto the hearth, Benjamin's eyes were lost against the glare of burning splinters, shadowed as his face was by curly black whiskers and locks. "I'd say set down, but..." He gestured around the room and Jedediah and George leaned against the table.

"How's little Benjamin?" Benjamin said.

"They all grow like bad weeds," Jedediah said.

"Wanna go fishin'?" Benjamin said.

Jedediah shook his head.

"Don't see much a' none a' you lately," Benjamin said.

"Busy times," Jedediah said.

"Whiskey work," Benjamin said.

"We set two jugs outside the door," Jedediah said.

A pink tongue wiggled from the murk of Benjamin's face as he wet his lips or rather the whiskers that covered them.

"I'm bein' hunted," Jedediah said.

Benjamin's head jerked up; the excitement of the chase. "You'd be a easy man to hunt," he said. "I could pick you off the creek most any week 'tween here and Williamsport."

"He needs to take me alive."

"So he's a trapper," Benjamin said. "That's a worse predicament for both a' you. Now you said just one he. You sure a' that?"

Jedediah nodded. "This kind always works alone."

Benjamin plucked at his beard. He pulled something out and held it in the firelight, flicked it away. "So you want to trap him instead."

"I want to hunt him."

Benjamin shifted such that Jedediah knew he studied the boy.

"Less I know a' this," Benjamin said, "the better."

"You don't need particulars to help me think this through. I know where he's camped in the woods. I know what he's about."

Benjamin still watched George. "You're doin' this alone, right?"

"Never mind that," Jedediah said.

"How old's he?" Benjamin said.

"I'm eighteen," George said.

"He's a man," Jedediah said. "This concerns them that'll take on my land and business as much as it concerns me."

Benjamin tipped his head toward the dirt floor. "I can't help with somethin' like this."

"I aren't askin' for nothin' but an idea I might not a' thought up. I got no choice but to hunt him. You think I could trap a man, then the law take my word against his?"

Benjamin withdrew his knife. He turned sidelong to the fire and used the point to dig beneath the tips of his fingernails. "I take no part in killin' anything I can't eat or trade," he said. "If you're carryin' this out anyways, I spose I'll speak a' huntin in general and you do what you want with it." He pointed the knife at Jedediah. "But you need to leave the boy outta it."

"He's in it already," Jedediah said.

Shaking his head, Benjamin went back to his fingernails. "Comes down to two ways a' huntin' anything. You stalk or you ambush. Now say you think the game's watchin' you. We don't have much a' that 'round here, but let's say it's so. You take a good hound. Like my Hercules. Where the hell is he? But you aren't takin' him, anyways. You take a good dog deep into the woods and 'ventually you make a big circle. Now when you come back on your trail, you watch that dog. He'll tell you if it's the quarry been trackin' you instead a' the way it's s'posed to be. You go on ahead and find cover where you can make a waylay."

"What about the other way?" Jedediah said. "If a man don't have a good dog and his brother-in-law won't loan his?"

"Stalkin'. That's the harder, my opinion. You know well as I do the advantage goes to the one sittin' still over the one movin'. But let's say you know where the creature's laid up. Then you take your time. You move so slow on him it hurts. One step, wait. One step, wait. Tree to tree. And you stay downwind."

"This animal I'm huntin' don't have a nose like others."

"Don't matter. Sound travels on wind. Broke branch. Graze a' your leggin on brush. But you don't let that happen anyways." He turned up the palm in which lay the knife handle. "Still."

"Day or night?" Jedediah said.

"Day," Benjamin said. "See, nighttime's when most woods creatures are about. Lot more for the hunter to put on alert. He'll hush the woods. A animal can feel that around him."

Jedediah started for the door. "I know how you mean," he said.

A plan was forming in place of the black cloud lifting from his mind. And he knew that despite the pang that remained in his gut, he had to eat to be strong, to have his wits. George, too. A little doze tonight would be nice, but he didn't count on it. Should he drink whiskey or not?

They found Sarah smoking from her clay pipe in her chair by the fire. Benjamin and Jimmy James were at her feet with slates on their laps, Benjamin writing while Jimmy James made the motions of a walking spider with his fingers on the hearth. Sarah smiled, wished Jedediah and George a good morning. Lately, she was less the wounded wife of this man who'd abandoned not just her bed, but her presence outside meals and the minimum necessities of keeping a home. She'd been offering pleasantries, inquiring of his business and his needs about the farm. She was telling him she tried to understand him, though he knew he was beyond understanding. Somehow she had heart enough to let the past go, she and that indomitable hope, that he might be moved by the effort. And he resented it all, for he supposed pity in her kindness.

"What's to eat?" Jedediah said.

"A stew of frog's legs and onions," she said. "I'll make johnnycakes."

He went right to a shelf and took down a bowl and a spoon. "George," he said, "eat up. It'll be a whole day huntin' tomorrow."

"What are you huntin' this time of year?" Sarah said.

"Rat," Jedediah said. "I'm goin' to get me a big white rat."

The hollow of the lower run fissured into the unmapped country so narrowly, its great pines and hemlocks shrouded its ceiling so densely, it wouldn't have mattered if the crescent of waning moon was enough to light a course. Jedediah carried a cresset of pitchpine knot and suspended over his shoulder his musket, George following, firelight flapping across the cockled bark of tree trunks as they picked their way among streamside boulders and deadfalls.

The night sky appeared when they attained the bare hardwoods of the plateau, a sheen on the starless eastern hemisphere telling of dawn. They turned back on themselves, angling over the flats toward the lip of the ridge. By sunup,

Jedediah warned George to mind any noise. "Walk Indian-like from here on. We're miles out, but we got to be a-guard a' him maybe about, away from his camp."

Two hours later, morning full-on but still gripped in the evening chill, they saw the break of the valley through the woods ahead. Jedediah's plan, gauged by watching the sun as they'd moved northeastward, had been to reach sight of the ridge downstream and downwind of the wolves' howling ground, and then work upwind just within view of the crest, sure not to misgauge their mark.

Jedediah pointed toward the valley. "We're not far down from your uncle Benjamin's," he whispered.

George peered that way. "Then why'd we walk ten mile to get here?"

"We'd a' been found out goin down the creek and up that wall. Now we'll stay back from the drop and outta the noisy laurel over there, sneak along through the open woods. Tree to tree like Benjamin says."

"Then what?" George said.

"When I see him, I'll say what," Jedediah said.

It was slow and painful walking, Jedediah snapping around at George for any misstep on twig or loose stone. As the sunrays drove in from the meridian, the woods of great oak and cherry, poplar, birch, chestnut and scattered red pine, closed in on them in a glare, tree bark taking on the burnish of Britannia and obscuring the distance. Jedediah, sweating, squinting as he looked out from tree trunks, doubted himself. Why hadn't he seen the opening on the ridge? He'd hunted this top a hundred times.

Damn his eyes. What the hell was that shining over by the edge? He sneaked behind a chestnut in that direction. "George," he whispered.

"What is it?"

"Quiet," Jedediah said. "Lean 'round me. Slow as a worm. Tell me if you see somethin' out ahead. Maybe twenty rod."

He waited.

"Hell, yeah," George said. "Camp set up right there. Not even ten rod. He's got some kind a' tarpaulin strung up in the trees. Back off the open piece."

"Shit," Jedediah said. "We're on top a' him. I wanted to send you around." He turned, studied the sky. "If I go straight at him, least he's lookin' into the sun."

"What am I s'posed to do?"

"Make sure a' the prime a' your musket. Follow behind ten paces or so."

"What'll I do with the gun?"

"You kill the son-of-bitch if you have to. You kill him dead."

George's eyes flitted everywhere but at his father. "I can't just—" he steadied his breath. "I can't kill a man I don't got a quarrel with. I don't know if I could kill a man I got one with."

Should've brought whiskey, Jedediah thought. "That bastard over there is watchin' for me. There's things you don't know 'bout your daddy. That man leaves here alive, you'll never see me again. And you'll lose that land I give you."

"For Chrisesakes," George said.

Holding his upper body stiff as a hickory sapling, Jedediah lifted and advanced each leg tortuously slow. If he felt a stick beneath a moccasin, he shifted his footfall, the thigh pain of keeping on balance burning into his back. Especially on the side of his bad leg.

His banded pistols were primed, the grips turned at the ready, and his thumb was on the hammer of his musket. He was half an hour walking tree trunk to tree trunk before he could make out details beneath the waxed tarpaulin: bedroll, knapsack, a ring of stone encircling cold coals. A rifle against a tree from which the canvas was tied. And out on the floor of sandstone stood a three-legged trestle holding a spyglass. Aimed into the valley, upstream at the farm.

He chanced sneaking to another tree and then others until he rested, leaning against an oak at the far side of the tarpaulin. When he saw him out there, the anger set in, as did a wish for whiskey, for he began shaking, convulsions wrung out of his chest by each heartthrob. There he'd been all the while. At the edge of the bald, squatted beyond a lone laurel. Watching the valley, that Jedediah might paddle downstream and a trap be set.

His teeth would have chattered were his jaw not clenched. He forbore the urge to shoulder his musket, that rush for action when he spotted game in the hunt. Too often he took a sloppy shot through brush, anxious the game might get away. Take it slow, he thought. He'll step into the open, maybe to study the farm through his spyglass.

Yet if Jedediah waited too long, the fury would further weaken his wits and handiness. And he could hardly hold his bowels, they quivered so. Better then to draw him out.

Leaning hard into the tree, he raised the musket and pulled back the cock. "Slave catcher," he said. "I'm over here."

The man made no move, probably weighing whether he was hidden and merely being called out.

"I see you there," Jedediah said. "I wanna talk to you,"

The slave catcher's hat inched around until one eye was visible. He turned and shuffled onto the sandstone. His mouth was snarled around a twig from which he'd whittled away the bark, a shot pouch slung over his shoulder and already a pistol in his hand. Jedediah knew it could not be loaded. Well, likely not.

Aiming at the brow beneath the stiff brim of a fresh beaver hat, Jedediah said, "You know who I am?" his voice as unsteady as the muzzle.

"Don't matter who you are," the slave catcher said.

"I figured that," Jedediah said. "You buy your niggers on the hoof, aren't that so?"

The slave catcher nodded. "Smart one, I see."

Jedediah noted the drawl, the lines at his eyes from years of squinting against southern sunshine as he led coffles sale to sale, the hoarseness of voice from his tobacco.

The slave catcher turned up his empty palm, forearm rested on his thigh. "I give any old nigger I bag the name some master that lost his slave wants it to be. Ya'all look the same." He shrugged one shoulder. "I'm just a man right'n a score."

Hot needles burned into Jedediah's left shoulder as he kept aloft the heavy barrel of the old Brown Bess, his hand going dull. The man's brass added to his ire, but in such a way that

262 · PJ PICCIRILLO

something rose to steel his voice and steady the musket. "Looks the nigger caught the catcher."

The slave catcher made a quick survey of the woodsline.

"I aren't alone," Jedediah said.

Shifting the twig from one side of his mouth to the other, the slave catcher grinned. "I only come all this way cause I was told you'd be a' easy take, boy. Seein' you understand that I don't need you in particular, why don't you slip on down this mountain and I'll call this one even."

"What I understand," Jedediah said, "is no one'd know to look for your body, huntin' someone like me."

The slave catcher eyed the muzzle. It waved again and dipped and lifted and Jedediah knew there was maybe half a chance he'd hit him. Keeping his aim as best he could, he eased the butt of the stock into his armpit and clasped it, the ache pouring out of his shoulder. "Who put you on to me?" Jedediah said.

Chuckling, the slave catcher chewed his twig and thumbed back the cock of his pistol. No way that's loaded, Jedediah thought.

"Was it Thomas Tillman or Peter Bakeraskin?" And Jedediah saw his answer in the briefest balk in the slave catcher's attention, a flit of the eyes at the unexpected suggestion of one or the other where it had been an alliance: Tillman, wanting Jedediah's wife and land, partnered with Bakeraskin for the means to such as this before Jedediah.

The slave catcher jerked his head at something in the woods.

"Never mind him," Jedediah said, but as fast as snakebite the slave catcher raised his pistol and fired past him, Jedediah returning the shot in a start without a thought of his aim. He called himself an idiot and dropped the musket and drew out his pistols, charging ahead while he screamed George's name.

The cap of his powderhorn already between his teeth, the slave catcher disappeared over the precipice. Jedediah crouched, peered down. There he was, sliding to the base of a black birch thirty yards beneath him. Raising both barrels as the slave catcher turned on his knees and rammed home a ball, Jedediah sighted the biggest part of his body and pulled the triggers. Smoke blew from the pans and muzzles, and just beside a button hole in the slave catcher's open coat, a singe mark formed in the linsey of his shirt. He grunted and bent, his hat dropping to the ground.

When Jedediah reached him, the slave catcher was pushing himself up with one hand, raising his pistol with the other. Jedediah stomped the wrist of this hand to the ground, dropped his own pistols, and wrenched away the one the slave catcher still clung to. Stepping off the wrist and cupping the man's throat in his palm, Jedediah forced his head against the black birch. The moaning blows of the slave catcher's lungs bubbled the blood at a corner of his lips before it ran in a frothy rivulet through the blonde stubble of his chin. As he keened out "please," a tawny backwash of dinner spurted then oozed from the hole at his middle, fume of gutshot fouling the air.

Then George was sliding off the bluff, stones kicking up leaves ahead of him until he got to his feet beside Jedediah. "We kilt him, Dad," George said. "Oh God."

Touching the muzzle to the temple of the slave catcher, whose breath was reduced to a fit of desperate and soggy in-sucks, Jedediah scowled at George. "We? Why didn't you shoot? I feared he got you."

George was in a palsy, eyes wide on the slave catcher. "He pulled so fast. I heard the bullet come by. I heard it whistle holy shit. He's kilt, Dad. I can't believe it's happened."

"Here's what I'm doin' first," Jedediah said, and George winced and twisted away for a finishing shot. But Jedediah released the cock of the pistol and stuffed it beneath his linen band. He let go of the slave catcher's throat, raised his right moccasin, and rested the sole against the man's chest. With all his loathing for the order behind this rat's errand, Jedediah thrust his foot. Out came ghastly wails and a drool of blood, out gushed the reeking bilious slop of the slave catcher's bowels. Jedediah ground his heel like a mortar, and George, in the grip of the awful cries, tried to pull his father away. But Jedediah cursed him and drove on until he lost balance and drew away his moccasin and blood-sodden stocking and the slave catcher collapsed before them heaving into his flux.

"For Chrisesakes," George said. "Now what?"

Jedediah looked at his son and pointed to the top of the ridge. "We drag him back up there," he said. "For the wolves."

By the time they tugged the dying slave catcher onto the sandstone, the coming otherworld had glaired his eyes and he could only mouth his pleas and laments.

Jedediah withdrew the pistol and presented it over the slave catcher, George's hand trembling as he took hold of the piece. He inspected it, he closed his eyes and shook his head back and forth, but in the end he stuffed the pistol under his own linen band. Then Jedediah pulled from his shirt the slave catcher's shot pouch and beaver hat and gave these to his son. The hat fit. And lifting his eyes to the stiff brim, the fine material and craft, George eased.

Sending George for the Brown Bess, Jedediah went and shouldered the knapsack and took up the rifle. It was a fine gun with a patchbox set into the stock, an intricate filigree of brass garland extending from the hinged door up to the comb and clear to the lock. There was an inscription he'd have to file away.

Back at the edge with George, Jedediah stuffed the spyglass into the sack and looked up the valley. The thread of the Sinnemahoning poured forth a-glitter in April's white westering sunlight. He caught tiny scintillations coming off the gray-weathered shingles of his house and barn. "We aren't done yet," he said, and started down the slope. They'd be home in less than an hour.

Stopping at the tree to retrieve his pistols, Jedediah turned back to the summit. He cupped his hands around his mouth. "Die slow," he shouted, his voice carrying upward on that breeze that forever battered this highland. "You die there knowin' you didn't take nothin' a' Jedediah James."

They stood in the bench of woods and watched the house, saw nothing out of the ordinary—just the littered yard, the cow and horse and hens meandering the pasture, the snuffling hogs rooting about a wall of the barn. Smoke rising from the chimney. When the girl Sarah, fourteen now, and Daniel, a year younger, walked with pails up the trail toward the spring, Jedediah and

George gathered their plunder. They passed the boy and girl without a word, Sarah keeping a goodly distance as she eyed Jedediah's arsenal.

After rounding the house, Jedediah ordered George home to tell his wife he'd be gone for the night. "Meet me at my canoe," he said. "Make sure you bring that new pistol and shot pouch. And the horn-window lantern you got at your weddin'. For while we're canoein' in the darktime."

Sarah and little Benjamin sat at a bench, facing away from the table, the churn between Sarah's legs while she plunged the dasher kern into cream. The house was dim but for a feeble fire where Jedediah charred cloth for the tinderbox he kept stuffed in his shirt. Then, as he rummaged for the candles he would not let Sarah light, taking as many as he figured necessary to re-plenish the lantern as it lighted their way from the prow of the canoe, he told Sarah he had business in Williamsport. Then he departed for the barn where he'd leave his rifle and musket and spyglass and get the money he'd need, freshen his shot pouch.

The doors were swung wide. He blamed Jedediah Junior and Jacob who'd probably taken their horse to their cousins'. No, more likely they'd wasted the day down on the river at the Sharpe's, pestering that girl Berneta they vied over. Should be at the still or about farm work.

Just inside, he caught by the milky daylight floating in be-hind him someone at the foot of the ladder to the haymow. Little Jimmy James. He was so black of face and filthy of linen that Jedediah wouldn't have seen him but for the whites of his eyes and the luster of that bulbous forehead. He'd catch this boy alone in the oddest places—beneath the eaves at the back of the barn, inside the springhouse, off in the woods. Quiet, a melan-choly little thing, the sight of him always annoying. And he was forbidden to be near Jedediah's room.

"What're you doin' in here?" Jedediah said.

The eyes shifted back and forth; the brat didn't even know what he was about. Or he was up to no good and fished for a lie.

"You answer when I talk," Jedediah said. Details emerged as his eyes adjusted. What was that the boy held? "The hell you got a corn knife for?" But Jimmy James would not look at him, and

Jedediah saw he was fixed on his stocking and moccasin where the blood had darkened and dried.

"What'd you kill, Daddy?" Jimmy James said, then studied the firearms in Jedediah's belt and hands. "When you gonna take me to kill somethin'?"

Jedediah realized when the boy cowered that he'd raised the butt of the rifle. Why did this child provoke him so? "Get outta here," he said. "Stay the hell away from me."

Riding the surge of the springtime swell, they made it down the creek and then the river in time to catch the evening horde at the Russel Inn. Halting George outside the place, Jedediah said, "Stay here. I got to make quick business of this and I don't want them pesterin' about whiskey."

George rubbed his forehead, groped the pistol at his waist. "I can't do no more killin'."

"More?" Jedediah said. "You've not done none yet." He started toward the cackles of laughter leaking out the loose panes of the un-shuttered windows.

A crowd was huddled around a corner table, everyone leaning toward cups, enthralled by the gossiper of the moment. A few heads turned to see what chum had stepped in from one or another of the taverns that had sprung up about town. "It's Jedediah James the distiller," a woman said, and noggins rose into the smoke. "To the maker of spirits."

Tonight's barkeep was a stout, bearded Prussian named Mikolay Schaade to whom the Jameses delivered their product in the publican's stead, even the Russel Inn now a customer. "Some of your own?" Schaade said, shoulders raised above his collar as he leaned into the bar with his great hands clutching its edge.

"No," Jedediah said. "I want high proof. I want four bottles."

Schaade lifted his chin. "One-hundred-and-ninety proof? Four?"

Jedediah nodded. "Four."

Wrenching up his lips, Schaade swung around and stepped through the curtained doorway. He returned with the necks of two bottles suspended between fingers of either hand. He set these on the bar, uncorked one, and bent for a noggin beneath the countertop.

Jedediah held up a hand. "Save that." He sucked down the pure alcohol until his forehead beaded with sweat and sawteeth coursed his throat. Pitching forward, he slammed down the bottle and exhaled like a bellows, for an arrow of fire had touched off an inferno in his gut. He straightened and bounced in a little dance. Accustomed as his stomach was to whiskey, the years of it chafing there had made him more sensitive to high proof.

The party in the corner had gone quiet. He looked over, saw them studying these bottles brought from the kitchen. Two men crept toward the bar, noggins in hand. Envoys.

The first to arrive at Jedediah's elbow sniffed the air, nodded at the liquor with deference, and said, "Me sees you're takin' on a jag with the white stuff."

For fear of fleas, Jedediah pulled his arm away, just as the second soak stepped up to his left side. "Which a' you," Jedediah said, "wants one a' them bottles for a piece a' information."

They leaned over the bar and looked at one another, the bred courtesy of vultures at the feast, sure the spoils would be shared. The one to the left rushed his etiquette. "I'll do it. If I can leave it corked. For later, you know."

Jedediah laid down his money, gathered all four bottles, and went to the nearest table. Sitting, he put down the spirits and waved away the man who hadn't spoken quickly enough.

"The name is Mathias Kerr," the other said as he drew up a chair, his words whistling between his few upper teeth.

Jedediah flapped his hand at this. "I wanna know where someone lives."

"Then ye've struck it lucky," Kerr said. "I know Williamsport like a lion knows he's den."

Jedediah looked around, whispered the name. "Thomas Tillman."

Kerr let forth a gummy smile and shot a finger into the air. But his eyes were vacant as he turned the soggy gears of his mind. When the name met recollection, the smile disappeared and Kerr drew the finger to his lip. "Ah, the newspaperman. Ye've got a complaint with 'im. Not so friendly to yer kind."

Jedediah took hold of Kerr's coat. "You're not to wonder what I'm about."

"Here, now," Schaade said from the bar.

"I'm only at yer service," Kerr said as Jedediah let go. "Tillman's got a sign hung by this same street. Going that way." He pointed east. "Says, 'Gazette.'" He raised his hands. "Well, I mean ye no insult if ye might not be read. But then I've an idea. I'll take ye there."

Jedediah was on his feet already. He picked up the uncorked bottle, guzzled, then bent until the searing of his throat eased. He squeezed away tears, pushed a corked bottle toward Mathias Kerr, and grabbed the other two by their necks. "Go away and drink," Jedediah said. "You'll be a sorry man if you're not liquored enough by daybreak to forget you saw me."

In the scant moonlight, Jedediah had George put his nose to signs along the street to read them. "This is it," George said, and Jedediah strained his eyes at the home of two stories. He guessed there were living quarters upstairs, the newspaper business beneath. All quiet. All dark. All right.

He finished his bottle and dropped it in the street, suppressed a cough. He bit out the cork of another, spit it away. "We're goin' 'round back," he said and staggered through the yard. Beneath the rear eave, he sized the distance to houses on the street closer to the river, to those of next-door neighbors, dogs barking within some now, without others.

George shook his head no when Jedediah held out the bottle.

"I don't want you to drink it," Jedediah said. "I want you to hold it." He uncorked the last one, and with sharp stabs, spurted the liquor onto the bottom clapboards as he walked to the far corner of the house. Swinging around, he tossed the bottle into the yard, nearly losing balance. Better hurry; he was about to vomit, and the nearest dogs were in a frenzy.

Returning to George, he took the last of the spirits and repeated the soaking to the front corner. Then he braced himself against the house, lest he fall as he lowered himself to his knees. He withdrew his tinderbox and swung open the lid as he set it on the ground. He wrapped his fingers through the oval of the steel, took up the flint, and fluffed his charcloth. Trying to strike the steel against the edge of the flint, he missed more than he hit, occasional flakes of spark falling, not the shower he needed. He glanced toward the river. Lamplight in a window. A woman cursing at her dog. "George," he hissed. "Come here."

"What in hell we doin'?" George said.

Jedediah handed him one of his pistols. "Fill the pan," he said.

"In the dark? Holy shit."

"Do it and hurry," Jedediah said. "Don't measure. Just enough for a flash. I'm gonna be sick."

"Good God," George said.

Jedediah dragged himself away and spewed pure liquid. Then some kind of acid sanies. The dogs went wild with the sound, the smell. Another neighbor railed at the commotion. Was that skylight to the East?

He crawled back to George, said, "I feel some better now." But Jedediah could not pull the cock of the pistol. He strained, got it. Touching the pan to the charcloth, he lowered his lips near it, fired. Upon the snap and flash, he puffed, his lungs taxed but blowing just enough that a meek yellow flame rose from the tinder. It disappeared into an amorphous blotch of ember. He held this to the soaked clapboards and exhaled upon it. With a woof and a scorching of Jedediah's forehead, a streak of fire combusted across the wall.

A day and half later, his body remained an aching capsule of nausea. Had George not pulled him along in the canoe the first day, through that night, through today, he would have collapsed in a plum thicket and hoped—or hoped not—that he might arise.

Lacking the energy to make his own fire, he'd stumbled right to the house and lay on the bed in a stupor, too miserable to sleep. Sarah feared he had the yellow fever, said she'd never seen him this crapulous.

Jedediah would not let George, who all through their return had repeated, "We'll be hanged for one or the other crime or twice for both," go home until they were sure no one pursued them. George paced around the table wringing his hands and wiping his brow with his shirtsleeve. He cast off his coat, his shirt soaked.

Sarah sent the youngest ones into the upper half-story and Jedediah Junior and Jacob to the haymow. As the last of daylight sifted through the bottle-glass windows, she lit two crusie lamps and her pipe. She sat in her chair, and between troubled glances, read from her Bible.

The knock at the door came an hour later.

"Oh, Lord," George said.

Jedediah sat up, dizzy by the effort while he waited for his reluctant heart to catch up. He drew a pistol and warned Sarah not to go to the door.

"What have you done, Jedediah?" She closed the Bible and set her pipe on the floor. "Have you gotten George into trouble?"

A horse blew in the yard. The knocking again. A muffled voice said, "Jedediah James. We're two deputies of the sheriff. You're to answer before a judge."

He pulled out his other pistol and went to the door, glanced back at George who bent now with his elbows on the table, his face in his hands. Jedediah looked at the pistols. Hell, they weren't even primed. Idiot.

"For murder?" he shouted through the door.

"Aren't you a funny one? Arson. You were fool enough to leave behind bottles empty of the rotgut you bought at the Russel Inn. I got papers to show it. But you can't read anyways."

"Me alone?" Jedediah said.

"Who else?" the deputy sheriff said.

This satisfied Jedediah. He went and tossed the pistols onto the table, returned and rasped back the bar. The door swung wide by the force of rifle muzzles.

As Sarah stoppered a cry, the deputies rushed past Jedediah to each side of his son who stood trembling with the two pistols before him and his own tucked into the band at his waist.

"Never mind him," Jedediah said. "I'm the one you're after."

One of the men held his rifle on George while the other stepped back to Jedediah. He creased his eyes and examined something on Jedediah's face. "I'll be hanged," he said. "This is our man. He's got no eyebrows."

Starting toward the bed for the blanketcoat he'd used as a cover, Jedediah found Jimmy James skulking by the ladder, mouth parted as he plumbed the scene with those eyes that had a look of knowing horrors beyond bearing. A glint of lamplight caught on tears tracing his nose, and though Jedediah could make no sense of why, these infuriated him.

"Don't let them men take you, Daddy," Jimmy James said.

"Git your ass outta here," Jedediah said, and the boy scampered up the ladder quick and frightened as a treed opossum.

They'd brought him a horse. Hands bound, he rode between the deputies. At the creek, Jedediah told them of the easier ford upstream. "These nice shod horses won't have to cross a deep part in the dark," and he surprised himself at the lightness of his mood.

The men appreciated the information, for as they forded in the thin starlight, the water at the horses' knees was black as rock oil. They proceeded upstream along the far path, followed the first fork past William's farm, then turned up the Ellicott Road whereby they'd avoid the old tortuous way of wading from one scant creekside trail to another.

Within the forest, they had not even starlight. The horses peered and bobbed their heads as they made their ways around deadfalls, the deputies fearing they'd lost the road altogether. They murmured about the fierceness of this country and the threat of catamounts and rattlesnakes, about the forlorn feel of the place even in daylight, what with such precipitous hollows, monstrous trees, dank under-canopy.

Then, after they'd gained the heights and the rising moon showed through twisting tree limbs, there came the cry of the wolves from their gathering place. So sharp was the cleft of valley the men flanked that the sound seemed too close to come from an opposite ridge, clear and threatening right down to the softest yip.

The first deputy pulled up his reins and the three men listened. The wolves were in a frenzy: gibbers and hoots of bliss, gruff fighting barks, belligerent snarls. The sound of blood.

The hullabaloo climaxed and the wolves paused to gather

strength. "That's a bloodcurdling song," the deputy in the lead said. "So close. Up in this goddamned mean country." He leaned and spat. "Jesus that scares the shit outta me."

Despite Jedediah's hands being bound, despite poor prospects and the poisoning of high proof, a comforting peace settled on him. Having miscarried this second venture, he felt all the more satisfied in his success with the first. He'd won the greater battle, if not the war.

The deputies sat their horses, taking sanctuary in the silence of hiatus. The fools—fearing that which let itself be known.

Then the wolves released with humanlike whoops of rapture. Grinning, Jedediah drove his heels into his horse's flanks, and so compelled the party to carry on.

He had a pile of moldy hay and a chamber pot, no communication beyond this stone gaol cell except a high window with the shutters thrown back and a barred slit in the door. He drifted between woken moments of remembering and catalepsy, interludes as close to restful sleep as he could recall. He knew not if he lay thus a day or days, moving only to shift in the hay, scratch where chaff breeched his shirtfront or sleeves, when a bar slid across the other side of the door and Caspar Roan and Jacob Lloyd entered.

"Get up," Roan said, jerking a thumb over his shoulder, the first Jedediah had seen the man angry.

Jacob Lloyd remained by the door as someone unseen shut and barred it. "Look," he said, "he's pissed himself."

"I said get up," Roan said, and Jedediah raised himself to sitting. Drawing his knees to his chest, he felt shifting against his thighs the chill of what Lloyd had remarked.

"Why would a man," Roan said, "slap the nose of a dog that at every opportunity bites him?"

"How many times I told you," Jedediah said, "I don't need your help?"

"Oh, you need our help," Jacob Lloyd said. "You're about to spend the rest of your days in such a hovel as this. And lose everything."

"You have a decision to make," Caspar Roan said. "And you're lucky for that because if that whole house had caught afire and killed Thomas Tillman, your only choice would be a rope around your neck."

Jedediah groaned. "It didn't burn?"

"For God's sake," Jacob Lloyd said.

Roan squatted in front of Jedediah, elbows on his knees. "You plead guilty, we can arrange for some gaol time and restitution—your payment for Tillman's damages. You plead innocent, you will lose and spend your days locked away.

"I aren't givin' Thomas Tillman a penny," Jedediah said.

Roan glanced back at Jacob Lloyd. Lloyd shrugged. "You realize," Roan said, "that if you don't plead guilty, Thomas Tillman will scheme and get your farm while you're in gaol?"

Jedediah sucked on whiskers that had grown over his lips, studied the far corner. "I can say 'guilty'," he said. "And you can tell 'em all you want I'll pay him. Tell 'em I'll pay him when I have the money."

On the morning of the trial two days later—the good prothonotary able to wedge the case into the docket of an old friend, Ex-sheriff and Associate Judge John Cummings—Sarah, carrying fresh clothes for Jedediah, was led into the cell by a deputy. Alone all this time, Jedediah still couldn't help irritation at this intrusion on his strange peace, the bear-like stupor.

She knelt before him, kissed his cheek, smiled. "Caspar explained the plan," she said. "I'll be there for you."

And so with Jacob Lloyd standing beside him, Jedediah answered "guilty" to the short, round judge.

Two days had been time enough for word to spread that whiskey maker Jedediah James was to be tried and hanged for arson. All agreed he'd done it in response to Thomas Tillman's newspaper articles, full of spicy calls for black codes and rants against ownership of land by Africans. The crowd was thronging even out the doors, Sarah, Caspar Roan and Thomas Tillman each squeezed into a respective pew among the reeking wags of the street.

Jedediah's plea drew delighted "hear, hears" followed by

whispers of, "we'll have us a hangin' by mornin'." Then everyone looked where the young deputy attorney general, Joseph B. Anthony, sat with the sheriff at the other side of the room. Jedediah thought Anthony a fop in his ruffles and long-tailed, violet coat with its collar starched to his ears. Court dress. Anthony stood, cocked hat in hand. "We accept the plea," he said. "We're ready to move on to sentencing."

Though the tavern-folk of Williamsport, practiced as they were in law, did not grasp all the technicalities of court, they understood by careful study of the best cases its moods. They smelled a conclusion contrary to their expectations, and where there had been a charge to the air of the room—necks extended, swollen eyes wide and flashing—came gloom. The thirstiest even left their pews and pressed through the bunch at the door.

The judge turned to Jedediah who had taken his seat. "Rise again, Jedediah James."

Jedediah stood.

"As has been agreed," the judge said, "between the Commonwealth and your counsel in the event you made such a plea, I sentence you to the following. Thirty days in gaol. Less time served. You will pay the county these reparations." He raised a paper to his eyes. "One. The cost of your summons and conveyance to gaol. Twelve dollars. Two. The cost of your incarceration. Thirty dollars. Three. Court costs. Four dollars." He set the paper before him, squinted until he found Jedediah. "Furthermore, you will pay restitution to Mister Thomas Tillman for the replacement of clapboards." He searched the other side of the room. "Where is the deputy attorney general?"

"Here, your honor."

"How much did you say?"

"Forty dollars."

The judge again addressed Jedediah. "Payable on or before…" He tapped his brow. "Have we agreed to that yet, sheriff?"

"No, your honor," the sheriff said. "It should be before release."

"Your honor," Jacob Lloyd said, standing. "Mister James is a yeoman of small means with six children in his household. He admits his guilt and I assure you regrets his actions. He is destitute of such a large sum and we request terms." Lloyd paused a moment. "After all, we wouldn't want him to default and burden the Commonwealth forever in gaol." He lowered his voice. "And his children be beggars in this county."

The judge leaned ahead and studied Jedediah. "No, we certainly can't have that."

Commotion erupted on the prosecution side of the courtroom. Thomas Tillman, florid, spectacles fallen to the edge of his nose, was leaning over the bar and hissing at the deputy attorney general. Ignored, Tillman shouted to the judge: "Don't you dare let him off like this. He has the money."

"I've enough of you miscreants disrupting this court," the judge said. "Be gone."

"I'm not one of them," Tillman said, waving a hand about the room. "It's me, Thomas Tillman."

"And I see that now," the judge said. "In any case."

Prothonotary Caspar Roan had stepped before the judge. "I'll draw up terms, your honor?"

"Ah, Mister Roan," the judge said. He pulled up his robe and glanced at his watch. "Without delay."

There came a rap at Jedediah's door on a sodden August afternoon in 1827. He was sore of back and limp of mind, in bed trying to rest off a jag while worrying about mash he needed to tend at the still. The boys were on a timber run, floating to mill pines from a piece this side of the round island. He spied the barnyard through the window, took a pistol from beneath the rumple of towcloth that was his pillow, pulled back the cock and waited. Silence.

"Jedediah?"

Sarah, for Christ's sake. "What?"

"I want to come in."

He let off the cock of the pistol but stopped himself before putting it back. Must be trouble—Sarah never came here. So he girded it under his linen band before going and drawing back the bar.

She was in a cap and apron, the shoulders of her butternut shortgown near black from rainfall. Frail, hands translucent as plate glass, the skin across her face so papery and weather-beaten it looked it might tear. Still comely, though, in her way.

He went back and sat on the bed while Sarah closed the door, took in the heaps of tattered shirts and stockings, the rotted buckskin thrown in a corner. The floor—carpet of dank hay to keep his feet out of the mud where rainwater leeched through the foundation. A leaking bucket of water, the stinking chamber-crock before him, fruit flies hovering above it. And the jars of money, paper and coin, beneath the bed, on the cross-legged table of slabs, along the walls. Who knew how much?

"I want to send Benjamin away," she said. "He is twelve years old and I want him to go the Sharpes."

Away? he thought. Why do you send a child away? Did he forget some ritual with all of them? "What about the boy a couple years older?" There, he knew better than Sarah. She missed one—the nettlesome one.

Sarah closed her eyes. "Even you can see there's somethin' awful wrong with that boy."

"Did we send any other'ns off to George's?"

Rare rage burned her cheeks. "I should've sent every child away long ago. I might've saved them. Or are you too soft of the head you can't recall what's become of the grown ones you didn't turn into whiskey peddlers, them that escaped to the country of my brother Stephen at the Hickory Kingdom only to wither into that trade anyway?"

She waited, sighed. "First Sarah. Then Jacob. Now Daniel. They saw the worst parts of your wrath rankle in Jimmy James and had sense enough to fear for themselves and run off. But it was too late, Jedediah. That bitter gall inside you'd sprouted in them. And it straightway infected the Sharpes they married— hard as George and Rosanna tried to stop it. I fear it will be in us people forever. I'm helpless even to protect our granddaughter Nancy over in George's cabin." Sarah let pass a tremor, looked to the joists of the loft. "Sendin' our boy away is all I can do more than prayers, that this scourge might someways, someday stop."

Jedediah had followed her eyes upward and now he gazed where the wallboards met the loft to separate him from the stench of the stock. Some. He concentrated, tried to lift the fog and recollect what she was getting at.

"In that twilight of the mind you live in," she said, "in that midnight world you run to, you've really forgotten what's come of your sons and daughter on that highland?"

He rubbed his forehead. How was he supposed to keep it all straight, forever hearing of trouble in the society he frequented? But now it was coming to him. They'd been at it with the law. Hadn't he paid bail for one of them? Had gotten Jacob out of gaol. Last year. No, it was springtime. Even Daniel—couldn't be more than 18—he'd been arrested. What for? Dammit, if they'd stayed where he could keep an eye on them.

Sarah stepped before him, so close he could see the faint tremble of hairs errant from those sheaves she wore over her brow—was that gray there? "You may not have the heart to regret all you let happen to this family," she said, "but I thought you'd at least take notice." She balled a hand and drew it before her face, it too somehow clenched, and Jedediah thought she might strike him. Well, I never did that to her. Did I?

Instead, she wiped away sweat at her lip, tears that had welled in her eyes. "Now you listen to what I wish to save our youngest child from, the violence and transgression my brother has witnessed up there of his niece and nephews. I'll start with your daughter, who's made a tipplin' house of her cabin where she and your sons sell liquor on Sundays, sometimes to mere boys, all the time to the drunken caitiffs of that backwoods. Word is they distill wood alcohol, but I've not heard of anyone goin' blind yet."

Jedediah raised a brow at this great insult to his reputation.

"Your sons have fornicated," she said, "with the wives of the local louse, and in the husbands' revenge have been beaten with stones and clubs—where they've not turned and beaten the husbands instead. The eldest of the two knifed a man of fifty and bit off his ear. I had to endure hearin' he ate it. You've paid their fines for battery in wars over the timbers they steal. A trade you taught them—though not in any interest in givin' them a trade, but by example. There's more, but I'm tired Jedediah, havin' to bear what runs through my mind always—that I lived just to see my children owned by the liquor and lawlessness they became heirs of while they tried to understand a man makin' battles he doesn't need to make to own a home he can't even live in."

Something about this turned like a gimlet in his gut. He looked up from where he'd watched his wrists dangling between his knees. "Aren't nothin' owns them."

She rolled her eyes. "They thought they left you, Jedediah, but they took you with them."

"Well," he said, looking around the room, feeling suddenly alert, more lucid. "I got me my four boys here."

"You have two whiskey-makin' timber thieves that way," she said, pointing toward George's cabin where now his bachelor brother Jedediah Junior lived. "You have skulking about this place a silent fourteen-year-old with darksome ways I can make no sense of. And then there's Benjamin—my hope. I won't let it be too late for that child. God knows what it will do to me to send him away, but he's all that's left to save."

Jedediah was shaking his head. "You aren't takin' my boy."

"Your boy? You've hardly said a word to him. Other than to tell him to mind your mash while you fell trees or to help with the farm work you leave to me and my brothers while roofs leak and this place grows over with weeds and rubbish." She squinted her eyes to look out the window. "No, has grown over."

"I got to have children about to pass down my land and livin'."

Sarah lowered herself onto a knee, reached beneath the bed and took up an earthen, lidless jar of money. Jedediah tried to snatch it as she stood, but he was slow and unsteady these days, Sarah still spry as a kitten. "The more you hoard," she said, stirring the coins, "the surer you'll leave nothin' but curses upon your children." She swung the jar, money tinkling out and pelting a wall as Jedediah leaned away.

He waited, watched out until she dropped the jar and it chinked into two pieces against the muddy hay. "I only got so many jars," he said.

She shook her head, drew her hands to her lips in the fashion of a prayer for patience. "I promised myself to you twenty-three years ago. I remain as much wife to you as I was then. Every mornin' I rise hopin' this is the day you come back to me. I will do that for as long as we live."

Against a holy hush left in the wake of this, the barn's ceaseless humming of flies swelled in Jedediah's ears. Without his helping it, there came a long-forgotten image: Sarah lying beside him in the pine woods, bashful and awkward while still eager for his kind regard. By the scarce power of mind he yet possessed, it struck Jedediah that she was just that girl despite all the years and children and whatever gray and wilt had come of her body, for that great heart had not diminished.

He had an urge to put his arms around her as he had long ago, that he could hold and be held against demons that lurked in every corner and at every horizon. As he deliberated rising to his feet, he felt all his decrepitness burdening him—unlike her, he was not the person he'd been in the pine woods. But Sarah, having mused some great sadness beyond a crack in the chinking, turned away.

In that instant, Jedediah wished that back in the pine woods, before all became poisoned with papers and lies and vengeances, he'd have seized that sweetness and kept it close forever, like a copper stitched into his shirt.

To avoid Sarah, Jedediah did not go to the house for food when he left the barn late the next morning, and so took a breakfast of whiskey as he worked in the stillhouse, the liquor burning pleasantly in his entrails in this early stage when drink cleared his mind of the ruthless fog. He was shirtless and hatless, slick with sweat and plagued by flies, what with the hot heft of August and the fire under the boiler. Have to be careful not to overheat the mash.

As he knelt before his cooling barrel holding a cowhorn measuring cup to the spout of his worm to catch the last of a cut of foreshots—he prided himself on never selling first cuts, which could kill a person—someone tapped on the frame of the open door. The boys were on another timber run and no one else was allowed up here without his say-so. He felt at his waist for his pistols only to realize they lay beside his shirt in the corner. Easing his head around, he found George Sharpe leaning in, hands in the air over his straw hat. "Just me," George said.

Jedediah dangled his head. "I should'a guessed," he said. "I'm far into it here, so we're gonna have to talk while I work."

George stepped inside and leaned against the wall where hung wooden stirring oars, an ash shovel, odd bits of copper. He waved away smoke that hadn't drafted through the roof hole Jedediah kept covered with a board when he had no fire.

Standing, stretching his back, Jedediah said, "You aren't takin' my boy." He turned to a shelf on the wall and poured the foreshot into a firkin—the stuff burned like hell when a man needed to get a fire going good. Then he placed a bottle on the board beneath the spout.

"Let's talk about somethin' else first," George said.

Jedediah touched the side of the copper boiler. Getting too hot, dammit.

"Caspar Roan comes to the mill," George said, "says he's runnin' out of ways to help you. Runnin' out of sheriffs friendly to him. Come a day they're gonna come after you for your debts to the county. Everyone knows you got the money."

"I aren't payin' them horseshit," Jedediah said as he squatted and moved coals with a length of iron rod.

"I told him I'd tell you," George said.

Dropping the poker and steadying himself with a hand against the cooling barrel, Jedediah rose, turned. The hair at George's hatbrim was grayer every time he saw him, the lines on his face clearer. That cleft in his chin, which he'd passed on to his sons, even his daughters, was so furrowed now he could have stood a nail in it. The eyes he shared with them hadn't changed—cool green like pools in the creek.

"Them scars never go away, do they?" George said.

"Which scars is them?" Jedediah said, but he knew which scars.

"They go way inside," George said. "They keep needling farther in. Like porcupine quills."

Jedediah tried to match George's stare but looked down at the meandering scrawl an insect had written in sapwood where bark had fallen from a wall-log. Through the doorway, over the snaps of the fire and the drip of whiskey, came the buzz of cicadas from along the field. He noticed the screechy, whinnying laughter of blackbirds in the creekbottom, the tweeting of the strange passing birds of August in the near woods, the rustle of squirrels cutting down the first green acorns.

"You know everything about me," George said. "Like I know everything about you. All but somethin' that happened in them days. I've felt it since you first came to the Farleigh mill. It makes you woeful. It makes you mad. You been tryin' to make it even."

Stepping to the corner, Jedediah took up his shirt and pulled it over his sweaty torso. This meddling vexed him. But he was indulgent, for he was lately of such a strange and brittle mind he craved the small comfort in the company of this person who understood at least some of it. He returned and touched the

282 · PJ PICCIRILLO

boiler. Still too hot. He bent and took up his poker and further spread the embers. They went to smoke and made him cough, a weak and dazing effort. Bracing himself with the poker, he straightened.

"You think you keep workin' at it," George said, "you'll make them scars go away. I thought by now you'd know they won't. You need to wake up to that so you can get by. It's nigh too late—you're goin' dull, man."

George reached out and put his hand on Jedediah's shoulder, calm and kinship settling in. "You got young ones debauchin' themselves up on the flats," George said. "We got young ones up there, I mean. Just like we got a little granddaughter down in George's cabin, and her father's another whiskey maker and timber pirate. I understand Sarah's plan. Let me take the boy Benjamin like she bid me. Do it just because old George asked."

Jedediah pointed the poker he yet held. But he could not muster the voice to argue. So he turned away in search of the bottle he'd been sipping from.

On a morning of foggy thaw in March 1834, humps of ashen snow ramparting the woodsline in the drifting places and describing the northern shade of evergreens, Jedediah stepped from the jakes to find his son George bursting out of the mist. He carried his rifle and was accompanied a step behind by his wife Rosa, one hand lifting her petticoat, the other yanking her wiry wild ringlets. They made for the house where George pulled the latchstring and kicked open the door.

Jedediah watched for company of further trouble, discounted the phantoms that lingered anymore in the tree limbs, lurked in the shadowy brush. Half curious, half fearful of what downstream menace they may herald, he went to the doorway and peeked in.

George held the butt of the gunstock over Sarah's head as she cowered in her chair beside her spinning wheel. "Tell me where the son-of-a-bitch is," George said.

At this, Jedediah slunk from the doorway. But he stopped at the porch step when he heard Rosa screech out, "Jimmy James is a monster, he's a devil-man."

Sarah begged George to please put down the gun, said she knew not where his brother was. And so the pair rushed out to the porch railing. Rosa, convulsing with grunting sobs, was like to pull her hair out while George scanned the field and pasture, the riverbank. "Where's Jimmy James?" he said.

Jedediah shrugged. "You know that man comes and goes."

"Yeah, he comes and goes," George said. "You know where he came and went to? My thirteen-year-old daughter Nancy, that's where. And she's pregnant."

* * *

* * *

They were all that remained in the pouch of hope he toted about his brain, George and Jedediah Junior and their birthright to what he'd amassed. But a week later, stumbling and calling about their dim and empty cabin, he discovered them gone, only to be further distressed as he realized his whole legacy fell now to a profligate, the very thing that had driven them away.

He returned to his room and sat and sipped until unbeckoned memories tumbled amusingly about his head like children in a haymow. Eventually, they diminished to the disjointed notes of a music box reaching the end of its wind, the sense of an old song in there somewhere. At daybreak, he changed his urine-soaked britches and searched his clutter for the covenant. He'd have to cut down the landmark trees he'd scored.

When he'd scattered his heaps and tired of pounding his forehead for where he'd put that document he must destroy, he went to the house.

There were no lamps burning so he left the door open for more light, finding Sarah in her chair by the cold hearth, a blanket over her legs. She must sleep there now, he thought, then heard Jimmy James snoring in the upper half-story.

He rummaged shelves, scattering tin cups, trenchers and pewterware. Sarah said nothing, even as he moved her clay pipes, distaffs and niddy-noddies, even when a pickling crock fell and shattered.

He went to the fireplace. "I need that paper." He studied the jambs. Was there a loose stone? "The one that says they aren't never to sell outta the family." He squinted at her. "Did you move it? Them boys take it?"

The blanched morning light slugging through the doorway drew out the lighter aspects of the room, how wan Sarah had become, her face the hue of a cup of mush-and-milk. Somehow she looked even thinner, her fingers on the blanket wisps of straw. A glint at her neck. She still wore that necklace?

"Where'd they go?" Jedediah said.

"Where do you think?" she said. "To the Hickory Kingdom with my brother and the other children. They ran to where they thought they'd leave all this." Which she summed by a turn of her palm.

"Aren't why," Jedediah said. "Those boys cleaned out the local timber. They left me so they could go into the log and liquor business with the rest of 'em." He blew between pursed lips. "Tipplin' houses."

Sarah stared on as though at infinity, the stare of the skull at the coffin lid.

The snoring overhead had stopped and now a shadow figure descended the ladder and faded into the dim perimeter of the room.

"They see you hoard," Sarah said, her voice distant as her eyes, "and they resent some depravity in it. So they think they're righting your wrong with the opposite error. They squander everything, right down to themselves with the rot of greed and misdeed. Excesses. They fled for an uncharted forest, their dark kingdom. And so they have transgressed the laws of God and the tide of mankind and think they are hidden from both. There is no freedom in that. They are owned now by their sins, and so they live."

"I told you there aren't nothin' owns my children," Jedediah said.

"You have but one child now."

Jedediah strained his eyes beyond the ladder, found him against the wall, arms crossed. "What'd you come back here for?" Jedediah said.

"S'where I live," Jimmy James said.

Sarah nodded toward him. "Who, Jedediah, do you think's goin' to run what's left of this place so you can be fed?" She lurched ahead, seized his wrist, the fingers icy lashes. "Let us leave here. All you fight for is gone. Your sons and daughters. What might have been a homestead. You've lost even your senses." She squeezed tighter. "There's time. You've plenty of money in those jars to start a farm near the children where they could relieve us in our old age. I tell you, it is our last chance. I feel it. This is the end of our lives otherwise."

The door shifted as a draft passed through the room, chilling his shoulders, drawn by some damned hole in the roof. He breathed in the muddy smell of March, looked outside. Talk of the children had brought to mind only a word. Betrayal. And leaving? Some vague tang of defeat that soured the warm whiskey in his gut.

He pried her fingers from his wrist and tried to locate Jimmy James, but the light through the doorway had shocked his eyes. "Boy," he said.

"What?"

The voice directed him to the faint form of a linen shirt. "You find me up the still. I'm gonna learn you the mystery of whiskey makin'." There came the sudden white of his son's teeth.

Jedediah turned away and Sarah released into shuddering gasps. When he paused in the doorway to let his eyes adjust to the daylight, she called his name.

"I see you will not go away from this place," she said. "I told you I will live by my promise." Her voice breaking, she drew long breaths. "I just didn't think it would be this hard. But that's the thing about promises. You keep them even if it means losin' everything. So no matter what, I am with you to the end."

The next morning, he hitched the horse to a sledge and led it around to the door of his room. After he loaded his boots, shirts and money jars, mattress, bearskin and blankets, his rifle and sacks of shot and powder, he started the horse toward his sons' former cabin. From there he'd have a better view of the creek. It was closer to the howling-ground of the wolves. And woe to anyone who came to claim that two hundred acres.

Stopping before a makeshift gate in a pasture fence of stump, brush and stone, he removed the poles of locust that blocked his way.

Turning back for the horse, he paused and looked out over his field gone fallow, a stubble of crabapple saplings and snow-broken weed stems. The day was calm, the air heavy, licks of fog hanging onto the steeps like the slow smoke of greenwood fires.

At odd times anymore, some bygone landscape would overlay the view before him. He stood now before a tobacco field he'd known of like contour. The mutter and sough of the swollen creek became the suck of swamp water, the earth of the near furrows gritty and buff as old buckskin. There came the smell of a smokehouse, the laugh of a seagull.

He knew this muddling of time and place was a thing of age— and of wisdom, for whatever power of mind remained in a man, he came to wonder whether there are distinctions in this world, whether life was the same no matter the path he took. And so he contemplated fate.

As part of this—or maybe of its own—a voice whispered out of the past. The face that tried to come to mind was dim and fleeting, as if in rising from that coffer he'd locked in his youth it had stirred a haze of dust. And though the words made no more sense than a breeze, they left him feeling a circle was about to close, the old years somehow drawing near.

Growing up, I'd drawn enough from my surroundings to have some sense of their history, so the story to this point had not shocked me. My response had been more a matter of slow dilation; that old balloon of uncertainty pressed now at my ribs. And the person lurking in the shadows of the account, he who'd haunted my childhood, had left me with a chill despite the barrel stove by the door of the passenger car onto which we'd transferred.

Between the waiter in our first train and then another after we'd boarded the Northern Central at Baltimore, we'd been grudged four hours in dining cars before Benjamin, slouched in his seat, had stopped his storytelling. We were taking on passengers at Bridgeport, across the river from Harrisburg, and he'd picked up his satchel and hat, trudged out to the platform, and led us to this car.

I had a clear view of Harrisburg as we left the Bridgeport station, a somber prospect in rank—rearmost, the brooding, leafless mountains and their foothills, back-cloth to the smug capitol building of sooty red brick with its phallic federalist dome and flanking, ostensible houses of democracy. All of it presiding over the church steeples, tenements, and shops of brick and board where they huddled and weathered there on the riverfront like bad teeth in that jaundice breath of urban coalfire.

What is the root of that dismal feel of capital cities?

The wooden seats of our rattletrap creaked as the train gathered speed and my attention went to the muddy brown Susquehanna, brimming from the snowmelt of the headwater country to which we were headed. In the faint window reflection, a ghost of Benjamin burrowed into his greatcoat, which appeared larger now, he smaller there on the bench with no table between us.

I tugged at my shawl and closed my eyes a moment. "In his very lurking," I said, turning to Benjamin, "he looms over the story—everything about it seems ready to converge on the yawning question mark of Jimmy James."

Benjamin shook his head back and forth in little lurches. "It does not converge on Jimmy James. But on what converges in him."

"Your account leaves riddles where mine begin." I waited, consumed in that stare, thinking he was not going to address this—though I know now he was calculating whether it was time.

"The child he begat," Benjamin said, "was named Absalom."

Even as I realized the likelihood of this, it took me aback. "All my life," I said, "I thought Absalom was Nancy's brother, and here he was..."

"A man you thought was brother," Benjamin said, "was son. Life can lead us to believe a person is who they're not."

"What are you suggesting?" But he ignored me, knowing, I suspect, he had to unspool it slowly so I would reckon it on my own, that I might stanch my error in all its incarnations.

"Jimmy James," Benjamin said, "had a look about him that did something to women. Some women. The dark charm of the devil." He turned his eyes from me, and I knew by the rarity of this he was about to utter something even he considered indelicate. "He was a regular lecher." Benjamin coughed and wiped his lips with the sleeve of his coat. He waited to gain breath, steadying himself with a hand on the bench where lay his dirty straw boater. "But like all men, there was that one woman. She took to him and him to her like sin."

"I never knew him to be married," I said.

His shoulders jittered in a silent chuckle. "Marriage? My brother? Her father forbade her around him anyway." He wheezed and fumbled for his bottle, gave up. "The violence. The outlawing. That anger he carried and spewed like venom."

I looked down to find my hands squeezed together on my lap. "Who was she?" I whispered this, more an expression of my willingness to surrender to truth than a question. For it was at this moment I accepted that fact is altogether different from truth. Truth, like evil, is absolute. Once we set it next to fact, we cannot deny they are antitheses. It amazes me, in light of what I was about to realize, how readily we yield to what others have us believe are facts. They piece them like quilts into whatever patterns suit their purposes, and spread these as a pall over the truth. And so we do not recognize what is before us. Or in us.

"Do you understand now, Anna Maria?" Benjamin said.

I turned to the window, the perimeter of which had fogged, and touched my fingers to the cold glass. We were at a place called the Dauphin Narrows, the train veering onto the iron-trussed Rockville bridge. Just upriver spanned the old covered Marysville bridge; I'd ridden many a clattering train through that smoky, tottering expanse, and wished we were now in it, that I could not look upon these waters flowing from home.

Curling my hand to warm my fingers, I said, "She was my mother. And I am a product of that man."

I pictured her. A silent woman, slow to smile. I recognized from Benjamin's story traits of the old warhorse Samson Starret, the deep-set brown eyes and long chin handed down through Stephen Starret, patriarch of the Hickory Kingdom. I had known nothing of my mother before she had become Rachel Sharpe.

"Good Lord," I said, looking at Benjamin. "That poor man Absalom was my half-brother. He was my first cousin, once removed, too. And some such cousin through my Starret side." I realized as well that my mother and real father were first cousins—but that that been accepted in those days, was expected in some places. And Benjamin was my uncle. A cousin through my mother, too. My.

We'd crossed the bridge. My view now was farmland and misted mountains, not that reminder of a river surging on in its assurance I was heading home—where I was less inclined to be than ever. I rummaged the old assumptions, the facts of my life, and laid these next to truth, reassigning terms of relationships to frightening faces. Still, relief was rippling through me, that paradox of peace in finding the name of one's disease.

Benjamin's head had drooped to his cape, his exhales stuttering. I bent to find his eyes open; he must have been waiting for me to digest it all. I leaned farther, my corset squeezing my words out as gasps. "What became of them? My grandparents Jedediah and Sarah down there along the creek?"

I eased back as Benjamin lifted his chin, nodded. A fair question. He patted for the bottle I knew was not there. I wished I had one for him—when he'd been drinking he'd carried a trace of the strength with which he'd moved about the station in Washington. A good sousing apparently invigorated him; maybe this was just delirium tremens. But in the heaviness of the lethargy, in how that sere skin had grown yet paler, I sensed that the whiskey had masked some deeper sickness. Had his eyes not blinked, I'd have thought him a corpse.

He had power enough, however, to consume me again in that stare. And to speak quite coherently. "In time, my mother and Jimmy James went to the Kingdom. They lived on the road to the river in that house you knew Jimmy James to have. I helped him build it. She died there."

"But..." Blood surged to my temples and I lurched forward. The conductor, holding his watch and leaning against an empty bench, glanced so sharply the shiny brim of his hat shifted over a brow. I was confused, disappointed, frantic that Benjamin would stop there when something told me that to make sense of it all, I needed to see Jedediah's story to the end.

"But what of Jedediah?" I said. "Sarah said she would never leave him."

"That is yet to come," Benjamin said, his voice weak as rice water. "There is what I know and what I can only imagine, and it is all true."

He woke from a rare bout of sleep in which he'd dreamt of his days in Virginia, where his mind so often went anymore. Never had he seen moonlight this brilliant; it poured through the un-shuttered window like sunshine. So luminous he could make out color—the yellow of his straw hat on a peg, the red glaze of the chamber crock there on the floor. But the light hadn't woken him—he realized someone was in the room; he heard breathing. An exhale of his own turned and caught in his throat, his pulse rocked the mattress. He shifted only his eyes, dared not reach for a pistol beneath his towcloth pillow.

Beside the window, a figure resolved, a frail thing in a coat. Something blue about the neck. A caged rabbit flailed at his ribs, drummed against his skull.

A whisper: "Jeddy."

He sucked for breath. That ghost always in the back of his mind had come to populate the phantom land that had washed over this place. When she stepped forward he sat up and pushed himself against the logs of the wall, thumping his skull, the few teeth remaining in the back of his mouth knocking together.

Vivid in the moonlight, standing before him, the ghost held out an arm. Except for the voice, there was no likeness to the girl he'd known, hair hanging gray to her shoulders, the once velvet cheeks dusky and chafed as an old boot. Where there'd been buttery softness was manliness in lips pulled tight to the gums, in rigidness of jaw. A catalogue of hardship hardened her eyes.

But ghost or not it was Juda, for she wore the indigo scarf around the collar of a patched surtout.

"In my heart," she said, "I's been a-comin' all dese years." And as she glanced into the moonlight, he caught that old readiness.

"Jes a big circle back to you." She smiled, the corners of her lips tugging aslant the hard lines of her face—a smile nonetheless, by which a recollection of old joy shivered through Jedediah. He reached out, her attention shifting to the hand, but he let it fall. Juda closed her eyes a second, then bent and took that hand and kissed its knuckles and he knew she was flesh.

She took a seat on the edge of the bed, Jedediah remaining against the wall. For a long while they sat thus, the calls of the valley's little peeping frogs fevered to a mass screech, Juda periodically breathing out, "I can't believe I's here. All dem years a' waitin's nuttin' now."

Lifting a leg onto the mattress, she turned to face him. "Dey's lots a' thangs happened wid me," she said. "I know dey has wid you. But I's always been yo wife."

Juda waited, went on. "I been a-watchin' you. Was up in dem woods since mornin'."

Jedediah looked away. The room had dimmed and all the warmth of the cabin seemed to have left with the moon trekking upvalley.

"Jeddy," she said, "thangs was bad when dey sold me Sout'. Massa and Mistress was away more 'n more to his gov-ment work. When dey'd come back, Massa was mean as a boar. Mistress... Hmm. I didn't thank she could hate me more. Now I always knowed Massa'd send me away. Someday. Rid hisself a' de troubles a' me and de 'minder I was to Mistress. I jes thought he'd honor his blood and keep me nearby. Or give me to Missy Cornelia."

She laid a hand on his knee. "But de farm was on hard times and dey was actin' rash. So you got to know dey would'a sold me Sout' anyways—no matta' what you'd done. You got to know it was a blessin'. 'Cause it was my way back to you. At Serendip, der was always eyes on me. Down Sout', no one cared much 'bout a old gal like me. Dat last Massa might not even been angry to see me gone, all I do was cry." She bit her lip. "And dem farms in 'ssippi, dem 'tations, dey so big, de overseers don't bother breedin' a gal if ders gone be a fight like I put up."

Pulling back her hand, she looked to the window. "I tell you Jeddy, I was joyful when Massa sent Old Shivsley to tell me you run off. Dat meant you'd be free to have me when I found you. And here I am."

Some somnolent longing stirred. Jedediah thought of reaching out to Juda, of holding her to stave the chill. Instead, he drew a blanket over his legs. "You walked clear from the South?" he said.

"I been comin' all winter. Dey's people help. White 'n black. Dey puts you up, talk 'bout stars and funny lookin' trees to go by. But I didn' fret none a' dat. I feeled my way to you. I knew 'bout a place called Williamsport—Mistress didn' thank we hear all dat talk where Missy went. I learnt as I come it were on de west branch a' de river Sus-quee-henna."

Juda raised her other leg onto the bed. "I found dat river, den de split—oh, Lawd, it were nice to walk in daylight in Pennsyvania. Den I come to Williamsport and I knowed finely I was close to you, honey. I went to de places a' de common folks." She smiled. "Jeddy, ebber-body in dat town, dey knows you. Dey says, 'you go up dat wild country and you'll find yer kind. Der's a big creek spills in de river,' dey says. 'It goes west and nort' into a forest blacker'n you ebber seen.' And so I wents up here where de wolfs howl so much and I found you."

She looked to his hands upon the blanket. There'd been less mannishness about her when she'd smiled. He wished she'd do it again, that he might glimpse the old loveliness, feel the sparks she'd earlier lifted out of the ashes in his gut.

"Who's dat white woman next-door?" Juda said. "Where you come and go. And dat black man. He looks like I 'member you. But with such a hard look. He looks sorrowful mean."

He didn't answer.

"Dat's what I thought, Jeddy." She reached and held his hands. "S'alright. Jes let yer Juda-girl be here dis one night. Den Ise'll disappear. And die happy cause I made it back to you."

"No," he said, and she closed her eyes. "You're stayin' here."

"You n' dat woman not tagetha'?" she said, peering at him.

The lameness of thought had become a comfort of late. Now she'd awakened his wit and he resented seeing a dilemma.

Several. "How do you think we're together," he said, "when we're not even in the same house?"

"I seen stranger thangs," she said.

"Never mind her. She knows nothin' about our days."

"We had more'n days," Juda said. She watched him, she probed him until she took off the scarf and laid it on the bed beside him. "Why'd you leave dat?"

"They made me throw it down," he said.

"Der's a lonesome feel 'bout dis farm," Juda said. "S'all grown over. Nuttin' planted but flax and rye. Rubbish ebber-where. And dat big house ready to fall in on itself." She looked around the room, studied Jedediah. "I see sumptin' a' all a' dat in you. Livin' here like a hermit. Goin' wid dat fierce-lookin' boy to dat still in de woods. You limpin' like yer spirit been plucked out. Guns sticked through yer cincture. Lawd, you're scraggy thin."

She pointed to shelves on the wall. "Jeddy, I don't understand. You're free, but udder'n all dese money jars and talkin' like a white man, you could be a broken old slave. Or one dem poor niggahs down Virginny, buy der freedom when dey too old for it, den nebber owns nuttin', just rents some piece and starves."

Jedediah took her wrist and jerked her toward him, her face a breath away. "I got every damn thing they told us we can't have."

Juda pulled loose of his grip. "You sound like dem white debils I spended my life 'round." She squinted about the room. "I's so hungry. All dem miles." She gave a throaty chuckle. "But fer what kind folk fed me, I 'et such thangs you likely don't 'member. Roasted quills a' some turkey a fox left me. Gum bark and seeds a' redbuds."

But Jedediah was shaking his head. "Don't need to remember. Times get hard in this country. We got long mean winters. Then floods that take our crops. We ate near the whole of chestnut saplings. Basswood buds, elm bark."

"Grass soup?" Juda said.

"Couldn't wait for it to get green," Jedediah said.

"You 'et unripe grapes?" Juda said.

Jedediah rubbed his stomach and they laughed.

"'Member lookin' for mosses to roast," Juda said, "when we was little'ns?" And they went silent.

"One winter," Jedediah said, "we ate the husks and stalks of corn—like cows. I even chewed on my moccasins."

"I come 'cross some boys butcherin' a deer," Juda said, "by a barn down in one dem Carolinas. I so hungry I waited 'til dark and found dem bones where dey throwed 'em in de woods. Lawd, dey hard to break, but I done it wid two big rocks. Den I sucked de marrow outten ebber' one dem bones." And Jedediah, laughing to the exclusion of words—since when, he could not recall—waved to show that yes, he knew what she meant. But he recalled he'd boiled their bones and fed all the marrow to their little starving children that winter while he and Sarah only sipped the broth, and he stopped laughing and stared out the window where the moonlight was but a haze now.

"At sunup," he said, "I'll get you some food."

"Where's yer stores?" she said, and he turned to find her squinting about the cabin. "And yer kettle and treenwares?"

"Never mind that," he said.

As if she'd done it here every night for the past thirty-five years, Juda rose, unbuttoned her coat and dropped it to the floor. She pulled over her head the thong of a reticule that hung at her side and set this on the edge of the bed. Then she reached behind her neck and untied the drawstring of her coarse frock. It dropped to show a design of stripes. Shivelley and the other overseers who'd whipped her had spared only her breasts—deflated and collapsed now like sacks of chaff. Spared them for themselves, he was sure. Without a word, she bent and lifted the blanket and crawled in beside him. She wiggled her hand behind his back and embraced him, resting her head against his chest.

"I can't," he said.

"Dat don't mean a thang," she said. "Dis all I wants."

Dawn was succeeding that great westering moon. The day crept in with the hush of the frogs as impatient robins *cheeped* in the nest. A breeze fetched through the cabin a sharp musk of creek muck.

"Life's jes a big circle," Juda said and kissed his shoulder. "We jes come back 'round to where we started 'fore it all ends."

Already guessing he'd raise suspicion by appearing this early—he never breakfasted anymore, rarely went to the house before midday—he spotted Sarah watching from a corner of the porch with an armful of firewood. "I'm after food," Jedediah said.

She knitted her brows. "Then I'll make you bannock. And there's trout meat and fiddleheads in the kettle from yesterday."

Jedediah followed her inside to the hearth. He stirred coals and blew embers to life, laid on the wood to heat the kettle. "You tell Jimmy James I'll come by later to take him to work at the still." He took an empty flagon from a shelf. "Put the bread in a sack and the stew in a big bowl 'cause I'm takin' it with me."

Sarah followed him to the doorway. Rounding the porch for the spring, he caught her watching him, head tilted. Then she squinted across the field to the cabin.

Crossing the field, steadying the bowl while he carried the flagon and sack, he saw Juda returning from the jakes, the indigo scarf bright in the sunshine. Inside the cabin, he found her hair wet, and as they sat at the table, she told him she'd bathed in the creek. Mid-morning, while Juda related the histories of his parents and the slaves he'd known, Jedediah caught Sarah in cap and apron circling the cabin. She peered through the window opening, then the doorway, Juda lifting her chin as she noticed her.

Not yet, Jedediah thought, I aren't ready for this. "Go on home," he said.

"You come out here," Sarah said.

"You best gets out der," Juda said.

He gripped the edge of the table, pulled himself up and went to the doorway.

"You gonna tell me that's your sister?" Sarah said.

He leaned on the doorframe, scuffed his moccasin over the pine sill.

"What've you to say?" she said, rare color in her cheeks. Then she looked over his shoulder as Juda approached.

"Jeddy, I jes go," Juda said. But he shook his head no and spread his feet.

"Jeddy?" Sarah said, and made a huffing sound. "I know who she is."

"You know nothin'," Jedediah said.

Sarah chuckled. "I always knew there'd been someone. A woman knows." She tipped her head and eyed Juda up and down. "She just don't expect her to come back."

"I's never left him," Juda said.

Sarah flung out a finger. "You mind your words."

Jedediah held up his palms. "There's things you don't understand about each other."

"I want to talk to her," Sarah said.

"No," Jedediah said.

"And I want to talk to her," Juda said.

He shook his head. "Uh-uh."

The air was alive with sunshine and mayflies and birdsong, the fruity smell of apple blossom and fern. He recalled days such as this with either of these women. Warm but incompatible images entwined before that strange new eye of his mind, wedding finally into a rope of reconciled remembrances, snug and fast as the cord of Indian hemp. But what did it bind?

Juda's breath feathered upon Jedediah's neck, her inhalations staccato with unease. Sarah brushed errant hairs from her eyelashes, seemed to sift for something lost across the years. He wanted to take each woman by the hand, to have no choices, to keep them both here with all else that was his.

Then Sarah nodded. "I got no cause to hate this woman for things that happened in another life. And her not knowin' any different comin' here." She watched Jedediah until he glanced away. "Nothin' changes the promise I made," Sarah said

Juda let out a mournful humming sound.

Sarah held still a moment, then smoothed the apron at her thighs. "If I'm hateful and jealous of this woman," she said, "I'm allowin' she's ruint everything I made of my life and all the lives we gave."

She stepped ahead, her toe touching the threshold. Jedediah braced the doorframe. But Sarah slipped her arm along his side and he turned to find her rubbing between her fingers a fray in the sleeve of Juda's frock.

"I'll be back." Sarah said. "With a clean petticoat and short-gown."

The mind's resilience is most remarkable. I learned that day how a person even grievously sick can betray death to the end. In the blink of an eye, he can go from complete cognizance to oblivion.

I do not know whether Benjamin died when I thought he'd fallen asleep a few miles back or when I suspected something wrong as we trundled up to the platform at Keating. But there at the fork of the West Branch and the Sinnemahoning, in the twilight shadow of that bluff beyond which lay the great hickory flats of home, I discovered with my hand beneath his lolling chin he was gone. I was as amazed as I was aggrieved: how could a man that close to death have been lucid? And so I couldn't help the creeping sense of some purpose in the courses of our lives.

I'd been gazing out at the valley, lost in the wake of the story he'd just told and which I am about to recount of the destruction of Jedediah James, the finale I should have seen coming.

Before Benjamin related that conclusion, I'd been struck nearly senseless by his revealing an intimate entanglement of his history with mine. This had followed miles of silence brought about by his account of Juda's return. We were stopped at the platform at Millersburg and I feared that the chance to learn the truth of his own shadowy past dwindled the farther we got from his last dram of whiskey. Looking out the far window, past railside sheds and across a mucky field to the Susquehanna slogging along in opposite tune to the ticking clock of my apprehension about approaching home, I forwent stepping slowly into the troubled waters of his life and simply dove in. "What will you tell me about the murder of my father, Jimmy James?"

He waited for me to turn to him, gave a prolonged blink, a nod; he'd been expecting this. "My brother was a bane to the

Kingdom and a heartbreak to my mother. If he wasn't being hauled off to gaol he was being chased away by a husband or someone he stole timber from. But everyone loved his whiskey like certain women loved him, and he always came back to do some vile thing or another."

Benjamin coughed, more a silent straining, sweat beading at his hairline. "My mother wanted nothing more than me to stay away from the Kingdom. But she couldn't keep up their home no matter the moneyjars she had or the ones Jimmy James added. I had to leave George Sharpe's mill. So I fixed up an old cabin nearby and helped her grow a garden and a little corn. I kept things in repair and cut and floated my own timber." He raised a pointer finger. "Legal."

The conductor came into the car and glanced around, leaving after he found it occupied by only us and a couple at the front. "We fought like hell, me and your father," Benjamin said as the train lurched into motion. "More and more after our mother died. Twenty-odd years we went back and forth fighting and tolerating each other."

I gripped the wooden armrest of my seat. "Then came that day," I said, "when we went to your cabin. Me. My mother. Those I thought were my father and full brothers and sisters."

I heard the calls for my mother at our home's windows, the calls that had precipitated the visit, *Rachel—Ra-a-a-a-chel*, saw the grinning black face looking in, something in the eyes saying he sought me as much as he did my mother.

I swallowed, my fingers going numb as I squeezed the armrest. "I never saw him again. Right after we went to you, he was murdered."

Those withered cheeks contracted in the faintest grimace. "I told them over and over—your mother, your stepfather David Sharpe—that me going to Jimmy James would stoke hellfire. Just make him more determined to come after you and your mother. But people persist with their notions."

"So you did it," I said. "You went to him."

He affirmed this with a trembling show of his palm. "Jimmy James had a lot of money. He'd floated thousands of stolen pines to mills and Maryland shipyards. He'd sold whiskey to every

302 · PJ PICCIRILLO

logger between the Sinnemahone and Lancaster. By then he was a man out of his mind, telling the world his fortune would be yours when you came of age. He thought it would change it all— he'd get back his Rachel and his little girl. He'd spite everyone. You see, Jimmy James could not stand anyone having something that was his, especially a Sharpe. Sharpes and Starrets barring him from his own blood."

The train slowed for another stop and Benjamin paused to catch his breath. "We weren't the only ones that feared for you," he said, then waited.

I let go of the armrest, inched my chin toward him. "I don't follow."

"A man that loved you because he understood the confusion of bastardy. How could he not? He lived with it, as you did, but with twice the shame."

"Who?" I said, vexed at this riddle-talk, the train stopping, the conductor stepping into the car and shouting, "Sunbury," which meant it was time to transfer onto the Philadelphia and Erie. Our last leg to Keating.

"Your half-brother," Benjamin said. "Absalom."

This car was crowded and stunk of sweat and damp wool. Children ran about the aisle as grumpy businessmen in billy-cocks scowled, the mothers knitting and chatting, the fathers staring out windows. Of course we, by privilege of our unprivilege, were left to our own facing benches.

Even after the locomotive tugged us from the station, Benjamin labored for breath from having ascended the coach's steps. The cape of his coat, which he drew closed despite the mugginess of our dungeon, quaked with his erratic gasps.

When at last his respirations tapered to sighs, I said, "I hardly knew him. Absalom. I vaguely picture him digging potatoes out back of his grandparents' place. But I recognize how he was my father's son." I turned to my reflection in the finger-smudged window. "And my half-brother."

I looked back to find Benjamin's head erect where it had sagged to one side or the other for the past few hours; he was ready to tell me something. "It was not just because he loved you," he said. "Absalom hated his father—and for more than promising all the money to you."

And at that, without even putting to words that my half-brother had murdered my father, Benjamin revealed another of the great mysteries of our past.

"So you're telling me he did it in part for me," I said. "To somehow protect me. But I shouldn't feel too guilty, being only one reason." I shook my head.

"I point out only that he lived knowing he was born from the rape of his mother. Such a man can't help hating that part of himself. So he tries to destroy it."

We rode in silence. At Williamsport people debarked, people boarded. Benjamin dozed, the train stopping at or passing little board and batten stations dotting the increasingly remote valley. Most of the passengers got off at Lock Haven where the conductor lighted the oil lamps, the day waning. Benjamin woke then. He became uncomfortable, shifting on his seat, sighing, pulling at his collar.

As for me, I wished I could blame my nausea on the rocking and knocking of the train. But on top of the whirlwind of emotions I'd experienced these nine hours, the usual reluctance to be returning home had increased to dread.

After ten or so miles, I touched Benjamin's knee—I was running out of time. "Why were you accused?" I said.

He made a feeble shrug. "When I went to see him that night, we argued until we threw punches and some woman staying there cussed me out of the house. He was dead fifteen minutes later."

Benjamin looked out the far window to the mouth of a hollow. I knew this was Ferney Run. He remained watching the woods until he began fidgeting again.

"How was he killed?" I said.

"Bullet in the head."

"So what I've heard is true. He was shot at his table through a window."

Again a shrug. "There were footprints in the snow. The window was broken and there was a ball in his skull."

"And the woman?"

"In bed. Said she saw nothing. I believe Absalom stood outside while we fought."

"You knew who did it from the beginning," I said.

He made no reply.

"You were to hang, yet you refused to call out Absalom."

Benjamin groped about his seat, took up his straw boater and thumbed the brim. I followed his gaze out the window. We were rounding a curve in the valley. They called this place Great Bend. The farms on either side of the West Branch had been built by Samson Starret and his sons, before his daughter Sarah—my grandmother—and those sons moved upriver to the Sinnemahone and Hickory Kingdom.

"Then your lawyer insisted on appealing," I said. "With no other suspect, how were you acquitted?"

He frowned out at the river. "They realized the bullet they dug out of my brother's skull would not have fit the bore of the gun they'd found in my house." He paused with his mouth parted, the better for breathing as he panted to get air. "The only thing Jimmy James ever gave that boy was one of my father's old muzzleloading pistols." His chin rose with the sweep of an escarpment across the river, the narrows steeper, closing in as we neared the Sinnemahone. "He died a year later at Gaines' Mill, Virginia."

"So Absalom went off to the war," I said.

"Gone the day after the murder," Benjamin said.

"You went after him, didn't you? To watch out for him."

Benjamin stopped fumbling with his hat. "I held him at the end." He turned to me. "Shot in the spine. Seen so many die. But none so helpless as that boy as he begged me to tell him he'd be forgiven." A glance away as he gathered breath. "But even more, beyond concern for his own soul, he wanted to know if he'd stopped the scourge on our family." He lost his voice to a whisper. "I would not answer that."

We passed Renovo's sooty engine shop and stopped at the town's depot, the portly, bearded stationmaster boldly but incuriously regarding us from a ladder-back chair on the platform as he sucked smoke from his pipe. I'd followed a chain Benjamin had fashioned. It ended where my link was bound to the lives of every person in his story, ancestor or not, right down to Madagascar Jack and Cornelia Bakeraskin, Thomas Tillman and Caspar Roan, each of them the impulse of some vice or virtue in my breast. To know myself, I needed to know Jedediah James. To know him, I needed to know his nemeses and lovers. I had to witness George Sharpe trying to save a man who could not be saved.

I had to realize the frustration of the wives of Jedediah James and the likelihood of the doom that befell my father, Jimmy James, and half-brother Absalom. And only by understanding the aggregate of it all could I reach the crossroads where the chain would either shackle or unbind.

Until then, I had defined myself by folklore, by Napoleon's history: a set of lies agreed upon. Even the means of my flight were the proceeds of my ancestors' shams. Benjamin concealed nothing, that I could understand the past impartially in my heart, and I looked out at that fearsome landscape and dared believe I was traveling toward truth.

"A question," I said, "echoed through the story. It was never resolved." I waited for Benjamin to finish coughing the croaks of an old crow. "Is the Sinnemahone," I said, "a godless place?"

He grunted—not an answer, rather acknowledgment of my question.

The river was mute as slate in the waning light. The far slope had been logged to its chine, quilled by the occasional limbless tree, the shorn boughs of hemlock strewn among fallen boles stripped of their bark for the tannin it provided the tanneries. For all its austerity, this was a place of bounty. The timber and coal, wild game and heart-stopping vistas. Abounding fresh water.

The water. It surged there in the river insistently away from here, moody in its turns from blue to green to its present opaque, threatening with every storm to rear beyond its banks. I knew intimately its sources, the headwaters of my homeland on the divide that split the rains between this river and the great tributary we approached, the Sinnemahoning. As a girl, I'd felt in my bones the iciness of those freestone streams as they'd lapped my thighs where I waded to swim or bathe. I'd tasted the zest of the mineral-rich springs that slaked the honest thirst of country living.

I studied the denuded ridge, plumbed the April-gray water. And then it struck me, struck me by the absence of verdure: I'd been conditioned to slight a beauty raw and rugged and frank. Perhaps—just perhaps—when my ancestors had arrived, they'd been moved by the brutish purity of this wilderness, but then they and the rest of us had come to overlook it during intervening hardships. I glanced to find Benjamin's eyelids sagging. I decided the picturesque was a motif intentionally unspoken in his account, a presence timed to suddenly and forcibly pronounce itself by his having crafted its un-presence, by his not calling attention to the abstruse, deceptive charms of our place. And so he had been addressing my question by not addressing it, letting it grow as a milt in my heart. The answer has redoubled my insights into the story, myself, my world. The elusive nature of God.

There in the wake of having every notion of myself destroyed, the old tension about moving homeward eased. It used to be that by this point, closing in on Keating, my innards were in knots. Now I was eager to see the people and place I was returning to. For the first time in my life, I gave myself over to a sense of homing.

Something else. Though I could not bring myself to feel gratitude for a brother having tried to protect me given his corrupt method, I saw him as the greatest of tragedies, a man somehow right in his heart, but horribly flawed in how he acted on it. It was by the depravity of his deed, of conditions deteriorating to where the mode of righting wrongs would reach perversion, that I avowed myself to the resolve that was budding in my breast.

Onward we traced the river, pathway of game and Indians, of settlers. Jedediah James and George Sharpe had with their wives fled by this route the lies that had shackled them. Their children, thinking they could escape the reach of a man's demon, had transgressed the ancient way and run farther, headlong to a highland hideout.

Benjamin's face was so wan and drawn. His eyes fluttered, his head bobbed. I still ruminate the providence in our meeting that day, magnified now by the momentousness of the effect, the uncanny circle that never would have closed had I not looked up to see him at the Baltimore and Potomac Railroad station. That compass, which made its course through Benjamin, was presciently set into motion by my grandmother, Sarah, the day she demanded that this youngest son be sent away from her collapsing family. I pause before my pupils at odd times and look out the window of the schoolhouse, across the cemetery where she lies, and sense that circle completed in me. I feel affectionately connected to my grandmother. I picture her along the Sinnemahone tending her flax, I hear her humming to her children, I feel the drift of a dream in her heart, enduring no matter when or where it might bear fruit.

The wonder of it only increases when I consider what might have happened had I chanced upon Benjamin James years earlier, before I'd gone off for an education. I suspect I would not have left, resigned to some fate of my blood, having heard such a story without the discretion and perspective that distance and the years afford us. Even if I'd left, it would have been to renounce this place. So either way, I would not be here teaching the children.

Beneath the gravestones and in plots unmarked lie many of the characters of this history. Not Juda, who, Benjamin explained, vanished after the end. But the bulk rest there with other forebears of this backwoods settlement, most of the interred at least cousins to me by some degree—Sharpes and Jameses and Starrets and those of a few other surnames.

So these are the family names of my students, many of whom share a feature or temperament with an ancestor. Through the years, I've glanced up to catch emerald eyes or a dimpled chin or great, flapping ears. I've seen again and again nappy hair or an aspect of severe sullenness, fought the independence of a bear or the irascibility of a rattlesnake. For them, I hold in my mind lessons of the past, our past, and in my breast lives my grandmother's dream.

We had not far to go to Keating—one intervening stop at Westport. Benjamin was slumped in his seat. He tried to right himself, gave up and leaned his shoulder against the window.

He rested his forehead on the glass and I followed his eyes to the dirt road on the far shore of the river.

"I looked across the valley," Benjamin said, "and saw the dust rising from the hooves of their horses…"

He faced Rosanna, each to a stool by the piers of the Sharpes' gristmill, and watched through the newly leafed trees the dust cloud advancing along the river. Across their knees rested a frame over which they'd stretched a silk bolting cloth that Benjamin had been scraping with an oaken glut. The morning, bright and minty fresh, was a good dry one for cleaning caked powder from the sieve, for using the magnifying glass to find which tiny openings needed brushed clear.

Rosanna turned to see what he studied. She rose and balanced her side of the frame on her stool, mounted the creekbank toward the doorway of the mill as she called for George. He stepped out, shaded his eyes against the daylight.

"There's trouble ahead of a party on horses," Rosanna shouted over the shuddering of the building's frame members and the whoosh of flumewater driving the turbine. "It's to do with Jedediah James and what we heard a' him. I'm sure."

George sent sixteen-year-old David, who'd been at the grinding stones, to the stable to saddle the horse. He called Benjamin to the floor of the mill. "You and David," George said, hanging his apron on a peg, "keep the stone running the rest of the day."

"What is it you heard about my father?" Benjamin said.

George tried to snatch a fly out of the air, looked past Benjamin to his stones. "Talk. Just talk."

"I'm nineteen years old," Benjamin said. "I can hear talk. Even something he did."

"Let me find out if this has to do with him." George turned for the door.

"He's my father," Benjamin said. "I'm going."

George stopped, frowned at a grain barrow. Then he went and

pushed the lever that raised his runner stone. "Go saddle the mule."

After they forded the river and gained the road, George got down and walked, studying the tracks. "Four horses," he said, stopping. "Good sharp shoes. Town horses." He eyed the valley, lime green up its flanks to the un-budded trees of the higher places. "If they're headed clear to your father's, they'll have to camp to rest those animals, even if they done so since Williamsport." He kicked dirt, raised a puff of dust. "They wanted to avoid the hills of the Ellicott Road. But they're ridin' too hard. Someone's in a hurry. And don't have sense."

He mounted and they walked their horses, crossing the river again wherever the road went to the other side. They continued through the day until the sun touched the ridge at the fork of the Sinnemahoning and George held up a hand. "I'm gonna ride ahead real slow and see what we got. They can't of gone much farther." He pointed into a grove of hemlocks darkening the near foreslope. "We'll sleep there tonight. You get a fire goin'." He waved away a halo of punkies. "The damned bugs."

An hour later, as Benjamin snapped off boughs to smoke up the fire, he caught two riders coming up the road. They were already looking about, what with the smell of campfire, which Benjamin ran to and kicked down. Now they watched the mule working grasses by the water. Benjamin knew they were town men—tall hats, waisted coats with more buttons than button holes. Trousers. So busy watching the obvious they never looked his way.

Within ten minutes they returned following George. The men tied their horses along the riverbank and came to the rekindled fire where Benjamin sat with his knees pulled up. The valley brimmed now with the white light of dusk in which millions of mayflies effervesced, swallows veering. But beneath the black ceiling of hemlock it was already as night.

One of the strangers stepped right to Benjamin, extending a hand and introducing himself as Caspar Roan, a name Benjamin recalled from his youth. He returned the handshake, as he did with the second man, presented as Jacob Lloyd. They lifted the tails of their coats and sat beside Benjamin while George squatted at the other side of the fire.

"They're camped on the round island," George said. "We'll follow them at daylight."

"Who are they?" Benjamin said.

George waited for Caspar Roan who pushed a stick farther into the fire. "The sheriff," Roan said. "Deputy. Man named Thomas Tillman. Another called Peter Bakeraskin." He looked up at Benjamin. "You know who that is?"

Benjamin nodded. "Tillman, too. What's it about?"

The three men looked from one to the other and then to the fire.

"It's about a lot of things," Caspar Roan said. "I just hope to God we can help."

They rode out before dawn, everyone silent, as men are among the unknowns of darkness, of confrontations to come. Benjamin had not slept, wolves real and remembered troubling him. Childhood incidents with his father had paraded through his mind—streaks of drunken violence striped between days the man had secluded himself quiet as a creek mussel in the shadows of their house, the perimeter of their farm.

Yet beneath that was a tenderness he could not help. In Benjamin's earliest years, while a fierce love hummed from his father's rare, sober caress, Benjamin had felt some greater hunger defile the passion. He'd figured out that hunger. And he hurt for his father. He feared for him. He wished he could simply touch the man.

As they closed in on the round island, Caspar Roan stepped his horse beside Benjamin. "Your two eldest brothers will come today," he said. "There might be trouble between them and your father."

"There's been for a long time," Benjamin said.

"Trouble will come at your father from a lot of directions," Roan said. "I don't know if we'll be able to help him this time."

Benjamin looked over at the moving silhouette—tall-hatted man on horse against a leaden backdrop of starlit creek valley. He did not tell Caspar Roan what he and George Sharpe had yet to realize: his father could not be helped.

At dawn, they were sitting their horses in a stand of pines where they could see out to the island. Passing figures eclipsed the coals of a campfire, one of the men coming to the creek, unbuttoning his breeches, voiding himself. They watched as the party forded to the road, gave them time to get ahead. Within an hour, they saw them crossing the creek to the James place.

Now they were in a hurry and made no effort to conceal themselves as their horses and mule splashed through the water and scrabbled up the bank. George led them across the field and through the shadow of the barn, the other group watching from where they remained mounted before the house, feathers of smoke puffing from the chimney. Thomas Tillman sneered. "You can't leave anyone about their business, can you, Roan?"

"Good morning, Thomas." Caspar Roan heeled the flanks of his horse and moved ahead of George. "Sheriff Winters," he said, pulling up beside the group, the others falling in with him. He nodded at the deputy and eyed the rifles stuffed in scabbards at the lawmen's knees, the pistols pressed beneath bands at their waists. "And you Mister Bakeraskin. It's been a while."

Peter Bakeraskin rolled his eyes and shouted toward the house: "Come out here, Jedediah James. You and the concubine."

As they waited, Sheriff Winters turned to Caspar Roan. Winters was hatless, thick black hair raked back over his skull. He wore side whiskers and a full beard that undulated as he worked the wad of tobacco in his cheek. His eyes were the transparent amber of maple candy—sluggish eyes that left the impression that everyone in his sight bored him. His deputy, on the other hand, a clean-shaven youth in a crisp felt hat, sat erect with a ready watch. The sheriff squirted a yellow streak of tobacco juice. "Tillman said you might show." He nodded toward George and Benjamin. "Who're they?"

"One a friend," Roan said. "The other a son of Mister Lloyd's yon client." He pointed to the house.

The sheriff raised his brows and bobbed his head. "Well,

well," he said. "We got a 'client' in that house. And his lawyer to the rescue."

The door opened and Sarah peeked out. "What is it?" she said, more weariness in her voice than wariness.

Both Tillman and Bakeraskin began speaking, but the sheriff held up a hand. "I got papers that concern Jedediah James. Send him out."

Sarah looked from man to man, lingering a moment on Benjamin, then settling on Caspar Roan. She waited. Roan nodded her on.

"He isn't here," she said.

The sheriff was scanning the property, kept watching the bank in back of the house. He glanced down-valley, squinted at something. Everyone turned to see Jedediah limping through the greening brush of the field, Juda behind him, keeping a distance.

"There's our man," the sheriff said. "But who are they?" He nodded toward the creek.

Benjamin twisted in his saddle to find his brothers George and Jedediah Junior approaching from where they'd moored their canoe. Each carried a rifle. They were scraggier every time he saw them, eyes hollow, vacant but for a thirst for whiskey.

"They're the ones I told you about," Thomas Tillman said.

When they passed the barn, the sheriff, who seemed to be at the same time keeping an eye on Jedediah, spoke out. "Easy with them rifles." And his deputy reached for his own. "You, too," the sheriff said.

"They carry them everywhere," Thomas Tillman said. "Like father, like sons."

The brothers went straight to Tillman at his horse. "You got the money?" George James said.

Tillman winced. "Patience, dammit."

Jedediah crossed the rill and stood 30 yards away, Juda approaching as far as the other side. He set the butt of his rifle in the weeded dirt of Sarah's flax patch and leaned with his hand on the muzzle, his breath wheezy after the walk. From beneath the brim of his straw hat, he surveyed the faces as if trying to add up all the trouble they might mean.

Peter Bakeraskin, to see better, was bending forward, his broad middle bound by his waisted coat—he'd become portly and bore the extra flesh of his aging face in the contour and wanness of a sour green apple. "That's the wench," he said, pulling from a sleeve tied to his pommel a golden handled truncheon. "The escaped slave." And he shook the tip at Juda before pointing it at the sheriff and telling him to seize her.

The sheriff's eyes lumbered to the baton, then to Jedediah. "Tell me your name," he said.

"Who the hell are you and what're you doin' here?" Jedediah said.

The sheriff leaned, pursed his lips and fired away. "I'm the sheriff of this county," he said. "Even this backwoods ass-end of it. I'll get to the reason I'm here in a minute. The name."

"If you're the sheriff," Jedediah said, "you know who I am. Probly drink my whiskey."

"You look like you come for a fight," Sheriff Winters said. "Two pistols and that rifle you're proppin' up."

Thomas Tillman squinted through his spectacles at the rifle's fancy brass-work. "I know where he got that gun. That makes him a murderer, too."

Jedediah described a circle with the muzzle. "Why don't you go ahead and tell the sheriff where I got this," he said, and Tillman mouthed something and spoke no more.

"Can you tell me differently who she is?" the sheriff said to Jedediah, and he pointed to Juda, her arms crossed against the chill of the yet cool and dewy morning.

Jedediah glanced at Benjamin then at Sarah who stood on the porch step now. He looked down at his moccasin scuffing the sandy loam. "She's my wife," he said, and Benjamin let out a moan and had to keep himself from falling off the mule.

"Then who's that?" the sheriff said and jerked his chin toward the house.

"My wife," Jedediah said.

Sheriff Winters worked his chew a minute, shifted it to the other cheek and spat precisely between the ears of his horse. Then he looked to the heavens. "We got a regular downpour of predicaments," he said. "Blue sky and all." He reached beneath his coat, withdrew a folded document. "We'll start with this. I have here a notice of sale."

"Let me see that," Jacob Lloyd said and began dismounting.

The sheriff pointed the edge of the document at him. "You go the courthouse and see it. One more move, I'll have your place of residence changed to the cold little building on its grounds." He turned back to Jedediah. "For two years you been notified of bein' in default to the county. That's after making no payments over ten years—for a mere forty-six dollars in court and gaol costs." He let forth tobacco juice and turned to stare a moment at Caspar Roan. "Strangely generous terms."

"Further," Sheriff Winters said as he deposited the paper beneath his coat, "you paid nothing of forty dollars reparations for Mister Tillman's clapboards. You been served twelve writs. I came clear up here and nailed a couple to your door myself."

Jedediah shook his head. "I aren't payin' no one for my own home. Or givin' that son-of-a-bitch a farthing."

"And so this land," the sheriff said, "and all that lies upon it has been attached to satisfy your debts—by the proceeds of a sheriff's sale posted at the courthouse yesterday. For sale tomorrow."

"Tomorrow?" Caspar Roan said. "How is there a sheriff's sale scheduled one day hence that I don't know about?"

The sheriff ignored him and pointed from Juda to Jedediah to Sarah. "You're to quit these premises immediately."

"Bullshit," Jedediah said and he took up the rifle, nesting the stock under his arm.

The sheriff laid his hand on the grip of the gun in his scabbard, the deputy coming to full draw. "Put that down," the sheriff said out of the side of his mouth. "Don't agitate him."

"Easy," Caspar Roan said as Jedediah petted the lock of the rifle, rested his pointer finger on the trigger guard.

Sheriff Winters glanced at Thomas Tillman. "And don't you get started, now that I explained things to him. I'm tired a' hearin it. My deed defeats whatever paper those brothers or anyone short of the Almighty says entitles them to sellin' half this land."

Jedediah took a step toward his two eldest sons. "What's that about?"

Tillman's face bunched with such a smile his spectacles lifted off his nose. "To clear what might or might not be a lien, I'm paying them a hundred dollars each for that piece down there," and he pointed toward the cabin Jedediah occupied.

"You could'a saved your money," the sheriff said. "There aren't no 'pieces'. It all goes to sale tomorrow."

Tillman shrugged. "I don't mind buying insurance against their covenant, keep it from coming back to trouble me."

Sarah, upon Jedediah advancing a few more paces toward their sons, came down from the porch step. "Jedediah," she said.

"The two a' you," Jedediah said, wagging his chin between George and Jedediah Junior, "are doin' business with him?" He lifted his barrel to indicate Thomas Tillman on the horse above them, the sheriff pulling out his own rifle. "You're sellin' my land to that bastard?"

"Our land," George James said. "We got a piece a' paper says so."

"Piece a' paper," Jedediah said, "that says you don't sell it outta this family."

Keeping an eye on the sheriff, George Sharpe dismounted and stepped before his horse. "Let this go," he said. "They can't take anything you won't have again."

But Jedediah would not look from his sons. "My own boys."

Thomas Tillman bent in his saddle, hissed at Jedediah: "I will have a deed to this property at sunup tomorrow. Everything." And he made a sweeping gesture spanning the barn and homes and Sarah there before the porch, hand to her mouth, a figure appearing in the doorway behind her.

"Boy," Jedediah shouted, "come over here."

Jimmy James, barefooted, wearing a sleep-wrinkled shirt and grimy buckskins, went to him, wary eye on the crowd.

Peter Bakeraskin's face had gone from a green apple to a red one, his eyes near to bursting from their sockets. "There's the other matter, Sheriff."

The sheriff sighed, flapped the hand that was not holding his rifle. "We'll see to the new thing first." He called to Jedediah:

"You understand there's a law against polygamy? Man can't have more'n one wife?"

"Laws," Jedediah said, and he glared with an intensity the sheriff must not have liked, for as he leaned to spit, the lazy eyes seemed to waken.

"I'm duty bound," the sheriff said, "to charge you and look into this further. Unless one of these women wants to deny you possess her." There was a hint of hope in his voice. But neither spoke. "So be it," Sheriff Winters said. "Jedediah James, you'll be goin' with me to Williamsport."

Jedediah's jaw locked. He looked back at Juda, then at Sarah, his house, the ridge.

"Now deal with her," Bakeraskin said, pointing his truncheon at Juda.

As Jedediah began mumbling and shifting on his feet, the deputy whispered something to the sheriff. He waved him off. "Wait until I figure out what all I got here." He studied Juda between glances at an increasingly unsettled Jedediah. "Gal," he said. "This man Peter Bakeraskin says his wife's family owned you once. That true?"

"Dat's so," she said, her eyes curses on Peter Bakeraskin.

"Did you run from a planter who bought you off a coffle in Alabama?" the sheriff said.

Juda shook her head no. "I run from de third 'tation I got sold to afta' dat. In Miss-ssippi."

Bakeraskin extended his truncheon behind the deputy and swatted the hind of the sheriff's horse. "Seize her," he said.

When the sheriff settled the beast, he reached over, grabbed the stick and tossed it away. "Rein it in," he said, "or you're off to gaol, too."

"She's contraband," Bakeraskin said. "And my old slave Jedediah harbored her."

"Shut it," the sheriff said, and turned back to Juda. "I'm obliged by federal law to put you in gaol until your owner comes for you."

"Oh, Jeddy," Juda said. "I told you it was a big circle." She looked off as a ragged queue of crows disappeared into some perch among the bare trees of the heights. "I jes didn't think it come 'round dis far."

Jedediah snapped his head back and forth as a dog quitting a pool. The straw hat fell and he buffeted his temple with the palm of his free hand as he let forth a wailing *no-o-o-o* that stuttered across the valley.

The sheriff shouldered his rifle, yet did not point it at Jedediah. With a downward motion of his elbow, he warned the deputy from taking up arms.

Jimmy James, who'd remained beside his father, protested some order Jedediah gave. "Do it, by God," Jedediah said. "Do it to that son-of-a-bitch." He stabbed the muzzle toward Thomas Tillman, and at this, Jimmy James went to the house, Sarah on alert as he passed.

"What're you sendin' him in there for?" the sheriff said. But Jedediah, wild of eye, ignored him.

"Get him now?" the deputy said.

Sheriff Winters for the first time looked concerned. He shifted in his saddle to take in every face around, spat. "Man can't handle things without prothonotaries and lawyers and every other kind of poke-nose." He regarded Jedediah—forehead slick with sweat, attention fixed on where his son had gone—then nodded toward Juda. "Start with the slave. Put her in manacles. Let's go one step at a time while I watch the madman."

"Look, the place is on fire." Thomas Tillman pointed where Jimmy James ran onto the porch, a lighted knot of pitchpine in his hand, smoke slugging through the doorway.

"Now the barn," Jedediah called. "Burn the hay."

Those still mounted braced themselves in their stirrups, yet no one moved further except Thomas Tillman to demand that the sheriff stop him.

The sheriff shook his head, said, "I don't think I can," and Jimmy James rushed from the porch, fending off Sarah as she tried to take the cresset.

"Dear God, no," she called, her son cupping the flame as he ran between Jedediah and Juda and into the barn, an ecstasy of sanctioned destruction in his eyes.

The deputy dismounted and started for Juda, the iron manacles dangling from a cincture at his waist. When Jedediah pulled back his hammer, the deputy halted and drew his pistol. Then came the click of another cock as Sheriff Winters took aim at Jedediah.

"Whoa now, Jedediah," Caspar Roan said, and George Sharpe, taking a step toward Jedediah, echoed this.

Jedediah waved his rifle at the men as Jimmy James led a horse from the barn, smoke already puffing from a side door.

"Sheriff," Caspar Roan whispered. "Let this go for now. We need to save what we can of this place."

The sheriff could not move to spit, lest he lose his aim, so his words gargled in his mouth. "Bullshit. I'm finishing the job I came to do."

"Aren't no Thomas Tillmans takin' Sarah," Jedediah shouted. He tilted his head back at Juda. "Aren't no Peter Bakeraskins takin' her."

The sheriff, coughing from his tobacco juice if not the smoke seeping across the yard to obscure the scene, placed his finger on the trigger. "Put down your arms, Jedediah James. You got no choice."

Jedediah looked at the those manacles. "I got a choice," he said and dropped his rifle. He withdrew both pistols, pulled back the hammers, and just before thrusting the muzzles into his mouth, said, "Nobody's gonna own Jedediah James."

Juda and Sarah reached him, each clutching an elbow to pull away a pistol, and Benjamin was off his horse and running, before the shots jolted his father's head and flared his eyelids into a look of astonishment, of shocking realization of the great irony summed in two pulled triggers. Benjamin passed George Sharpe who moved with wooden steps toward the collapsing body, reached his father who lay now with his calves folded beneath his thighs and blood trickling onto his throat where a hand had come to rest, Juda propping one shoulder, Sarah the other, each imploring that he come back, *oh please come back*, Sarah's necklace fallen from beneath her shortgown and swaying over the face arrested in amazement, sunlight, even through the smoke, glinting off the jewels of polished glass.

As Benjamin knelt, the breath of inferno roaring from the barn burned in his nose. The women grieved with gulping sobs,

Juda wiping Jedediah's mouth with a blue scarf she'd pulled from beneath her shortgown.

"Daddy," Benjamin said, the word faltering out as gutturally as he might have first spoken it. He took up his father's hand, the blood seeping between his fingers. "Oh daddy."

THE END

ABOUT THE AUTHOR

Photo by Molly O'Bryon Welpott

PJ PICCIRILLO'S stories and articles have appeared widely. He is the author of the novel *Heartwood* and has twice won the Appalachian Writers Association Award for Short Fiction. He lives with his wife and three sons in north-central Pennsylvania, which has always been home.

ACKNOWLEDGEMENTS

This work is a crossroads. The great generosity and gifted minds of storytellers and genealogists, historians and scholars, business owners and plain friendly folk intersect here. To the following people who took time to help me fathom an earlier age, I hope I have returned a tale equal to its parts.

Lou Bernard, Curator, Clinton County PA Historical Society

Eric P. Burkhart, PhD., Program Director, Plant Science, PSU Shaver's Creek Environmental Center

Jeanne Callahan

James R. Caola

Katie Cordek, Educational Coordinator, Somerset PA Historical Center

Edward Dix, Forest Program Specialist, PA Department of Conservation & Natural Resources

Ron Edwards, Plain Dealing Plantation, Center Cross, VA

Curt Falck, Grove's Gristmill, Union Township, PA

Chris Fenwick

Roberta Firestone

Bob and Jean Floyd, and Carol Floyd Pavlis

John Louis Ford, Curator, Writer and Historian, Soldiers & Sailors Memorial Hall & Museum Trust, Pittsburgh

Bill Gibbons, Lycoming County PA Genealogical Society

Ray Harmon, General John Burrows Historical Society, Montoursville, PA

Tammy Higgs, Historian, Sully VA Historic Site

Carey Huber, Environmental Education Specialist, PA Department of Conservation and Natural Resources, Parker Dam State Park Complex

Frank H. Hurst, Newington VA Plantation and The Tavern Museum

Michael A. Inzana, D.M.D.

Karen James, Pennsylvania State Archives

Robert Krick, Richmond National Battlefield Park, Richmond, VA

Chris Kunzler, Allen Gaines Homestead, Burnside Township, PA

Ginger Maine, Proprietor, Silverbrook Fiber Arts and Sheepskin, Marchand, PA

John J. McGovern, Esq.

Page McLemore, King and Queen County VA Historical Society

Mengle Memorial Library

Penn State Cooperative Extension, Elk County PA Office

Lori Potter, Karthaus, PA

Tom Rich, PhD., Professor Emeritus, Bucknell University

Linda A. Ries, Head, History and Archival Programs, Pennsylvania Bureau of Archives and History

Teresinha Roberts, Wild Fibres, Birmingham, UK

Mimi Schmitt

Sandy Smith, Penn State Cooperative Extension Agency

Jean Soderlund, PhD., Professor Emeritus, Lehigh University

Jonathan R. Stayer, Head, Reference Section, Pennsylvania State Archives

Randy Stoudt

Dee Styer

Dave Wallace

Ellen White, Sally Walker and Pete Glubiak, King and Queen County VA Historical Society

Aaron Williams, Pennsylvania State Archives

Sue and Mike Williams, Farley Estate, Allenwood, PA

I extend special thanks to Rosemary Nicosia, friend, educator and researcher who taught me to trust the efficiency of intuition.

At last I acknowledge the elusive freedom seekers who inspired this story. May it credit the legacy of courage they ushered into the heart of wild Pennsylvania.

.

www.ingramcontent.com/pod-product-compliance
Lightning Source LLC
Chambersburg PA
CBHW020534020726
47494CB00006B/1763